AND THE REAL BATTLE BEGINS ...

The burning fighter struck the BattleMech like an outsized missile, and in a roar of fire and thunder the 'Mech came apart. Secondary explosions ripped through the ruin, spreading burning wreckage over hundreds of meters and setting a nearby building aflame. Carlyle stared at the sight in horror and sick revulsion. It had all happened so fast ... And Christiano de Villar was gone, just like that. He hadn't even had time to punch out. Vargas shook Carlyle, hard. "Snap out of it!" he shouted. "You've got a job to do! Now move!" Alex Carlyle tore his gaze away from the smouldering hulk that had been de Villar's *Rifleman* and forced himself to act. But as he led his squad up the steps to the Residence doors he felt like a robot, detached from the action, going through the motions. No simulation had ever prepared him for the reality of battle.

BATTLETECH®

BLOOD OF HEROES

Andrew Keith

A ROC BOOK

ROC

Published by the Penguin Group
Penguin Books Ltd, 27 Wrights Lane, London W8 5TZ, England
Penguin Books USA Inc., 375 Hudson Street, New York, New York 10014, USA
Penguin Books Australia Ltd, Ringwood, Victoria, Australia
Penguin Books Canada Ltd, 10 Alcorn Avenue, Toronto, Ontario, Canada M4V 3B2
Penguin Books (NZ) Ltd, 182–190 Wairau Road, Auckland 10, New Zealand

Penguin Books Ltd, Registered Offices: Harmondsworth, Middlesex, England

First published in the USA by ROC, an imprint of New American Library,
a division of Penguin Books USA Inc. 1993
First published in Great Britain 1993
10 9 8 7 6 5 4 3 2 1

Collection copyright © FASA, 1993
All rights reserved

Series editor: Donna Ippolito
Cover: Boris Vallejo
Interior illustrations: Rick Harris
Mechanical drawings: FASA Art Staff

ROC Roc is a trademark of Penguin Books Ltd. BATTLETECH, FASA and the
distinctive BATTLETECH and FASA logos are trademarks of the FASA Corporation,
1026 W. Van Buren, Chicago, IL 60507

Printed in England by Clays Ltd, St Ives plc

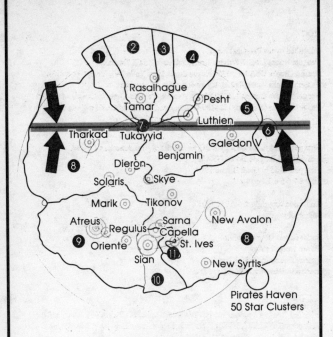

MAP OF THE SUCCESSOR STATES
CLAN TRUCE LINE

1 • Jade Falcon/Steel Viper, 2 • Wolf Clan, 3 • Ghost Bear,
4 • Smoke Jaguars - Nova Cats, 5 • Draconis Combine,
6 • Outworlds Alliance, 7 • Free Rasalhague Republic,
8 • Federated Commonwealth, 9 • Free Worlds League,
10 • Capellan Confederation, 11 • St. Ives Compact

Map Compiled by COMSTAR.
From information provided by the COMSTAR EXPLORER SERVICE
and the STAR LEAGUE ARCHIVES on Terra.

© 3054 COMSTAR CARTOGRAPHIC CORPS.

Prologue

It is the year 3056. Six years after the Clan invasion, Prince Victor Steiner-Davion of the Federated Commonwealth faces bloody revolution. Angry citizens of the war-torn star empire rise up against their lord, even as Clan raiders continue to attack portions of the mighty Successor State. Without a united realm, Prince Victor cannot hope to stand against the superhuman Clan warriors and their superior war machines. Nor can he hope to defend his realm against his rivals for power, those other leaders of the Great Houses of the Inner Sphere who have ever feared and envied his great star empire. Victor Davion must fight for his nation's survival at any cost, against ancient hatreds as well as the deadly Clan enemy.

If he fails? the Federated Commonwealth will fall—and a new Dark Age may engulf the Inner Sphere.

1

"I'm hit! I'm hit! Half my board's gone red!"

Listening to his frantic lance mate, Alexander Durant Carlyle cursed under his breath and keyed in his taccom link. "Ghost Three, this is Ghost Leader," he said, striving to keep his voice crisp and businesslike. Meanwhile he was calling up a sensor map on his main display screen. "Damage assessment."

Harrison Gates sounded calmer now, but his voice still betrayed an edge Alex didn't like. "M-malfunction in my left hip actuator. I think it's in the primary feedback coupling. The targeting computer's off-line, and my heat build-up's redlining. Blake himself couldn't get this bitch moving!"

"What about your jump jets, Three?" Alex asked sharply. He wished he knew Gates better. Was the man just blowing off steam or was he really in trouble? Gates was neither a regular member of Carlyle's four-man lance nor was he as experienced as the rest. "Can you jump clear?"

"Not with this hip, skipper," Gates replied. "Soon as the bitch comes down, the leg'll go for sure."

Alex cursed to himself again. The map showed four hostile BattleMechs closing in on Gates' fifty-five ton *Shadow Hawk*, while four more were sweeping around the flank to cut off the only line of retreat open to Alex's outnumbered lance. "Listen to me, Three. Reroute the circuits and get that piece of junk moving again! Hell, get out and push if you have to, but get going! We've got to get out of here before those bastards block the pass!'' He swallowed and tried to get a grip on himself. It wouldn't help the rest of the lance if he lost it now.

"I—I can't! Pull out and leave me here, skipper!''

"That's not an option, damn it,'' Alex growled, thinking was just the kind of situation every MechWarrior dreaded. The BattleMech, standing as much as thirty meters tall and massing anywhere from twenty tons to more than a hundred, was the most potent fighting machine in all of humanity's bloody history. Machines notwithstanding, most 'Mechs looked roughly human, with two arms and two legs and an intricate neural hookup that allowed the pilot of the monstrous vehicle to move and fight almost as if the metal giant were his own body.

Though BattleMechs were far superior to any other type of armored fighting vehicle, high technology also brought high tech problems. A damaged hip actuator like the *Shadow Hawk*'s was the equivalent of a broken leg. The 'Mech couldn't walk, couldn't even use its powerful Pitban LFT-50 jump jets to bound away out of danger. In short, the war machine was virtually immobilized until Gates could find a way to repair or bypass the electronics knocked out by the enemy attack.

That would take time, and time was the one thing they didn't have right now.

But abandoning Gates to the enemy wasn't an option either. The cardinal rule of the Gray Death Legion was and always had been firm: "The Legion takes care of its own.''

Alex examined the map again. His lance had come down out of Brander Pass, eight kilometers to the north. If they could just make it back to that narrow gap in the mountains they'd be reasonably safe while their supply of ammo held out. At this point their main problem was to beat the enemy flanking force to the mouth of the pass.

The attackers were mostly light, fast 'Mechs, while Alex's lance was a mix of mediums and heavies that were more powerful but slower than most of their opponents. And at least one of the 'Mechs closing on Gates was an assault class, an eighty-five-ton BLR-3M *BattleMaster*. The *BattleMaster* was more than a match for any of the Gray Death 'Mechs, and would easily make up for the weakness of the lighter attackers if Alex's lance was cut off and forced to face the enemy in a slugging match.

Gates was furthest from the safety of the pass and virtually immobilized until he could reroute the hip actuator circuitry. Alex's seventy-ton *Archer* was the nearest support for the damaged *Shadow Hawk,* while the lance's other two 'Mechs, Clay's *Griffin* and DeVries' *Centurion,* had the least distance to cover to reach the safety of the pass. If simple geometry was the only concern, the answer would have been easy.

Alex bit his lip. Simple geometry wasn't the only thing he had to take into account. According to standard combat doctrine Caitlin DeVries and her *Centurion* would have been the best choice for close-in defense of the damaged 'Mech. The *Archer,* with its batteries of long-range missiles, was designed for stand-off attacks. Under ideal circumstances Alex would have laid down a barrage of covering fire while DeVries gave close support and Gates got his *Shadow Hawk* moving again.

But that would only expose DeVries to the same danger Gates was already facing. The only sure way for her to get clear was to continue withdrawal.

Besides, Alex didn't like the idea of ordering a comrade into harm's way while he stayed comfortably clear of danger. One day he would take his father's place at the head of the Gray Death Legion, and he knew that no commander could hope to keep his people's loyalty if he wasn't willing to share in the risks. Grayson Death Carlyle had proved the truth of that on countless battlefields of the Inner Sphere over the years, and Alex Carlyle was determined to be the kind of leader—and the kind of son—who would carry on that legacy.

"Ghost Leader to all Ghosts," he said firmly over the general taccom channel, coming to his decision at last. "Two, Four, continue withdrawal as previously ordered. Three, hold on until I get there. We'll get out of this mess yet."

"Ah . . . Leader, don't you think I should—" Caitlin DeVries managed to sound angry and diffident at the same time.

"Negative on that, Four," he shot back harshly. "You have your orders. Execute them!"

Alex turned the *Archer* back toward the clearing where

Gates had taken his hit, but had gone only three steps before the *Archer*'s threat indicator lit up. With practiced ease he identified the potential target, a twenty-ton *Commando* working its way around the fringe of his effective combat range. Maneuvering the joystick until the targeting cross hairs locked on to the target, he triggered both his LRM launchers simultaneously.

The *Archer* staggered back a pace as the volley of forty missiles arced skyward, the 'Mech only keeping its balance because Alex's neurohelmet linked his nervous system with the onboard computer. The machine was back in motion even before the first missile reached its target.

His sensor readouts recorded the strike, and the BDA analysis scrolled across the top of his head's-up display. To a *Commando,* which relied on speed rather than massive armor for protection, the effects of such a heavy barrage could be devastating. The computer's best estimate showed that the target 'Mech had taken at least twelve direct hits in the upper torso, enough to tear through the armor and into the internal structure. Whether or not the attack had disabled the 'Mech, the machine was certainly hurting.

Alex smiled grimly. One less flanker to worry about.

The *Archer* forged on, covering the rugged terrain in long, ground-eating strides. As Alex manipulated the twin foot pedals with practiced ease, keeping one eye on the primary screen and the other on the sensor map, he couldn't quite suppress a small thrill of pride. Piloting a 'Mech was what he'd been born to do, what he was meant to do. Sometimes it seemed like his ability to get the most out of a Battle-Mech, even one as ponderous as the *Archer,* was almost instinctive. It was common among Alex's classmates in the Gray Death training cadre to joke admiringly that Carlyle maneuvered the seventy-tonner the way most MechWarriors handled a scout 'Mech.

The *Shadow Hawk* was engaged again, holding off a trio of light 'Mechs that Alex's computer was tentatively tagging as twenty-ton *Wasp*s. The mammoth *BattleMaster* hadn't entered the lists yet, but the 'Mech would be close enough to start pounding Gates by the time Alex got there. In a toe-to-toe match the two Gray Death BattleMechs should, theoretically, be able to stand off the *BattleMaster,* but Alex wasn't inclined to bank on theory. For one thing, the smaller enemy 'Mechs would continue to be a nuisance that couldn't be ignored. And Gates was still too much of an unknown quantity. Trying to repair his damaged 'Mech while also trying not to let down his guard might be too much pressure for the younger pilot.

Alex would have to play it as though he was fighting the battle on his own.

He locked on to one of the *Wasp*s at long range and opened fire with his port-side LRM, waiting until his target was well clear of Gates before thumbing the launch control. Almost immediately he fired his starboard missiles at the same target.

This time the volley wasn't as effective. The *Archer*'s Battle Damage Assessment sensors registered a pair of missile hits to the *Wasp*'s left arm, but the rest had gone wide of the mark. Cursing silently, Alex quickly reestablished the target lock. But even as the red cross hairs glowed over the image of the enemy 'Mech, the *Wasp* had triggered its jump jets and bounded behind the cover of a nearby ridge. The cross hairs faded to white again before Alex had a chance to fire.

As he dropped his cross hairs over another *Wasp*, they went red again in a lock, but Alex held his fire until the target moved clear of the *Shadow Hawk*. Then he pressed the firing stud once more.

The missiles were right on target. At least ten found their mark, the BDA reporting a whole cluster of hits on and around the enemy 'Mech's poorly protected head. At the very least, a head shot would almost certainly cause multiple failures in sensors, controls, and other critical systems. Even if the pilot somehow managed to survive, he'd be badly shaken up.

The third light 'Mech followed the first, withdrawing out of harm's way behind the ridge. Alex shifted to a flat out run, a dangerous way to travel during combat conditions because of the problems of balance and uncertain footing. But he wasn't likely to get another respite like this one, with the enemy regrouping out of sight, and he hoped to get into position to defend Gates before the fighting resumed in earnest.

"Ghost Three, this is Leader. What's your situation?"

There was a long pause before Gates answered. "Rerouting to tertiary circuits," he reported. "The secondaries are out too."

"ERT?" Alex snapped.

"Computer says . . . four minutes."

Alex nodded to himself. That was about what he'd have expected for estimated repair time, though he'd been hoping for less. "All right, Three," he said slowly. "If the tertiaries fail too, lay down covering fire and then punch out."

"Acknowledged," Gates replied, his voice grim. It was the only possible order Alex could give if the damage proved too extensive for emergency repairs, but the younger pilot's reluctance to go through with it was understandable. Alex could rescue Gates if the other man was forced to abandon the *Shadow Hawk,* but no MechWarrior liked to contemplate the idea of leaving his 'Mech to the enemy. In the war-ravaged star empires of the Inner Sphere, BattleMechs were hard to come by, and once a pilot joined the ranks of the Dispossessed he might never get a second chance. Even a wealthy mercenary outfit like the Gray Death had only a limited number of spare machines on hand, and those extra 'Mechs weren't likely to go to a warrior who'd already lost one.

Nonetheless, if the 'Mech had to be abandoned, Alex would make sure Gates had a chance to eject, and he'd fight just as hard to rescue the man as he would to cover the retreat of the machine. Despite the old Inner Sphere maxim that life was cheap, but BattleMechs weren't, technology took a back seat to human life in the Gray Death Legion. That was something Grayson Carlyle had preached since the earliest days. With or without the *Shadow Hawk,* Alex would do everything in his power to bring Gates off the battlefield . . . or go down fighting as well.

He slowed as he approached the damaged 'Mech, which Gates had maneuvered behind the partial cover of a tumble of jagged rocks. It was a good tactical position, shielded from the best enemy line of approach and commanding an excellent field of fire across a broad clearing. Seeing this, Alex's regard for the rookie MechWarrior went up a few notches. Gates had apparently moved the BattleMech into the rocks after the hip actuator was knocked out, and that couldn't have been an easy job.

A hint of movement at the far side of the clearing caught Alex's attention, and he focused the *Archer*'s visual sensors there. The image that suddenly sprang to life on his primary screen brought a savage curse to his lips.

It was the enemy *BattleMaster,* its squat shape and high-domed cockpit distinctive. The massive assault 'Mech mounted a mix of lasers, short-range missiles, and antipersonnel machine guns, but the machine's most lethal weapon was the Donal particle projection cannon in its left hand. Because of the PPC's range and awesome destructive power, MechWarriors feared it above all other weapons in the 'Mech arsenal. Like the *Archer*'s missiles, the PPC was a long-range weapon, largely ineffective for fighting at close quarters.

Unfortunately for Alex, however, the *BattleMaster* was also well equipped with medium lasers designed specifically for fighting at shorter ranges. The larger machine outclassed both Gray Death 'Mechs when it came to close-in fighting, and the enemy 'Mech's heavier armor only increased its advantage.

The *BattleMaster* moved slowly behind the same ridge line the smaller 'Mechs had used for cover, disappearing from view. The blocking terrain would screen its approach for a minute or more, but after that the machine would be right on top of its opponents. They had to be ready with some kind of defense before that happened.

Alex bit his lip, trying to force himself to remember everything he'd ever learned about the *BattleMaster*. He also remembered how often the Gray Death's weapons master, Major Davis McCall, would admonish the cadets with his favorite saying: You can always find an equalizer. All Alex had to do now was identify that equalizer and act on it. Quickly, before it was too late.

Then he had it. His fingers were already preprogramming the *Archer*'s targeting computer as he keyed in his taccom system to pass orders to Gates.

"Three, we're going to need that ace-gun of yours," he said quickly. The *Shadow Hawk* mounted an Armstrong J11 autocannon, a rapid-fire projectile weapon that combined superior accuracy with striking power. There might be bigger autocannons available in the Inner Sphere, but few systems were better overall. And right now Alex was counting on accuracy rather than brute force to take this trick.

"Drop your repairs and get ready to engage the big guy

on my mark.'' He paused, punching in a final sequence on his fire-control computer. Because a preprogrammed barrage could be completely invalidated by some unexpected development in the chaos of battle, it was a risky proposition at best. But as long as the target's behavior conformed to the parameters punched in, the subsequent attack would be much more accurate overall. It would also be easier to coordinate the actions of the two defending 'Mechs more closely when the firing data was worked out in advance. ''Transmitting targeting data now.''

The younger pilot's response was edgy. ''Ah . . . skipper, I don't know about this . . .''

''Damn it, Gates,'' Alex grated through clenched teeth. ''We don't have time for arguments now!''

''But you're asking me to let loose everything, skipper! My heat's still pretty far up the scale.''

Heat was probably the main problem of the awesome energies contained within the bulk of a BattleMech. Just moving the machine made the 'Mech's power plant and engines generate hellish amounts of it. Discharging weapons, especially high-powered energy weapons like the *Shadow Hawk*'s two lasers, compounded the already serious problem. BattleMechs were equipped with heat sinks to dissipate heat, but no 'Mech had ever come off the assembly line with enough cooling capacity to entirely solve the problem. Too many other things were just as vital—armor, weaponry, electronics—and it was often necessary to make tradeoffs.

The trouble was, generating too much heat too fast could do a lot of damage to a 'Mech's electronic systems, even overload life support and fry the pilot. An integral part of the coolant subsystem was a governor that would shut down the entire machine if the heat problem became critical. And if the *Shadow Hawk* suddenly shut down it would become a sitting duck. There wouldn't be time to restart it. Gates would have no choice but to abandon the 'Mech.

Alex didn't hesitate this time. ''Drastic times, drastic measures, Three,'' he said curtly. ''Lock on to the assigned targets and get ready. We'll take the bastard when he tops the next rise.''

''Yes, sir,'' Gates responded, still sounding reluctant. Alex understood why. Not only was the other pilot courting a battlefield shutdown, but there was always another fear nagging at the back of a MechWarrior's mind. An over-heated 'Mech could become a deathtrap if the machine's safety measures failed. Dancing around the red line was something no sane MechWarrior wanted to do.

"Guess that makes me insane," Alex muttered to himself, focusing all his attention on the primary screen. If his guess about the enemy's intentions was correct, the *BattleMaster* pilot wouldn't waste time and effort on a fancy indirect approach. He would count on size and firepower to overcome the two Gray Death 'Mechs. That meant he should be appearing at the top of that ridge any time now . . .

"Target! Target!" Gates was shouting the warning even as the *BattleMaster*'s rounded cockpit swam into view on Alex's monitor. He fought down the urge to override his preprogramming and take a quick shot at the exposed head. 'Mechs were most vulnerable to a head shot, but a miss now would spoil any chance of carrying off his original plan. And that would go against another of McCall's rules: Never trade a sure hit for a chancy kill. Alex held his hand poised over the targeting joystick.

Time seemed to slow down as the *BattleMaster* clambered slowly up the slope and into full view. "Wait for it," he said softly, as much for his own benefit as for Gates'. "Wait for it . . . Now! Fire! Fire!" His finger stabbed the firing stud as he shouted the order.

After a moment's hesitation, the onboard computer evaluated its targeting instructions and locked on to the enemy machine. A 'Mech's fire control systems could pick individual target points with great accuracy, but only at the cost of considerably slowing down the rate of fire. In a typical fire-fight situation that was an unacceptable tradeoff, but in these circumstances he could afford it. Alex had preprogrammed the computer to fire the *Archer*'s full arsenal, concentrating on the *BattleMaster*'s torso area, site of all its lasers and short-range missiles. Even with the heavy chest armor to protect those weapons, such a massive barrage would still do some damage. A cluster of hits would also drive up the enemy's heat levels, though not as fast as Alex's own were climbing.

Gates fired at the same time, his lasers and autocannon adding to the fury of the attack. Overall, the *Shadow Hawk* would probably be more effective than the *Archer,* because the smaller 'Mech's weapons mix was better suited to the range. The computer's BDA was already confirming Alex's estimates, showing that few of the LRMs had been on target. The range had just been too short for the missiles to lock on.

But the short range would also limit the effectiveness of the enemy PPC, which was a vital factor at this stage. Double-checking the damage projections, Alex allowed himself a smile of satisfaction. The lasers had burned through armor in two places, and there was a high probability of damage to the *BattleMaster*'s missile storage bay. Another hit or two might detonate the stored warheads and rip the whole left torso open.

Alex's heavy fire must have thrown the *BattleMaster* pilot off, for all three of his opponent's return laser shots went wide. Misses or not, Alex was sure the other warrior was going to be mustering every ounce of skill—and counting on every bit of luck—at his command trying to even up the odds against the two Gray Death MechWarriors. From here on, it was likely to be an out-and-out slugging match, pure and simple.

He fired the *Archer*'s two arm-mounted lasers again, opting now for speed over accuracy. Gates fired another autocannon burst, pouring out high-velocity shells as fast as the *Shadow Hawk*'s ammo feed could dump fresh rounds into the chamber. "Discontinue firing, Three," Alex ordered curtly, taking aim for a third laser shot. "Resume repairs." The faster Gates could get his machine moving again, the sooner both of them could break off this fight and try to escape.

The *BattleMaster* kept on coming, hardly seeming to notice the Gray Death fire. As it stalked toward them with inexorable purpose, the torso lasers flared again, scoring a hit on the *Archer*'s left arm. Alex cursed and returned fire, cursed again when the shot went wide. The enemy 'Mech was almost on top of them now, close enough for him to pick out the individual scars on the torso armor.

And still the giant 'Mech kept on coming. In a sudden rush of understanding Alex realized that the pilot wasn't going to stand off and engage in a firefight at all. With the damage around the missile ammo bay, it was only a matter of time before the *BattleMaster* took a dangerous hit, and the pilot was too smart to bank on those odds. He was planning to turn the fight into a literal hand-to-hand engage-

ment, in close where even laser targeting systems would be
all but worthless and where all that counted was mass and
power.

Alex retargeted his lasers. With the *BattleMaster*'s left
arm encumbered by the massive PPC, the two-fisted *Archer*
had a slight advantage in a close-in fight. He had one chance
left to magnify that advantage before his opponent reached
him.

Firing the *Archer*'s twin lasers almost as one, Alex barely
contained a whoop of triumph. Both shots had struck their
target perfectly, just below the right elbow joint. If they
hadn't shattered the whole lower arm, they had certainly
penetrated the armor enough to damage the control circuitry
and bundles of myomer fibers that served the 'Mech as in-
organic muscles. With one arm damaged and the other one
virtually useless, the other pilot was suddenly in too close
to use his weapons effectively.

Alex stepped the *Archer* forward, bringing the Mech's
powerful arms to the ready. Even the strongest armor
wouldn't hold up to the punishment a 'Mech could deal out
with the weight of seventy tons behind each titanic punch.
He drew back for the first blow, then froze in horror at the
other 'Mech's response. He had forgotten, in the excitement
of the moment, that the *BattleMaster*'s PPC was not a built-
in weapon like the *Archer*'s arm-mounted lasers, but more
like a gigantic rifle that could be jettisoned at will. Which
the enemy pilot had just done. Even as the *Archer* was stepping into range, the *BattleMaster* had dropped its PPC and
was raising its massive left fist now clenched tight. Before
he could react, Alex realized that his opponent had timed
his strike perfectly. The huge hand was aimed directly at
the *Archer*'s vulnerable head, and the force behind the swing
was enough to crumple the armor and shatter the whole
cockpit.

As the punch landed, Alex knew the sour taste of failure,
followed instantly by the crackling of his taccom circuits.

"All right, all right, exercise over," came the voice.
"Shut it doon, lads. 'Tis nae point in continuing the noo!"

The huge fist in Alex's viewscreen shimmered and vanished as his sensor arrays once again projected the real world
outside rather than the falsehoods of the training program.
Alex Carlyle slumped in his control chair, sweating from

more than just the BattleMech's heat. The exercise was over, and his trainees had lost the battle.

"Bring your bairns in tae the HQ and report to the debriefing room," the heavily accented voice of Major Davis McCall continued gruffly.

Then came Caitlin DeVries' voice over the lance's private radio channel. "And Heaven help us all," Alex heard her mutter.

2

Glengarry, Skye March
Federated Commonwealth
31 March 3056

"I dinna ken what tae dae aboot ye, Alex. In twenty years there hasna been anither MechWarrior in this auld outfit who could match ye when it comes tae straight 'Mech handling, but 'tis nae enough. Nae enough by a long shot, laddie, and ye ken it weil a weil."

Alex Carlyle shifted in his chair, wishing he was anywhere but here. The office was small and sparsely furnished, with a single window looking out over the cluster of low buildings that made up the Brander Wilderness Training Center where the Gray Death Legion practiced field operations and trained cadet MechWarriors. The trainees often joked that the room's single chair reserved for cadets had been deliberately designed for maximum discomfort, and today Carlyle was ready to believe it. Worse yet, there'd been no time to shower or change after the morning's exercise and the humiliating debriefing of the fiasco. Sweaty, dirty, clad in his MechWarrior's shorts and a lightweight mesh tunic instead of the regulation cadet uniform, Carlyle wanted nothing more than to crawl into a hole and hide—but only after an hour or two in a sonic shower stall.

He forced himself to focus on the words of the Gray Death Legion's weapons master. Major Davis McCall had been one of the unit's first 'Mech pilots, back in the days when Alex's father and his men were still cutting their teeth as a struggling mercenary company. McCall had fought in most of the great battles of those early days, on Verthandi and

Sirius V, Helm and Baldur and Gram and all the other scattered worlds of the Inner Sphere where the mercenaries of the skull banner had drawn and shed blood in the seemingly endless Succession Wars. The veteran from Caledonia had the scars to prove it, too.. The red hair and beard were streaked with gray now, his right eye was a glittering bionic implant, and his left arm, like that of the 'Mech he had piloted for so long, was an artificial assemblage of plasteel and myomer fibers, but he was still an integral part of Grayson Death Carlyle's innermost circle of lieutenants and friends. The burly McCall rarely climbed into a cockpit these days, but his tactical skill and years of experience in the field went to good use in his role of weapons master supervising the training of young recruits preparing for a career with the Legion.

"Your auld faither winna be pleased with this quarter's TE reports, laddie," McCall went on, shaking his head slowly. "When he returns from his wee junket tae Tharkad he'll be aye upset tae see ye hae fallen sae far behind."

The regular training evaluation reports were the measure of each cadet MechWarrior's progress in the Gray Death's ongoing training program. A poor TE could end a trainee's hopes of permanent employment even before he was fairly started.

Alex had never really considered the prospect of a bad evaluation. He made higher academic marks and handled his BattleMech better than any of the other cadets. Besides, he was Grayson Carlyle's only son and heir.

He opened his mouth, then thought better of it. Anything he said now would sound like he expected some kind of special treatment, a favorite son trading on his father's name. And that was one thing Alex would rather die than do.

McCall stopped pacing behind his desk and leaned over it, stabbing a finger at the younger man for emphasis. "Aye, lad," he said, seeming to read Carlyle's mind. "Tis nae special dispensation for ye just because of who your faither is. In fact, laddie, ye hae higher standards tae measure up against than any o' the ithers in your class."

"Higher standards!" Alex broke his stoic silence at last, unable to contain himself any longer. He didn't look for special favors, but he'd always expected a fair deal. Catching himself, he added lamely, "uh, sir."

McCall's smile was thin. "Aye, lad. Higher indeed." His voice was gentle now, the thick Caledonian accent lilting instead of harsh. "I've kenned weil that ye were a natural-born 'Mech pilot from the day ye first climbed into a cockpit. As an ordinary MechWarrior, lad, ye would be ain of the best, someone I'd want as my ain lance mate. But as the colonel's only bairn, the Gray Death will be yours someday, young Alex. That's nae small responsibility, and ye hae tae be prepared for it. Not just as anither pilot, but as commander. That's ain skill ye havena learned the noo. Ye must learn tae be a leader fit tae tak over from your faither. And 'tis there that ye still dinna make the grade."

Alex found his voice. "No one could do that, sir," he said slowly. "My father . . . he's one of a kind. He forged this outfit from nothing but raw talent and a few lucky breaks. If you expect me to be half as good as him you're kidding yourself."

"Aye, the colonel's always been a braw laddie," McCall agreed with another smile. "But dinna sell yourself short, young Alex. Ye hae the potential tae be just as good as Grayson Carlyle, maybe better, some ways. But it winna just happen. He was as raw as ye are once, but he learned. First from his faither's people, and then on his ain. And he's never stopped learning, either, laddie. And nor will ye."

Alex looked down at the desk. "Maybe you should be grooming someone else for the job," he muttered darkly. "Dave Clay, maybe." He didn't bother to hide his feelings now, his tone as bitter as his words. It had taken more than an hour for the trainees to return from the mock battlefield after the morning's exercise. The long trip back through the pass to the training center had given Carlyle ample time to brood over his mistakes, putting him in a dour mood by the time the four 'Mechs and their escort of trainers had been turned over to the technical staff. Step by step, he'd tried to make the best possible choices, yet each one had only made things worse.

And the hell of it was that this wasn't the first time he'd failed. It seemed that every exercise designed to test his ability to make snap judgments in the field ended the same way, in failure and another lecture from McCall on the responsibilities of command. The rest of the recruits had finished their debriefing and headed back for the cadet quarters, but as usual Alex was left to face his mentor alone in this same small, spartan office, feeling like a fool.

McCall shook his head. "The Gray Death winna follow anyone but a Carlyle, laddie. Ye ken that. 'Tis your faither's skill that brought us together, and 'twill always be a Carlyle at the helm."

Despite his personal doubts, Alex knew that McCall was right. In the era of the Successor States of the thirty-first century, ties of personal loyalty and feudal allegiance went deeper than any other bonds. A man pledged faith to a leader based on blood ties or proven abilities rather than outmoded concepts like nationalism or ideology. And that held as true among a mercenary unit like the Gray Death as it did for any of the Great Houses of the Inner Sphere. The men and women who signed on with Grayson Death Carlyle would remain loyal to his name, to his heirs. But without that essential core of leadership, the unit would probably just melt away.

"Even if ye never tak the field in person, ye will be the man in charge," McCall went on. "Owner if nae commander. But 'twould be a waste for ye tae be some faceless owner relying on the likes of my wee godson tae run the unit in battle. Ye hae too much tae offer, laddie, tae end up anywhere but at the head of these troops."

Alex shrugged. "If you say so, Major," he responded listlessly. "But I just don't see how I'm ever going to get it right. I was sure I was doing the right thing today, but obviously I was wrong from start to finish."

"Aye, maybe ye were." McCall sat down heavily and flexed the fingers of his bionic hand absently. "Do ye ken where ye went wrong?"

Alex pursed his lips. "Forgetting that the *BattleMaster* could drop the PPC was a pretty damn stupid thing, for starters. I might've had a chance if I'd disabled that arm."

"Ye wouldna hae been able tae do it," McCall said. " 'Twas nae time, and ye were lucky with the first arm hit, anyway. Computers gave it less than a thirty percent chance." Both the regular BattleMechs and the trainer

'Mechs had used onboard computers to predict and calculate damage and to provide bogus sensor information, killing onboard systems to match the hits they projected in the theoretical combat. Live-ammo exercises were too costly in men, materials, and man-hours of repair work to be viable for normal training.

"And that last fight wasna the real problem. Ain-tae-ain, the odds were well-nigh even. Had ye nae frozen up, ye might hae won that fight, but ye still wouldna hae won the battle."

"But the others made it to the pass," Alex protested. "And if I'd beaten the *BattleMaster,* Gates and I would've been in the clear!"

McCall shook his head. "By the time ye were engaged wi' that big behemoth, lad, the rest of the lance was aboot tae be swamped by the flankers ye barely touched on the way tae cover Gates. That was why I ordered the halt. The situation was hopeless by then, because ye wcre too damned stubborn tae delegate the rescue mission tae the ithers."

Alex's shoulders sagged. "I couldn't order them to do something I wasn't willing to do myself. I figured I was the only one who could hold that *BattleMaster,* and it didn't seem right to sacrifice more than one 'Mech if the rescue went sour."

McCall's eyes glinted. "And did it nae occur tae you, lad, after that stunt ye pulled last week Tayside, that there might be a good reason why we gave ye a 'Mech designed for stand-off fighting?" McCall looked genuinely angry now, and his accent seemed to fade as he tried to make his point plain. "No one doubts your bravery, lad. Or your compassion for your people. 'Tis more important that you learn to handle your assets effectively than it is tae score cheap popularity points by wading into the thick of the fight. A commander canna become bogged doon in combat sae much that he loses sight of the whole battle. DeVries or Clay could have covered Gates up close, with you in support at longer range and the fourth 'Mech moving tae secure the pass. Your *Archer* could hae supported in both directions at once, and that would hae turned the tide not only against the *BattleMaster* but at the pass as weil. But ye chose tae ignore doctrine and gang your ain glay, didn't ye?"

Alex took a deep breath. "You've always said that doctrine could be a strait jacket to trap a second-rate commander, Major. My father was never one to worry about doing it by the book, so I didn't think—"

"Aye, that's it, isn't it? Ye didna think. Doctrine untempered by imagination is a danger, aye, but there is always a good reason for that doctrine tae be there in the first place, and woe tae him who ignores it! Combined arms tactics are the very heart of a successful battle, where ye use all of your available units to the fullest possible advantage. Wasting an *Archer* in a hand-tae-hand fight isna using those assets wisely, is it?"

Alex looked away. "I guess not," he admitted reluctantly.

"Weil, then, today's wee scrap did ain thing, anyway, if it taught ye that lesson. I expect better of ye on the next exercise, young Alex. Dinna let me doon. And dinna let your auld faither doon. Understand me?"

"Yes sir," Alex said.

"Good. 'Tis the end of it, then, for the noo." McCall glanced at the old-fashioned clock on the office wall between the door and the engraved coat of arms on its tartan background that was the only decoration in the small room. "Ye'll just have time tae shower and change before the emelt gets in. Dinna miss it, laddie."

"I won't, sir," Alex replied, checking his wristcomp against the wall display before picking up his cooling vest from the back of the chair, saluting McCall, and leaving the office. After the mess he'd made of the exercise today, the last thing he wanted was to be late for the maglev transport heading from the training compound into the capital. His father was off-planet, and Alex was supposed to deputize for him at an important ceremony tomorrow. If he missed that . . .

Alex was still brooding when he reached the cadet quarters block. He was used to being on top, at the head of his cadet class in every course and on every training maneuver, but over the last few weeks he'd become ever more unsure of himself as the focus had shifted from ordinary operations to these more difficult command exercises. Lately it seemed as if he couldn't do anything right. Today had been bad, but last week's exercise, when he'd tried to push across the Tay River against heavy opposition, had been a genuine disaster.

The failures were sapping his self-confidence more and more, which only led to fresh failures. It's a no-win situation, he told himself angrily. Whatever McCall thinks, I'm just not cut out for this.

He barely noticed the pair of cadets who hailed him as he started down the hall to his room, and probably wouldn't have responded to his roommate if his friend hadn't opened the door and stood directly in his path.

"Aye, laddie, and ye look like ye've had a right royal reaming!" Davis Carlyle Clay mimicked McCall's accent to perfection. Showing a lopsided grin that accentuated his boyish good looks, he was freshly groomed and clad in his dress gray cadet's uniform.

Dropping the phony Scots accent, Clay kept up the banter as Alex pushed past him into their room. "I was just getting ready to check the medbay to see if they'd admitted anyone with his butt in a sling."

Alex's only answer was a distracted grunt as he stripped off his tunic and grabbed a towel from his locker. He wasn't in the mood for Davis Clay's particular brand of heavy-handed humor.

But Clay didn't give up. Still talking, he followed Alex into the washroom they shared with the two cadets in the next room, Farquhar and Galleno. "Hey, come on, man, say something! Auld Mac kept you in there for an hour after the debriefing and all you do is grunt at me? Let off some steam, for the love of Blake!" Clay laughed. "If I'd been through the Scottish Inquisition I'd be dying to share the grief. What did he say? Just the stuff you understood, of course, the ten percent in anything like English." He grinned again.

"Look, Dave, I don't want to talk about it, all right?" Alex said wearily. "I'm running late, and I'm just not in the mood for all this . . . nonsense."

Clay stepped back as if he'd been struck, then shrugged. "Sure, Alex. If you say so. Sorry." His voice was flat, neutral, but the look in his eyes was wounded.

As Alex closed the door to the stall and switched on the sonic beam, he was frowning. He'd known Dave Clay all his life, and they'd been best friends almost from the start. The other cadet was the elder by almost six years, and his irreverent, devil-may-care attitude contrasted sharply with

Alex's more thoughtful manner, yet their bond remained unshakable.

Until now. Lately Alex had found his friend's jokes a little too barbed, hitting a little too close to home. He'd been keeping Clay at arm's length for weeks now, and Clay was obviously upset by the wall that had grown between them.

Not that Alex wanted that wall. He just didn't know how to keep it from getting higher and broader with each passing day. It was one more thing he couldn't seem to get right. One more thing to worry about.

By the time Alex finished showering and had donned his dress grays, Clay had already gone. The whole cadet unit, fourteen would-be MechWarriors waiting for a precious slot to open up in the Legion's five-company roster, would be attending the ceremony in the capital, and Clay had probably already headed for the maglev terminal with the others. Checking his wristcomp again, Alex realized he had precious little time to make it there himself. He found his kit bag, prepacked before the exercise and ready to go, and slung it over his shoulder. Perhaps there would be a chance later to take some steps toward solving the Davis Clay problem—if only Alex could figure out what those steps might possibly be.

But he wasn't the only one left in the barracks block after all. Cadet Caitlin DeVries was just outside his door, leaning against the wall with a frown creasing her usually attractive features. "It's about time you got moving," she said, picking up her own kit bag and falling in beside him. "I was sure we'd both be gigged for missing the emelt."

"You should have gone with the others," he said curtly.

"Somebody had to make sure our star speaker found the terminal," she said. Even though her tone was light, she was still frowning. "Dave left a while ago. Looked like he'd lost his best friend." She held out an arm to stop him and looked straight into his eyes, challenging. "Did he?"

Alex looked away. "He probably thinks so," he said softly. He pushed past her, his long legs carrying him out of the building and across the tarmac at a ground-eating pace. Caitlin strained to keep up.

"You want to tell me about it?" she demanded.

"Come on, Caitlin, you know what he can be like. I was

in a hurry getting ready and he just kept on with the jokes. I was short with him. So shoot me.''

''I might just. You're leaving a few things out, aren't you? Like the fact that you were mad about being raked over the coals by Auld Mac, and you were taking it out on Dave. Right?'' She didn't let him answer. ''For Blake's sake, Alex, you of all people should know not to take Dave seriously. You're the one who told me that, back when I joined up. Or don't the same standards apply to the colonel's son?''

''Don't say that!'' he snapped, immediately on the defensive when anyone accused him of trading on his father's position. As Grayson Carlyle's son he was destined for command some day—unless he failed to measure up, as seemed all too likely right now—but the idea that others might believe he thought himself better than the rest always galled him. Though he knew Caitlin was only trying to make a point, her words still rankled.

But she was right about Davis Clay. He was the oldest cadet with the Gray Death, and had been in the training program for almost a decade now. Since the Legion's last reorganization to become a mixed regiment of infantry, light armor, and BattleMechs, the process of recruiting new personnel had firmed up. The reputation of Grayson Carlyle's elite outfit made it one of the most sought-after mercenary billets in the Inner Sphere, but the unit also had some of the toughest recruiting standards anywhere. No matter how experienced or gifted, any MechWarrior who wished to join the Gray Death Legion went into the training program first. But only those who proved they had what it took, mentally, physically, emotionally—even morally— wound up in an active-duty unit. Grayson Death Carlyle set high standards for his men, and especially for his MechWarriors.

Empty billets in the Legion were filled by cadets on the basis of a competitive test. Clay, despite an excellent training record, had failed the last three times he'd had a shot at advancing into one of the active-duty units. Anyone else might have given up and struck out on his own in search of another merc unit with less exacting standards, but Clay was a special case. His father, Delmar Clay, had been one of Grayson Carlyle's original MechWarriors, a member of the inner circle almost from the beginning. The elder Clay had expected a lot from his son, but his demands for performance had never been matched by praise for the boy's accomplishments. When Delmar Clay died in the desperate fighting during the Legion's withdrawal from Sudeten, he left his son a hard legacy. Davis Clay was determined to live up to his father's expectations, no matter what it took. But his inability to win a permanent place with the Legion had taken its toll. His sardonic humor masked a fear that he would never be quite good enough to reach his goal.

In a way, Alex mused, Clay's problem wasn't that much different from his own. They were both trying to live up to a standard that might well be beyond their grasp.

"Dave just wanted you to know he was there for you, Alex," Caitlin told him, her voice softer now. "That's what friends do, you know. He deserves a little friendship in return."

"Yeah, I know. I wasn't thinking . . . Guess that mess this morning still had me wound up."

"Next time maybe you'll listen to your officers, huh?" She grinned for the first time. "Some of us actually know what we're talking about at times."

Alex mustered a feeble answering smile. "Go ahead, get it out of your system. I was a bad boy. I admit it. Can't we move on to something more pleasant now?"

"Is there anything pleasant to talk about in this pit?" she asked, her free arm taking in the training center with an expansive gesture. "I think the real reason this morning was so tough is that Auld Mac's been reprogramming the simulation computers. Did you get a load of the way those *Commando*s were scoring hits? No way that was a fair fight!"

Their talk drifted to technical matters as they hurried to the terminal. The PA speakers were blaring out the final boarding call just as Alex and Caitlin reached the MLT car. Their wristcomp transponders reported their arrival as they climbed aboard, checking them off the computer roster so that McCall would know that all were present and accounted for.

The emelt was already pulling away from the platform and gathering speed as the two found seats across the aisle from a group of senior technicians from the training center's maintenance unit. Leaning back in his seat, Alex swung up one of the entertainment vidscreens provided for passengers, and ran a hardwire lead from his wristcomp to the vidscreen's external input jack. A moment later the text of the speech he was supposed to give appeared on the screen. He would spend the hour-long trip studying it, but a part of his mind was still on the failed exercise, on Dave Clay, and on what it all meant for his own future.

3

Glengarry, Skye March
Federated Commonwealth
1 April 3056

Davis Carlyle Clay sat alone in the MLT car, staring out the window at the rolling hills of Glengarry's Braemoray District and thinking of home. He had been born on Helm, the Gray Death's first landhold. The planet had been awarded to the Legion by House Marik in exchange for the unit's service to the Free World's League at the height of the Succession Wars, but the mercenaries had been driven off Helm by their employer's treachery while Clay was still an infant. For as long as he could remember home had been Sudeten, a planet of House Steiner's Lyran Commonwealth—until the day the Clans had come.

It was ironic, he thought bitterly, that what had finally brought an end to centuries of continual warfare among the Great Houses of the Inner Sphere was another kind of war, this time against a common foe from beyond the vast reaches of human space. It was an even greater irony that the external threat had been spawned by exactly the same circumstances that had fueled the centuries of Succession Wars. In all its expansion among the stars the human race had yet to encounter another intelligent species, yet men never failed to find new excuses to wage war against one another. For centuries the Star League had united and ruled the stars, until that golden era had collapsed in civil war and chaos. In a mass exodus led by the most famous general in the history of mankind, most of the League's military had simply abandoned the Inner Sphere, disappearing forever into the unmapped space of the Periphery.

Left behind were the five Great Houses and their rulers, each of whom claimed to be the rightful heir to the throne of the Star League. For almost three hundred years the militaries of the Great Houses had fought one another to a standstill. The wars had been ruinous, with an inevitable decline in technological know-how and a virtual stagnation of cultural growth. The leaders had fought on regardless, Steiner and Kurita, Liao, Marik, and Davion, each one determined to emerge as the sole ruler of all human-settled space. Alliances shifted, leaders changed, ordinary people died in droves, but still the Succession Wars went on.

Then occurred a single political maneuver that had almost changed all that. In the year 3028 two of the Great Houses had actually united in more than just a temporary alliance of convenience. The marriage of Hanse Davion, Prince of the Federated Suns, to Melissa Steiner, daughter of Archon Katrina Steiner of the Lyran Commonwealth, had in one stroke united those two realms into a single overpowering political unit, the Federated Commonwealth. The mighty F-C army scored massive victories over their major rivals, and for a time the stalemate seemed ended. But even the Federated Commonwealth's drive stalled eventually, and a period of uneasy peace settled over the Inner Sphere.

It was at that juncture that the Clans appeared on the scene. Descendants of those who had followed General Alexsandr Kerensky into exodus after the fall of the Star League, the Clans had developed an entirely new society far from the rest of humankind. Their technology had moved forward while that of the Successor States had been losing ground, and their methods of training and motivating their fanatic soldiers were unlike anything the Inner Sphere had ever imagined. In a space of three years the Clans overran a third of the Successor States, forcing the leaders of the Great Houses into an uneasy alliance to fight the new enemy. Somehow the Inner Sphere had survived the onslaught, but only at tremendous cost.

After the betrayal of the Gray Death Legion on Helm, the mercenaries had sought service with House Steiner. Like Helm, Sudeten was awarded them as a planethold in exchange for their services, a base of operations for the Legion between missions. Clay still thought of the planet as home, the world where he had grown up, where he had first joined the Legion's MechWarrior training cadre. The world he had shared with his father.

Those had been happy days for him, once the shadow of his mother's untimely death had passed. He remembered how proud his father had been the day Davis announced his decision to join the Legion and carry on the family tradition. And he remembered the anticipation in the weeks before his first scheduled test for a permanent posting to his father's own command.

But the test had never come. Just days before it was scheduled, the Clans had launched their invasion of Sudeten, and in the desperate fighting that followed there was no time to consider cadet promotions. Along with the rest of the cadet class, Davis Clay had been ordered to assist in evacuating the noncombatants while Colonel Carlyle and his troops tried to hold back the foe. In the meantime Delmar Clay had fallen in battle while piloting his battered old *Wolverine,* trying to rally his troops for one more counterattack against a seemingly unstoppable enemy.

The Gray Death Legion, acknowledged as one of the best mercenary units of the entire Inner Sphere, had barely emerged from the campaign intact. Nearly half their men and machines were lost in the fighting on Sudeten and then on the nearby world of Pandora, where the Clans caught the Gray Death a second time.

So the Legion became homeless again, forced to evacuate Sudeten when the Federated Commonwealth government decided there was little to gain by sending reinforcements to support the shattered mercenaries. Instead Prince Davion had reassigned the Legion to a new world, this world, Glengarry, and here the Gray Death had tried to start anew.

The Legion had replaced its losses and restored its tarnished reputation in a half-dozen small campaigns against various minor opponents along the Federated Commonwealth's long border. But Davis Carlyle Clay had been unable to forget the past. His performance in training had suffered, and time after time he had just failed to make the cut when the opportunity came to advance into the Legion's fighting arm.

It was three years now since his father's death, and still

Dave Clay hadn't accomplished the one thing that would have meant the most to him.

He watched the hills of the Braemoray District hurtling past the emelt and bit his lip. There would be no more failures. The next time he had a chance, he would make his father proud.

4

Tharkad City
Tharkad, Federated Commonwealth
1 April 3056

"**Y**ou'd think a chance to attend Court would make a man happy. But I guess you're going to be the exception to the rule . . . as usual."

Grayson Death Carlyle tugged at the tight collar of his dress gray uniform and frowned at his wife's words. "It was a mistake to come," he said gruffly. "And not just because of the situation back home. Damn it, Lori, we haven't missed a Day of Heroes celebration in a quarter of a century. It wasn't right to miss this one."

"I know, Gray," Lori Kalmar-Carlyle said. "But you don't turn down the Archon Prince."

Carlyle nodded, glum. It was late evening here on Tharkad, but back on Glengarry it would still be the middle of the night. And in a few more hours it would be time to begin the Day of Heroes ceremonies, the Gray Death Legion's most important holiday. It marked a chance to remember the legionnaires who had fought and died for the unit over the years, and he hated to miss this opportunity to commemorate those lost comrades. There were damned few of the old Legion left, and it wouldn't be much longer until all the original band was gone.

But instead of being on Glengarry with his men, Carlyle had come to Tharkad, feeling like a hick tourist on his first trip to the big city. It took all the iron will that had forged the Gray Death Legion from a handful of misfits into one of the most celebrated mercenary units in the Inner Sphere just to keep from gawking at the grand architecture or the throng of gaudily clad courtiers lining the Grand Hall of the Royal Court.

"There are more people here than in all of Sigurd-shaven," Lori said quietly, echoing his thoughts with the same uncanny accuracy that had made her invaluable as the Legion's executive officer. Her hand slipped into his.

Carlyle glanced again at his wife, a woman still slender and blonde and more than a little bit vulnerable even after so many years together. She hardly ever mentioned Sigurd, her home world out in the sparsely settled Periphery. Adjusting to the crowds and confusion of Tharkad had to be even more difficult for Lori than for him, making her think of the home she had lost.

Before Carlyle could respond, the PA blared a trumpet fanfare. "His Highness, Victor Ian Steiner-Davion, Archon Prince of the Federated Commonwealth, Supreme Marshal of the Armed Forces of the Federated Commonwealth, Duke of Tharkad, Duke of New Avalon, Duke of Donegal, Landgrave von Bremen, Minister of the Crucis March, First Lord of the Star League."

The trumpets blared again, and the enormous double doors at the far end of the Grand Hall opened ponderously to admit the most powerful man in the Inner Sphere. Prince Victor was a short, square-jawed young man of twenty-six, with blond hair and piercing blue eyes. He wore the dress uniform of the Tenth Lyran Guards: high-collared, red-and-gold trimmed dark blue tunic, powder-blue trousers with red piping, and matching red sash. Despite the gaudy uniform, Grayson thought the Prince cut a figure that was neither impressive nor dignified as he stalked down the center aisle a shade too fast. He looked, in fact, exactly as Grayson Carlyle had imagined him, an impatient man with little time for empty forms and ceremonials.

The prince of the Federated Commonwealth nodded from time to time as he made his way down the aisle, acknowledging nobles, military officers, and ministers who bowed low as he passed. He took no special notice of the Carlyles, but that was no surprise. There was no reason why Victor Davion should have singled them out. Although the Carlyle name was now well known throughout the Inner Sphere, Grayson had never previously visited Tharkad, nor had he ever set eyes on the Archon Prince.

Another officer in the Legion's somber dress grays received more attention, or at least her family did. Tracy Maxwell Kent was the daughter of one of the Federated Commonwealth's wealthiest nobles, Lord Rodney Howard Kent, who had only recently been named to the prince's Advisory Council. Lord Rodney was one of a score of prominent Federated Suns nobles accompanying the Archon Prince on his tour of the Lyran portion of his domain. Tracy had finally made peace with her family after years of estrangement, and Carlyle was happy to see father and daughter together again after so many years of bitterness. It seemed that being a captain in the famed Gray Death Legion was, after all, a respectable enough position even for a Kent. With the old breach healed, Tracy had again become heiress to the Kent titles and property, and she would almost certainly be called home to the capital to take up her aristocratic obligations as soon as she could honorably wrap up her affairs with the Legion.

One more of the Companions gone, Carlyle thought, suddenly nostalgic for those early days when the Gray Death had still been a struggling merc company trying to earn its spurs. It reminded him again of the Day of Heroes celebrations he would be missing. Time had wrought too many changes in the Legion. Most of the old outfit was gone now, killed or retired or just plain moved on. He hardly knew most of his officers the way he'd known those first comrades, and these days it seemed like he spent more time behind a desk or off on junkets like this one instead of piloting his 'Mech into the thick of a fight.

The prince ascended the five steps to the raised dais at the end of the Great Hall, then paused. Set under the three banners of the realm were two empty thrones, one under the sword-and-sunburst emblem of the Federated Suns on the left, and one under the mailed fist of the Lyran Commonwealth to the right. Placed between and above them both was a banner with the fist-and-sunburst emblem of the Federated Commonwealth. After a moment's hesitation, Victor bowed stiffly to the throne on the right, then took his seat on the left, under the Federated Suns banner. A murmur ran through the crowd, and not all the words Carlyle could hear were approving.

For better than two decades those thrones had belonged

to Prince Hanse Davion and Archon Melissa Steiner-Davion, Victor's parents. The pair had been the architects of the alliance that had altered the balance of power in the Inner Sphere and nearly ended the long stalemate in the struggle to restore the Star League. Although the pair had governed a united realm, the Prince Hanse and the Archon Melissa had each retained their respective thrones, an essential balancing act to keep both sides of the alliance content. After Hanse Davion had died of heart failure four years before, Victor had inherited his father's crown but continued to honor his mother as co-ruler of the realm.

Now Melissa Steiner-Davion was dead as well, victim of an assassin's bomb blast. Since that tragic day almost a year ago, Victor had been facing a growing political crisis that threatened to shatter the fragile Federated Commonwealth alliance, and he needed to do everything possible to boost his waning popularity. The idea of power passing irrevocably into the hands of the Davion family was still anathema to some Lyrans, particularly certain nobles of House Steiner who had never fully accepted the marriage alliance. Victor's bow to the throne that had belonged to his mother might have been intended to signal his respect, but by seating himself under the Federated Suns banner he had clearly proclaimed the realm to which he gave priority in his government.

Here on the old Steiner capitol world Victor should have seated himself on the Steiner throne, Carlyle thought. In these troubled times, that single slighting gesture might have cost the young prince far more than he could afford.

Perhaps if Victor's sister Katherine had been here, she would have found a way to smooth things over. Taller than Victor, with a regal beauty that owed as much to her grandmother's strength as to her mother's loveliness, Her Grace the Duchess of Sarna, Katherine Steiner-Davion, was much beloved by the people of the Lyran Commonwealth and she was easily the most popular of Hanse and Melissa's three children. Perhaps it was just that she so resembled the beloved Melissa, or perhaps it was the fact that she seemed to one most concerned for fate of the Lyran Commonwealth.

But Katherine was not here today to take her place along-

side her brother in the Grand Hall. Where she would surely
have bestowed grace and charm, Prince Victor suddenly
gestured impatiently. Two huge doors behind the dais swung
slowly open, and a pair of 'Mechs stepped into the hall.
The tradition of 'Mechs guarding the Lyran throne went
back more than five hundred years, but today the appearance of those two BattleMechs made many in the assembled
crowd gasp. Traditionally, the two 'Mechs had always been
*Griffin*s painted in the colors of one of the Archon's favorite
Lyran Guard units. Today the one on the left was a *Marauder* painted in the black and gold colors of the First
Kathil Uhlans, a unit fanatically loyal to the Federated
Commonwealth. On the right stood a *Crusader* painted with
the red torso, black legs, and black trim of the Kell Hounds
mercenary unit.

That, Carlyle thought, was another major mistake. The
last thing Victor needed was to emphasize the alliance between the two realms here on Tharkad, where pro-Lyran
sentiment ran deepest.

The Grand Marshal of the Palace silenced the noise with
another PA announcement. ''In the name of the Unfinished
Book, let all who have business before the throne of the
Archon Prince draw nigh. May the Divine Power give His
Highness wisdom to preserve and protect the realm!'' That
drew more comment. The Unfinished Book was the central
symbol of the unofficial state religion of the old Federated
Suns, and had no place in Lyran society. Carlyle wondered
if Victor was even aware of how much he was trampling
on the feelings of half his subjects with these blatant attempts to impose outside culture on a proud people like
the Lyrans.

Carlyle's attention wandered as the first petitioners or
honorees were led before the throne. He wondered if any
of these carefree court dandies had even an inkling of the
events unfolding beyond the narrow confines of their shel-
tered lives of pomp and privilege. The assassination of the
Archon Melissa was only the latest in a string of blows
that had left the Federated Commonwealth teetering on the
brink of collapse, yet none of these overdressed courtiers
seemed aware of any change from the great days of Prince
Hanse.

Of course, the rot had set in slowly, over a period of
many years. It had started with the failure of Hanse Dav-

ion's drive to unite the Inner Sphere. Chief obstacle in the
way of victory had been the Federated Commonwealth's traditional rival, the Draconis Combine of House Kurita. No
matter the combined power of the Davion and Steiner resources, success had remained just out of reach. In the end
the Combine had managed not only to survive but to mount
a counterthreat sufficient to force a truce and a return to the
old Inner Sphere stalemate. Then came the stunning shock
of the Clan Wars, which hit the old Lyran Commonwealth
frontier worlds particularly hard. Carlyle still shuddered at
the memory of Sudeten, where so many of the Legion had
fallen against the Clans. Though the war had lasted but three
years, its consequences were both tragic and grave, adding
fuel to the Lyrans' growing discontent with the Federated
Commonwealth's weakened economy and overstretched, in-
adequate bureaucracy.

Now Archon Melissa was dead, and that would only add
momentum to the Lyran separatist movements. All the evidence in her murder pointed, in fact, to one of the most
prominent of those separatists as the author of the deed.
Ryan Steiner, Duke of Porrima, was both a cousin of Prince
Victor and a man of shrewd cunning and a wide following
among the Lyran dissidents. He was also, as it happened,
the major political power broker in the Isle of Skye region,
and that made Grayson Death Carlyle nervous. Even more
dangerous was the fact that Richard Steiner, military commander of the Isle of Skye, seemed to be taking orders from
Ryan rather than from his Federated Commonwealth superiors. Glengarry was in the heart of the Skye March, and
that put the Legion squarely in the middle of the growing
political firestorm. Indeed, Prince Victor had assigned
Glengarry to the Legion as part of his effort to counter the
power of the separatist movement with his own loyal forces
even before the tragedy of his mother's death.

It all struck Carlyle as too little and too late. Even if it
turned out that Ryan Steiner had not been behind Archon
Melissa's assassination, tightening Federated Commonwealth security in the Skye March was only fueling the separatist cause. Sooner or later the separatists would make
their move, and the chain reaction of a rising in the Isle of
Skye would trigger risings throughout the Lyran Commonwealth, perhaps to the point of all-out civil war. And that

would be the end of the Federated Commonwealth. Of that Carlyle was certain.

Had the orders summoning Grayson Carlyle to Tharkad not been unequivocal he would gladly had deferred the trip even without the excuse of the Day of Heroes. Until the political situation was less murky and uncertain, he wouldn't feel comfortable with the way matters stood back in the March. There had been the sudden crisis on the border with House Marik, for instance, that had cropped up shortly before the assassination. Richard had sent two of the F-C's best regimental combat teams from the Skye March to mount an active defense around Ford, probably on direct orders from Ryan. At the same time nearly half the Gray Death Legion had also been redeployed out of the Skye region, sent to Borghese in the Tamar March to relieve the Black Thorns after a Jade Falcon raid. Units from other, quieter sectors were supposed to be coming in to relieve those troops, but so far none had materialized. Meanwhile the Tharkad rumor mill hinted that not all the relief forces were as loyal as those that had been sent away from the heart of the March. That left trustworthy garrison forces few and far between in the Isle of Skye, a state of affairs not at all to Grayson Carlyle's liking.

But Victor had insisted that the famous Colonel Carlyle and a small contingent of his senior personnel must be in attendance at this Court. In addition to the strategy conferences the legionnaires were scheduled to attend, the prince also seemed determined to thrust them into a round of social and ceremonial functions designed to demonstrate both the power and the unity of his government. The Gray Death had already participated in a military parade the day after arriving in Tharkad City, marching the four BattleMech's of Carlyle's command lance through the heart of town.

And now there was this bit of pomp and circumstance to get through . . .

"Colonel Grayson Death Carlyle," intoned the Grand Marshal of the Palace. Though he mispronounced Grayson's middle name, making it rhyme with "teeth" rather than "breath," the mercenary was too startled by the summons to really notice. Straightening the edge of his uniform jacket, he stepped forward, conscious of the whole Court's attention.

In a daze, he approached the foot of the dais and bowed respectfully, but without the obsequious air of some of the more accomplished courtiers who had preceded him. He was, after all, a mercenary soldier, not a Federated Commonwealth aristocrat, and that made him an employee rather than a true subject. Nor had his contract ever officially been with House Davion. He had signed on with Katrina Steiner before her abdication in favor of her daughter Melissa, and his current allegiance to the F-C government derived from that agreement.

"Ah, Colonel Carlyle," Prince Victor said with a faint smile. "A pleasure to meet you at last."

"The pleasure is mine, Your Highness," Carlyle replied formally.

"You have served the Federated Commonwealth well over the years, Colonel," Victor went on. "A distinguished record indeed. And even if that were not so impressive? the Gray Death Legion's discovery of the computer core on Helm would by itself entitle you to a place in the history books. The Federated Commonwealth is most grateful for the service of commanders such as you." While the prince spoke, a liveried servant had come forward carrying an archaic broadsword like the one on the Federated Suns banner. Pausing but a moment, the prince took it in with both hands.

"Ceremony demands of you what I would not request," he continued. "If you would kneel please, and place your hands on the hilt of this sword."

Carlyle hesitated briefly, then dropped to one knee. When his hand clasped the sword just below Victor's, the prince resumed speaking. "Let it be known on every world of the Federated Commonwealth, in the councils of the Clans, and among our enemies, that I, Prince Victor Steiner-Davion, do hereby recognize the many services of Grayson Death Carlyle to the Houses of Steiner and Davion. I hereby name you a Baron of the Federated Commonwealth. I bestow upon you and your heirs, in perpetuity, the fief and planethold of Glengarry in the Isle of Skye."

The two men stared at each other for a moment, then the prince whispered, "You have earned it, Carlyle. For your sake and mine, I hope you are able to hold it."

The announcement set off a new wave of murmurs among the crowd. It was rare for a mere baron to hold an entire planet in fief, and in the few cases where such an award was made, it was generally a backwater world like Glengarry. Even rarer, though, was the advancement of a mercenary colonel into the peerage of one of the Successor States. Until now the Gray Death Legion had enjoyed the planethold on Glengarry as a part of their contract with the Lyran Commonwealth, with the world providing money, manpower, supplies, and land to both present and former members of the outfit. But that hold was valid only for the duration of the Gray Death's service contract. This grant from the prince was something totally different. It made of Colonel Grayson Carlyle a mercenary leader who could take his Gray Death Legion to the service of another employer, while still remaining Baron Carlyle over the fief of Glengarry.

Grayson Carlyle looked up into the prince's ice-blue eyes. He knew what would come next, and for a moment he was inclined to end the proceedings here and now. Content to remain his own man, Carlyle had been on his own since the day his father had died in battle on far-off Trellwan. Accepting a Barony from Victor Davion would change everything.

It was obviously another step in the prince's plan to maintain control over the troubled Skye March. By binding the Gray Death that much closer to the twin thrones, Davion was tightening his grip on Ryan Steiner and the Skye separatists. Besides that, it was well known that the Gray Death was engaged in a long-term feud with the Draconis Combine. While the gossips prattled on about whether Prince Victor had become overly fond of Omi Kurita, daughter of the Combine's brilliant Coordinator Theodore, Victor's honoring the anti-Kurita Gray Death Legion would help negate the idea of him toadying to the realm's oldest and most inveterate foe.

Carlyle wasn't sure he liked being a pawn in the Archon Prince's political chess game, but if any power in the Inner Sphere stood for civilization, for order, for an end to the wars that had crippled humankind for too many centuries, it was the Federated Commonwealth. All his life Grayson Carlyle had seen himself as standing against the barbarians at the gate. If the price of maintaining the Federated Commonwealth against its enemies was his fealty, how could he refuse to pay it?

Slowly, deliberately, he nodded his head, and Victor Davion smiled. "Please, Baron von Glengarry, repeat after me. Before these witnesses here assembled I, Grayson Death Carlyle, Baron von Glengarry, do hereby take you, Victor Ian Steiner-Davion, Archon Prince of the Federated Commonwealth, to be my lord of life and limb, and I your man, for my planethold of Glengarry."

"Before these witnesses here assembled I, Grayson Death Carlyle, Baron . . ." As he repeated the words, Carlyle couldn't help but notice that it was a revival of an archaic fealty oath. Nobles generally swore fealty to the realm and its legitimate government, but the prince had chosen to emphasize the personal loyalty of master and man. That was somehow typical of Victor Davion.

"Moreover," the prince went on solemnly, "I swear to support and uphold the Federated Commonwealth, in peace and in war, with all the strength of my land, and to adjudge the enemies of the realm as my enemies, for as long as I shall live."

Slowly, Carlyle repeated the formula of defending his liege to the death, still wondering if he was doing the right thing.

Then Prince Victor spoke again. "I, Victor Steiner-Davion, take you, Baron von Glengarry, to be vassal of heart and hand and mind, to support and sustain you, for as long as I bear this Sword of State." The prince handed the ancient weapon back to its custodian and resumed his throne. "Rise, Baron Carlyle of Glengarry, and let citizens of the Federated Commonwealth look upon the rewards of selfless duty and devotion to their nation."

A cheer went up from the assembled court. Though resentment of the Archon Prince would be further fanned by his peculiar combination of the old oath of fealty with many of the traditional titles and forms the hidebound aristocrats of Tharkad would have expected, the act itself was sure to be popular. The Gray Death Legion had been a stalwart bastion of the Commonwealth for years, and both the unit and its commander were well respected.

Grayson felt a new weight of responsibility across his shoulders as he stood and bowed again. Until now his only obligation had been to his people, to the Gray Death Legion. Now he would have to balance their good against his new fealty to Victor Davion. The Archon Prince must have known that Carlyle was a man who would always take his oath seriously, no matter what the personal cost.

5

Dunkeld
Glengarry, Federated Commonwealth
1 April 3056

The magnificent sunrise of Dunkeld was one sight Alex Carlyle never tired of seeing. A brilliant orange ball rising out of the mists of the Firth of Dunkeld, Glengarry's K Class star shed its light over the harbor and across the old, dignified capital city. Despite the emelt's late arrival from the training center the night before, Alex had made a point of rising early enough to watch the sunrise from the balcony of the Residence, the Gray Death's fortified base on Castle Hill. Sudeten, the world where Alex had been born and raised, circled its brilliant sun at a distance of nearly three astronomical units, which made its dawns far less spectacular than here on Glengarry.

Alex leaned against a thick stone parapet and took a sip of blackroot tea as his gaze wandered down onto the streets and colorful rooftops of the Dunkeld's wealthiest residential neighborhood spreading out at the foot of the hill. From here, distance and morning mist obscured the less savory details, and it was possible to imagine the city as it must have been in its prime, before war and neglect had marred its antique beauty.

Dunkeld was nearly as big as any capital city on the major worlds of the Inner Sphere, including even New Avalon or Luthien or Tharkad, but appearances were deceiving. Its population, like that of the whole planet, had been declining steadily for generations. Glengarry had once been a thriving colony, one of Terra's eldest daughters, but it had been hit hard in the early rounds of the Succession Wars. Dunkeld still possessed vestiges of Glengarry's onetime greatness, things like the fine architecture of the Municipal Center in the heart of town or the massive bulk of these old Star League fortifications on Castle Hill northwest of the town, but the city was no bustling metropolis. Many of its buildings were empty and decaying, and still-occupied sections were often shabby, dirty, and run-down.

Alex wondered if the city, the entire planet, would ever return to anything of its original glory. His father had always been outspoken on the subject of humanity's losing struggle against the decline of civilization, but it took the images of Dunkeld, past and present, to bring the truth home. Grayson Carlyle and the Gray Death had been dedicated to holding the line against the forces that were dragging humanity down, but how much could they do in the face of overwhelming odds?

Sudeten, with its numerous industrial centers and burgeoning population, was a thriving planet, seeming impervious to the ravages of war. Like most worlds of the Inner Sphere, it had lost a certain amount of high technology over the three centuries of Succession Wars, but the arrival of the Gray Death Legion had led to a small technological renaissance. With them had come copies of the ancient Star League computer core salvaged on Helm in the last days of the Legion's fight against House Marik. The so-called Gray Death computer core held many lost secrets from the golden era of the Star League, not all of them military, and the dissemination of that information had helped create a genuine economic boom on Sudeten as well as across the rest of the Inner Sphere.

But Glengarry had proved a tougher proposition altogether. The original colony had done well enough for a time, being close to the valuable Terran trade routes. Homegrown products exported to the hungry markets of Terra brought in a healthy revenue to fill the planetary coffers. Unfortunately, Glengarry's first colonists had never seen fit to diversify and build self-sufficient heavy industries. When the Star League collapsed and intersteller trade declined during the First Succession War, the planetary economy suffered a mortal blow. Glengarry was as much a casualty of war as any of the border planets that constantly changed hands between the warring armies of the Great Houses of the Successor States.

In fact, the world had not seen much fighting in more than a century, at least not the kind that had characterized the Succession Wars overall. The rival leaders of the Inner Sphere had not found sufficient reason to attempt to conquer the world, nor did Glengarry's location make it the target of the constant raiding endemic on worlds closer to the border. There were just no suitable strategic or economic targets worth attacking on Glengarry.

In consequence, the Lyran Commonwealth had not seen fit to garrison the planet with regular military units. Except for an ill-trained planetary militia and the private armies of a handful of ambitious noble landowners, there had been no effective fighting force on the planet for years. Private wars between the aristocrats, and the depredations of home-grown marauders driven to violence by poverty and despair had substituted for the large-scale conflicts that plagued more noteworthy worlds. These local problems had been enough to keep Glengarry from recovering from the downward spiral that had begun with the fall of the Star League. The decision to bolster the strength of Federated Commonwealth forces in this region of space, the so-called Isle of Skye linking the old Federated Suns to the worlds of the Lyran Commonwealth, was what had brought the Gray Death to Glengarry and given the citizenry hope at last.

With the Legion's arrival on Glengarry, the population had looked to the mercenary unit as a panacea for all the planet's ills. Carlyle's troops had easily suppressed the outlaw gangs and defanged the ambitious noblemen, but it would take more to restore Glengarry's lost glory. One mercenary regiment with its dependents wasn't enough of an influx of people to spark a financial boom, and the lost knowledge of the old computer core was worthless without the means of production to turn out the high tech wonders revealed there. The population of Glengarry was too small, too scattered, and too deeply rooted in a subsistence-level agrarian economy. Though Grayson Carlyle had done everything possible to help, he had been unable to do more than slow down the planet's continuing decline.

There was ample room for expansion, if only the colonists could develop their world. Most of Glengarry's population was concentrated on the smallest of the planet's three major continents, dubbed Scotia by the Scots-descended pioneers who had first settled there. Dalraida and Pictland, two larger land masses in the northern hemisphere, had never attracted much attention, partly because of their harsher climates, but mostly because the original colonists had been drawn to the abundant resources of Scotia. The mountain ranges that dominated much of the continent were rich in a variety of ores, while the open ground of the valleys and lowlands had been judged ideal for farming and ranching. If not for the wars, later colonial expansion might have opened up the other land masses, but as it was, most of Glengarry was still virgin wilderness.

It was too bad the odds were stacked against the locals, Alex thought bitterly. Under different circumstances Glengarry would have been one of the jewels of the Inner Sphere. Instead it was a quiet backwater condemned to a long, slow, ignominious death.

"Sir? Will you have breakfast now or would you prefer to dress first?"

Alex glanced back at the figure standing in the doorway leading into his apartment. Dressed in a kilt of the Dunkeld Servant's Guild, the big-boned man was a local, ruddy-faced and with the light hair and eyes common to the Celtic stock of Glengarry. Alex was still not used to the full-scale VIP treatment, especially after spending so much time as a cadet. Cadets at the Brander training center shared rooms and did without servants, but in Dunkeld, and especially in the Residence, things were different.

On Sudeten this man's duties would have been performed by a host of machines slaved to a household computer system, but on Glengarry personal service was a major source of employment for people who would otherwise have been condemned to abject poverty. As far as the locals were concerned, even the lowest-ranking astech of the Gray Death rated as a VIP entitled to all the comforts of the aristocracy. Back at the Brander center, Carlyle shared a room with Clay, and a bathroom with two other cadets as well, but here at the Residence his family had a large block of apartments reserved for their personal use, with a staff of retainers to look after their every need. Alex had a four-room suite all to himself, stocked with old but well-cherished furnishings. The luxuries, and the temptations that went with them, made a sad contrast to the unhappy conditions that prevailed among the common folk of Glengarry, and Alex often found it hard to keep things in perspective.

"Thank you, er . . ."

"MacDonald, sir," the man supplied helpfully. There was a note in his voice that was anything but subservient, despite his job. Glengarry's population, mostly descended from Scots, Welsh, and Irish stock from Terra's British Isles, displayed a notable streak of pride and independence. They reminded Alex of old Davis McCall, though they were less prone to slip into the completely unpronounceable dialect McCall was so fond of.

"Thank you, MacDonald. I'll shower and dress first. And I'll only be wanting a light breakfast, please."

The man clucked disapprovingly. "Och, you're all alike, you Carlyles," he said, half to himself. "Best kitchen on the whole planet and all you want is something light." He looked directly at Alex. "Service in the main dining hall in thirty minutes, sir."

Alex handed MacDonald his empty teacup and followed the servant indoors. The Residence was the largest, grandest building in the warren built on and into Castle Hill. The rest of the complex was given over to fortifications extensive enough to house the whole Gray Death, with plenty of room to spare, but they were now occupied by no more than a single company of the Legion's elite armored infantry plus a larger body of planetary militia. Most of the heavier weaponry originally mounted in the fortress had long since been scrapped, leaving Castle Hill better suited for ceremonial than for military functions. But the Residence itself was still the seat of Glengarry's planetary government, as it had been almost from the birth of the colony. As landholders-contractual, the senior officers of the Gray Death had quarters and offices here, together with officials of the planetary government.

That government was essentially unchanged from the days of the First Succession War. Glengarry had been held by a whole succession of different feudal overlords, mostly Lyran aristocrats but with a sprinkling of corporations and an occasional merc unit like the Legion as House Steiner had seen fit to reassign the planet for short-term political or economic advantages. Through all those regimes, in which most of the titular rulers were not even resident on the world, the local population had been administered by a council of twenty leading citizens who appointed one of their number to the archaic post of Governor General once every five years. The Council of Twenty was a tightly held oligarchy that had remained within the same tiny circle of families for generations. The planet's government was plagued by corruption and petty jealousies, and it was only with the utmost care and caution that Grayson Carlyle could approach reforms. Several long-time members of the council had been forced out soon after the arrival of the Gray Death. The current Governor General, Roger DeVries, was a new man. Unconnected with past abuses, he had vowed to reorganize the planetary administration and break the power of the oligarchy. He was also Caitlin's father.

Alex mused over the chances of real reform as he went through his morning routine. Roger DeVries struck him as an honest, well-intentioned man, but he was also definitely an individual with his own agenda. He wasn't even a native of Glengarry. DeVries had started out as a small time free trader plying the intersteller space lanes. Eventually settling on Glengarry with the profits of his merchanting career, he'd married a local girl twenty years his junior. Though he had quickly become an important and influential figure on Glengarry, the man's off-world birth had barred him from an active role on the Council of Twenty. On the theory that DeVries was less enmeshed in local politics and ancient feuds, it was Grayson Carlyle who had sponsored the man for the Council, working behind the scenes to secure him the Governor-Generalship. The alliance between the merchant and the mercenary was not always an easy one, however. DeVries held the good of the planet above all else, and resented the drain on resources and manpower represented by the Legion. And although Grayson Carlyle wanted nothing but good for Glengarry, the Gray Death still came first and foremost in his mind. It was a situation that inevitably led to clashes between two strong-minded men, a tension only heightened by the political infighting among nobles who missed the good old days of an absentee overlord and the freedom to resolve their differences by force if they deemed it necessary. Probably the only thing that had kept matters from getting completely out of hand was the inability of the aristocrats to decide who they hated more, the mercenary planetholder who wouldn't let them rearm or the interloping off-worlder Governor General who refused to play politics the way the landowners wanted.

Alex finished his shower—a real-water shower, a luxury

not often enjoyed at Brander—and dressed in his best uniform. By the time he was seated at the long, empty table in the main dining hall waiting for MacDonald to bring his breakfast, his thoughts were back on the speech he was to give this afternoon. Today was one of the most solemn holidays observed by members of the Gray Death, and Alex would be representing his absent parents at the ceremonies marking the occasion. Like the bungled leadership exercise the day before, this was part of the process of grooming him for the day when he would take command of the Legion. Legionnaires and civilians alike would be listening to his words, making their own estimations of what kind of successor Grayson Carlyle had chosen. What Alex said today could set the tone for the future of Legion and planet alike . . .

Above all he wanted to make his parents proud. He only hoped he would.

6

"**A**ll is in readiness, Herr General. The last DropShip has docked, and Weltalloberst Glushko reports jump preparations underway around the fleet," reported Hauptmann Johann Albrecht to the commander of the Free Skye Expeditionary Force.

"Excellent." General-Kommandant Wilhelm Freidrich von Bulow studied his aide for a long moment. Sitting aboard the command DropShip *Asgard*, he had the Free Skye fleet's entire sophisticated communications system literally at his fingertips, but von Bulow was essentially an old-fashioned officer. He preferred to let his staff sift through the routine matters and report to him in person. There were some who scoffed that he was an eccentric old fool, but after years as a staff man himself von Bulow regarded his methods as a tried and true alternative to the chaos that generally resulted from micromanagement from the top. "Excellent, Johann. I must remember to commend the Logistics Master for his fast work."

"Yes, sir," Hauptmann Albrecht replied, pausing to enter a notation on his wristcomp. Like the good aide that he was, the officer would no doubt remind von Bulow of the commendation in due course.

Von Bulow continued to regard the man with a cold, expressionless stare. "And what is the opinion of our plan on Deck Four, Johann?" Deck Four of the Command Drop-Ship *Asgard* housed the junior and mid-level officers of von Bulow's staff, along with the leadership of the Duke of

Skye's Own Huscarles, the elite infantry guardsmen pledged to the support of Duke Richard Steiner.

The aide's smile was almost predatory. "Conditions for the strike could not be better, Herr General," he said. "Half of Glengarry's garrison is deployed off-world, while the Gray Death leadership is off attending some court function on Tharkad. The enemy is wide open."

"They have quite a reputation, Johann," von Bulow reminded him, playing devil's advocate.

"Mercenaries," the aide sneered. "Good enough for raiding or set-piece battles, perhaps. But how well will they fight when there's no profit in the conflict? They have no cause, nothing to rally behind—and no one to lead them. How much of a threat can they be?"

"Be careful of overconfidence, Johann," von Bulow said quietly. "These aren't just ordinary mercenaries. Always remember that. They fought the Clans to a standstill on Pandora, and that was no mean feat. The Gray Death Legion is an opponent to be respected."

"Yes, Herr General." The younger man's tone was subdued, but there was still a gleam in his eye.

Von Bulow favored him with a smile. "Still, you're right. The situation will never be more favorable. His Grace has planned well." He gestured at the transparent plasteel window behind his desk, where six *Invader* Class JumpShips hung motionless at the system's zenith jump point, awaiting the order to engage their hyperspace drives for the jump from Skye to Glengarry. The *Asgard* was docked with a larger vessel, the Star Lord Class *Gotterdämerung*. Together, the ships represented a formidable armada.

Ever since the death of Archon Melissa Steiner, the pride of her eldest son and heir had swelled unchecked, and the Davion presence in the Isle of Skye was becoming more intolerable with each passing week. Prince Victor had all but accused Duke Ryan Steiner of complicity in the assassination of his mother, but that was no excuse for the arrogance his troops had been displaying these past months. And if Victor Davion's lackeys believed that the Duke would cave in under their pressure, they were sadly mistaken.

Discontent with Davion rule had flared into open protest and even some riots all over the Isle of Skye at virtually the same moment? And though Richard Steiner held the rank of Field Marshal and Commander in Chief of the Federated

Commonwealth forces in the Skye March, he had chosen to throw his lot in with Ryan Steiner's Free Skye Movement rather than attempt to put the risings down. Von Bulow, as one of Richard Steiner's closest supporters, had advised against Richard allying with Ryan, but it seemed now that Richard had done the right thing after all. As Field Marshal of the Skye March, he controlled most of the region's military assets, but as the new Duke of Skye, his political power was even greater. The former Duchess, Margaret Aten, had been handicapped by the twin impediments of low birth and close personal attachments to Katrina and Melissa Steiner, but the political marriage between her young daughter Sarah and Katrina's nephew Richard had been a popular move. Even more popular had been Margaret's decision to step aside and allow the new generation to take over.

No one outside the new duke's inner circle knew that the abdication had been anything but voluntary. Even the young Sarah remained blissfully ignorant of the coup Ryan and Richard Steiner had staged to win virtually absolute political power with the Skye March.

Besides having the Steiner name to his credit, Richard had immediately made it clear that he was no slavish supporter of the Federated Commonwealth. In a hotbed of separatism like the Isle of Skye, the new Duke's position on the issues of local rule and regional sovereignty had earned him many allies at all levels of society. And where Margaret Aten had been a vehement opponent of Skye secession, her daughter, only half Richard's age at the time of the marriage, was meek, mild, and easily dominated by her forceful husband.

Once Ryan Steiner had obtained Richard's support, he had Richard send two full regiments of dedicated pro-Davion troops from their base on the key world of Hesperus II to aid Richard's cousin, Marshal Caesar Steiner, deal with the tensions on the Marik border. This removed a major obstacle from the path of rebellion. Richard also secured the return of the Fourth and Seventeenth Skye Ranger regiments, which had been shifted out of Skye space during earlier Davion efforts to tighten their grip on the region. The two units still retained their old pro-Skye sympathies. Added to the Tenth Skye Rangers, which made up the core of von Bulow's command, they formed a solid nucleus around which the insurrection would be able to rally.

Most of the garrisons the Davions had planted in the Skye territory were of indifferent quality and uncertain commitment. A few, like the Skye Rangers, were actually controlled by Ryan Steiner's Free Skye Movement, and many of the others would be easily dominated by Duke Richard. After all, he was already their rightful commander, and in the first few weeks of the uprising, to what other clear, legitimate authority would they turn? That had been the case with the loyal but green Eleventh Federated Commonwealth, the regiment garrisoning Skye. On the duke's orders, the unit had stayed in garrison when militia armories on Skye were opened to the cadre of reservists and promising trainees who formed the rest of von Bulow's strike force, the Skye Guards. They were green, but eager.

Of the handful of pro-Davion units that might offer real resistance, only the Gray Death Legion remained as a genuine force to be reckoned with. The mercenaries were already weak from detachments, and their leadership was currently far from the unit. If von Bulow could overwhelm their base on Glengarry quickly enough, the Legion could be neutralized right from the start, and the rest of the Skye March would fall easily. Yes, von Bulow thought, His Grace had planned this well.

The strike on Glengarry would be the first overt military operation of the campaign. Even so, Duke Richard had taken care to avoid an outright confrontation. Instead, he had exercised his undoubted right as Duke of Skye to reaffirm von Bulow as the rightful Baron of Glengarry. By thus using his authority as duke and Field Marshal to uproot the Gray Death from Glengarry and plant von Bulow and the Tenth Skye Rangers in their place, Duke Richard would have almost all of the Isle of Skye in sympathetic hands and a solid body of legal right on his side when the Archon Prince protested. Let Victor actually start a war by challenging Ryan and Richard Steiner. Given the divided loyalties throughout the old Lyran Commonwealth, the prince would soon be bogged down in civil war.

The dawn of new independence for the people of Skye was at hand. And perhaps more, too. Richard Steiner wasn't that far off the principal line of succession of the Lyran Commonwealth. Once Katrina's heirs were cast out, what would stand in the path of Richard becoming the next Archon of a revived House Steiner?

"Pass the order to Weltalloberst Glushko. All ships to continue preparations for jump. I want the fleet ready to move out in three hours. And inform Glushko that I will be transferring my standard to the *Gotterdämerung* prior to jump. Understood?"

"Yes, Herr General." The aide saluted stiffly and left von Bulow alone to contemplate the fleet and the scattered stars beyond.

Stars that would soon be free of the Davion tyranny.

7

"**G**ray Skull, Antelope. We are clear. Preparing to go to main drive on your signal."

Before responding, Captain Einar Rodland of the JumpShip *Gray Skull* carefully checked over the instrument repeaters around his bridge station. The risk of a catastrophe soared astronomically any time two massive ships tried to maneuver in close proximity to each other. In the absence of atmosphere and gravity, the laws of inertia reigned supreme, and the tiniest mistake in applying thrust could end in a fatal collision.

It was doubly risky when one of the vessels was a JumpShip. Designed solely for the purpose of traveling the light years between star systems, the huge vessels lacked conventional space drives. With nothing beyond thrusters for station-keeping purposes, they were essentially huge, free-floating targets that couldn't evade trouble if a ship under power did run wild.

Rodland double-checked the navigation display and keyed his comm circuit at last. "Antelope, Gray Skull. Concur. You are free and clear to navigate."

"Thank you, Gray Skull," the DropShip skipper replied. "Happy drifting, Captain."

Nearby, Ilse Martinez snorted. She had taken a vacant bridge position to observe the *Antelope*'s departure, a common courtesy extended by JumpShip captains to visiting officers. She was commanding officer of the DropShip *Io*, which was docked with the *Gray Skull* for the hyperspace

jump to the Skye system, where her ship would get badly
needed repairs.

She glanced at Rodland and raised a quizzical eyebrow.
At his nod she touched her own borrowed console to respond to the DropShip. "Safe planetfall, Captain Drake.
And don't let the dirt clog your jets." She looked at Rodland and smiled. "Now I've done it. Sold out to the enemy
and insulted my own kind."

There were appreciative chuckles from the rest of the
Gray Skull's bridge staff. The mostly friendly rivalry between JumpShip and DropShip crews was an old one, and
exchanging appropriate insults in lieu of well-wishing was
a time-honored tradition.

Rodland waited for the laughter to fade before speaking
again. "Engineer, what is our charge status?"

"Ninety-eight percent, Skipper," Lieutenant Haugen replied. JumpShips were incapable of normal-space travel
without the assistance of tugs, saving all their mass for the
Kearny-Fuchida hyperdrive system. Between jumps they
used gigantic sails to gather and store solar energy. The
Gray Skull had carried a full charge for weeks now, except
for the small drain to power life support and other onboard
systems. "Nominal for jump."

"Good. I didn't want to have to redeploy the sail." The
process of furling and unfurling the kilometer-wide sail was
slow and cumbersome, and Rodland didn't like to waste
effort unnecessarily. But when ships were docking or de-
parting, he insisted on striking the collector array. It was
one less thing to get in the way.

"What about it, Captain?" he asked Martinez. "Is the
Io secure for jump?"

She nodded, but looked reluctant. "All set, but I was
hoping we could delay the jump for a few hours."

Rodland rubbed his forehead. "Any special reason?"

Martinez shrugged. "The Day of Heroes celebration is
still going on back in Dunkeld. We're recording the newstrans. I kind of wanted to get the whole thing, that's all."

Ilse Martinez had been with the Gray Death Legion for a
long time, and she took her connection to Carlyle and his
men in deadly earnest. Rodland studied her for a long moment, then nodded. "It'll take almost an hour to plot the
jump to Skye anyway. We'll wait until you've got everything
you want."

"Thanks, Captain. I appreciate it."

Captain Rodland turned to Lieutenant Dag Ullestad, the ship's executive officer. "Make all preparations for hyperspace jump, Mister Ullestad. Designate destination as Skye system zenith jump point. Start your computations."

"Aye aye, sir," the exec responded smartly.

Rodland noticed Martinez watching the by-play on the JumpShip's bridge with an expression of bemusement. It was the first time she had traveled aboard the *Gray Skull,* and she was probably finding the military demeanor of the crew vastly different from what she was used to. She had started out as pilot of a merchant DropShip attached to Renfred Tor's *Invidious,* and had wound up in the Legion's pay almost by accident after Tor and Carlyle began their long-term friendship back on Trellwan so many years ago. So, ironically, the fervent supporter of everything to do with Grayson Carlyle was less inclined to the military life than Rodland, who cared little enough about the identity of his employer but who ran a tight ship.

Rodland had been a ship captain in the service of the Free Rasalhague Republic before the Clans had virtually exterminated that small nation of stars. Rather than face further combat against the fanatic Clan armies he and his crew had chosen the freelance life. That might technically be classified as mutiny and desertion and any number of other capital offenses against the Republic, but Rodland and his men hadn't been alone in fleeing the wreck of Rasalhague. Soon afterward they had taken on the one-shot contract to help evacuate the Gray Death from Sudeten. Grayson Carlyle had offered an ongoing contract afterward, and in honor of the new deal Rodland had rechristened the old Rasalhague *Stolthet* with its new name, *Gray Skull.* But that had been good politics, nothing more. Rodland regarded his stay with the Legion as a temporary stopover on his way to something better—perhaps even a fresh commission with one of the Successor States. The mystique of the Gray Death Legion was nothing new to Einar Rodland, and it wasn't about to claim his soul as it had so many others.

He unstrapped from his command seat and pushed off from the chair arms with practiced ease. JumpShip crews spent most of their time in zero-G, and quickly became accustomed to working in weightlessness. Rodland snagged the back of the navigator's chair and peered over the man's shoulder to double-check the jump calculations he was making. The repeaters at the captain's position would have showed Rodland the same information, but he preferred to let his people know when he was taking a direct interest in their work.

The crewman at the sensor station suddenly broke the reassuring calm of routine. "Contact! Contact!" he said excitedly. "Bearing three-five-two by one-oh-one!"

"Identify!" Rodland snapped, turning away from Rischel and propelling himself with a quick push back to the command station.

"Radiation signature . . . hyperspace field emissions . . . Trace is definitely a JumpShip, inbound," Ullestad reported briskly. ". . . Range sixty-seven thousand kilometers—"

"New contact!" The sensor operator broke in. "Bearing one-one-six by two-five-one!" There was a pause. "Two new traces . . . three . . ."

"God in Heaven," someone said. "It's a bloody fleet!"

"They're coming out all around us!" Martinez said unnecessarily. "We're right in the thick of it!"

Rodland ignored her. "Can you get me a transponder idee?" he asked the communications watchstander.

"Negative. No transponder code. They're running silent." Ships engaged in lawful business transmitted a constant signal establishing the identification, ownership, and affiliation of the vessel. Any ship not transmitting the coded signal could be regarded as potentially hostile.

"Goddamn," Rodland muttered, strapping in. "Ensign Rischel, speed up those calculations. Communications, signal to Dunkeld control. Report multiple JumpShips, inbound, no transponders. Go to constant sitrep updates until further notice. Mister Ullestad, sound the battle alarm."

The raucous sound of the klaxon filled the bridge. Over the noise, the exec's voice sounded almost inhumanly calm as he triggered the intraship address system. "Now, general quarters, general quarters. All hands to action stations. Secure for possible battle conditions. General quarters. This is not a drill."

Aboard the Free Skye Jump Ship *Gotterdämerung*, General-Kommandant von Bulow rubbed his forehead and eyes, trying to force his disoriented faculties into some semblance of normalcy. From the very beginning of his military career he had suffered from the effects of jump shock, the physical and psychological affliction that sometimes accompanied the transition through hyperspace. For most people it was a minor discomfort, but von Bulow found it almost crippling at times. It was also an embarrassing ailment for a commanding general, but he had never been able to cure it. If his presence hadn't been essential on the bridge of the command JumpShip during and immediately after the jump to the Glengarry system, he would have stayed in his quarters aboard the *Asgard* to avoid betraying this weakness to his men. But the moments right after a hyperspace transition were often critical, and von Bulow had to be on hand to make decisions.

He was still blinking his eyes and fighting down the nausea in the pit of his stomach when the JumpShip's captain, Weltalloberst Ivan Glushko, turned to face him.

"Transition complete, Herr General," Glushko reported. "Coordinates confirmed."

"All ships have reported in," the commtech added a moment later.

Von Bulow nodded acknowledgment, but didn't answer.

"Your orders, Herr General?" Glushko pressed, a look of concern crossing his craggy features.

The general found his voice at last. "Status . . . status of shipping in the area?" he croaked.

"A JumpShip in the position predicted by our scouts," the sensor technician reported. "*Invader* Class, transponder verifies it as the *Gray Skull,* as expected. Configuration suggests one attached DropShip. One additional ship under power. Warbook analyzes it as a *Gazelle* Class armored company carrier. Vectoring for Glengarry, range seventy thousand kilometers, opening."

"Carlyle has a *Gazelle* in his aerospace contingent," Glushko added helpfully. "The *Antelope,* Lieutenant John Drake commanding."

Von Bulow nodded impatiently. "I know," he said. "All right, Weltalloberst, order the fleet to begin launching DropShips. Priority to the *Merkur.* Execute Operation Blackout, as planned."

"Yes, Herr General," Glushko replied, turning back to issue a flurry of orders to the *Götterdämmerung*'s bridge crew. Operation Blackout called for the neutralization of any enemy targets that presented themselves in the area around the jump point. Spies had been active in the Glengarry system for weeks now, and von Bulow had been confident they would have only one JumpShip to deal with in the system.

Still feeling sick from jump shock, von Bulow unstrapped cautiously. The zero-G condition on the JumpShip bridge weren't helping his stomach any. ''Weltalloberst, I am transferring my standard to the *Asgard,*'' he said. ''Carry out your instructions, and retain squadron control until I transfer command.''

''Yes, Herr General,'' the JumpShip captain repeated.

Propelling himself toward the nearest hatch, von Bulow tried not to let his continuing bout of nausea show. The next few hours would be critical for the invasion force, as they launched the massed DropShips and formed up for the trip to Glengarry while making sure that the Legion ships in the system didn't have a chance to escape and carry warnings to other pro-Davion worlds. It wasn't the time for any doubts about von Bulow's health.

Soon enough, he knew, the symptoms would clear up. The prospect of action would occupy his full attention, and von Bulow would again be at his best.

8

Standing on Castle Hill, overlooking the city of Dunkeld on Glengarry, Major Davis McCall tugged at the high collar of his dress uniform tunic. Muttering a lengthy Gaelic curse at the restrictive garment, he remained unaware of the threat to the very ground on which he stood. McCall had never been one to enjoy formal functions, preferring action to ceremony and the MechWarrior's informal garb of shorts and cooling vest to the stiff attire reserved for parades and special events. But the Day of Heroes was one time when he didn't begrudge the uniform. He must look his best today. He owed it to the men whose memory the Legion would be honoring.

Of course, McCall remained too much a rebel to adopt the complete Legion dress uniform, even on the Day of Heroes. His kilt and sporran made him look more like one of the locals than a member of the Gray Death, but that was a point of pride on which he wouldn't compromise. McCall was a native of the planet Caledonia, right here in the Isle of Skye, and had been a card-carrying member of the planet's Jacobite Party until circumstances had forced him to seek a new life as a mercenary. He'd been with Grayson Carlyle almost from the beginning, and his record over the years was more than enough to justify McCall's occasional eccentricities.

Much had changed in thirty years with Grayson Death Carlyle. When McCall had first joined up on Galatea, the mercenary clearinghouse world, Carlyle had been a youngster barely out of his teens. His handful of BattleMechs and cadre of infantry trained in radical new anti-'Mech tactics had just survived a desperate struggle against House Kurita on the remote world of Trellwan. McCall hadn't been too sure of the scratch unit's prospects, but Carlyle had been the only commander willing to hire a maverick with a checkered past and a reputation for more independence than most officers liked to see in their troops.

The fighting on Verthandi and afterward had led both men to reassess their initial wary views of one another. Grayson Carlyle had proved to be a genuine tactical genius, with a flair for doing the unexpected and turning hopeless situations into incredible victories. And Davis McCall, stubborn, independent, outspoken, had stood firm beside Carlyle in every battle. Unquestioning loyalty was something McCall didn't offer very often, but Carlyle had earned it a dozen times over.

Now the Gray Death Legion was no mere understrength company. It was a mixed regiment today, with five full companies of BattleMechs and a substantial force of infantry, armor, and aerospace support. There were more men drawn up this morning on the large parade ground behind the Residence than had shipped out to Verthandi during McCall's first mission, and half the Legion was currently off-planet defending the Tamar frontier against a rumored Clan attack. The mass of officers and men in their somber dress grays made an impressive block, framed on either side by the more colorfully dressed troops of Glengarry's Planetary Guard in their kilts and light-colored tunics. Behind them an honor guard of four BattleMechs, the recon lance of the Gray Death Companions, loomed over the parade ground like huge monuments to the vanity of men.

McCall took a last look across the parade ground, then turned his critical gaze toward the reviewing stand. Senior Legion officers, members of the Governor General's staff, and a few selected dignitaries from Dunkeld filled most of the seats. His glance stopped as it met the piercing, dark eyes of Major Gomez Cristobal de Villar, another of the Gray Death's long-service veterans who had risen to senior rank. De Villar had once led the Legion's recon lance and doubled as the resident expert in explosives and demolitions. Today he was commander of the First Battalion and Chief of Operations on Grayson Carlyle's staff, acting CO

in the colonel's absence. The saturnine MechWarrior from
Bolan gave McCall a thin-lipped smile that still showed a
hint of the old recklessness that had made him a Gray Death
legend.

The man who had once relished living on the edge had
mellowed quite a bit since the days when he'd enjoyed playing with live explosives just to see the startled looks of his
fellow Legionnaires. Marriage, and the three children that
had followed, had helped de Villar set down solid roots.
One of those children was in the current cadet class, and
another was attached to Colonel Carlyle's personal staff as
an aide. The third had died on Sudeten.

De Villar's wife, Freya, sat beside him. Also there was
her brother, Master Tech Major Alard King, another of the
old Legion hands. To King went the credit for the Gray
Death's success in copying the old Star League library core
back on Helm. Older and grayer now, King was still a top
technician who frequently grumbled about the administrative duties that fell to the Legion's ranking support services
officer. He still preferred to get down and dirty with his
men instead of being chained to a desk. As for Freya, she
had joined the Legion after Helm, recruited by her brother
as one of the unit's scouts. Though she still held a commission as captain, these days she devoted most of her time to
her husband, rarely appearing at Legion functions. She
would be reliving some bitter memories today, McCall
thought. Enrique de Villar, the youngest of her sons, had
been taken prisoner by the Clans, but had died under inter-
rogation rather than reveal what he knew about the unit's
evacuation plans.

Standing beside Alard King was another familiar figure,
someone McCall would never have expected to see here.
Charles Bear, the big Amerindian from Tau Ceti II, had left
the Legion soon after the reassignment to Glengarry. Having dreamed all his life of performing the traditional act of
bravery of his people, counting coup on an enemy in battle,
Bear had finally achieved his goal on Pandora. Afterward
he had simply retired, accepting from Grayson Carlyle a
huge estate in the Glencoe Highlands in the southern uplands of Scotia. He withdrew there to live as a recluse,
seeing no one, apparently content to leave the old life behind. Bear noticed McCall's look and gave a curt nod of
acknowledgment, his face expressionless. McCall couldn't

help but wonder what was going on behind those blank eyes. What memories did these ceremonies stir in the big man's heart?

His quick visual survey finished, McCall took his own seat near the podium and gave the signal for the ceremony to begin. To a fanfare by the Legion's band, the junior cadet MechWarrior, Harrison Gates, walked to the podium. It was traditional for the newest 'Mech pilot in the outfit to begin the Day of Heroes with a short introduction of Colonel Carlyle or, in this case, his surrogate.

"Legionnaires!" Gates said, looking nervous but trying to cover it with loud enthusiasm. "Colonel Grayson Carlyle and his lady have been honored with a summons to Tharkad, and so cannot address us today. But the colonel's son and heir is here to represent his father. I'm proud to say that Alexander Durant Carlyle and I serve together in the Cadet Company, and though I've only been a member for a month I have already come to respect Alex Carlyle as a fine MechWarrior, a dedicated legionnaire, and, I hope, a new friend. I give you . . . Cadet Alexander Durant Carlyle."

The younger Carlyle stepped to the podium, pausing to shake hands with Gates and say something too quietly for McCall to hear. Alex looked every bit the soldier in his crisp dress grays, and McCall gave a quick, approving nod. Despite the young man's problems back at Brander, he carried himself like a born leader. Once he overcame his current difficulties he was sure to go far. Watching Alex slip the memory chip of his speech into the electronic teleprompter on the lectern, McCall was reminded of the young Grayson Carlyle, masking his personal doubts behind an aura of confidence and ability back on Galatea. Now Alex was speaking, his voice quiet and even, his words all the more forceful for the calm authority of his tone.

"Today, by the old Terran calendar, is the first day of April," he began. "Twenty-eight standard years ago on this date the Gray Death legion fought a series of battles on the planet Helm that ended in a retreat from that world, but it was in no way a defeat. On that day, the Gray Death recovered an important Star League computer core while holding off superior forces sent by House Marik in a treacherous attempt to crush the Legion. The unit then withdrew to successfully escape from the planet's surface."

Alex paused to look around the gathering before going

on. "The battles on Helm showed the Gray Death Legion at its finest. Betrayed, we refused to surrender. Pressed to the limits of endurance, we did not abandon the knowledge of the Star League to be destroyed or misused by our enemies. And, outnumbered, we still fought on. That is what it means to be a part of the Gray Death Legion.

"Many good men lost their lives in the fighting on Helm, and others have died fighting for the Gray Death before and since that fateful day. My father chose to set aside this anniversary of the struggle on Helm to honor those heroes who have fallen in the service of our Legion. Their names and their deeds will live in our hearts forever, whether they were foot soldiers or MechWarriors. And though it would be impossible to recount all their stories here today, we can remember them all, honor them all, as the heroes they proved themselves to be."

As the speech rolled on, McCall's eyes were on young Carlyle, but in his mind he was seeing other men and women he'd been proud to call his comrades. Delmar Clay had been his lance mate and best friend before the last battle on Sudeten. And Isoru Koga, the ronin MechWarrior driven out of Kurita space by the false accusations of a rival in his old regiment. Koga had perished in 'Mech-to-'Mech fighting with his old enemy, delivering the attack that destroyed his opponent's machine while his own life trickled away from a mortal wound in his gut.

Blake and Sharpley had died in action on a pair of obscure Kurita frontier worlds during the War of 3039, while Sharyl, the tech-turned-MechWarrior from Dahar IV, had decided to move on after the conflict had wound down. The only active MechWarriors out of the original band were Grayson and his wife Lori, Tracy Kent, de Villar, and Major Hassan Ali Khaled, away with Second Battalion on far-off Borghese.

Other names, other faces came to mind. Tough old Ramage, who had commanded the infantry in the early days, then moved on to become weapons master before McCall, had died as he had lived, fighting, watching Grayson Carlyle's back in the middle of a savage clash with the Clans on Pandora. And Renfred Tor, the merchant JumpShip captain who had been one of Carlyle's first companions. He was the only one of them who had died in bed, leaving a daughter to carry on the family business. As captain of the old *Invidious,* Katrina Tor was the Gray Death's senior ship captain. Like Khaled, she was away with the other half of the Legion.

And there had been so many others. Sometimes these Day of Heroes remembrances made McCall wonder why he stayed with it. A mercenary's life was a grim one, filled with danger and discomfort and the certain knowledge that unending war would surely claim every comrade, if not today, then perhaps tomorrow. Once McCall had seen nothing but the glory and the honor. Now he knew better. He had lost his first BattleMech, an eye and an arm, and countless people he had once called friend.

He closed his eyes for a moment, still seeing those others. Sometimes he thought of giving it up, like Bear. He was fifty-five years old. The life of a MechWarrior was for young men who still had the reflexes and eagerness of youth. It had been almost two years since McCall had piloted a BattleMech in combat, though he still got in cockpit time in the trainer 'Mechs he took out against his cadets. These days he often wondered if he could still measure up in a real battle.

It was a life that was slipping out of his grasp, but it was still the only life Davis McCall knew.

"The Day of Heroes is a day of remembrance," Alex Carlyle was saying. "Not to mourn lost friends, but to celebrate their deeds and keep their memories alive. For as long as there is one member of the Gray Death Legion who remembers his comrades from days past, those legionnaires will remain a part of our grand tradition."

He stepped back from the podium, giving way to Cadet Gates again. As Alex took his place in an empty chair between McCall and de Villar, he heard an insistent beeping from the latter's wristcomp. De Villar frowned and touched a stud on the device.

"It is not normally the custom for civilians to address the Legion on the Day of Heroes celebrations," Gates was saying. "Today, at the suggestion of Colonel Carlyle, we are relaxing this tradition to permit the Governor General of Glengarry to join us. His Excellency, Governor General DeVries . . ."

Alex studied de Villar, only half hearing the cadet's introduction. The major's frown deepened as he listened to the voice being transmitted through his wristcomp to a tiny speaker adhering just behind his ear.

Then de Villar rose abruptly, touching McCall on the shoulder. Without hesitation, the Caledonian rose too and followed his superior off the platform. Alex watched them leave with a sense of foreboding. Only the most urgent problem would prompt any of the Gray Death's watchstanders to interrupt these solemn proceedings.

Alex wasn't the only one to notice the two majors leaving. A faint stir passed through the crowd and the Governor General paused before taking his place at the lectern, his eyes narrowed. Then he stepped forward, as if dismissing the interruption.

Roger DeVries was tall, silver-haired, and distinguished, with a thin gray mustache that made him look all the more aristocratic. He gave a half-bow as he gazed out at the assembled legionnaires. When he began to speak, his words were measured and smooth, but delivered with a grave dignity.

"Soldiers of the Gray Death Legion," he began, "I cannot convey in words my pleasure at being here with you today, saluting your fallen comrades and remembering the past deeds that have made yours one of the premier mercenary units in the Inner Sphere. Your colonel has honored me by permitting my attendance. But while we remember the past, let us also look to the future, to what we can do to forge new hope and new prosperity for the world of Glengarry."

Alex Carlyle barely heard the Governor General. His mind had traveled far from the parade ground podium, was focused instead on McCall and de Villar and on a hundred questions about what kind of crisis might have called them away.

9

The Planetary Defense Command Center was buried deep beneath the rock and earth of Castle Hill, a reinforced ferrocrete bunker that served as the military nerve center for all of Glengarry. Normal access was severely restricted, with a single elevator shaft connecting the underground warren with the complex of buildings and barracks that made up the outer works of the Castle Hill fortifications. There were a number of emergency exits, tunnels carved through the rock to distant, well-hidden doorways, but these were intended for use only as a last resort.

The buried chambers that made up the command center had been designed to coordinate the efforts of entire armies engaged in planetwide campaigns, back in the days when Terran colonies were still capable of the kind of mass warfare become virtually obsolete in this day of BattleMechs and small, elite strike forces. Guarded jointly by the Gray Death and their opposite numbers in the Planetary Guard, the chambers were packed with the high tech instruments of modern warfare—detection gear, bank after bank of computers, battle simulators, communications consoles, and all the rest.

As the elevator doors snapped open and Davis McCall followed Gomez de Villar into the Combat Coordination Room, a pair of Guardsmen in kilts and powder-blue tunics gave crisp rifle salutes. Because most of the Gray Death had been relieved of watchstanding duties so they could attend the Day of Heroes ceremony in person, the usual complement of Legion armored infantrymen was not present.

The technical posts in the CCR were being filled by volunteers from the crew of the Legion DropShip *Medea,* with the ship's captain, Lieutenant David Longo, acting as Officer of the Day. The *Medea* was currently grounded at the Dunkeld spaceport. Together with her sister ship *Io,* the DropShip had taken heavy damage in a recent raid against the Jade Falcons, and both ships would require extensive refitting at the dockyards on Skye before they could re-enter service. The *Medea* had been cannibalized to get the *Io* spaceworthy enough to make the voyage, and was slated to be patched up and sent to Skye when Ilse Martinez returned.

So Lieutenant Longo was temporarily a captain without a ship, and seemed pleased at the chance to serve the Legion in some other capacity until it was time to leave for Skye. He looked relieved, though, to see a higher authority to whom he could turn things over.

"Report," de Villar rasped as McCall and de Villar crossed to the central well, known fondly as the Snake Pit, which served as the master coordination position for all activities in the CCR. McCall noticed that one monitor, muted now, was carrying the newstrans from the ceremonies topside. At the moment, however, no one in the chamber was paying attention to it.

"No further voice messages, Major," Longo replied, looking up from his position in front of the main monitor. "We had the routine report that the *Antelope* was inbound under thrust, then the warning call. Multiple traces, positively ideed as JumpShips, no transponders, potentially hostile. Nothing more since then, except an open CAT feed."

The battalion commander sank into an empty chair, jabbing a finger at the technician manning a nearby console. "You—Communications. What's the time lag to the *Gray Skull*?"

"Twenty-eight minutes, Major," the commtech stammered.

"So long? Damn . . ." De Villar frowned more deeply than before. "Well, I guess there's no help for it."

The time lag in communications over interplanetary distances was something ground-based soldiers tended to forget. Because it was impossible to maintain a hyperspace field within a significant gravity well, JumpShips had to remain a long way out from a star. Moreover, magnetic fields also had a way of disrupting hyperspace transitions, and so most jumps were made between specific jump points at an appropriate distance from the star's zenith or nadir poles. The *Gray Skull* was at Glengarry's nadir jump point, just under four astronomical units away, and it would take signals moving at the speed of light almost thirty minutes to cross that void. With an hour between transmitting a signal and receiving a reply, an ordinary conversation was impossible. The only practical way to communicate was by sending long blocks of information or instructions, then hoping the situation didn't change so radically in the meantime that everything in the last transmission became invalid.

"Are you getting anything useful from the CAT?" De Villar asked Longo, sounding irritable. That was a sure sign of his concern, McCall thought. As a young lance leader, De Villar had been volatile yet seemingly impervious to doubts or fears, and these days he rarely revealed any kind of emotion openly. If his mask was slipping this much, McCall assumed it meant that de Villar was plenty worried.

"No, sir," the OOD said. "But it's pretty early for anything worthwhile to be coming in." The CAT—or communications and telemetry—feed from the JumpShip included a wide range of data, including constant computer-generated situation reports, scanning logs, and other information that might reveal a lot about the new arrivals. But it would take time for the *Gray Skull* to learn anything significant. The light-speed lag would be slowing the collection of data on the JumpShip's end, too, unless the newcomers had appeared right in Rodland's lap. Scanners would be getting data seconds or minutes old, and at deep-space ranges the kind of information the scans brought in would be essentially trivial until the ship was close enough for detailed visual examination of the unknown fleet.

And then everything would take nearly half an hour longer to reach the Glengarry command post. . . .

"Right," de Villar said, tight-lipped. He gestured toward the commtech again. "Send the usual standby, orders-to-follow message." Then, to McCall, he added, "I hope we can give him enough to cover all the possibilities. Never cared much for long-range direction in a mess like this."

De Villar started tapping on a computer keyboard, jotting

down notes for his message to Rodland. As the acting CO worked, McCall found a seat at an empty tactical planning station. During the elevator ride down from the surface De Villar had filled him in on the warning from the *Gray Skull*. Not that they had much information as yet. Just the one sketchy report, and it left a lot of questions to be answered. The Caledonian didn't like fumbling in the dark, and that was precisely what they were doing now. And would be doing, until they discovered who was out there and why.

So many incoming JumpShips, all arriving together in a backwater system like Glengarry, could only be a military task force, and the silence of the JumpShip transponders certainly suggested hostile intent. Still, the evidence wasn't conclusive by any means. Those ships might be a legitimate Federated Commonwealth fleet on some lawful mission, in transit to or from another part of the Skye March, and maintaining transponder silence to avoid giving away information to prying enemies who might be interested in F-C troop movements.

Or the ships might belong to ComStar, the independent, Terra-based organization that was part technological repository and part mystic, semi-religious order dedicated to the maintenance of communications between worlds. Up until twenty-five years ago no one outside ComStar had suspected that the organization was any kind of a military power at all. But it turned out that for centuries they had possessed a secret arsenal of Star League-era BattleMechs; it was those 'Mechs and the ComStar military that had finally ground the Clans to a halt at the Battle of Tukayyid.

Since then ComStar had fallen prey to internal disputes that had stripped the Order of most of its power and prestige, but they could still field those powerful 'Mech forces almost anywhere inside the Inner Sphere, and they were notoriously secretive about their movements and intentions. Moreover, there was the ComStar splinter group, the so-called Word of Blake movement now based in Marik space and rumored to be planning some kind of mischief against their onetime comrades in ComStar. The Word of Blake threat had already weakened the defenses of the Skye March by siphoning off a pair of regiments to reinforce Marshal Caesar Steiner's army down on the border. Perhaps one of their fleets had broken through to Glengarry on its way to

harass some ComStar strongpoint in what was left of Rasalhague.

Even if those newly arrived ships were manned by enemies of the Federated Commonwealth, it was quite possible
that they were simply passing through the Glengarry system
on their way to some more important target, such as Skye.
Until De Villar had more data, the Gray Death couldn't be
sure of anything.

But by the time they knew more, it could be too late.

10

Deep Space, Glengarry System
Federated Commonwealth
1 April 3056

"**D**amn it, why don't they do something?" Weltalleutnant Sean Ferguson, nickname "Shadowcat," muttered aloud. His nerves were stretched taut by the prospect of battle, and the seemingly endless wait cooped up in the narrow cockpit of his aerospace fighter wasn't improving his mood.

He checked the clock on his control console for what seemed like the hundredth time since strapping in. The Free Skye armada had made the jump to Glengarry more than half an hour ago, and the klaxon calls summoning the fighter squadron to the launch bay had come even before they'd had time to recover from the effects of jump shock. But all the rush to man the six *Lucifer* Class fighters had been merely a prelude to boredom. The *Merkur*, the fighter-carrier DropShip, still hadn't even separated from the *Gotterdämerung* mother ship. Meanwhile Ferguson and his Free Skye comrades sat trapped in the *Merkur*'s fighter bay somewhere in the Glengarry system's deep space.

"Take it easy, Junior," admonished squadron leader Weltallhauptmann William "High-six" Hobart. "The bus drivers know their job. Just settle down and try to relax. And next time you feel the need to make a comment, make sure your comm system's off."

Ferguson felt himself blushing under the bulky flight helmet. Hobart, the only veteran in the squadron, had an uncanny way of making him look and feel the fool. He knew he was raw by Hobart's standards, but somehow none of the other pilots in the outfit managed to draw attention to them-

selves the way Ferguson seemed to. And it didn't help that
his training record made Ferguson the squadron's exec.

They were all excited, of course, even Hobart under the
grizzled veteran's calm he affected. For days the only subject of conversation had been the orders activating the First
New Glasgow Aerospace Squadron, Skye Guards Regiment,
for the Glengarry mission. The squadron had been formed
only recently after the armories on Skye were opened and
equipment became available to the local training cadres
maintained by the various Ranger regiments on Skye. As
yet the new aerospace unit was unblooded, but now they'd
have a chance to show their mettle under real combat conditions.

The squadron had been designated as the principal attack
force for Operation Blackout, the first stage of the invasion
of the Glengarry system. The exact nature of their mission
was still a matter of conjecture. Their fighters were fully
loaded with weapons and ammo, and the tactical data had
been stored in the onboard computer, but the pilots would
not know their specific target until the moment came for the
strike. Before the jump, MacGillivray, Ferguson's wingman, had bet him that the op would involve interdiction of
a JumpShip to prevent enemy DropShips from reinforcing
the planet. Judging from the nature of the last few simulations back on Skye, that made a lot of sense.

Ferguson checked the chronograph again. The worst thing
about the long wait to detach the *Merkur* from the JumpShip
was the time it gave him to contemplate the prospect of
battle. He hoped he wouldn't let his squadron down,
wouldn't crack when he got into a real shooting war. The
idea of facing living, breathing opponents instead of electronic simulator targets aroused fear as much as excitement.

But his homeworld, like so many others, chafed under the
rule of House Davion, and this conflict was the only way
Skye would ever be free. It was war—war to the knife, if
need be. And Sean Ferguson was determined to play his
part, no matter what it required of him.

In the Castle Hill command center on Glengarry, Major
Davis McCall stared at the newstrans still coming in over
the main monitor as if it could give him a better solution
than the one he had.

"I dinna ken any ither option," he said slowly. "Withoot

yon JumpShip we're cut off. 'Tis nae ither way tae deal with that fleet.''

''If they're hostile,'' de Villar answered, more to himself than the major. ''If we're the target. Too damned many 'ifs' for my taste. Rodland will just have to hold position until we know more.''

''Aye,'' McCall agreed with a frown. ''And with the time lag, 'twill be up tae him tae decide if they hae tae jump oot—and when. We canna manage it frae here.''

The acting CO looked sour. ''I wish it was Katrina Tor making the decision out there. Or Ilse Martinez. I don't know if Rodland's the man I want calling the shots.''

''Ye could order Martinez tae tak command.''

De Villar shook his head. ''This is too important to start messing around with the T-O. Most of Rodland's officers have been with him since they left Rasalhague. I don't want to risk a showdown that might blow up in our face. We need the *Gray Skull* if we expect to get help.''

McCall nodded slowly. It was a devil of a situation, he thought, with the possibility that all the Legion's hopes might end up riding on one JumpShip and a captain with a dubious reputation. Lacking an HPG communications station, Glengarry was completely dependent upon JumpShips to maintain contact with other systems.

Before the arrival of the Clans, every human-occupied world had been part of ComStar's web of faster-than-light interstellar communications. These stations had been in the hands of ComStar for generations, until the organization's former leader had attempted to seize political power over the Inner Sphere in the wake of the Clan war. The attempt had failed, and Primus Myndo Waterly had been deposed, but in the process the whole communications network had been thrown into chaos. On many worlds, the ruling Successor State had taken over the hyperpulse stations, while permitting ComStar techs to continue running them. At the lesser stations ComStar sill operated the stations on their own. But not on Glengarry. The HPG site near Dunkeld had been sabotaged by a fanatic ComStar acolyte who feared that the Gray Death Legion, with its reputation for disseminating knowledge, might learn enough of ComStar's secrets to put them out of business forever. So the only remaining link between the planet and the rest of the Federated Commonwealth was via messages passed by JumpShip. And the *Gray Skull* was the only friendly JumpShip in the system.

"All right, then," de Villar said quietly, entering another note on his terminal. "Without an HPG, the only way we're going to warn anybody of the situation here is to send word out by way of the *Gray Skull*. Rodland can alert the F-C authorities . . . maybe hook up with Khaled and Second Battalion, too."

"Aye, 'tis our ain option," McCall said, frowning unhappily. Like de Villar, he wasn't happy at the thought of Rodland calling the shots out there. There had been a lot of unanswered questions about the circumstances of Captain Rodland's departure from service to Rasalhague. "As long as the laddie at the helm kens his duty . . ."

"Aunt Ilse will keep him on the straight and narrow," Lieutenant Longo interjected. He wasn't really related to Ilse Martinez, of course, but most of the aerospacers in the Legion regarded the DropShip skipper with a mixture of familiarity and awe as the one ship captain who had been with Grayson Carlyle since the unit's earliest days. McCall wished he could share the younger man's optimism.

"My question is, which authorities do we order him to alert?" De Villar said grimly. "Hell, we still don't even know who's out there, so how do we know who to inform? Who's trustworthy?"

"We'll ken better soon," McCall said. "If Rodland doesna jump until he maun dae it, he'll hae aye time tae learn who they are oot there."

"Yeah, but it doesn't help us on this end," de Villar observed. "We have to frame the orders now."

"Weil . . ." McCall stared at a blank monitor screen on the wall behind de Villar, lost in thought for a long moment. "Weil, if it turns oot tae be hostile, I dinna think 'twil be a Davion fleet. Young Prince Victor has nae reason tae turn on us. And even if he did hae something agin us, I dinna think he'd attack withoot hearing us oot first."

"Don't forget Helm," de Villar said flatly.

McCall thought of his feelings before the ceremony had started. Had it been only an hour ago? It was hard to believe the Day of Heroes memorial was still going on in the compound far above their sanctuary. "I never will, laddie," he said. "But Victor Davion, whatever else he may be, isna one tae act withoot kenning a' there is tae ken. He winna be fooled intae blaming us for something we didna dae . . . and we havena done anything tae himself. No, I think we can trust that one, but I winna want tae be trusting any ither.''

"Especially Richard Steiner," Longo put in carefully. "Looks to me like he's in Ryan's back pocket, so if anybody local's behind that fleet out there, I'd bet on him. And His Grace of Skye has a hell of a lot of influence in this part of space. If he's hostile, he'll have a long reach.''

"The ain thing we can do is tae order Rodland tae hook up wi' the HPG net," McCall said. "New Earth's the closest A station tae be restored, if ye discount Skye—an' I think we hae best assume Skye's aye hostile when we send these orders, just tae be sure. Our best bet is tae send a message tae Colonel Carlyle on Tharkad. He can judge how tae pass it on tae the authorities at Court.''

"It'll be chancy," Longo said. "One hostile commtech could sabotage the whole thing.''

De Villar shrugged. "That's true of all our options. That's why Rodland needs to go from New Earth to hook up with Khaled's people on Borghese. That way we're sure of some help.''

"It'll take weeks," Longo said.

"Months, more like it," de Villar corrected. "But we don't have much choice, do we?''

"Nae," McCall concurred. "Nae choice at a'. Sae we'd best be getting yon message off, while there's still time. *If* there's still time . . .''

11

"**N**ew contact! New contact at bearing zero-four-two by one-three-three."

Captain Rodland called up the navigation plot on his console. Where there had been a single blip a few minutes earlier, there were clearly two now. "Mister Ullestad . . ."

"New contact is definitely under power, skipper," the *Gray Skull*'s exec said before Rodland had even finished. "It's a DropShip, all right."

"Type?"

"Working . . . Warbook confirms it's a DropShip. *Leopard* Class . . . bearing is constant, range sixty thousand kilometers, closing. She's coming our way."

Ensign Rischel turned to face Rodland. "He's running on a steep acceleration curve, Captain. I'd estimate three gees. That'll put him alongside us in about . . . twenty-four minutes."

"That's assuming they want to match delta-vee with us," Ullestad added. "If they don't turn around and decelerate at midpoint, they'll be here sooner."

"Not much point in that," Ilse Martinez said. She had left the bridge to check on the *Io,* but now she was back, strapped into the tactical coordinator's position.

The exec looked across at her with a raised eyebrow. "There is if you intend a shooting war. No need to match course and come alongside if you want to blast a target out of space."

"You don't think they'd do that," she protested. "I mean

. . . these aren't Clan ships. They'll observe the rules of war.''

Rodland shrugged elaborately. "Rules of war or none, I don't want to play sitting deck if a bunch of hotheads decide we're a target.''

It was an unwritten but long-honored law of modern warfare that JumpShips of all types were sacrosanct, protected from attack by any belligerent party. The widespread loss of Star League-era technology had made the starships such a precious commodity that few combatants in the Inner Sphere were willing to risk the loss of their own fleets by attacking anyone else's JumpShips. But lately that unwritten law had been losing force as new technologies had revived the shipbuilding industries of the Successor States. The Clans, who didn't have the same tradition of restraint, had pointed the way to waging war against JumpShips during their assaults on the Inner Sphere. The political fanatics of the Inner Sphere might take their cue from that, especially in a civil war or among true believers like the Word of Blake movement. The accepted rules of war could break down damned fast in such situations. And even if the intruders didn't come in shooting, they might be planning to try to capture the *Gray Skull* with a boarding party.

It looked like history might be about to repeat itself. Once again Einar Rodland was looking down the wrong end of a military mismatch.

"We have to assume that *Leopard* isn't just heading over here to snag an invite to tea," he told Martinez. "Mister Ullestad, progress on those jump calculations?"

"Still working, sir. Ten minutes. No more."

"Good. Expedite it. I want to be able to get the hell out of here before he gets close enough to start taking potshots.''

"You're not pulling out without permission, are you?'' Martinez demanded. She knew Rodland's history, and she'd made no secret of her distaste for a man who would abandon his comrades to their fate. "It won't be long until we have fresh instructions from the planet. And don't forget the *Antelope*.'' Just after the appearance of the mystery armada, Lieutenant Drake had decided to return to the JumpShip instead of running the gauntlet of those unknown ships. He was still out there.

"I'm hedging our bets," Rodland replied absently, studying the monitor on his control board, which carried a duplicate of the nav plot. "I want everything programmed before those bastards get close enough to cause trouble. We'll wait to recover the *Antelope*."

Martinez pushed off from Rischel's chair and ended up in front of him, her dark eyes boring into his. "You just make sure you keep your hands off the button, Rodland," she said, voice soft but level. "Until we know what they want from us down on Glengarry. I've been with the Legion too long to walk out on them now."

"We'll wait for orders," Rodland replied coldly. "Or until we run out of other options. But remember one thing, sister. This is my ship . . . and my crew. They come first. And if you don't like it, you can cut loose in that rustbucket of yours and take on the bad guys all by yourself. You read me?"

She nodded, a curt, sullen nod. "I understand," she grated. Without another word she pushed off again, sailing through the zero-G to the hatchway in a graceful, easy motion. Then she was gone, and Rodland looked back at his repeater screen. The intruder ship was still closing.

"Gray Skull, Gray Skull, this is Antelope," Drake's voice said from a comm speaker. "We have long-range visual acquisition of the intruder DropShip that just detached. Do you copy? Over."

"Antelope, Gray Skull. Copy that. Can you patch through a video signal?"

"Affirmative, Gray Skull. Stand by." There was a long pause. Then one of the monitors on Rodland's comm panel lit up. At first it was fuzzy, then Drake started applying magnification to his long-range telescopes. Suddenly an image sprang out from the blackness.

Ullestad had the same image on his monitors. "Wait a minute, skipper!" he said. He tapped the keypad in front of him. "Warbook's got a new estimate . . . that's a *Leopard* CV! See the fighter bay doors?"

"Fighters," Rodland said, tight-lipped. The standard *Leopard* Class DropShip carried a lance of BattleMechs or a small contingent of troops, but the CV variant was specifically designed to carry aerospace fighters. "That's no damned boarding party."

"That cuts our safety margin," Rischel said. Fighters capable of six gees of acceleration could coast longer at the ship's current speed and then use that higher acceleration curve to brake, getting them to the *Gray Skull* well ahead of their mother ship. They'd probably launch when the DropShip hit the midpoint and turned to start decelerating.

Rodland's fingers tightened on the arm of his chair. "Antelope, we're making that target as a CV type. Do you concur?"

"Affirmative on that idee, Gray Skull," Drake said, sounding unconcerned. "Doesn't look good, Captain." The communications channel cut off abruptly.

No, it didn't. And they were fast running out of options. Rodland didn't want to cut and run if he could avoid it. With his reputation, another unordered retreat would be the end of his career. But the alternative didn't look too good either just now.

"Sir . . ." The sensor technician sounded perplexed. "Sir, I'm reading an aspect change on *Antelope*. Her deltavee is changing. . . ."

The symbols on the tactical display were changing subtly as the computer, compensating for time lag, tried to predict the velocity and course of the DropShip as she unexpectedly changed her thrust. Rodland stared at the screen in dawning recognition.

And horror. There was only one thing that change of course could mean.

"God *damn,*" Ullestad said softly. "Drake's no match for a CV and a fighter squadron."

"No, but he can sure throw a glitch into their battle plans," Rodland said. "Let's hope to hell it's worth the cost."

= 12 =

"**R**ange, twelve thousand kilometers, closing."

Lieutenant John Drake checked his status board and nodded approval. They were as ready as they would ever be.

The *Antelope* was a *Gazelle* Class DropShip, designed to transport a company of armored vehicles and attached troops. Today she had been pressed into more mundane service, transporting a mixed batch of cargo the *Gray Skull* had brought in on her last run from Lyons. But in any role she wasn't entirely without teeth. Drake hoped his ship could give a good account of herself.

A part of him was protesting that this was no part of a DropShip captain's duty, that right now he should be withdrawing at top acceleration. That was the accepted role of a DropShip, especially one running empty. Life was cheap, but technology wasn't. Save the hardware for a later fight.

But Drake owed his life and position to the Gray Death Legion. His father had commanded the *Antelope* before him as a part of a Kurita armored regiment stationed along the Rasalhague frontier. When the Clans came, the *Antelope* had been damaged in action and barely escaped by docking to a merchant JumpShip fleeing the hostilities. They had come out in the Sudeten system, Federated Commonwealth territory and where a Kurita vessel would have been fair game. It was bad enough for a ship belonging to the Federated Commonwealth's hereditary enemy to risk showing up within F-C territory, but the Gray Death Legion had been waging a long-running feud with the Kuritas ever since the sneak attack on Trellwan that had killed Grayson Carlyle's father.

The *Antelope* had crashed on Sudeten, killing Drake's father, but Grayson Carlyle had not been hostile. Instead he'd given Drake the option of repairing—and keeping—his ship in exchange for assistance in the Legion's evacuation effort. The Clans had just beaten them, and Sudeten would be the Gray Death's homeworld no more. Another man would probably have commandeered the stricken DropShip, but not Carlyle. Drake had been with the Legion ever since.

And today, at last, the time had come to repay his debt.

"Incoming message from Gray Skull, sir," the *Antelope*'s chief commtech reported. "Captain Rodland."

"Transfer to my panel here," Drake ordered. Inwardly he cursed the interruption. He needed to stay focused, and explaining himself to the JumpShip captain was a distraction he didn't need right now.

"Drake, what the hell are you playing at?" Rodland demanded as his features filled the monitor.

"Gray Skull, you guys need time," Drake said carefully. "Time for the orders HQ promised to send us, and time for you to get ready to jump. I might be able to buy you what you need. All I've got to do is slow them down a little. If they start messing around with their acceleration curve to get at us, it'll play havoc with their timetable."

"One DropShip won't last long against a whole damned fleet, Drake," the JumpShip captain protested. "Hell, if they launch their fighters they'll outclass you even without help from the rest of that bunch. Call it off, man! Before it's too late!"

Drake shook his head. "No can do, Gray Skull. Let me do what we both know I've got to." He paused. "Check your tactical board, Captain. Nothing I could do would get me docked with you before these bastards are right on top of you. So I'm in deep trouble either way. Best thing now is to make sure we're the only ones."

There was a long silence on the other end. Drake could picture Rodland running simulations on his tac board, but he already knew what the computer would say. He'd always been able to outguess a tactical situation even without computer assistance. This one he'd summed up the moment he'd seen the distinctive *Leopard*-CV configuration in the telescopic image.

Then Rodland's face was back on his screen, features grim. "Computer says you're right. But you can't just throw your lives away."

"We'll see. Maybe we'll hand 'em a surprise or two." Fat chance, Drake added silently, but he wasn't about to admit to any doubts now. "I'll try to buy you as much time as possible. Antelope, out."

He signaled to the commtech to cut the channel and then turned his full attention back to the tactical display. It was a simple task, really. All he had to do was get the enemy captain's attention. . . .

Every motion, every movement was a strain under three gravities of acceleration, and aboard the Free Skye Drop-Ship *Merkur,* Weltallkommandant Otto Jaeger moved his hands over the control board with exaggerated care. It would be too easy to drag a stray digit across the wrong pressure pad, and every space officer knew that speed had to take second place to caution in high-grav situations like this one.

He punched up the sensor-array repeater screen and studied the pattern of lines and symbols that interrupted the region of deep space around the DropShip.

"Do you have him, sir?" the sensor technician asked, sounding worried.

Jaeger studied the red trace that represented the hostile ship moving under power straight toward the *Merkur.* "I've got him," he acknowledged. "Looks to me like a *Gazelle* Class. He's not seriously thinking of attacking, is he?"

"Looks like it, Captain," the exec responded.

"Suicide," Jaeger pronounced. The *Gazelle* was actually bigger and better armed than his command, but not when you added the *Merkur*'s contingent of fighters to the balance. No one in his right mind would try to pit an ordinary transport DropShip against a fighter carrier with a full complement of fighters. Unless . . .

"Intelligence data," Jaeger snapped. "What do they have on the Gray Death's space assets?"

"Only one *Gazelle* Class listed, Captain Drake," the exec replied promptly. "She's the *Antelope.* Standard configuration as of two months ago. No indication they've done any conversions or modifications since then."

Jaeger stared thoughtfully at the monitor. "That man is

either very brave or very stupid,'' he said, almost to himself. ''All he can do is delay us.''

''Perhaps that's all they want, sir.''

''Well, the sooner we deal with him the sooner we can deal with the JumpShip. Order the fighters to launch. Handle him. And quickly.''

''Aye aye, Captain,'' the exec acknowledged.

Jaeger contemplated the sensor display and smiled coldly. The opposition was badly mistaken if they thought they could win with delaying tactics. This was one fight that would be over in short order.

''And five! Four . . . three . . . two . . .''

In the cockpit of his *Lucifer,* Weltalleutnant Sean Ferguson gripped the control stick with both hands and braced himself as the countdown ticked off the seconds. A few minutes earlier he'd been complaining at the inaction. Now he felt a cold chill settling in his gut as he thought about the order to launch. This would be no simulation, no quiet practice fight. This was the real thing. . . .

''Launch!''

Acceleration slammed him back into his contoured cockpit seat as the fighter bay catapult flung his aerospace fighter into the void. Ferguson had only the briefest glimpse of the *Merkur's* elongated hull rushing past. Then the carrier DropShip was out of sight astern.

He counted off the prescribed number of seconds before cutting in his engines. The DropShip had maintained acceleration throughout the launch operation, so that the delta-vee values of mother ship and fighter were diverging moment by moment. Once the larger craft was clear of danger from the fighter's engines, Ferguson could go to powered flight.

''Red Squadron, this is Red One,'' Hobart's voice crackled in his headset. ''Set your navputers to take a CAT feed from Red Mother.''

Ferguson's fingers played over the console beside his left leg. The cockpit displays shifted as the feed started. The *Merkur* mounted a far more sophisticated array of sensors than any fighter could carry, and her computer was bigger, faster, and smarter. Using unjammable tight-beam laser links coordinated by computers on both the fighters and the mother ship, it was possible for the ships of Red Squadron to use those superior command and control facilities to good advantage. Of course, if things got dicey and the tight-beam links went down, he'd have to rely on his own instruments, but for now all six ships of Red Squadron would be working in tightly coordinated harmony.

"Red Three," he reported. "Link established. Showing one hostile, range ten thousand, closing."

"That's confirmed, Shadowcat," Hobart said a moment later. "All Reds, close up and alter course to intercept the hostile. Standard diamond formation."

"Red Three, aye," Ferguson acknowledged. He moved the stick with smooth precision, marvelling at how ordinary it all seemed. It was just like a drill after all.

Except for the fact that the hostile target out there was real—and in a matter of minutes so would be the missiles and beams coming at them.

=== 13 ===

Deep Space
Glengarry System, Federated Commonwealth
1 April 3056

"**F**ighters! Fighters! Fighters!" the *Antelope*'s weapons officer chanted. "Target is launching fighters."

"What does the Warbook make of them?" Captain Drake demanded.

His exec, Linda Fowler, was quick to respond. "They're *Lucifer*s. Sixty-five tons, an LRM and seven lasers for armament."

Drake pursed his lips. "Well, I guess medium fighters are better than heavies."

"If you ignore their speed and maneuverability," Fowler countered grimly.

He ignored the comment. DropShips weren't supposed to engage in space battles voluntarily, and six medium fighters would pose a serious threat even under the best of combat situations. The *Antelope*'s weapons and armor were more than a match for any mere fighter, but they were designed for self-defense and as support for troops during a landing operation, not for a standup fight. Aerospace fighters designed specifically for interception work could fly rings around a DropShip.

Anyway, just engaging the *Lucifer*s wouldn't accomplish much. He might destroy one or two of them, but that wouldn't change the basic situation. Meanwhile the *Leopard*-CV was maintaining its heading and speed, closing on Rodland's *Gray Skull*. The only way to buy Rodland the time he'd need to wait for the orders promised from the Gray Death commanders on Glengarry was to distract that DropShip.

Drake's eyes roamed over the sensor display and the ship's status monitor. There really was no choice but one. "Helm, start random variations on the acceleration curve," he said at last. "Weapons Officer, power up the PPCs and prepare to engage."

"Target, Skipper?" Takashi Akiyama glanced over his shoulder, a quizzical expression on his fine-boned face. "Or do we stick with CTA?"

He shook his head. This time they wouldn't turn the weaponry over to computer fire control. The computer threat-assessment program was effective in most cases, but it made its judgments based on narrow tactical considerations. A longer view was needed here.

"Override computer fire control," he ordered. "We want you to concentrate everything on the *Leopard*. Helm, maintain a direct course toward that ship. Match maneuvers, but close up the range." That wouldn't be easy, with both ships using random thrust variations to fool each other's targeting systems, but they didn't have to get close enough to board. All they had to do was present a sufficient threat.

Startled gasps from around the bridge greeted his orders. "The CV isn't the threat," he heard someone say aloud.

"Our job is to keep the bastards tied up for a while," he told them bluntly. "We do that best by harassing the mother ship."

"Aye aye, Skipper," Linda Fowler said for all of them.

She knew as well as he did what the decision would mean.

"*Allmachtiger Gott!* The DropShip is still on intercept with us!"

Aboard the Free Skye DropShip *Merkur,* Weltallkommandant Jaeger turned in his chair to study the enemy ship's tactical plot. The ship's vector data had not really changed, except for the minor fluctuations of random drive-variation to throw off targeting systems. With six fighters closing rapidly on the ship, it took guts for the enemy captain to maintain such a single-minded attack posture.

A brave man, indeed, this DropShip captain. A pity he would have to be killed . . .

"Flight Control!" he rasped. "Order Red Squadron to close the range and attack."

"Missile launch from the target," the sensor technician reported. "Incoming missiles! Incoming missiles!"

"Point defense!" the exec snapped.

The weapons officer responded with a crisp "Aye, aye," and bent over his board. Bursts of thousands of high-velocity slugs probed the void around the *Merkur,* searching for the streaking warheads locked on to the carrier DropShip.

"Two . . . three . . . five warheads neutralized," the sensor tech reported. "Still . . . twelve incoming."

"Brace for impact! Damage control parties, stand by!"

Jaeger could feel the rippling detonation of the swarm of LRMs against the ship's armored hull. The *Merkur* seemed to shudder under the attack, and Jaeger's fingers dug into the arms of his acceleration couch. "Report damage!" he ordered sharply.

"Reports coming in now, sir," the exec replied. "All decks secure. They scoured away some armor, but nothing serious. No breaches."

"Main comm array is out. Switching to secondaries," the communications station keeper reported a moment later.

"Minor damage to Number Three laser turret," the weapons officer added. "The weaponry still reads nominal, but the turret mechanism's showing an amber light."

"Damage control has it," the exec said. "I've got a team on the way."

"Good," Jaeger said, pleased at the crew's smooth responses. That first salvo hadn't been anything more than a test of the *Merkur*'s reactions, and worse would surely follow if the enemy captain had even half the brains Jaeger suspected. Still, he was confident his crew could handle anything a *Gazelle* Class ship could throw at him.

And meanwhile the fighters were coming into range too. That would settle this fight.

"Missiles incoming! Range five hundred, closing!" shouted the *Antelope*'s weapons officer.

"Brace for impact!" Drake ordered. "And maintain your fire on the *Leopard*!"

An instant later the Gray Death DropShip seemed to stagger as the enemy missiles detonated along the *Antelope*'s stern. The bridge lights faded for a moment, then came back up. At the same time a string of red warning indicators glowed bright on Drake's status console.

"Six . . . no, seven hits, skipper," Fowler reported. "All to the stern section. Engines are redlining, and we have a pressure drop in the upper drive room, port side. Containment doors are in place."

"We can't take much more of this," Drake said, sick at the thought of what he was doing to his father's beloved *Antelope*—and to the nine crewmen who trusted in him as captain.

"PPC hit on the *Leopard*!" the weapons officer exulted. "Bastard felt that one, guaranteed!"

"How much time have we bought for Rodland?" Drake asked. He'd lost track of time ever since the first *Lucifer* had crossed the DropShip's stern and opened fire.

"Twelve minutes, skipper," the exec told him. "More, really. We've shot their whole maneuver profile to hell. Once they finish us off they'll have a lot of delta-vee to make up." Linda Fowler's voice was even. It was as if she had already accepted death as the only possible outcome.

And she was right, of course. The DropShip was well armored and heavily armed, but the enemy fighters had the advantages of speed and maneuverability, and each time they closed to the attack they ran up more damage to the DropShip's hull armor without suffering any themselves. As long as Drake ignored them in favor of the mother ship, they could keep up those unanswered attacks. It was only a matter of time before the *Lucifer*s finally finished off the *Antelope*.

Drake slammed his fist down on the chair arm. "If we're going out, let's do it in style," he said harshly. "Lieutenant, I want every gram of thrust you can squeeze out of those engines. I don't care if you have to go back there and hold them together with your hands!" Drake looked at the pilot. "Helm, alter your delta-vee again. I want a collision course with the *Leopard*."

"Aye, aye, sir," the pilot responded, grim-voiced. No questions, no protests, just simple obedience. It made Drake feel proud, proud of all his crew. They deserved a better fate than the one they would meet today.

Drake hesitated a long moment before speaking again. "I can take the helm myself . . . and I'd like a volunteer to ride herd on the engines. But the rest of you can abandon now and take your chances on a pickup. Even if the bad guys grab you, POW is better than KIA any day of the week. And mercs usually get better treatment than house troops.''

No one moved or said a word. Finally Linda Fowler spoke. ''We all go together,'' she said, then after a pause, ''. . . Captain.''

''Another *Lucifer* coming up on our six!'' the sensor technician broke in. ''Missile launch! Missile launch!''

The captain of the *Antelope* gripped his chair arms and waited for the impact.

=14=

"I'm on him! I'm on him!" Free Skye Weltalleutnant Sean Ferguson let out a whoop and triggered a second salvo of missiles. The *Gazelle* Class DropShip was no match for a well-handled fighter, especially a *Lucifer*.

"Keep it chilly, Red Three," squadron leader Hobart admonished. "You'll live longer. Don't lose your head over small fry while we've still got the big boy to tackle."

Ferguson reined in his enthusiasm even as the first missile salvo rippled across the mercenary DropShip's tail section. His sensors gave him a satisfying BDA report: critical damage to engineering, another likely hull breach to go with the one Red Five had scored earlier, even some damage to the control surfaces on the tail assembly, which wouldn't matter until the ship tried to enter atmosphere. If she survived that long.

"Score five more hits for Red Three," he said, trying without much success to sound calm and matter-of-fact. This first taste of battle was exhilarating, and Ferguson felt more intense, more alive than he ever had before.

His last salvo had missed the enemy DropShip. She'd been varying her acceleration to throw off the *Lucifers*' targeting systems, but this time the sudden surge in velocity looked more like the uncontrolled fluctuation of the damaged drive system.

"Damn," he muttered aloud.

"Don't worry about it, Junior," Hobart said reassuringly. "That's combat. Now drop back and see what a vet can do."

Ferguson triggered his forward thrusters and watched the Gray Death DropShip start to pull away. An instant later Hobart's *Lucifer,* its red and gold wing markings distinctive, flashed above his cockpit, driving in to the high trailing position that had given Hobart his nickname. A position to the rear of the target—six o'clock, by the old analogy to the Terran standard clock—was valuable in any battle, but Hobart's favored "high-six" spot gave him an especially commanding view of his victim.

Unlike the rookies, Hobart didn't choose long-range missiles for his attack. His fighter's heaviest laser pulsed once . . . twice . . . a third time, probing at the shattered stern of the DropShip. Secondary explosions ripped through the ruined hull plating. Ferguson's BDA panel lit up with a constellation of red and amber lights as his sensors took in the damage Hobart was inflicting.

"That did it!" Hobart said calmly. "That sucker's power plant is dead! Looks like he's down to batteries for life support, but that's about it."

"Red Squadron, Red Squadron, this is Merkur," the fighter controller's voice crackled over the commlink. "Thanks for the assist. Now that he's lost his power he won't be a threat. Break off the action and head for the primary target."

"Roger that, Merkur," Hobart's voice acknowledged. "You heard the man, Reds. Let's pull some gees!"

As Ferguson started feeding the new instructions into his navputer, he could see the squadron's mother ship maneuvering. The enemy ship had been trying to match course, presumably for a kamikaze maneuver. With its power plant shut down and engines useless, the Gray Death DropShip wouldn't be able to maneuver further, while the *Merkur* could change her delta-vee and dodge the cumbersome hulk. The enemy ship would simply drift on its present course until it was clear of the battle zone or until they decided to surrender and take a tow.

The *Merkur* was turning ponderously, its twin PPCs opening fire. A moment later Ferguson's sensors picked up a swarm of missiles streaking toward the crippled enemy DropShip. So much for escape or surrender, he thought. Obviously, Captain Jaeger wasn't taking any chances.

Sean Ferguson swallowed and reminded himself that this

was, after all, a war. War to the knife, with the freedom of
Skye at stake . . .

"Gray Skull, Gray Skull, this is Antelope . . ." came the
words over the *Gray Skull*'s commline. A crash of static
masked the weak signal for a moment. "That last salvo . . .
did for us. Four dead . . . power's gone . . . I'm afraid . . .
failed . . ."

Captain Rodland leaned forward and stabbed his comm
panel savagely. "Abandon ship, Drake! You can't do anything else now!"

"Too late, Captain," Ullestad said quietly. "He's taking
fire from the *Leopard* now. There's no time to abandon—"

"God damn . . ." Rodland's fists were clenched. Drake's
Antelope had been outclassed from start to finish, and
though he'd scored a few hits on his opposite number the
damage had been insignificant. Drake had thrown away his
life and his ship in an empty gesture.

"Gray Skull . . ." The signal was suddenly stronger, as
if Drake had pumped his last battery reserves into the
comm system. "Fifteen extra minutes . . . hope it was
enough . . ."

Then there was nothing but static.

In the silence, the sensor technician's voice was star-
tlingly loud. "Multiple hits. The *Antelope*'s taken her last
jump, sir."

Rodland looked at Ullestad. "Prepare to execute jump,
Lieutenant," he said quietly. "It's time we got the hell out
of here."

"But what about the orders from Glengarry?" the exec
protested. "They told us to stand by and await instructions.
You know the signal's on its way by now."

"And while we wait, those bastards are still closing!"
Rodland grated. "You think they're going to leave us alone?
I'm not hanging around to find out! Order jump stations
now, Mister!"

Ullestad started to reply, but the communications technician cut him off. "Incoming message from HQ, sir," he
said. "Coded priority one."

"Sir, I've got additional targets now," the sensor tech
chimed in a moment later. "Multiple targets under thrust.
Looks like our friends out there are launching every
DropShip they've got."

Rodland hesitated for a long moment. Every instinct cried out for him to clear out of the danger zone as soon as possible, to save the *Gray Skull* from the enemy threat. He would have been long gone already except for Drake and the *Antelope*.

But if he cut out now, Drake and his people would have died for nothing. The DropShip had bought precious time so that the *Gray Skull* could wait for instructions from the planet.

"Belay the jump order, Lieutenant," he growled at last. "Maintain readiness. Communications, record the transmission." He rubbed a hand across his forehead. The new orders might have instructions for the *Io*. He hit the intraship address stud. "Captain Martinez to the bridge. Repeating, Captain Martinez to the bridge."

=== 15 ===

"**E**yes . . . right! Present . . . arms!"

Alex Carlyle drew himself to attention and touched one hand to his cap as the Gray Death Legion passed in review before the speakers' platform in the Castle Hill parade ground. The music, courtesy of a planetary militia band, was a raucous noise of pipes and drums that produced no tune he could recognize. Bagpipe music had never been to his taste, especially after the time Davis McCall had blasted a recording of some pipe band over the training company commline to test how well the cadets could handle distractions while piloting their 'Mechs.

The thought of McCall made Alex wonder again where the Weapons Master and Major de Villar had disappeared to, and why. Only a major crisis could have taken either man away from the Day of Heroes celebration. Nearly an hour had passed. What was going on?

As if in response to those questions, Weapons Master Davis McCall appeared at his elbow, holding a hand salute as the troops paraded by. When the last of the ranks had passed and the officers on the reviewing stand could drop their salutes, McCall drew Alex to the rear of the platform and spoke in low, urgent tones almost drowned out by the pipes still wailing on the field.

"We hae a problem, lad," McCall said without preamble. As usual in tense situations, the broad Scots accent was much less noticeable than in the major's ordinary conversation. "An unknown fleet jumped insystem about an hour ago. It could be nothing at a' . . . or it could be an invasion. We winna know for anither hour or sae."

"A fleet . . ." Alex swallowed. With his father on Tharkad and half the Legion away on Borghese, Glengarry was vulnerable. "What do you think it is? A raid?"

"Dinna make assumptions until the data is in," the Caledonian advised sternly. "We're monitoring the situation from Command. But 'tis nae point alarming anyone until we ken more."

"I understand, sir," Alex said, nodding. "Is there something I can do to help?"

McCall nodded grimly. "Aye, there is. Pass the word tae Tech Major King. As soon as the ceremony is aye over, Major de Villar wants a' forces tae return tae their posts and gae on full alert. Major King tae tak command at Brander meantime, sae I can remain here."

"Full alert, sir?" Alex asked quietly. "What about the cadets?"

"Aye. Cadet 'Mechs tae be serviced and fully armed. If thir turns oot tae be an attack, we'll be aye wanting every 'Mech we can put in the field." McCall paused. "Full instructions will be posted in the bulletin board, but you tell Major King what's happening. Quietly. We dinna want tae start a panic if this turns oot a false alarm."

"Yes, sir," Alex acknowledged. "But . . ."

"Spit it oot, laddie," the weapons master prompted him impatiently.

"Sorry, sir. I just . . . wondered why you didn't brief him yourself."

"There's been comment enough over de Villar and me leaving. I winna interrupt the ceremony further tae talk to Major King direct. And by the time 'tis over, I'll be needed doon below again. And anyway, young Alex, passing orders and messages is one of the principal duties of an aide-de-camp, is it not?"

It took a moment for the words to sink in. "Your aide? You mean. . . ?"

"Aye. 'Tis time you learned the ither side of command, and where better?" McCall fixed him with a black frown. "Even if a' this is for naught, 'twill be good experience for you. When the rest of the cadets gae back tae Brander, I want you tae remain here. Report to the Command Center after you hae spoken tae Major King."

"Yes, sir," Alex said. "Thank you."

But McCall was already striding away, leaving Alex to contemplate the man's words with mixed emotions. On one hand, the prospect of an invasion fleet somewhere out in deep space confirmed Alex's worst fears. But if battle did come, at least he wouldn't be in a 'Mech cockpit. Alex wasn't sure he could face a real battle yet, not with his training failures weighing so heavily on his mind. As McCall's aide, he wasn't likely to end up facing any life and death decisions—and that suited Alexander Durant Carlyle just fine.

Ilse Martinez pushed her way through the hatch onto the bridge of the *Gray Skull,* anxious to find out what was happening. She had monitored the *Antelope*'s signals from the *Io*'s bridge, listening in horror to Drake's last words. The *Antelope*'s sacrifice probably affected her more deeply than anyone else aboard the Gray Death JumpShip. It was on her advice that Grayson Carlyle had offered young Drake a place with the Legion after the Sudeten evacuation. She'd seen talent there, and considerable courage with it.

Now Drake had proven how much he had of both, paying the ultimate price to do so.

Another name for the rolls on the Day of Heroes, she thought grimly. Martinez had been with Grayson Death Carlyle for thirty years now, ever since the unit's first days. Few would have guessed it, though, for she didn't look her age. Space crews who spent a lot of time in zero-G didn't show the years the way their ground-bound comrades did, and Martinez could have passed for a woman of forty standard years.

But she was past sixty, and today she was feeling every one of those years, and more.

Rodland looked up as Martinez drifted to his side. "They're finally transmitting orders," he said without preamble. "So maybe now we can get the hell out of here."

"I'm glad you stayed," she said gruffly, hardly bothering to conceal her feelings. Martinez didn't like Rodland, didn't like the stories she'd heard about how he'd deserted his friends and the service of Rasalhague when the fight with the Clans got too hot for him.

But at least he'd stayed this time. Drake's sacrifice hadn't been in vain.

Rodland gestured to his commtech. "Start the playback," he ordered.

The monitor at the command position swirled for a moment, then settled down to reveal the face of Major Cristobal de Villar.

"Gray Skull, this is Headquarters," he began immediately. "Your transmission has been received."

Then he paused, as if glancing at some notes out of range of the video pickup. "At the time of your first call, you reported seven JumpShips arriving in the system. According to the current CAT feed data, this hasn't changed as of the transmission time, but I have no way of knowing your situation by the time you receive this. Without additional data my orders cannot be very specific, but I'll try to cover the major contingencies."

"Bloody decent of him," Rodland growled.

"Quiet," Martinez snapped. Rodland might be in command of the ship, but thirty years with the Gray Death Legion gave her the right to speak her mind. Not that she had ever been particularly reluctant to do that, even in the early days.

"Whatever they do, we need more information," de Villar was saying. "If you haven't done so already, concentrate every possible effort on gathering full particulars on those ships. Get us everything you can think of, but especially try for an idee. That goes no matter what else happens." De Villar paused again. "If they don't take any aggressive action, I want you to stay put and monitor the situation as long as possible. Maybe they're just passing through. If all they do is roll out their sails for a recharge, we can be fairly confident they're not interested in us. But I want their activities monitored until they leave, or until we get some kind of proof they aren't hostile. You may want to send in the *Antelope* to get a closer look, but don't provoke anything."

"Yeah. Right." Rodland shook his head slowly. "Fat chance of that now, Major."

"If they launch DropShips, especially in any kind of numbers, everything changes. That will mean they're almost certainly hostile, and that we're the target. In that event, Captain, get as much data as possible, transmit it to us, but under no circumstances allow your ship to be endangered."

"Amen to that," Rodland commented, drawing another glare from Martinez.

"Remember," de Villar continued, "your ship is the only link we have with the rest of the Inner Sphere. We don't have a working HPG, so we can't call for help. We have to assume an enemy would have scouted us out well enough to know that. And that means you're at risk. They'll want to capture you, maybe even destroy you, to keep word of an attack from spreading. So, if those ships are hostile, it's vitally important that you jump out before they have a chance to hit you. Once you're clear, your orders are to make for the Class A hyperpulse station on New Earth. Send a complete message in code to Colonel Carlyle on Tharkad.

"We don't know who's behind this attack—unless you've found out more by now. But the colonel knows enough about the political situation to decide whether he wants to call in any FedCom authorities. You'll be running a bit of the risk on New Earth, of course, but it's a chance you'll have to take. Last we heard here, Davion had taken over the HPG station and has it back in full service. Odds are it's safe."

Rodland hit the button to pause the playback. "There are working communications stations closer than New Earth," he said, sounding irritated. "We could cut a lot of time by sending the messages out of Skye."

Martinez shook her head. "We do it his way," she said. "Don't forget, the Duke of Skye isn't exactly a bastion of support in the Federated Commonwealth cause. Until we know who we're up against, we have to take the least possible number or risks. Hell, Skye rebelled back in thirty-four. They could be doing it again."

"Better hope not," he said, noticeably pale. "We're programmed to jump to Skye, and there's no time to calculate another destination now."

"Then we forget the safety margins and make a second jump out of Skye without waiting for a full recharge," she told him. "I won't be happy until we're well clear of this part of space."

"When you've finished at New Earth," the message from de Villar went on, "I want you to proceed to Borghese. Major Khaled should still be based there. Get word to him about what's happening here, and then follow whatever orders he gives you."

The rest of the message was more elaboration on the basic instructions. When it was finished, Rodland shut down the comm panel and turned to Martinez again.

"Looks like we've got our marching orders," he said.

She nodded unhappily. "I don't like leaving them like this. You don't need me to deliver your message. Maybe I should take the *Io* back to Glengarry and see if I can help out there."

"Bad idea, Captain," Rodland said. "Pointless."

"What's that supposed to mean?" she demanded.

"Well, first off, your ship may be patched up enough for routine flight ops, but you know that bucket of bolts will never make it through any opposition."

She nodded reluctantly. The *Io* was in serious need of an extensive overhaul since the Altair raid. Martinez had improvised some temporary measures to keep her ship flying. But in action against aerospace fighters, the *Io*'s makeshift repairs would be a poor substitute at best for the refit the ship needed so badly. Even if the DropShip could run the gauntlet and make it to Glengarry, she wouldn't be much use once she got there. "Yeah, you're right. But I don't like it."

"Sister, I haven't liked anything I've seen yet today," Rodland said with more feeling than he'd shown since the beginning of the crisis. He turned toward the exec. "Mister Ullestad, I want all our communications and sensor logs compressed into a fast squeal for transmission before we jump. Can do?"

"Aye aye, sir," the lieutenant responded smartly. "Five minutes."

"Good. Then in ten minutes we're out of here. Anything else? No? Then get to your station and make sure that rust-bucket is good and ready."

"Merkur, this is Red One," said Free Skye squadron leader Hobart. "Target in range in six minutes. Any special instructions?"

Listening to the comm chatter, Weltalleutnant Sean Ferguson eased back on his thrust. Hobart's question sounded worried, and anything that worried the squadron's veteran leader made Ferguson nervous.

"Red Squadron, Merkur," came the reply a few seconds later. Ferguson recognized the voice, and it didn't do anything to make him feel better. If Weltallkommandant Jaeger, the *Merkur*'s captain, was becoming personally involved in the fighter squadron's operations it could only mean trouble. "Your orders are to destroy the enemy JumpShip."

"D-destroy, sir?" The slight quaver in Hobart's voice was audible even to a rookie like Ferguson.

"Those are your orders, man. Now carry them out." Jaeger's voice was flat, harsh.

"They . . . they may surrender, sir," Hobart said. "When they see us coming."

"You will offer no quarter, Red Squadron," Jaeger ordered. "Whatever that JumpShip does, it is to be destroyed."

"Aye aye, sir," Hobart responded slowly. The commline fell silent.

Ferguson's chest felt tight. The squadron's training had dwelt more on the practical matters of fighter combat than on any sort of military philosophy, but Hobart had been strict about instilling a knowledge of the rules of war in his charges. And one of the first rules of space combat was that a JumpShip was inviolate. The technology represented by those interstellar transports was all but irreplaceable today. So much so that many superstitious pilots attributed almost mystical powers to the hyperdrive's ability to twist space around itself to move a JumpShip instantaneously between stars. Ferguson wasn't prepared to believe all the stories he'd heard, but he knew Hobart could never have conceived of the idea of attacking a JumpShip. It was even worse if the enemy ship should surrender. The Fourth Ares Convention, one of the written rules of war, guaranteed that mercenaries who surrendered in combat would not be subject to reprisals.

But Jaeger's orders left no room for doubt. And Ferguson had to admit there was good reason to strike hard and without mercy. After all, the Free Skye Movement was only a tiny resistance organization compared to the size and power of the Federated Commonwealth. The only way to make up for that disparity was to prevent the enemy from using its superior assets.

War to the knife. In a fight for freedom, there might not be room for the niceties of a civilized war.

"All right, Reds," said Hobart, his voice sounding gruff but determined over the channel. "You heard the orders.

Arm all weapons, and increase to full thrust. Commence attack run on my mark.''

Ferguson eased his throttles forward, feeling the weight of the increased gee-force settling across his chest. Lucky or unlucky, it didn't make any difference now. They were committed to the attack.

"*Lucifer*s coming into firing range, Captain. Estimating thirty seconds.''

"Damn,'' Rodland muttered. "Guess we cut it a little too fine.''

"Weapons officer!'' Ullestad snapped. "Plot a firing solution and open fire when ready. Mister Rischel, your attention to your terminal, if you please. . . .''

Rodland swung to face the JumpShip's communications station. "I want a full replay of the CAT logs ready to send out, Gundersen,'' he ordered. "Just in case they lost anything we transmitted in real time.'' In theory, it was impossible to jam a tight-beam laser link even over interplanetary distances, but the *Gray Skull*'s captain wasn't taking any chances. Not after all the risks run, all the costs paid for lingering this long. Now the information the *Gray Skull* had been collecting and sending out in a steady stream for hours would be reduced to a set of signals that could be transmitted at high speed in a last, single burst before the JumpShip triggered her hyperdrive. "Compress the data we've gathered and get the transmitter on line. I want a zip-squeal at a thousand to one.''

"End the sensor feed, Captain?'' the commtech asked.

Before Rodland could reply, Petty Officer Lund, the JumpShip's sensor technician, broke in. "Sir, I think I can get a VE on those fighters.'' He hesitated before plunging on. "It might be important, sir.''

Rodland nodded reluctantly. A visual enhancement of the incoming *Lucifer*s might give them a view of any markings or emblems the fighters were displaying. Even if there wasn't time for the *Gray Skull*'s crew to identify whatever the long-range visual sensors picked up, the data could be very useful back on Glengarry. "Right. Gundersen, maintain the feed. Keep processing the condensed signal as the data comes in, and be ready to transmit on my word. Got it?''

"Yes, sir,'' Gundersen said. "I'll set up a tie-in to the

jump countdown. It'll go out automatically at J-minus-five seconds.''

"Good . . . good." Rodland nodded curtly. "But be ready for a manual transmission, too. Just in case." He didn't add that a single missile could get through their defenses, take the computers off-line before they could jump. The data had to get out, even if the *Gray Skull* couldn't escape.

The thought made Rodland frown. He still hated this whole mess. But he couldn't run. Not this time. Not after what Drake and his crew had done.

"Do we jump, Captain?" Ullestad asked calmly.

"Start the final check list," Rodland replied, trying to match his exec's apparent detachment.

"Final check list," the lieutenant echoed, then hit the intraship speaker control. "Jump warning! Jump warning. Five minutes! All hands, jump stations! Report status and stand by!"

Rodland tapped an intercom key on his board. "Io, confirm jump warning."

Ilse Martinez replied quickly. She had returned to the bridge of her own ship, apparently content to trust Rodland after all. "Confirmed," she reported. "Io now at jump stations, four minutes, fifty seconds . . . mark!"

"Navputer confirms coordinates for jump," Ensign Rischel announced.

"K-F drives on line and reading nominal-to-profile," Haugen chimed in. "Auto-sequencers engaged. Charge reading ninety-six percent."

It was the standard litany of a bridge crew preparing for the trip through hyperspace, though Rodland was conscious of the edge in all their voices, the atmosphere of tension that underlay everything they did and said.

Then the routine was shattered.

"Missile launch! Missile launch!" Lund chanted. On Rodland's board, dozens of tiny blips representing enemy missiles suddenly appeared like clouds of tiny insects around the six fighters.

He checked his clock. Four minutes . . .

"That big bastard's just hanging there! Target practice is on for today!"

Sean Ferguson could hear the excitement in Archie

"Wildfire" Strachan's voice even through the distortion and static on the commline. The Weltallfähnrich had the point position in Red Squadron's diamond formation, and sounded like he was back in the simulators on Skye instead of leading the six Free Skye ships into combat.

Ferguson couldn't muster the same enthusiasm. He kept thinking about the orders to violate the rules of war by destroying the JumpShip. None of the simulators could ever have prepared them for this situation, because an attack on a JumpShip was simply unthinkable, even in practice. So there was no telling what to expect from this battle.

He kept telling himself the attack was a necessary measure, but his mind rebelled against the thought. His fingers clutched tight around his joystick in what Hobart contemptuously called a "rookie's hold." Ferguson was barely conscious of it.

"Rein it in, Four," Hobart's voice cut through the static sharply. "Concentrate on flying and shooting, and save the chatter for the party when we make pickup."

The enemy JumpShip was still too far away to be visible to the naked eye, but Ferguson's instruments showed it still hanging all but motionless in space. The squadron's first wave of missiles streaked toward the target, and Ferguson found himself holding his breath.

For an instant half his sensor readouts broke up, then reformed. An energy discharge . . .

"Skipper! Skipper! I'm hit!" Strachan shouted.

"PPC fire from the target," Hobart said, voice level. "Spread formation. Attack pattern Beta. Now . . . talk to me, Wildfire. What's the BDA?"

"S-systems nominal . . . l-light damage to port wing armor . . ." Strachan sounded surprised to be alive.

"Right," Hobart said. "At this range we're still pretty safe. But watch yourselves." He paused. "Shadowcat, Chevalier, fire your loads and go to Beta! Execute."

Ferguson hit the stud that triggered his Holly LRM rack for a second barrage, then pushed his joystick hard to starboard and advanced his throttles to full thrust. Hobart's order for plan Beta called for Ferguson and his wingman, Ian "Chevalier" Henderson, to fire and then peel off. From here on, each pair of Skye fighters would make separate attack runs in waves to maintain constant pressure on the enemy.

Ferguson let out his breath slowly. Maybe this mission wouldn't be so bad after all. He'd had visions of the enemy's weapons being able to take out the heavily armored fighters with single hits, but evidently the JumpShip didn't mount anything more sophisticated than any other vessel in the Inner Sphere.

The knowledge brought a measure of relief, but Ferguson's grip on his joystick was still tighter than it had ever been in practice.

"Concentrate all fire into the missile swarm! Execute!" Captain Einar Rodland gripped his chair arms, every nerve focused sharp on the sensor monitor in front of him. JumpShips weren't supposed to engage in direct combat, but most mounted a number of laser and PPC batteries to aid in repelling boarders. He'd heard of ship captains employing their offensive weaponry for antimissile work, using a targeting program originally developed to deal with meteor swarms that could destroy a JumpShip's solar sail, but this was the first time he'd ever had to use it for the *Gray Skull*. He prayed that Ensign Wingate, the JumpShip's weapons officer, would be up to the task. She was the only one on his bridge today who hadn't been part of the original crew, and she'd had precious little opportunity to practice her craft these last two years.

"Firing," Ensign Brooke Wingate responded, unruffled. Seconds passed, each an eternity for Rodland.

He saw the results on his board before Lund started reporting. "Multiple hits," the sensor technician said. "I count nine . . . ten . . . twelve missiles knocked out. Still eight zombies incoming."

"Continue firing!" Rodland snapped.

"Weapons are cycling, sir," Wingate replied, some of her calm gone now. "If you want enough heat sinks on line when the drive kicks in, we can't push it—"

"Brace for impact!" Ullestad's voice overrode the other noise on the bridge. An instant later the first missile struck the JumpShip. Rodland winced with each successive explosion that shook his command.

"Damage assessment!" he ordered.

"Three missile hits," Ullestad replied. "Section

twenty-four . . . Docking Ring Three is out of action. Hull breach in the docking area. Looks like a hit on the *Io* as well.''

"Status?"

''Nothing serious that I can read, Skipper,'' the exec said. "We were lucky. Jump countdown is still on . . . forty-five seconds now.''

Rodland stabbed a button on his console. "Io . . . report status!'' If the DropShip had been seriously damaged by the strike, it could complicate the jump, perhaps even endanger the *Gray Skull*.

''We're in one piece, Captain,'' Martinez reported. "But we didn't need another hole in our armor.''

A ragged cheer went up from the rest of the bridge crew. Aunt Ilse, it seemed, was winning friends aboard Rodland's ship as she already had throughout the rest of the Legion.

''Thirty seconds,'' Ullestad reported.

''Another wave of missiles closing fast,'' Lund said. "It's going to be tight . . .''

''Power down all unnecessary systems,'' the exec ordered. A klaxon alarm shrilled a warning through the ship. "Navputer is feeding coordinates. Jump field is now forming . . .''

''Sensors off-line,'' the petty officer said.

''Message compressed and in the slot,'' Gundersen added. "Counting down to transmission . . . Transmission beginning . . . now!''

''Go for jump! Go for jump!''

The last seconds seemed to stretch into infinity. . . .

''Power discharge from the JumpShip!'' Sean Ferguson shouted as his instruments registered the expansion of the enemy ship's hyperdrive field. "Get the hell out, High-six!''

''Too late, kid,'' Hobart replied. "Too late . . .''

The expanding bubble of hyperspace around the JumpShip swelled to its maximum diameter. Ferguson heard shouts, then an inhuman scream, over the commline as the four fighters still pressing the attack were caught in the field and literally torn apart.

''Sweet Jesus,'' his wingman muttered, sounding as horrified as Ferguson felt. Four men and their high tech fighters, all destroyed in an instant.

The price of daring to attack a JumpShip . . .

And then the hyperspace field was gone, and with it the ship itself. Gone as if it had never been there.

Ferguson closed his eyes and fought back tears at the loss of his comrades. He barely heard the recall orders from the *Merkur*.

= 16 =

Dunkeld, Glengarry
Free Skye March, Federated Commonwealth
2 April 3056

Governor General Roger DeVries had returned to his office in the Residence after dinner, as he usually did when some ceremonial duty forced him to neglect his work during the day. The Gray Death's Day of Heroes celebration was long since over, and DeVries was thankful to be done with it. He owed his position to Carlyle's Legion, but he still didn't care for any of them, personally or professionally.

He stared glumly at his computer monitor, with its reports of the new business to be taken up by the Council of Twenty in the week ahead. There were drawbacks, he thought, to serving as the governor under a contracted planetholder like Grayson Carlyle. In this day and age, many nobles paid little attention to their fiefs as long as the governor met his obligations for taxes and manpower. Glengarry's titular holder, for instance, had never visited the world, even when local conflicts had threatened the security of his domain. Baron von Bulow seemed to regard Glengarry as just another holding, more to be ignored than a territory to be exploited.

It would have suited DeVries much better if Prince Victor had ordered the Glengarry grant transferred from Baron von Bulow to an ordinary mercenary unit. Certainly it had taken MechWarriors to put down the rival thanes who had gained their fiefs from the Baron and then used them to build their personal power, not to mention the gangs of desperate men who had terrorized the countryside. Any normal merc leader would have been content simply to restore order and then use the planet merely as a base of operations for his unit. Mercenary planetholds were supposed to provide food, industrial support, manpower, and the occasional wild vacation for weary soldiers. In such an environment, real local power would have rested squarely with the governor.

Unfortunately, Grayson Death Carlyle was not the average mercenary, by any means. He kept a much closer eye on local affairs than DeVries would have liked, always promoting improvements in everything from industrial output to home sanitation. A laudable enough program, DeVries thought, but it made for almost continual interference by the planetholder—backed up by his mercenary army—in the affairs of the government.

Carlyle's involvement was hampering the work DeVries had pledged himself to. After years as a merchant plying the interstellar spacelanes, he had a good idea of what was needed to make his adopted home a viable member of the intersteller community. Where the mercenary colonel was apt to treat Glengarry as a kind of hobby, dabbling in whatever improvements seemed useful at any given moment, DeVries had set out to harness and efficiently exploit the planet's potential. With a successful stint as governor, he had hoped to prove that his stewardship would benefit not only Glengarry, but the Federated Commonwealth as a whole. After all, Prince Victor would one day be looking for a new planetholder for the Glengarry fief, wouldn't he? It was in the nature of things for merc units to raise ship and move on every so often. The Legion's assignment here would end one day. Then the Gray Death would be gone, reassigned to some other Federated Commonwealth world that needed a military presence more then Glengarry, or perhaps turning to a new employer outside Federated Commonwealth space entirely.

Why shouldn't Glengarry's next holder be the successful administrator who had reformed the corrupt government and made the planet a contributing member of the interstellar community again? Someday it would happen. . . .

But not as long as Carlyle muddied the waters. When the colonel returned from Tharkad, the two of them would settle this matter once and for all, DeVries thought as he cleared his monitor screen. However sympathetic the governor might be to Carlyle's attempts to improve the lot of Glengarry's ordinary people, what was necessary now was a massive program to bring the planet squarely into the thirty-first century, even if it took harsh measures to make it work. It was time to stop squandering planetary assets in a haphazard way, time to put a real reform program into operation.

A knock on his door interrupted the governor's reverie. He frowned. His secretary and the Planetary Guards who were normally stationed outside the office were not present tonight to screen unwanted visitors. But it was probably just one of the servants, easily dealt with. DeVries hit the control on his desk to open the door, then turned in his chair to face it. As he swiveled, he slipped one hand into the drawer that held his Mydron autopistol. One must always take precautions when serving in public office, particularly given the number of disgruntled thanes and council members who still resented Carlyle's backing Roger DeVries for the governorship.

But this was no enemy.

"Sorry to bother you, Dad," his daughter said, giving him a tentative smile as she entered the office. "But I figured you'd be locked away in here."

DeVries studied Caitlin with an upraised eyebrow. "What's with the military rig, Kit?" he asked. She had changed out of her dress uniform, but was still wearing cadet grays. "Don't tell me you've forgotten how to wear civvies?"

She came through the door, shaking her head. "We've got orders to cut the visit short and take the emelt back to Brander. I leave in another ten minutes, so I wanted to say goodbye."

He frowned. "Back to Brander already? But you just got here last night. I thought you said they'd let you have a few days . . ."

"Something came up, Dad. It's all hush-hush, but orders are orders." She shrugged. "Guess it's back to the salt mines for us cadets."

DeVries didn't answer right away. First there had been the mysterious coming and going at the Day of Heroes ceremony. Then most of the Gray Death's high command had been out of touch all afternoon, even when he'd tried to contact their acting CO about his request for some 'Mechs to root out the outlaw band that had been terrorizing Carrick, a subject the Legion people had been hot about a week back. Now the cadets were being ordered back to Brander early, and with no reason given. . . .

DeVries realized suddenly that he'd been staring at his daughter without really seeing her. He cleared his throat. "Look, Kit, tell you what. Why don't I put in to have you assigned to the Residence for a little while. Aide or liaison or something. Your class can get along without you for a week or two, can't they?"

She looked uncertain. "I don't know, Dad. There must be a reason for these new orders."

"If there's a real need, you can be back at Brander in a few hours. But let me pull a few strings to keep you here in the meantime." He forced a smile. "What's the use of being governor if I can't use my influence to keep my daughter around for a few days, hmm?"

Caitlin nodded, smiling. "I guess they won't miss me that much. Alex has already been detached as an aide to Major McCall."

"Well, if it works for the colonel's kid, it works for mine too. Go on back to your room and I'll see what I can do. If I can't manage it, I'll let you know in time for you to catch the emelt."

He kept up the smile until Caitlin was out of the room, frowning again once the door had shut behind her. Something was going on, and he aimed to find out what it was. In the meantime, he wanted Caitlin safe at the Residence. He'd always opposed her decision to sign on as a Gray Death MechWarrior cadet, but she was stubborn and he'd finally given in. That didn't mean he'd given in entirely. If trouble was brewing, he'd protect Caitlin.

Still frowning darkly, DeVries called the Gray Death headquarters to arrange for the new orders. Then he put in a call on another line to the Planetary Guard duty officer, instructing him to start a full check of the current situation on and off Glengarry. DeVries would find out what was going on in short order, or find a new staff come morning.

He was determined to protect Caitlin, of course, but he was just as determined to protect himself and his position. And information was the best kind of armor he could think of.

The Gray Death's command center buried deep below the Residence on Castle Hill was well stocked with the high

tech instruments of modern warfare—detection gear, bank
after bank of computers, battle simulators, communications
consoles, and all the rest—but the very heart of the facility
was a quiet room paneled in genuine oak imported from
Terra. A massive table and plush chairs dominated the conference chamber, the display screens and computer monitors discreetly hidden behind drapes at either end of the
room. This might have been the inner sanctum of some
powerful corporation, except that the group assembled there
were uniformed men considering the news of an approaching armada.

Better than twelve hours had passed since the *Gray Skull*
had first sighted the intruders, and it was now dark again
outside. But there was a timeless quality to the Command
Center that defied concepts of day and night. Everyone at
the table had been working for hours now, but the planning
and discussion was still going strong. In the absence of solid
information the Gray Death Legion's senior officers had to
prepare for a variety of contingencies while their specialists
in the control area outside continued to gather intelligence
and process probabilities—all in the hope that they might
be ready for whatever would come next. It was an impossible task.

Alex Carlyle felt out of his depth. While the discussion
continued around the table, he contented himself with staying quiet and listening to McCall and de Villar run the
meeting. The rest of the cadets, together with the soldiers
and technicians from the Brander WTC, had already been
dispatched by emelt back to the training facility, where Tech
Major King would take command in McCall's absence. The
departure of his classmates had left Alex feeling distinctly
alone, but he took some comfort in the fact that Caitlin
DeVries had also remained behind here in Dunkeld. McCall
had distractedly approved a request filed by her father just
before the emelt was due to leave.

"We've milked the burst from the *Gray Skull* for everything its worth. The unit markings on those fighters weren't
anything I've seen before, but the fuselage insignia is a
revival of the emblem the Skye separatists used back in thirty-
four." Captain Ethan Radcliffe, the young, aggressive commander of the Legion's armored company, had been drafted
to serve as S-2 in the absence of the usual intelligence officer, Major Khaled. He looked tired and a little disreputa-

ble after a long shift hunched over a computer terminal trying to evaluate the information Captain Rodland had transmitted before the JumpShip's escape. "Computer gives it a ninety-four percent probability. They're almost certainly Free Skye forces . . . rebels. No way of telling from here how good they are."

"There's a hell of a lot of them, that much is sure," Lieutenant Longo commented. "Seventeen DropShips minimum. That's no raiding party. Those boys mean business."

"Their lead ships have been ideed as carriers," said Captain Julio Vargas, senior officer of the Gray Death's aerospace fighter contingent, and uncharacteristically subdued. Like most fighter jocks he had a reputation as a hotshot in the air and a womanizer on the ground, but today he was all business. He'd helped Radcliffe with the threat estimate, focusing primarily on the enemy aerospace assets. "They've got three *Leopard* CV-Class fighter-carriers over and above the one that launched the attack on the *Gray Skull*. That's eighteen more fighters if they're all fully loaded. No way we can challenge that in space. No way."

Aerospace fighters were like BattleMechs in many ways, the product of a high tech, man-machine link capable of outperforming any conventional air or space vessel in a combat situation. The Gray Death had two companies of fighters on its TO and E, but one was attached to Khaled's battalion off-planet. That meant Vargas had six fighters on hand to deal with perhaps three times that number aboard the intruders' fighter-carrier DropShip—not to mention others possibly held in reserve aboard other DropShips in the intruder fleet. The handful of conventional military aircraft in the arsenal of the Glengarry Planetary Guards was no match for aerospace fighters even under ideal conditions.

That left no question as to who had aerospace superiority, which was the first requisite to any major planetary invasion.

"What about the rest of the fleet?" The question came from Captain Guillaume Henri Dumont, the elegant, dapper CO of de Villar's First BattleMech Company. "Any more information yet?"

Radcliffe shrugged. "Best estimate gives them three 'Mech battalions—nine *Union* Class DropShips, twelve 'Mechs each. There are a couple of smaller ones, too, maybe *Leopards*. They might be fighter-carriers, or they might be carrying extra 'Mech lances. There's no way to tell until we get a visual ID. They've also got a pair of troop transports and what we think is a cargo ship with extra supplies and ammo to support the op.'' He paused. ''We've also identified a *Fortress* Class DropShip. Given that Free Skye insignia, it's probably the *Asgard*.''

''*Asgard*,'' McCall repeated, letting out a low whistle. ''I dinna like the sound of that.''

The *Fortress* Class DropShip was relatively rare in the Inner Sphere these days, a dinosaur that was falling into disuse because of the scarcity of spare parts. But in the days before the *Union*, House Steiner had outfitted a number of old *Fortress*es to serve as command ships for the Lyran Commonwealth's largest and best-trained strike forces. Though slow and hard to repair, the *Fortress* ships had the twin advantages of heavy armor and a mix of weapons that included powerful ground support artillery. In space and on the ground alike, a *Fortress* DropShip was a ready-made strongpoint.

Only one was stationed in the Isle of Skye, the *Asgard*. It was headquarters ship for the Duke of Skye's regiment of Huscarles, and everyone knew that Richard Steiner, the current Duke, had joined the camp of the Skye separatists.

''Then we can probably figure on the Tenth Skye Rangers,'' Dumont said, managing to sound languid and unconcerned. ''Good outfit. Usually based on New Kyoto watching the Marik border.''

''I'd say that was likely.'' That came from Captain Eddie Ross, who commanded the elite armored infantry company attached to de Villar's battalion. Ross was a native of the Skye March, and had served in the Tenth Skye Rangers for a time before gambling debts had made his homeworld too hot. Of everyone in the conference room, he was probably the one man who best understood the politics of the region—assuming, Alex reminded himself, that the man himself wasn't in sympathy with the separatists.

''I wondered about it when the Tenth wasn't ordered to join the rest of the expedition at Ford. Most of the regiment was recruited on Skye, and the unit's definitely in Duke Richard's hip pocket.''

''It might not be the duke's forces at all,'' said Lieutenant Andrei Denniken. In the absence of Grayson Carlyle and the rest of the command lance he was ranking officer of the

Gray Death Companions, the colonel's own company of MechWarriors. Denniken was a confirmed optimist, but even he didn't sound convinced of his words. "They might be a different bunch of separatists. Or even outsiders using the Free Skye insignia as a smoke screen."

"Enemies from outside wouldn't have penetrated this far without being challenged," de Villar said flatly. "And a *Fortress* Class DropShip does suggest the *Asgard* and the Huscarles. Best to assume we're up against Duke Richard's boys. If not, we can all be pleasantly surprised. But I don't think we will be."

"Question is, what do they want from us?" Captain Hannibal Simms of Hannibal's Cannibals, de Villar's Second 'Mech Company, leaned forward across the table as if in emphasis. "Have they started a rebellion? And where the hell do we stand if they have? Maybe it would be best if we tried to stay out of the whole mess, at least until the colonel gets back."

"Our contract is with the Federated Commonwealth government," Major John Owens, the blunt-featured commander of the Legion's Third Battalion, put in. He was an infantry soldier, not a MechWarrior, and his unit was made up of a mix of armor and groundpounders. Owens was something of a heretic in his poor opinion of BattleMechs, the universally acknowledged kings of the battlefield, but it was for that very reason that Grayson Carlyle had recruited him during the last expansion of the Legion to its present strength. Carlyle himself had started his career proving that a well-trained, well-motivated force of infantry could take on 'Mechs and win, a philosophy that continued to be a major part of the Gray Death's fighting philosophy.

"Yeah, but does that mean the FedCom?" Simms shot back. "Or House Steiner?"

"And who really represents House Steiner now anyway?" Ross asked. "Duke Richard might not be in the main line of descent, but people in the Skye March look to him before anybody else. And he's been taking the line that Katrina and Melissa were traitors to the old Commonwealth for agreeing to the Davion alliance, and therefore should be repudiated as the heads of House Steiner. Remember, Katrina overthrew Archon Alessandro, and claimed the throne because she was his older sister's daughter. Richard's the son of the younger sister, so his claim is really just as valid as Melissa's or Prince Victor's. If you allow that reasoning, then Richard has as good a claim on the top spot as anyone. He'll find plenty of people to say it's better."

De Villar held up a hand. "Enough . . . enough. We can't afford to get bogged down in this."

" 'Tis a tangle, and that's a fact," McCall said. "I dinna think—"

The buzz of an intercom cut him off. De Villar tapped a key recessed into the table top before him, and a curtain drew away from a monitor screen on one wall. The Nordic features of Lieutenant Freida Bergstrom, another lance commander from the Companions, filled the screen. "Major, we're monitoring a general transmission from the intruder fleet."

"Pipe it through," de Villar ordered.

The monitor swirled with color for a moment, then settled down to reveal a heavy-featured man in the midnight blue and red tunic of House Steiner's armed forces. His insignia identified him as a captain-general.

"I know him," Ross said. "He was chief military adviser on Duke Richard's staff . . ."

"People of Glengarry, I am General-Kommandant von Bulow of the Free Skye Expeditionary Force and rightful Baron of Glengarry," the man began ponderously. Alex noted his use of a rank designation completely outside the accepted Federated Commonwealth structure, despite his insignia. Presumably Duke Richard had organized his new military force to purge it of any Davion elements. "By order of His Grace the Duke of Skye, the Skye March has been declared in an official state of emergency. Forces of the Federated Commonwealth have committed wanton acts of violence against citizens of the Skye March on Kimball II and elsewhere. In response to these actions His Grace has signed orders declaring the Isle of Skye free and independent of the illegally constituted Federated Commonwealth."

The general paused for a moment, his eyes cold and staring. "Pursuant to the proclamations made by His Grace, I call upon all citizens of the Skye March to cooperate with the military forces under my command. Our intention is to secure the worlds of the Isle of Skye against Davion aggression. These measures are purely defensive in nature, and will not interfere with the peace and prosperity of any world under His Grace's provisional government. The only ones who have anything to fear from my command are the lackeys of the corrupt New Avalon regime, which has perverted the traditions and justice of the Lyran Commonwealth and the glorious House of Steiner.''

That brought a snort from across the table. Vargas, Alex thought, or perhaps Owens. Von Bulow continued in the same slow, heavy tone. ''To the soldiers of the Gray Death Legion mercenary regiment, we extend the hand of friendship and Duke Richard's offer of continued employment under the auspices of the Provisional Government, according to the terms of your contract with the Steiner family, which dates to before the illegal Federated Commonwealth alliance created by renegade elements of the family. Your renowned Legion has a long tradition of cooperation with House Steiner, and His Grace welcomes the opportunity to continue that mutually profitable association despite this current crisis.''

The general smoothed his tunic before continuing. ''My fleet will take up orbit within the next seventy-two hours. By that time, I expect to receive communications from the civil and military authorities on Glengarry to arrange for a smooth transition to the administration of the Provisional Government of the Isle of Skye. We hope to avoid any clash with the lackeys and hirelings of Davion, but resistance will be met by overwhelming force. And in the end, it is the citizenry of Glengarry who will suffer most from such a clash. The path of cooperation is by far the preferable choice.

''All glory to His Grace and to the cause of freedom!''

The screen went dead, and the assembled officers sat in silence for a long moment.

''Well,'' Lieutenant Denniken said at last. ''At least we know we were right about what we're up against.''

''I'm not sure it helps much,'' de Villar said. ''The Tenth Skye Rangers are damned tough opponents. They outnumber us, and they'll have other troops in support. They'll also control the planetary approaches, with a free hand to land any time and any place they please.'' He shook his head slowly. ''Where does that leave us? How do we organize a defense? Hell, *do* we even organize a defense in the first place? Ross here has a good point about the legal questions.''

" 'Tis a policy decision," McCall said quietly, his eyes on Alex Carlyle. "Not a military matter at all, at all. D'ye nae agree, young Alex?"

Alex swallowed and nodded slowly. "I suppose so, Major," he said.

"If your faither was here . . ."

"My father would say that the contract was with the Federated Commonwealth government," Alex said with a confidence he didn't feel. "Prince Victor is heir to both House Davion and House Steiner, but how can we be sure Duke Richard is involved? For all we know, von Bulow might be a renegade. One way or the other, whether he speaks in Ricahrd's name or not, the declaration puts him in rebellion against Glengarry's lawful authority."

"I agree," McCall said quietly, nodding. "And that being the case . . ."

"That being the case," de Villar picked up McCall's line smoothly, "we're left with the original question. If we intend to put up a fight, how do we organize against everything they've got?"

No one answered, but a moment later the intercom buzzed again. "I have Governor General DeVries requesting a line to you, Major," Bergstrom said.

"Right," de Villar responded. "Put him through." He looked around the conference room. "We'll need all the help we can get from the local boys if we're going to keep these bastards from taking us. Let's see what ideas the esteemed Governor General has, eh?"

Roger DeVries couldn't believe what he was hearing. The officers from the Gray Death actually claimed that they could defend Glengarry against what they thought was a Free Skye armada. And if that weren't enough, they seemed determined to drag the civil government down with them. It hadn't taken his own people long to discover the presence of the invasion fleet at Glengarry's nadir jump point, but General von Bulow's announcement had caught him off guard nevertheless. Still, it was nothing compared to what he was hearing from the legionnaires now.

His mind raced as Major de Villar outlined the Legion's need for support from the Planetary Guard. The appearance of the Free Skye fleet changed the entire situation on Glengarry. The invaders obviously had the military power to overcome any defense Carlyle's people could muster, especially with their much-revered leader and many of their best troops away from Glengarry, and far out of reach. But DeVries believed the only thing the mercenaries could accomplish by resisting the invaders was to bring the full horror of war to the planet. The issue of victory or defeat wasn't in doubt—only the issue of how much damage the Free Skye rebels would inflict before they won.

And the kind of damage a modern army could inflict on a planet wouldn't leave Roger DeVries much to rebuild. What was the use in aiming for a landhold if the fief would be devastated in some useless campaign?

But plainly the Gray Death people didn't see it that way. Their acting commander was talking as if mounting a futile resistance was the only option they were even willing to consider.

"We won't have much time to prepare," de Villar was saying. The intercom picked up a babble in the background, probably other officers debating. "But every armed man can count for something. How many do you think we can mobilize in two days?"

"Ah, look, Major, I'm not so sure about all this," DeVries stalled. "I mean, do you really think we can fight these people? Wouldn't . . . wouldn't some kind of negotiations be a better idea?"

The saturnine major frowned. "There are precious few grounds for negotiation here, Governor. It's either surrender or fight . . . and we believe our contract obligates us to fight."

"I . . . ah, see." DeVries hesitated. "I'm not sure just how much we can muster, Major. Let me put my staff on it and get back to you as soon as we know what's feasible. Say, three hours? It's the middle of the night, you know, and I'll have to get my staff organized before they can do anything."

"No more than that," de Villar said gruffly. "Every minute counts, Governor." The screen went blank.

DeVries leaned back in his chair. His office suddenly seemed very small. These mercenaries were pushing him into a damned tight corner, and he didn't like the feeling. He couldn't see any point in offering resistance to the invaders, but if he didn't go along with the Legion, he'd be nothing more or less than a traitor. He had taken an oath of fealty to Grayson Carlyle as landholder, and if he violated that oath no one in the Federated Commonwealth would raise a hand in his defense.

There has to be an option, he told himself. If there was one thing free traders and politicians had in common, it was the certainty that there were always alternatives. You just had to know where to look . . .

DeVries leaned forward again and stabbed the button on his intercom terminal. "Kennedy. I want a commlink with the invader flagship, right away." He paused. "And make sure it's a secure channel. I don't want any eavesdroppers. Understand me?"

Yes, there had to be another option. And DeVries would find it, one way or another.

17

Deep Space, Glengarry System
Skye March, Federated Commonwealth
2 April 3056

"**W**hat is it, Johann?" General-Kommandant von Bulow asked irritably, looking up from his trideo planning display and the preliminary plans for Operation Firestorm, one of the options he had to review in case an assault on Glengarry became necessary. It was tiring work, and he'd had little sleep the past few days, but von Bulow had never been fond of delegating authority for anything as important as a major military operation.

"Communications has just filed a message for you, Herr General," his aide said as the door slid shut behind him. "From the planet."

Von Bulow frowned. "So . . . the Gray Death negotiates? Somehow that doesn't sound right. Not their style at all."

"Not the mercenaries, no, Herr General," Albrecht said. "The Planetary Governor General."

"Ah . . ." von Bulow tapped a set of keys in front of him and scanned his file on the man. "An off-worlder. Merchant background. Interesting. I had not considered the possibility that the civil government might respond. Any mercenary leader worth his water would keep their administrators under tight control."

"But perhaps not Carlyle," the aide commented. "He is weak, that one."

"Not weak. Merely sentimental. He truly believes that a feudal military society must somehow be answerable to the common rabble, even serve them." The General-Kommandant made a dismissive gesture. "I've met many who claim to believe it, Johann, from Victor Davion to Richard Steiner. But I'm beginning to see that with Carlyle it's more than just words."

"Do you really think the locals will negotiate, Herr General? Or is this some kind of trick?"

"That will only be clear after we are firmly in place. But any sign of dissent, any group willing to treat with us rather than fight, is to be encouraged. Promise whatever concessions seem most likely to win them to our side."

"His Grace would not approve of granting too many concessions, Herr General," Albrecht pointed out.

"Not would I, Johann," von Bulow said with a half-smile. "Nor would I. Concessions may be promised, to weaken the enemy. If we can encourage the government to break with the mercenaries, even fight them openly in the name of Free Skye, we weaken their resistance. And we gain a better excuse for intervention to liberate our valiant friends on Glengarry from the oppression of Victor's band of hirelings. That will play well elsewhere as we consolidate our hold. But as for actually granting concessions . . . well, promises aren't worth much to a leader who is dead. Or sitting in His Grace's correctional facilities on Skye. True?"

"Yes, Herr General." The aide matched von Bulow's smile.

"Well, I suppose I should review this governor's message, eh? See what might have inspired him to contact us so quickly. Set it up on my monitor, Johann, and then turn in. I will not need you for a few hours, at least."

General von Bulow looked down at the three-dimensional terrain display once again. If all went well, he thought, Glengarry might yet fall into His Grace's hands without a blow being struck.

Roger DeVries leaned back in his chair, frowning at the monitor screen in his main office. He didn't like conducting long-range negotiations. His preference was always for face-to-face dealings, where he could read the body language of his opposite number and pounce quickly on any opening or perceived weakness. That wasn't possible here, with the lengthy interplanetary time lag still turning each transmission into a set-piece speech rather than an interactive conversation.

On the screen General von Bulow had his head cocked to

one side, his sound pickups muted while he apparently reviewed something DeVries had said in his last message. Then, abruptly, the man began to speak.

"I understand your . . . dilemma, Governor," von Bulow said with a faint smile. "Loyalties can become very tangled when you start mixing politics and policy, wouldn't you agree? The best policy for the administration on Glengarry is surely to avoid hostilities. Even with the protection of the Ares Conventions, war is brutality, pure and simple. We want to spare Glengarry that kind of misery. It is certainly not in our best interests to destroy a planet that could be an important part of an independent realm of Skye, after all. So I would hope to avoid bloodshed, and I am delighted to learn that you share my point of view. That leaves your mercenary planetholders as the sole obstacle to a settlement that will benefit all of us."

The general held up a hand. "Please don't misunderstand me, Governor. I don't preach a betrayal of loyalties lightly. After all, I would expect you to be loyal to the Provisional Government if and when we do reach an agreement." He smiled again. "But I think I can safely say that it is on the issue of loyalty that this whole matter hinges. It is the Duke of Skye's position that the grant of Glengarry to these mercenaries was invalid from the very beginning, in that it originated with the lackeys of House Davion. Everyone saw how even the Archon Melissa fell under the complete domination of her so-called husband and later their fool of a son. His Grace maintained that the Davion alliance and all its works are illegal, against the Lyran Commonwealth's constitution, and hence cannot be considered valid."

There was a pause before von Bulow went on. "What does this mean to you? Simply this, Governor. First, Duke Richard Steiner has claimed the mantle of leadership over House Steiner in lieu of the discredited line of Katrina, Melissa, and Victor Davion. He repudiates the Federated Commonwealth alliance, which has placed Lyran territory under the jurisdiction of the false F-C government. As the legal head of House Steiner and the Lyran Commonwealth he may now dispose of all property and contracts belonging to either the House or the government.

"Second, Colonel Carlyle's contract was and always has been with House Steiner, which means that his men are answerable to the authority of the rightful leader of that

House—again, His Grace Duke Richard. Third, the grant of Glengarry to Carlyle's Legion is not recognized as valid by His Grace, and in any event can be revoked by His Grace at will. In fact, it already has been. His Grace of Carnwath has reaffirmed that I am the legitimate holder of the fief of Glengarry, for the better order and governance of the region. Therefore, you need not be concerned with the implications of the planethold arrangement. It is, in fact, triply invalid. Pro-Davion elements might attempt to argue the matter, but the truth is that there is ample legal precedent for you to renounce the Gray Death Legion's authority if you so desire.''

The general smiled. ''In other words, my dear Governor General DeVries, if you are sincere in your desire to spare your planet the horrors of war—and who except professional soldiers would want such conflict?—then you have at your disposal all the legal justification you need to protect Glengarry's civilian population. I would be more than happy to accept your declaration of neutrality in this dispute between His Grace and the usurpers who have betrayed his family. That is all I seek, your declaration of neutrality . . . with your acceptance of a few minor safeguards to guarantee that neutrality hereafter. And if you are bold enough to take the steps toward that neutrality, the Gray Death Legion will be hard pressed to go against your decision. They depend on your civil government for their very existence, and with sufficient dedication on your part at this juncture I think we can see to it that these military men do not sabotage the cause of peace on Glengarry.''

DeVries paused the playback and settled back into his seat, regarding the general's frozen image on the monitor with a wry smile. General von Bulow, according to the governor's computer database, had spent the last several years as part of Duke Richard Steiner's personal staff, and it was obvious that he had learned the language of diplomacy in those years. It was equally obvious to DeVries that the man's smiles and platitudes and carefully framed legal arguments were all a smoke screen to hide his real intent. The rebels from Skye needed to neutralize the Gray Death Legion, based so close to the heart of their nascent realm. It was in Richard Steiner's best interests to take the Legion out of action with a minimum commitment of time and resources, especially since the planet Hesperus, a second major center of Davion resistance, would also require Free Skye attention in this early stage of the rebellion.

The question confronting DeVries was whether it was also in his own best interests to go along with the rebels. Before receiving the general's reply to his message he had spent a long time examining the strategic map of the Federated Commonwealth seeking a better understanding of the overall situation. Everything he saw tended to sway him to take the side of Free Skye in this rising. The Isle of Skye region was the sole connecting corridor between the old separate states of the Federated Suns and the Lyran Commonwealth. If the Isle of Skye managed to secede from the Federated Commonwealth alliance, it would effectively cut Victor Davion's empire in half. And that, in turn, would likely trigger other former Lyran regions to rise in revolt. With the continuing threat of the Clans on the Lyran border, and the ongoing tensions with House Kurita to occupy Davion forces on the old Federated Suns borders, a chain-reaction of secession and revolution would be hard for Victor Davion to counter. In all likelihood, then, despite the disparity in strength between the rebels in Skye and their Davion overlords, Skye would likely end up free, no matter how much resistance the Gray Death Legion offered.

So if Duke Richard was to become the new overlord anyway, what could Glengarry—or its governor—gain from resistance?

Still, there were dangers. DeVries was not about to accept everything the Free Skye general said at face value, no matter how attractive it sounded. And it would be impossible to make a move without first accounting for the Legion itself. That would take finesse.

He turned to another monitor screen and punched in the intercom code for his legal department. It was still the middle of the night, local time, but all his advisors and senior staffers were at their posts in response to his earlier orders. Passing a copy of the general's transmission and strict orders for secrecy on to the head of the department, DeVries cut the man off with a minimum of explanation. Before actually making up his mind, he'd get his own expert opinion on von Bulow's claims of neutrality as a legal, viable option for the planetary government.

His next call was to Colonel Max Walthers, a tough off-world mercenary who served as commander of the Residence Guard. "Walthers, double all security details inside the Castle Hill compound, effective immediately. All of them."

The colonel's scarred face registered surprise. "But Governor, the Gray Death is already on alert. We've got equal contingents of Legion and Guard troops at every post as it is."

"Precisely. And I want the Guards to hold the upper hand." DeVries paused. "In case of a . . . dispute."

The mercenary was quick to take his meaning. "As you wish, Governor. Should I brief the men to be expecting some kind of . . . trouble?"

"Not yet," DeVries said. "But I would suggest you put together a pool of senior NCOs who can be mobilized quickly to take command of key positions in case something comes up. I'll let you know when and how to brief them."

Walthers nodded. "I'll see to it, Governor. If anyone from the Legion questions the orders, I'll inform them that you've increased the Guard watch to ease the pressures on the legionnaires. That should commend itself to their officers."

The governor smiled coldly. "Very good, Walthers. Exactly what we need. For the moment, that is. I'll have some special orders for you later." DeVries cut the connection. Walthers had been his personal choice for command of the Residence garrison, and it was good to see the decision paying off. The man wasn't committed to any of the local interests, to other members of the Twenty, or the thanes, or even Carlyle's people. His loyalty was entirely to his paycheck—and to the man who issued it.

DeVries turned back to the first monitor and let the general's message resume. The pieces were in place now. All DeVries had to do was play the game out carefully, and he could outmaneuver the other players without risking his own position. He'd bring Glengarry and its people through this crisis intact. And after that? The possibilities were still wide open to the man who was willing to seize them.

18

Alex Carlyle walked purposefully into the briefing room of the Castle Hill command center. "Here's the information you asked for, sir," he said, putting a data disk on the table in front of Major de Villar. "Captain Vargas sends his apologies, but he hasn't had time to put together a full summary yet. He said he hopes this would give you everything you needed."

De Villar regarded the disk with a weary eye. "More reports to go through," he said, sounding as tired as he looked. The briefing conference had broken up, but only to the extent that the various officers had scattered to attend to their own duties. Vargas and Radcliffe, with Ross adding his local knowledge of the enemy's potential, were back at work gathering intelligence and making threat projections, while Major Owens had been assigned to deal with the logistical problems of mobilizing the depleted Legion for active duty. Most of the other officers, those not needed to actively monitor the situation in the Snake Pit, were at work pouring over the variety of operational plans on file in the headquarters computers, trying to adapt them to the present circumstances so that they could meet the invaders with at least some preparation behind them.

That left de Villar and McCall alone in the briefing room, on call to handle problems as they arose. And Cadet Carlyle, as aide, to run errands and generally try to make himself useful.

It was a side of leadership Alex had never really considered before. In a training exercise, there was a single quick briefing, and then it was into the 'Mech cockpits to wait for the ''Fight's on!'' call. Classroom work covered such diverse matters as strategy, operations, logistics, and all the rest, but they were always secondary to the immediate question of learning to fight a BattleMech. Now Alex was beginning to realize that complex military situations required a great deal of preliminary work long before two forces ever drew up on the field of battle.

''Did the captain hae any specific comments on this lot, young Alex?'' McCall asked him, gesturing toward the data disk.

''The Doppler readings are constant, sir,'' Alex replied. ''At least, that's what I heard Captain Vargas telling Captain Radcliffe. He didn't say anything else to me. But I overheard him saying that the entire intruder fleet was making a constant three gees.''

''They're in a hurry,'' de Villar said. ''You don't burn double-H at that rate unless speed is damned critical. Especially when there's no friendly refueling station or gas giant handy. If they cut too deep into their reserves they'll be hard pressed to redeploy if they don't knock us off fast.''

McCall shrugged. ''If 'twere the colonel up there they'd be counting on landing on ain of the ither continents and processing seawater. Or ain of those DropShips could be fitted as a wee tanker.''

De Villar nodded agreement, looking glum. ''Either way, they're moving fast. Which cuts down on our reaction time. Three days isn't much time to get ready, especially with that damned DeVries dragging his heels.'' He darted a glare Carlyle's way. ''Keep in mind, Cadet, that what you hear in this room doesn't go any further. Not to anyone. It isn't generally considered good diplomacy to curse the Governor General if there's a chance he might get to hear it.''

''Yes, sir,' Alex responded dutifully.

''Fact is, he's ducked four calls in the last hour. And we can't afford to keep putting this off. We've got to start mobilizing the Planetary Guard if we're going to have a chance of turning the bastards back when they make orbit.'' De Villar paused, rubbing his eyes. ''Well, I'll go over this report from Vargas, but then His Excellency is going to give me some answers, if I have to stand on his desk and shout to get them.''

The major slipped the data disk into a receptacle on the table top in front of him and turned his attention to his computer display monitor. Alex found a seat well away from his two superiors and settled down to wait for his next task. It had already been a long night. And he knew it was far from over.

Governor General Roger DeVries leaned back in his chair with a satisfied smile. His legal experts had agreed with the reasoning of General von Bulow's last message, and that gave him a clear line to follow in his dealings with the Gray Death Legion. Walthers had reported the guards fully prepared for action, ready in their doubled numbers not only at each of the regular guard posts but also in key positions around the portion of Castle Hill given over to quarters for the families and retainers of the Legion's senior officers. That should be enough to easily neutralize the bulk of the mercenary unit. Of course, a few would manage to escape the net, especially the ones at the Gray Death's Brander outpost. But they were no immediate threat, and would soon be brought into the fold once the main leadership was in his hands.

DeVries had good reason to feel satisfied. His plan would safeguard Glengarry with minimal risk of a serious confrontation. Above all else, he didn't want trouble. Neither with von Bulow's troops nor with the Gray Death Legion. Glengarry must be spared the calamity of war.

The intercom buzzed insistently.

"What is it, Campbell?" he asked, keying the speaker.

"Major de Villar to see you, Governor General," his secretary responded. The man sounded unhappy. DeVries had left strict orders not to be disturbed, and only a matter of the greatest urgency could have made Campbell violate those instructions.

DeVries stroked his thin mustache thoughtfully. Why was the Legion's acting commander here now? Was he still looking to talk about coordinating a defense, or had something leaked? Aside from Walthers, the team down in Legal and a pair of commtechs were the only ones who had any idea of what was really going on. Could someone else from the Guards have guessed what was going on and leaked it?

"Send him in," he said at last.

As the major entered, DeVries rose from his chair, smil-

ing and extending his hand. This was the time for some
good old-fashioned politicking.

"Ah, Major, good to see you," he said smoothly. "I'm
surprised anything could pry you out of your bunker—given
the situation."

"It's the situation I want to talk about," de Villar said
bluntly.

"Your request for Planetary Guard deployments . . . of
course." DeVries gestured toward a chair. "I still haven't
been able to get all the reports assembled, Major. You know
how it is trying to get staff people moving. But have a seat
and I'll see if I can run down some preliminaries for you
to work from."

De Villar sat down, and the governor returned to his desk
chair. Under his bland trader's smile, DeVries was worried.
He had planned to hold off on all of his options until he had
a better idea of the situation overall, such as a summary of
the intelligence estimates the Legion had been passing on
to his own military people for the past several hours. The
mercenaries had better resources, better information at their
disposal than he did, and he would have preferred to discover some unknown factor that might alter the equation
before he was committed to any definite course of action.
But the kind of mobilization effort the mercenaries were
calling for would surely be noticed by whatever intelligence
assets von Bulow already had in place on Glengarry, and it
would be foolish to think that there weren't plenty of prying
eyes out there. It would jeopardize everything DeVries had
negotiated if he was seen ordering his own troops to mobilize, as de Villar was ordering.

That left him thoroughly boxed in. He slipped his hand
under his desk and pressed the security stud there. It would
alert Walthers of a potential threat in the governor's office,
but the guards wouldn't respond unless he triggered the
alarm a second time.

With his visible hand DeVries reached for the computer
keypad, then paused and looked directly into the major's
eyes. Fanatics though these legionnaires were known to be,
it might still be possible to convince them to do the right
thing. De Villar, for one, had always struck him as a sober,
thoughtful man. "Major," the governor said slowly. "I understand your dedication to your unit, to your people. I know
it's popular to think otherwise, but politicians and admin-

istrators like me have the same kind of commitment to our people.''

"Never had many dealings with politicians, myself," de Villar said. "That's always been the colonel's job. What's your point, Governor?''

"I, uh . . . I wonder if you've considered all the ramifications of this . . . this mess. The legalities? If Duke Richard has declared himself rightful head of House Steiner, and it sticks, then it could be argued that your contract is with him, and not Victor Davion. That would put you in rebellion against legal authority, wouldn't it?''

De Villar shrugged. "It's been my experience that it's the winners of a war who decide what's legal and what isn't, Governor," he said. "The odds against Richard Steiner are pretty damned long, after all. Prince Victor controls a third of the Inner Sphere and more 'Mech regiments than Skye has planets. Steiner would have to win some spectacular victories to even have a prayer.''

"The odds against the duke might be long, Major. But here and now the odds against your legionnaires look longer. That fleet out there will crush the Gray Death sooner or later, no matter how many Planetary Guards you have helping you.''

"Maybe," de Villar admitted. "Nothing's certain in war, but I'll admit I'd rather be betting on his side." He gave a thin, humorless smile.

"Then why resist? Why sacrifice yourselves and your 'Mechs if even you suspect it may be a lost cause." DeVries paused, then plunged on. "At least think before you expose Glengarry to a full-scale battle, Major. I mean, innocent people will suffer if von Bulow's men invade. But he's offered us a deal. If we take it, we spare the people the ravages of an invasion.''

"The general's offer sounded pretty useless to me," de Villar responded. "Resistance is useless, so throw down your weapons and accept Richard Steiner as your new overlord. That's no deal. That's surrender.''

"No . . . not surrender. A simple declaration of neutrality, Major. In exchange, we agree to a token occupation. Surrender aerospace assets for the duration, agree not to fight Free Skye. Temporary demobilization of your 'Mechs, just until the immediate crisis is over. It's a perfectly reasonable price to pay, if it will keep the peace.''

De Villar rose halfway from his chair in a surge of motion, leaning menacingly over the desk. "Von Bulow didn't go into those details in the broadcast I heard, Governor," he said, voice taut. "Just what's been going on up here?"

Stroking his mustache again with a nonchalance he didn't feel, DeVries leaned back in his chair. But behind the easygoing air he was on his guard. "I'm just a poor old trader trying to hold down a desk job, Major," he temporized. "But I'm sure that if we tried, we could win just those kind of terms from the general."

The Legion officer leaned further forward. "Let's stop fencing, Governor," he said sharply. "You've been in communication with the enemy. You wouldn't have such a detailed idea of possible terms otherwise. What have you done to my legionnaires?"

DeVries stood up, meeting the man's steely glare. "Look, Major, I'll admit I've been looking for an angle to keep Glengarry from getting sacked. I know the realities even if I'm no professional soldier. Your troops are under strength, and the Planetary Guard are just militia. Von Bulow's got a huge task force out there. Even if you put up the best show since Tukayyid there'll be a lot of collateral damage. Surely you don't want that?"

"No one wants it," the legionnaire shot back. "But we have our duty."

"Your duty?" he demanded. "But it's just as possible that your real duty is to the Steiner family. And if Duke Richard turns out to be the legitimate representative, where does that put your duty?"

"General von Bulow is happy to interpret things that way," de Villar replied harshly. "Sophistry, pure and simple, to help you get out of your obligations with a reasonably clean conscience. I'm not buying it, DeVries." His hand strayed toward the holster at his hip. "I'm declaring you in violation of your oath of fealty to the Gray Death Legion and suspending the civil government. I suggest you cooperate—"

DeVries leaned heavily on his desk, as if suddenly overcome. His finger strayed to the security stud and pressed it a second time. His personal guards would have assembled in the outer office by now. The second alarm was their signal to make their move.

The door slid open suddenly as de Villar pulled his Mydron autopistol. Five guardsmen poured into the room, weapons at the ready. Walthers came in behind them, weaponless but with an air of swaggering confidence.

"I'm afraid I can't allow you to destroy Glengarry, Major," DeVries said sincerely. "A declaration of neutrality is the only solution. I'm sure General von Bulow will agree to observe civilized terms. It's for the best, really." He gestured to his guards. "The major is under arrest. Please treat him with respect, but confine him until further notice. Walthers, it's time. Pass the word to tighten security throughout the Residence. From this moment all personnel of the Gray Death Legion are denied access to all sensitive areas of the Administrative Wing. Place their dependents under close confinement, and arrest all Legion officers you encounter. Understood?"

"Yes, sir," the guard captain said, nodding acknowledgement.

As they disarmed de Villar and escorted him out of the room, the Governor General returned to his desk and sat down wearily. There was still so much to do . . .

══ 19 ══

"**C**itizens of Glengarry! Your attention, please, for an important announcement from the office of His Excellency the Governor General!"

"It's DeVries," Alex Carlyle said over his shoulder to the others in the Castle Hill command center. "On the public information channel."

The pace of activity in the Legion's headquarters complex had slackened in the last few hours. Most of the planning and preparations had passed from the hands of senior officers to their aides or to the computer banks, and it would be hours before new decisions would be necessary. Some of the senior staff had found time to snatch catnaps, and a few even returned to their quarters far above the underground bunker to seek out families or more comfortable surroundings while they waited. Alex, with no better job at hand, had caught a few hours' sleep before being assigned to replace an exhausted Lieutenant Bergstrom in monitoring communications channels in the Snake Pit.

Despite the fact that there was less to do now—or, perhaps, because of it—the atmosphere in the command center had been getting tenser by the minute since de Villar's departure. They'd had no word from him, although it was obvious that the Planetary Guards were assembling in strength at last around Castle Hill. But neither the governor nor his staff were taking calls, even from the Legion, and de Villar had seemingly dropped off the face of the planet.

McCall loomed behind Alex's seat to watch the monitor

as the announcer's chiseled face was replaced by the heavier features of the Governor General.

"Citizens of Glengarry," DeVries began gravely. "No doubt many of you are aware of the war fleet that has jumped into the Glengarry system and will be taking up orbit above our fair world within the next three days. This fleet of military DropShips has proclaimed itself under the authority of the Free Skye Provisional Government, a separatist movement that has raised the standard of rebellion against the Federated Commonwealth government under the leadership of His Grace the Duke Richard Steiner of Skye.

"The commander of the task force, General von Bülow, has made his intentions clear. This fleet is here because Glengarry is the planethold and principal base of the Gray Death Legion, which has not committed itself to the Free Skye cause. The Free Skye Provisional Government believes that the Legion, as a mercenary unit with contractual obligations to the Federated Commonwealth, could constitute a threat to their rising. The general's orders are to make sure that Glengarry and the Legion are not in a position to interfere, and he will do whatever necessary to carry out those orders."

DeVries looked directly into the camera with an expression of sincere concern. "Citizens . . . friends . . . no one wants to see our fair planet become a battleground. The Succession Wars and the Clan invasions both passed us by, but anyone who has seen off-world news reports knows that modern warfare is a horrible, brutal thing. Even a successful defense of Glengarry would be devastating to our people, our economy, our environment. And the odds are very much against a successful defense. A large contingent of the Gray Death Legion is away on a military mission, and Colonel Carlyle, the unit's well-respected commander, is also off-planet. Perhaps the Legion at full strength and under the leadership of their legendary colonel would be a match for any invader, but against the overwhelming numbers of the Free Skye forces, the shrunken garrison left behind to defend us is simply not equal to the task. Even their own acting commander has admitted doubts about his ability to protect Glengarry from this foe."

Now De Vries was smiling. "Fortunately, it is not necessary for our world to deal with this threatened invasion. I have discussed the situation seriously with the Legion's temporary commanding officer, Major de Villar, and also with General von Bulow. It seems that the Legion's current contract is ostensibly with the government of the Federated Commonwealth but may prove to be invalid because of potentially conflicting duties to House Steiner. We believe that these legal questions make the Legion's role in the face of this civil disturbance foggy enough to warrant taking a step back and looking things over very carefully before acting.''

''The bluidy Sassenach bastard!'' McCall swore. '' 'Tis a lie! Gomez de Villar winna agree tae any sich thing!''

''Hold a second, sir!'' Alex burst out. ''Look . . .''

''. . . to confirm this,'' DeVries was saying on the monitor. ''I give you the Acting CO of the Gray Death Legion, Major Cristobal Gomez de Villar.''

The governor's image gave way to de Villar's. The major had replaced the rumpled outfit he'd worn since the Day of Heroes celebration the day before with a clean, crisp, new full dress uniform, with all his decorations and awards. His expression was tense, strained, but he looked straight into the camera and spoke in a low, calm voice. ''As acting commander of the Gray Death deputizing for Colonel Carlyle, I hereby confirm my full agreement to the provisions that Governor DeVries and General von Bulow have worked out. These will be fully outlined in due time. For the moment''—he paused, his eyes straying to something or someone out of the camera's range, then took a deep swallow and went on—''for the moment, the Gray Death Legion is hereby ordered to stand down from alert status. All personnel are to cooperate fully with Governor de Vries and his staff in implementing the agreement with the Free Skye forces . . .''

Alex Carlyle slumped in his chair, hardly able to believe what he had just heard. Behind him, McCall's whispered ''I canna believe it'' summed up his own feelings perfectly.

''I'm sorry, Miss. The comm center is closed by order of the Governor General.''

Caitlin DeVries frowned at the kilted Planetary Guardsman blocking the door to the Residence's primary communications complex on Castle Hill. After watching her father's announcement on the monitor in her suite, she had hastened to find him, wondering why he hadn't sent for her if he'd been working on this crisis all night. She was supposed to be his aide now, after all. If he and Major de Villar had been negotiating with the separatists she should have been involved somehow, even if only keeping notes or making sure they had enough tea to keep them running. Wasn't that what an aide was supposed to do?

The announcement itself bothered her, too. It didn't sound like something the Legion would agree to. She wondered what Alex Carlyle thought of these negotiations. His father was famous for refusing to compromise his principles, not even to guarantee the safety of the Legion itself . . .

She pushed that thought out of her mind and concentrated on her immediate problem. "Do you know who I am, Corporal?" she demanded.

"The Governor General's daughter, Miss," the Guardsman replied, looking uncomfortable. "But that doesn't—"

"I'm also a MechWarrior cadet, and any MechWarrior rank outranks any Planetary Guard rank, at least the last time I looked."

"Er, yes, Miss, but my orders—"

She tapped the armband she'd added to her uniform, the crescent planet against the red and green plaid banner of Glengarry's armed forces. "I am also His Excellency's acting aide-de-camp. You can check the orders in the computer logs if you wish." Caitlin paused. "Are you going to suggest, now, that the Governor General's orders are supposed to keep me from having access to him? My father would be very interested to hear that. Wouldn't you say so?"

"Y-yes, Miss . . . I mean, no, Miss . . ." The guardsman stepped aside and hit the control stud that opened the door beside him. His tone had shifted from condescension to stiff, military respect as he drew himself to attention and gave her a rifle salute. "I'm sorry I held you up, ma'am. Pass."

Caitlin gave him a cold smile and went through the door. She turned to the left and headed up a half-flight of stairs to the control booth that overlooked the Residence video studios. She could wait there for her father to finish his message without disrupting the broadcast itself.

The booth was a long, narrow room overlooking the studio through a transplast window. A single bank of controls crewed by four technicians controlled all the functions of the studio, from robotic cameras and sound to computer-generated special effects. No one even looked up as Caitlin entered, and she did her best not to distract anyone from their work. Instead she craned her neck to study the studio itself.

Major de Villar was still speaking, spelling out the need for the Gray Death's officers to work closely with the Governor General to make sure that the final arrangements for the neutrality agreement went smoothly. He was reading from a teleprompter in very careful, almost stilted tones, quite unlike the animated delivery Caitlin had heard from him in a few lectures he'd given the cadets at Brander. From time to time his eyes would stray from the teleprompter and the robotic camera mounted above it to fix on something Caitlin couldn't see from her present vantage point. The look in his eyes bothered her, too. Something wasn't quite right . . .

She leaned further forward and finally saw the other occupants of the studio. First, her father, leaning forward in a chair out of camera range, watching and listening to the major with an attention he rarely gave to anything.

And then she saw the trio of guards surrounding Freya King de Villar.

The major's wife was wearing a torn nightgown and slippers. Her hair was in disarray, and her mouth was gagged. One of the guards was holding a needler pistol against the side of her neck, while another held her hands behind her back in a rigid, painful grip. The third, standing further back, cradled an autorifle that was pointed in the general direction of the major himself.

Caitlin's intake of breath was sharp, audible.

"Miss DeVries! What are you doing in here?" The director was halfway out of his chair, looking flustered. "This area is off limits . . ."

"My . . . my father wanted me to . . . to let him know when a message came in . . ." Her stammered reply didn't sound convincing even to her. She took a step back. "Er, from the Thane of Carrick. I . . . er, I thought he was finished, but I guess he's still busy with the broadcast. I'll give it to him when he's . . . when he's free."

"He's not on the air now," the director said, frowning at her. "Here, I'll put you through on the intercom." He turned away for the instant it would take to put through a call to the tiny earpiece receiver her father would be wearing to get cues from the booth. Caitlin didn't hesitate. She was through the door and down the stairs in that instant, pushing past the corporal outside to walk briskly down the corridor away from the communications center.

It took all her self-control to keep from breaking into a run until she was out of the Guardsman's line of sight.

The tiny receiver in his left ear crackled, and Roger DeVries straightened in his chair and raised a hand involuntarily to touch the slick plastic of the device. A moment later the voice of the broadcast director, tinny and distorted, began to speak hesitantly.

"Your Excellency, your daughter was just in the booth looking for you. Er . . . she said something about a message you'd been waiting for from the Thane of Carrick. But she wouldn't wait to talk with you . . . just left all of a sudden . . ." The director sounded nervous, but whether it was because of the possible security breach he'd allowed or the idea of questioning the activities of the Governor General's daughter wasn't clear.

DeVries stood up quickly. The major had at least another minute of text to read, and that would give the governor time to deal with this matter without interrupting the broadcast.

He wasn't expecting a call from Carrick or any of the other regional lords this morning, and that lie, coupled with his daughter's sudden departure, could only mean one thing . . .

Outside the heavy, insulated studio door, DeVries pulled his personal communicator from his shirt pocket and thumbed in a code sequence. "Walthers," he said curtly. "DeVries. Order your people to locate my daughter and detain her until further notice. Accept no excuses or delays. It's vital that I talk to her. Pass the word to all posts."

He hated to think that his daughter's first loyalty might not be to her own father, but he had to assume it. She'd thought of nothing but the chance to be a MechWarrior for years, and he knew that Carlyle's people underwent intense indoctrination from the time they started cadet training. DeVries couldn't afford to take chances now. He wasn't going to let anyone, not even his daughter, ruin things for him—or the whole future of Glengarry—now.

That was why he had to make sure she didn't so something foolish, like telling her Legion superiors what she'd seen in the studio. In a few more minutes it wouldn't matter, but until DeVries was sure he had the Legion's leadership rounded up and neutralized, Caitlin couldn't be allowed to run loose.

DeVries didn't wait for his security chief's acknowledgment. He returned the communicator to his pocket and went back into the studio, putting all thoughts of Caitlin out of his mind.

Right now, he had to focus all his attention on the task at hand. Later he'd bring his daughter around, and together they'd forge the kind of future Glengarry deserved.

Down in the Snake Pit, Alex Carlyle slumped back in his chair, feeling lost and confused. After everything Major de Villar had said about their duty to resist, how could he have changed his mind so fast? And without consulting McCall or the rest of the staff?

Now DeVries was back on the screen, every gesture and inflection conveying nothing but calm and reassurance. "Let me conclude by urging all of you, again, to remain calm and await developments. Glengarry is in no danger, I assure you, and with a little common sense on everyone's part I'm sure we can weather this disturbance with hardly a ripple. Thank you, and God bless you all."

McCall muttered something under his breath and reached past Alex to shut off the monitor. "I dinna ken what changed his mind," the Caledonian grumbled.

Before he could go on, an intercom line buzzed insistently. Alex hit the stud, and found himself looking into the bland features of one of the Legion's duty NCOs, Sergeant Yu.

"Sir, this is Checkpoint Four. I've got a dozen officers and technicians here who say their orders are to take the watch in CCR. Orders from Governor DeVries."

Major McCall leaned forward, waving Alex into silence. "This is irregular, Sergeant," he began.

A new face filled the screen. "Major, this is Captain Holmes, Planetary Guard. The Governor General and your Major de Villar are requesting that you and your staff join them in the Residence for a conference. We're supposed to keep an eye on things while you're topside." He smiled. "You know, spirit of cooperation and all that."

McCall seemed reluctant to answer, but finally nodded.

"Aye, 'tis time we sorted a' this mess oot. Pass them in, Sergeant." He nodded to one of the nearby technicians to release the elevator. It had been locked in place when the command center went on alert, and could only be activated from inside.

Holmes and his technicians arrived in moments, and formally relieved McCall of duty with instructions to take the staff up to the surface. Alex joined McCall and the other officers in the elevator for the ascent to the Residence. From the ragged conversations swirling around him it was clear that the other Gray Death officers were no more comfortable with the situation than he was. He hoped de Villar would be at the top of the shaft to meet them. Maybe he could explain what was happening.

But the major wasn't there when the doors snapped open. Instead Alex and the others faced a whole squad of Planetary Guardsmen, clad in full combat armor instead of their accustomed tunics and kilts, and leveling automatic weapons at the Gray Death party. Behind them more armed troops were visible herding Sergeant Yu and the other Legion guards from the checkpoint into the corridor at gunpoint.

"By order of the Governor General, you are hereby under arrest," the leader of the group said harshly. "Turn over your sidearms and wrist computers immediately. Cooperate and all will be well. Make trouble, and you'll be sorry. We have thirty-two Legion dependents in custody already, and they will pay the price for any misbehavior on your part. Do I make myself clear?"

No one answered. Then, slowly, McCall stepped forward, arms raised, and the others quickly followed suit. There was nothing else any of them could do.

20

Dunkeld, Glengarry
Skye March, Federated Commonwealth
2 April 3056

Caitlin DeVries clenched her fists in sheer frustration, wishing she could take out her feelings on someone, *something,* before they consumed her entirely.

How could her father have even considered betraying the Legion? The very thought made her ill.

She had always known that his feelings toward the Gray Death were mixed at best. Grayson Carlyle and his mercenaries had catapulted Roger DeVries into the Governor General's office. He'd held the post for the past two years, working closely with the Legion and apparently seeing that they could do a lot of good for Glengarry.

But at the same time, he'd let slip plenty of comments that betrayed his essential dislike for the mercs. They had done much to restore order on the planet soon after their arrival, but now the relationship was more one-sided. Glengarry provided everything they needed, but gained very little in exchange. So her father maintained. And he had been reluctant to give his blessing to his daughter's decision to sign up with the unit.

It was all she had ever wanted to do with her life, and in the end he had seen that he could either yield gracefully or watch her defy him. Faced with that choice, he'd given in at last.

Now Caitlin suddenly wished she'd never even *heard* of the Gray Death. Or maybe it was her father she wanted to reject. Right now she wasn't sure about anything.

Caitlin's fist slammed into the wall stud that locked the

door behind her. She had come back to her suite in the Governor's Wing of the Residence, not knowing where else to hide her face from the world. Every ornate piece of furniture, every elegant wall hanging reminded her of her dilemma now.

"We stand for order," she said aloud. It was the unofficial motto of the Gray Death, reputedly coined by Grayson Carlyle years before. The training program emphasized the notion that the Legion, unlike so many of the Inner Sphere's mercenary units, fought not so much for pay as for their leader's ideals of civilization standing against the barbarians at the gate. For two long years she had been hearing words like those, and she had always believed in them. The Legion . . . they were supposed to be the good guys, the new knights riding metallic steeds into battle against the people who wanted to pull civilization down.

What did that make Roger DeVries, if he was trying to negotiate a separate peace?

She swallowed and tried to get a grip on herself. Breaking down now wouldn't settle anything.

Caitlin raised her arm and punched in a code combination on the tiny keys of her wristcomp. The Gray Death's well-worn military models included the kind of personal communicators that were carried as separate pieces of equipment by the civilians in the Residence. Major McCall had to be told about her father's treachery.

There was no answer. She cursed and tried another code, Alex Carlyle's. Nothing.

The smartest way to mount a coup would be to neutralize the Legion leadership while they were still taking in de Villar's apparent support. Were they already out of action, prisoners . . . or worse? That was the only explanation she could think of for not getting through.

Which meant the Legion forces here in the capital were leaderless. Maybe she could still warn some of the outlying Legion units. Brander, for instance . . .

To do that she was going to need more than a wristcomp. Maybe she could still get out of the Residence and make a call from a comm terminal in town . . .

She was halfway across the living room when movement at the bedroom door made her spin around, dropping into a fighting stance with all the instincts of a trained Mech-Warrior.

If she was startled, the other was even more so. He jumped back from the door, then grinned sheepishly. "Och, lassie, dinna do that! I thought you were up to no good!"

Caitlin relaxed. "Sorry, MacDonald. I didn't know anyone was here."

The servant smiled apologetically. "Just helping Maggie out with the cleaning, lass," he said. "With all the extra people in town for the ceremonies, some of us are havin' tae pull double duty."

She answered his smile despite her turmoil. Ian MacDonald and his wife Maggie were two of the most trusted servants in the Residence. They had been there for years, through four administrations, and they had helped make Caitlin feel at home in the turbulent days right after her father's appointment. MacDonald, who had put in five years as an infantryman in the private army of the Thane of Buchan before the Legion had put an end to the feuding between individual noblemen, had been the one person in the Residence who'd urged her to follow her dream of becoming a MechWarrior. She'd known him only a few months before going out to Brander, but sometimes MacDonald had seemed more like a father than the man in the Governor General's office. At least the servant had always listened, had always offered a sympathetic ear.

She didn't know what to say to him now, though. She wasn't even sure how much MacDonald knew about the Free Skye separatists, or whether the legionnaires were allowed to talk about it with civilians. And what could she say about her father?

A loud knock rattled the door before she could find any words. "Miss DeVries!" She knew the voice. It belonged to one of the Guard sergeants assigned to the Residence security staff. "Your father wants to see you! Please come out right away."

She looked around the room, almost instinctively searching for a way out that she knew wasn't there. She couldn't see her father now . . .

MacDonald recognized her fear almost before she admitted it to herself. "What's the matter, lassie?" he asked quietly. "Is something wrong between you and your father?"

Caitlin nodded, a curt, almost explosive gesture. The knock sounded again, louder this time. "Security monitors saw you going in there, Miss DeVries. Please come out, now. Your father's instructions were very clear.''

Her mind was racing furiously. Father or not, what he was doing was a betrayal of the Gray Death, and she had pledged her life to serve the Legion. Once she let these soldiers escort her to her father, he would see to it that she didn't pass any warnings to Major McCall or the others. Not until it suited him. She had to get the warning to them first . . .

But how? She couldn't get to them in person, and a cadet couldn't just call up a major on the intercom and expect to get through. Not without a lot of obstacles. Besides, she wouldn't have time for that. She was running out of options.

She bit her lip. Her only hope was MacDonald.

Caitlin grabbed his arm. ''Ian . . . Ian, you must do something for me. I think the Legion's in trouble, and my father doesn't want me to warn them. Go back into the bedroom and wait until I'm gone. When they've taken me, find a way to get off Castle Hill and into town. Call Brander. Major King . . . no, make it Dave Clay. Cadet Dave Clay. Tell him it's important. Tell him . . .'' She trailed off. How could she let Clay know the message really came from her? ''Tell him it's straight from the *Centurion*'s mouth. Major de Villar's not cooperating with my father willingly. His wife is being used as a hostage to make him agree to surrender to the separatists. And I think the rest of the Legion officers have been rounded up, or at least cut off from outside contact. Do you have that?''

MacDonald stared at her for a moment, then repeated the message back to her, looking grim. ''I canna believe it,'' he added. ''Your father . . . Look, now . . . will you be all right, lassie?''

''I'll be fine. He's still my father . . . I'll be fine.''

The knock was louder still as MacDonald left the living room. Outside Caitlin heard more voices. New arrivals, probably with the cardkey that would override the electronic lock.

The door slid open to admit five soldiers in the kilts and light blue tunics of the security branch of the Guard. They looked angry, and had their weapons at the ready.

''Damn it, why didn't you answer!'' The sergeant had dropped all pretense of deference now. ''Your father wants you in his office right away!''

"And if I don't want to go?" she asked coldly.

He shrugged. "My orders are to take you there, Miss. Please don't make things awkward." He gestured with his pistol, and two of the soldiers started forward as if to seize her.

Caitlin DeVries stepped back, holding out her hands as she nodded reluctantly. "All right. I'll come." She brushed past the guard and out of the room without a backward glance.

Now it was up to MacDonald . . . and Dave Clay.

Davis Carlyle Clay looked up as the comm terminal on the duty officer's desk chimed to announce an incoming call. He was tired from the long emelt ride back to Brander, followed immediately by a shift as Cadet OOD looking after the Brander Center duty office while King and the other senior staffers worked to carry out McCall's orders for re-equipping the cadet 'Mechs for active duty. That at least could be canceled now that Major de Villar had announced the stand-down orders. Clay had screened the 'Mech bay with the news as soon as someone had brought word of the broadcast, and King was on his way back now. Maybe Clay could get some quality sack time today, after all . . .

He hit the Accept stud. The image that appeared on the monitor was obviously transmitting from a public comm booth in one of Glengarry's larger towns. He could see buildings in the background, and there was a drone of traffic noise under the voice of the caller.

"My name is MacDonald," the man on the screen began. His accent and dress put him down as a local, probably working class. He looked vaguely familiar, but Clay couldn't remember where he might have seen the man before.

The caller was also breathless, but his words tumbled quickly from his lips as he spoke. "I'm calling from Dunkeld on behalf of Cadet Caitlin DeVries. Are you Cadet Clay? Your commtechs said they'd put me through . . ."

"Wow, easy, there," Clay said with a smile. "I'm Clay. What's all this about? Is Caitlin too good to talk with us ordinary cadets now that she's got herself an aide's slot? Never thought she'd start using secretaries to send messages to her buddies."

"*Please,* Cadet. This is urgent. She said to tell you it came straight from the *Centurion*'s mouth. This is the message she asked me to give you. Major de Villar's cooperation with her father was not given willingly. His wife's being used as a hostage . . .''

Clay listened to the words with a growing sense of horror. He could hardly believe any of it, but who except Caitlin or someone else from Brander could know the type of 'Mech she piloted? ''There's no time to waste,'' the man concluded, his voice taut and urgent. ''Young Miss DeVries was . . . was detained. By her faither's men. Planetary Guards . . .''

Clay looked up as King came into the office. ''Sir, I think you'd better hear this,'' he said. ''MacDonald, please repeat your message for Major King . . .''

For an instant he tried to convince himself that it was all some kind of mistake, a cadet prank, maybe. But no cadet in the Gray Death would pull a prank like this, not even Clay himself. Deep in his gut he knew that the message was true, bitter truth that it was.

And he knew just what it was going to mean for the Gray Death Legion . . .

═══ 21 ═══

Alex Carlyle stirred restlessly in the narrow cot and tried to force himself to relax, but the effort was useless. Two days of enforced inactivity had left him nervous and moody, and that took a toll on his sleep. Dawn would come soon, the second sunrise since Governor DeVries had ordered the Gray Death's leadership confined in the Castle Hill military detention center, but Alex doubted he'd been able to get more than an hour or two of fitful rest through all of Glengarry's long night.

He finally gave up the uneven struggle and swung his feet onto the cold floor. The cell was barely large enough for the cot, a washstand, and a toilet screened off from the bed but not from the corridor outside. Most of the officers taken during the governor's carefully staged coup had been locked up in these old cells, which normally served as a temporary holding area for military detainees. No one had seen McCall or de Villar since they'd been rounded up, and married officers were apparently being held somewhere else. Alex wondered briefly, as he had many times already, where Caitlin DeVries might be. Had she betrayed the Legion, like her father? The thought would never have occurred to him just a few days before, but now anything seemed possible.

Alex rose and walked over to the narrow reinforced transplast window that overlooked the Castle Hill parade ground. It was hard to picture the Day of Heroes ceremony taking place out there, harder still to accept that it had happened just three days back. So much had changed . . .

And so much more would change in the next few days. The Free Skye armada would be in orbit in another day or two at the latest, and then it would all be over. From overhearing the guards talk, Alex gathered that most of the Legion's junior officers and the rank and file were still free, but those troops weren't likely to act on their own, especially after hearing Major de Villar's broadcast. Most of them probably thought the command staff was still hard at work, never imagining them locked up out of harm's way.

That meant the Free Skye force would be able to move in virtually unopposed, with the Planetary Guard ready to guarantee a peaceful transmission of power from the Gray Death to von Bulow's armada. Staring out into the predawn darkness, Alex wondered how his father would take the news that the Gray Death had been forced to surrender without offering even token resistance. It was a sad fall from the glory days they'd celebrated on the Day of Heroes.

A sudden flash off to the southwest caught his attention. For a moment he thought it might be lightning, a storm moving across the plains of Atholl out of Braemoray. Then he saw another, brighter flash. It was much closer this time, and Alex could hear the rippling sounds of explosions even through the transplast.

Explosions . . .

Gomez Cristobal de Villar heard the far-off but unmistakable *crump* of an explosion through the window, and jumped to his feet in one smooth motion. He checked his instinctive desire to throw open one of the windows and peer out into the darkness. The windows in the third-story suite in the Residence where he and Freya had been detained were only open a few centimeters, enough to admit fresh air, but any attempt to tamper with them would set off a half-dozen alarms and bring every Planetary Guardsman on the floor running to the room.

Freya sat up in the bed. "What's going on?" she asked, sounding fully alert. They were both veterans of all too many nights in the field, and the undeniable sounds of combat were enough to instantly wrest them from the arms of sleep.

"Heavy weapons fire," he said, cocking his head slightly to listen. Now he could hear another sound, faint and muffled but distinct to the trained ear. A rhythmic thumping . . . "Mechs, too."

"The Free Skye troops?" Freya's features creased in a frown. She got out of bed and went to the closet, pulling out fatigue coveralls for herself and tossing another pair across the room for de Villar to catch. "They shouldn't have made orbit yet."

"Yeah," de Villar said, starting to pull the garment over his legs. Somewhere, a siren was wailing its high-pitched warning, and he thought he heard the sound of booted feet running down the corridor as the Residence troops responded to the alert. "Unless they sent some fast transports on ahead. The reports didn't mention any sign of that before . . . before that bastard DeVries . . ." He trailed off. Frustration and guilt were waging a pitched battle inside him, and no words could express what he was feeling.

A fine leader he had turned out to be. In all his years with the Legion, de Villar had wanted nothing more than the chance to show what he could do as a commander. Despite his reputation for wildness back in the old days he'd always viewed himself as a man with leadership potential. Lori Kalmar had proven herself a capable exec, but lacked the drive to be a real leader in her own right. McCall was too fiercely independent and unpredictable, and Hassan Khaled was always a shade too bloodthirsty for his own good. So de Villar had worked hard, hoping for the chance to rise to the top, and finally, in the wake of the Clan Wars, he'd achieved his long-time ambition.

And now . . . now he'd thrown everything away.

"Take it easy, Cris," Freya said softly. She knew what he was going through, but she hadn't passed judgment on him. He'd done that for himself . . .

He could still see the guards holding a needler to her throat, forcing him to cooperate in the governor's broadcast. De Villar hated what he'd had to do that day, but in all honesty he knew nothing would change even if he had it to do it all over again. The Legion had been like a family for more years than he cared to remember, but Freya . . . Freya was his wife. The mother of their children. She wasn't just family, she was a part of him. He would never willingly let her come to harm.

"Could those be Legion 'Mechs?" she asked suddenly. "They surely didn't take out everyone, did they?"

He shrugged. "Maybe. With the whole damned staff locked up, I don't know who could have put together any kind of coherent resistance. DeVries claimed he had all the company commanders, and McCall . . ." de Villar sat heavily on the bed, frustration turning to a feeling of helpless rage. "Hell, I don't know. I can't take being in the dark! If only I could get out there and *do* something!"

Freya touched his shoulder fleetingly, a simple, reassuring caress. "Let it go, Cris," she said softly. "You've got to let it go . . ."

Dave Clay smiled and pulled back on his *Griffin*'s left-hand joystick control. He could feel, through the feedback from his neurohelmet, the subtle shift in balance as the 'Mech's left battle fist responded, drawing back with a faint whine of servoactuators.

Clay rammed the stick forward, felt the BattleMech follow the motion, its fist slamming into the high perimeter wall that marked the outermost defensive line of Castle Hill. The wall had been built as much for aesthetic reasons as for defense, and was no match for the force of a BattleMech. Masonry shattered, and a broad section of wall simply collapsed under the massive blow.

He used the massive hand to widen the gap, then kicked at the stray piles of rubble lower down. In less than a minute the breach was complete, wide enough for a 'Mech or a pair of vehicles to pass through easily. The *Griffin* stepped ponderously through the gap.

"Ghost Two," he said. "I'm in."

"Understood," Major Alard King's voice responded crisply. "Proceed according to plan."

As the *Griffin* started up the steep slopes on the north side of Castle Hill, Clay felt it almost a relief to be in action at last. Ever since receiving Caitlin's message from Ian MacDonald, Brander's cadets and technicians had been working overtime. Even with that, they'd only had enough time to load five of the cadet 'Mechs aboard an odd assortment of emelt cargo cars. All during the trip from Brander to the open country a few kilometers up the Earn River from Dunkeld, the techs had been swarming over the battle machines trying to finish prepping and arming them. King had decided that was the best place to unload them. And despite all that work, the *Shadow Hawk* piloted by Cadet Gates had broken down even before the move to Dunkeld was properly under way.

That had been typical of the whole ill-prepared operation. The Brander contingent was forced to rely on improvisation for practically everything, from logistics to planning to the actual troops to carry out the mission. Most of the soldiers in the two hover carriers accompanying the 'Mechs were a long way from being combat veterans—a few guards plus some of the support staff equipped with extra weapons scraped up from the Brander arsenal. Even the CO, Major King, was more at home in a 'Mech repair bay than on a battlefield. And the 'Mech pilots, of course, were all cadets.

But that was the way it had to be. They'd discussed trying to bring in a few other outlying Legion garrisons, but the need for surprise and speed made that option too risky. So they would go in with what they had.

Four 'Mechs should have been enough to go through the Planetary Guard like air through a hull breach, even with the defenses on Castle Hill to bolster the defense. But Clay wasn't so sure how the 'Mechs would fare today. Four cadet pilots backed with amateur infantry, following a plan no real tacticians had ever looked at—It didn't bear thinking about.

Clay's sensors picked up more incoming missile fire from the southern side of the complex. Cadet Galleno was posted near the Earn in his fifty-five-ton *Dervish,* using the 'Mech's long-range fire support weaponry to maintain a ragged barrage. If all went well it would keep the defenders focusing on the southern end of Castle Hill for the critical minutes the other three 'Mechs and their improvised infantry back-up needed to penetrate the northern part of the base and reach the Residence and the military compound near the crest. Not much further now . . .

In the dawn's half-light, Clay distinguished a clump of men running toward the *Griffin.* They were dressed in an assortment of combat battle dress and the kilts and tunics of the more usual Guardsman uniforms, and most carried autorifles. They could be safely discounted.

But one of them was humping a portable SRM launcher, and that, at least, was a threat.

Clay hesitated for a moment. No one in the Brander contingent had been happy about the prospect of fighting the Guardsmen. It wasn't as if these were genuine enemies, like

Kurita regulars or the Free Skye separatists. They were just local militia obeying the orders, illegal though they might be, of the duly constituted planetary government. Dave Clay didn't want to kill any of those men, but they stood between him and his objective.

In the time it took him to consider that thought, the Guardsman had his SRM unlimbered. Before Clay could react a rocket streaked from the tube.

As the warhead struck the *Griffin* square in the chest, the 'Mech staggered backward, but Clay caught himself and kept his balance. The Guardsmen seemed surprised at the outcome of the attack. Except for some scars on the *Griffin*'s chest armor, there was no damage. One of the soldiers threw down his longarm and ran, but the SRM gunner hastened to reload his launcher for another try. It was a pity that a brave man should die for no good reason.

Clay stopped the 'Mech in its tracks for a long moment, his mind racing. The *Griffin* was ill-suited for close-in combat, its arsenal limited to a plasma cannon and a battery of long-range missiles. It didn't mount any anti-infantry weapons, and Clay was reluctant to simply wade in with the machine's huge metal hands and feet. Maybe he'd have to do that to someone, someday, but he couldn't bring himself to crush these locals like so many insects.

Maybe that's why you're still a cadet, a voice in the back of his mind sneered. But Clay ignored it. There were some things he just wouldn't do.

He saw a possible solution and acted on it just as a second missile leapt from the muzzle of the launcher, trailing smoke and flame. Clay's fingers danced over his controls, cutting in the *Griffin*'s jump jets for a quick leap into the air. The thrust pressed him deeper into his chair as the ungainly behemoth jumped straight over the SRM gunner's position.

The cadet had a brief view of upturned faces and running figures as the Planetary Guard troops dispersed. The sight of Clay's massive armored machine passing overhead would have been enough to panic even hardened combat veterans, not to mention the backwash those below must be feeling from the 'Mech's jets.

The *Griffin* landed smoothly, with Clay's neural link controlling the machine's balance almost instinctively as it touched down. His video displays showed no sign of the defenders anywhere nearby, except for one fleeting look at a man running straight into Major King's mounted infantry platoon as their hover carrier passed full speed through the gap Clay had made down below.

Clay scanned ahead, using light intensifiers to turn the dawn as bright as full daylight. The *Griffin* was just outside the inner fence that marked off the Castle Hill military compound. The Residence itself lay beyond. Figures were scurrying across the parade ground, but resistance here seemed no better organized than what he'd already encountered.

Maybe, just maybe, Major King's crazy plan was going to work after all . . .

22

"I don't care what they look like, goddamn it!" Colonel Max Walthers shouted into the communicator. "You get your men to put up a fight even if you've got to personally shoot down the ones who run! You get me, Lieutenant? Or do you want me to demonstrate the technique—on you, maybe?"

Walthers cut off the channel without waiting for the Guard officer to reply. Damn it anyway, he thought bitterly. Looks like His High and Mightiness really botched this one up.

Walthers crossed the room to a window that overlooked the Castle Hill military compound. He didn't know what bureaucrat usually used this office in the Residence, but right now it was the closest thing to a command post he had. A pair of nervous-looking lieutenants and Corporal O'Leary, a scar-faced merc who'd been with him since his Kurita days, were all his staff so far, but even a dozen Kerenskys with a battle computer wouldn't have helped the odds much at this point. 'Mechs against local militia wasn't a fight, it was a slaughter, pure and simple.

It couldn't be the Free Skye force. They weren't due in orbit for another thirty-six hours. Besides, the planetary sensor net would have picked up any early arrivals and passed the word before the invaders could land. These had to be some of the Gray Death troops, probably from one of the outlying garrisons. Somehow they'd learned about the governor's hoax and had put together an operation despite the capture of their top leaders.

DeVries had claimed that he'd neutralized the Legion, and refused Walthers' suggestion to use the hostages to force a complete disarmament. Now the bitter fruits of that decision were ripe.

There wasn't much the Guards couldn't do except try to buy some time. A few people could still get out, maybe stay out of the Legion's reach until the Free Skye fleet arrived. That was the only ticket Walthers could see now. General von Bulow probably wouldn't see much use in DeVries if the man couldn't deliver the planet, but an experienced mercenary officer with firsthand knowledge of how the Gray Death operated might get a warmer welcome.

So the overriding need now was to keep the attackers at bay long enough to organize an escape plan. There was a small VTOL transport reserved for the governor's use on the rooftop helipad, but it would take time to round up a pilot and get it ready to launch. Time the defenders just didn't have.

Walthers saw the flicker of small-arms fire in the compound, and grunted in frustration and impatience. He'd have to expend a few more pieces to pull off this gambit.

His fingers tapped a new call-code into the communicator. "This is Colonel Walthers at the Residence," he said. "How soon can you get some jets into the air?"

The reply came back quickly. "Already taking off, Colonel," the watch officer at the Dunkeld Aerospace Port said. "Who the hell are they, anyway?"

"Beats the hell out of me," Walthers lied. "We'll worry about it later. Just tell those pilots to get here and *do* something. You got me?"

"Yes, sir."

He cut the channel, unwilling to waste time in idle chatter. Conventional aircraft wouldn't be much better than Planetary Guard infantry against those 'Mechs, but they'd slow down the attack while they lasted.

Now to take advantage of the delay.

"O'Leary," he said, turning on the corporal. "I've got a job for you . . ."

"Ghost Two, in position," Clay announced, studying his tactical display. The other two BattleMechs in the attack force were moving up to join him, and the two hover carriers had negotiated the difficult ground between the perimeter wall and the winding road that led to the Residence.

"Strike One, ready and waiting," Cadet Cristiano de Villar replied promptly. Better known to his fellow cadets as "Headshot" for his uncanny 'Mech-to-'Mech marksmanship, he was the third son of First Battalion's CO, and his sixty-ton *Rifleman* was the biggest 'Mech in the scratch unit. The younger de Villar was acting lance commander of the cadet company's fire lance, and under other circumstances might have been inclined to take charge of the whole op. But Clay was older, and his cadet commission predated de Villar's. That had been the deciding factor in Major King's placing Clay in command. He hoped the *Rifleman* pilot would accept the decision and follow his orders. Though calm and rational in battle situations, de Villar also tended to denigrate his fellow cadets, and he chafed under the restraints put on him by leaders he disagreed with.

"Strike Four," Cadet Farquhar added a moment later. "On station. When do we do it?" James Edward Farquhar piloted a *Phoenix Hawk* in de Villar's cadet lance. Like his commander he was excitable and eager for action.

He was also the son of the Thane of Moray, a local, and Clay had been concerned about letting him take part in this battle. But King had overruled his concerns, pointing out that Moray was one of the most ambitious of the landowners on the Council, and hence one of the governor's most constant opponents.

"Tinker to all units," came Major King's voice, sounding tense. "Commence Phase Three."

Clay reached out with the *Griffin*'s huge left hand and gripped the fence, pulling the nearest pole free from the ground. The steelloy mesh tore like so much paper, leaving a wide, ragged gap. He tossed the piece into the parade ground, scattering a handful of Guardsmen there, then pushed through the opening. Checking his side camera displays he saw that the other two 'Mechs were also moving into the compound. Machine gun fire hammered from Farquhar's *Phoenix Hawk,* and there was a flash of laser light as the *Rifleman* opened up on an autocannon emplacement near the northeast corner of the base.

"Targets! Targets incoming!" That was Cadet Galleno, from his *Dervish* on the city side of Castle Hill. "Three, no, five targets, airborne, coordinates Delta-Six, closing . . ."

Clay checked his map again and saw the blips Galleno was reporting. They were heading in from the aerospace port at high speed, and would be arriving in the fight in a matter of seconds.

For an instant Clay felt a flash of fear. Aerospace fighters were a MechWarrior's worst nightmare, the only weapon other than another 'Mech that could crack one of the huge combat machines. It had been a flight of Clan Omnifighters that had delivered the coup de grâce to his father in the final battle on Sudeten.

Clay swallowed and forced the thought from his mind. The only aerospace fighters currently on Glengarry belonged to the Gray Death, and even if the Guardsmen had confiscated them there was no way an untrained pilot could handle one. These had to be conventional jet fighters from the air arm of the Planetary Guard. They would be more dangerous than anything the attackers had met so far, but still a comparatively minor threat to BattleMechs.

"Strike One, this is Ghost Two," he said, trying to sound confident. "Keep those fighters off our backs, Headshot."

"I'm on 'em," Cadet de Villar replied. The *Rifleman*'s combination of lasers and autocannons, along with a sophisticated target-acquisition system, made it a favorite air defense platform, and the fire lance had spent long hours practicing just this kind of situation. De Villar's 'Mech drew back a few paces while Clay and Farquhar continued across the compound.

A moment later the jets were screaming overhead, breaking from a tight diamond formation to commence their first attack run. Laser and gunfire flashed from the left of Clay's 'Mech as de Villar opened up, and the lead jet burst into flames just as it released a missile. The warhead smashed into a blockhouse half a kilometer away from the fighting, but another fighter got off a whole flight of SRMs in Farquhar's direction. They impacted all around the *Phoenix Hawk*, and the young pilot reported a pair of hits on his rear torso. That was dangerous. The 'Mech's rear armor was comparatively weak, and a few more such hits would burn through to the critical internal systems mounted in the machine's chest.

Farquhar didn't seem much worried, however. "I've reached the detention center," he reported, sounding excited. That was the main objective for this phase of the attack, based on the best intelligence estimates they'd been able to make on the location of the Gray Death's captured leaders. Their contact in the Residence, old Ian MacDonald, had managed to get in touch only once after his initial call. He hadn't been able to learn much, but his wife had overheard some Guardsmen discussing the prisoners in the military cell block.

"Right," Clay said over the taccom. "I'll cover you. But watch for those fighters."

He glanced nervously at his tactical display. De Villar was still firing, but except for that first hit he hadn't done much damage. At least those pilots were circling away from the battleground, unwilling to risk the deadly hail of fire rising from the *Rifleman.*

A heavy machine gun rattled, loud enough for Alex Carlyle to hear it even through the sealed window of his cell. He craned his neck, but except for the distant light of a fire somewhere near the perimeter wall of the detention center he could see no sign of fighting. The missile barrage from the south must have been a diversion, he thought, with the real attack coming from the north. The battle had already drawn all the sentries out of the detention center, leaving the officers of the Legion alone and unwatched. But they were still locked in, forced to follow the fighting outside mostly by sounds and inferences.

"Good God!" someone shouted from across the corridor. Alex thought it was Captain Guilaume Dumont, CO of one of Major de Villar's two 'Mech companies. "They're fighting a full-fledged battle out there."

"Who's doing the attacking?" Vargas demanded from another cell.

"I can see two 'Mechs," Dumont said. "A *Phoenix Hawk* and a *Griffin.* The *Griffin*'s wearing a Companions insignia!"

"But no one in the Companions pilots a *Griffin!*" someone else protested.

Alex crossed to the door of his cell. "Maybe not," he said with a grin. "But Dave Clay drives a *Griffin,* and he's entitled to the badge." The emblem of the Gray Death Companions, the Legion's skull impaled on an upraised broadsword, was used by any member of the unit's Command Company, and by their heirs as well. With the exception of a few of the old-timers like Charles Bear or Major McCall, Dave Clay, Cristiano de Villar, and Alex Carlyle himself were the only people outside the regular Companions entitled to display that device.

Alex's spirits soared. Somehow, the cadets at Brander had learned the truth and decided to strike back. Maybe, just maybe, there was hope for the Legion after all.

"Attention in the detention center!" a voice boomed over the PA. Alex recognized Farquhar's boyish tones even through the distortion of the amplifier. "Stand back from the north wall!"

He could see Captain Dumont and a couple of the others whose cells were visible from his door move back as far as possible from the outside wall. A moment later light flashed and rippled through Dumont's window, and in seconds the duraplast wall just below it was glowing white-hot. Then the surface was running, melting. The stench was sharp, acrid, but to Alex it was the smell of freedom.

"Stand back from the opening!" Farquhar warned. The 'Mech's hand reached into the hole that had opened up in the structure, grasping the superheated duraplast to yank a whole section of the wall free. Some of the imprisoned officers gave voice to a ragged cheer.

Seconds later armed men in Gray Death battledress were dismounting from a hover carrier outside and swarming through the shattered wall. They made short work of the cell doors, and quickly released the rest of the prisoners. More troopers shepherded the freed hostages into the rear of the carrier as the battle raged on. Farquhar stood watch over it all from his *Phoenix Hawk,* releasing an occasional burst of machine gun fire to discourage any Planetary Guards from interfering in the operation.

Major Alard King was in the rear of the hovercraft, looking distinctly out of character in combat fatigues and a holstered laser pistol. Scanning each new arrival as the former prisoners piled aboard, his face was creased in a deep frown. "Where is Major de Villar? Or the weapons master?" he demanded as Alex climbed in.

"Haven't seen either of 'em since the first day," Julio Vargas said as he strapped on a pistol belt passed back from the front of the passenger compartment by an astech in battledress. "Or Major Owens, either."

"They separated out the married officers and Major

McCall right after they captured us, sir,'' Alex told King.
''I think they're allowing families to stay together under
guard in the Residence.''

''Damn,'' King cursed softly. ''Our intel didn't say anything about that.''

''We've got to get the rest of the Legion mobilized,''
Dumont said crisply. ''Turn out First Battalion now that the
Guards are falling back from the 'Mech bays.''

''Our first priority ought to be the safety of the rest of
the hostages, Captain,'' Alex protested. ''Without Major de
Villar or the others this whole jailbreak won't mean a
damned thing!''

The elegant captain gave him a disdainful look. Colonel's
son or not, Alex Carlyle was only a cadet, and Dumont's
opinion of his meddling in command decisions was all too
clear. But Alard King was nodding slowly. ''I agree with
young Mister Carlyle. The other hostages have to come
first.''

The senior tech looked worried. His sister was one of
those hostages, after all.

Dumont's expression was unhappy. ''I still think—''

''Do what you think is best, Captain,'' King said with a
shrug. ''Take a party and get to the Legion barracks. The
rest of our people were probably locked in there when the
battle started. But I'm taking my boys to the Residence, and
the 'Mechs are coming with me!''

Captain Dumont nodded abruptly. ''That'll do it,'' he
said. ''Vargas, Simms, let's move!''

Alex watched them scramble to the ground, then turned
back to King. ''What can I do to help, Major?'' he asked
quietly.

King's eyes had a haunted look. ''Pray, Mister Carlyle.
Pray for all of them . . .''

RICK HARRIS ©93

23

"**G**host Two, this is Ghost Leader. Report your status."

Hearing Alex Carlyle's voice over the comm channel made Davis Clay smile with relief under the faceplate of his neurohelmet. Thank god Alex was all right. "Ghost Leader, Ghost Two," he replied. "Welcome back. Hope you enjoyed your vacation!" His fingers were punching up a full sitrep from the *Griffin*'s computer as he spoke. "All systems nominal. Haven't had to use any ammo yet. That means I can cover the withdrawal if Galleno's running low. Ah . . . he's posted—"

"Three kilometers south," Alex's voice cut him off. As usual he seemed to have the whole tactical situation right at his fingertips, even though he couldn't have been out of his cell for more than a minute or two. "Using the *Dervish* to stir up a ruckus. I'm helping Major King coordinate now, and I've got the tactical computer right in front of me."

"Great, skipper," Clay replied. "We'll start Phrase Four right away."

"Negative on that, negative. We've got a change in plans, Two. All units to converge on the Residence immediately. Repeat, converge on the Residence. Some of our people were moved there."

"Christ on a crutch," Clay muttered. "Ah . . . roger that, Ghost Leader. May I suggest you let Headshot hold his current? We need him to keep off those damned jets. They're coming around for another string of attack runs."

"Yeah, I see 'em," Alex said. "Right. But you get it in

gear. We've got to get to the Residence while we still have some momentum.'' Unspoken was the thought that had plagued King and the whole strike force from the very beginning, the possibility that DeVries might decide to use the hostages as bargaining chips. Judging from Caitlin's secondhand warning, the governor had already threatened some of them to get Major de Villar's cooperation. If DeVries thought he had nothing left to lose . . .

"Understood, Leader," Clay said, his pleasure gone in an instant. "We're on it! Strikers, Strikers, this is Ghost Two. New orders! Repeat, new orders . . .''

Inside the Residence, Corporal O'Leary faced the Governor General. "We have to go *now*, Governor! We don't have much time left, goddamn it!''

DeVries studied the grizzled mercenary with a sinking feeling deep in his gut. Corporal O'Leary had been with Walthers for years, and it was never any secret that his first loyalty lay with the colonel rather than with his adopted world. Now the man's tone, abrupt, almost menacing, made it clear that the mercenaries weren't planning to let their employer interfere with Walthers' evacuation plan.

What the Legion had done was incredible. DeVries had thought all their units were accounted for, but they'd somehow scraped an operation together anyway. And without the benefit of any of their senior leadership. The only officer above the rank of lieutenant who hadn't been rounded up in the first hours of the coup was King, their technician, and he shouldn't have been able to mount an attack.

But the attack was going on right now, and the whole world was crumbling around Roger DeVries. The Legion was going to fight no matter what he did, and that meant the Free Skye armada would launch its attack after all. War would come to Glengarry . . .

And whoever won, the Governor General whose plan to keep peace had failed would be persona non grata with the victors. The Gray Death would never trust him again, and General von Bulow wouldn't be likely to renew negotiations once the Legion started fighting back.

"Governor," O'Leary repeated, making the word sound more like an epithet.

"All right, all right. I'll give the orders," DeVries said. Maybe the plan Walthers was hatching, as relayed by

O'Leary, would work after all. If they could escape and link up with von Bulow's landing troops, they might salvage something yet. "I'll have the VTOL ready to lift in, say, fifteen minutes."

"Make it ten. We don't have much time before the bastards are knocking on the gates."

"But—" DeVries saw O'Leary's expression and bit off the protest. "Ten minutes, then. I'll pass the word back to the colonel. But I need *you* to do something for me while I'm getting things together here."

The corporal looked suspicious. "What?" There wasn't even the pretended courtesy of the title anymore.

"My daughter. She's been confined to her rooms in the south wing until she . . . decides to accept the inevitable. If we're pulling out, she goes with us. I want you to get her and bring her to the helipad to meet us."

O'Leary started to open his mouth in reply, then his face took on an expression of thoughtfulness. "Your daughter, huh. All right, Your Excellency. I'll bring her. Just make damned sure you have that VTOL ready to go."

The look in the man's eyes made it clear that Caitlin would pay a heavy price if anything went wrong. DeVries swallowed and nodded. Walthers and his mercs had already demonstrated the power of hostages in their handling of Major de Villar. He knew they wouldn't hesitate for an instant to use Caitlin if it would get them what they wanted . . .

As O'Leary hurried out of the office he was already punching in the call-code to alert his pilot and the VTOL ground crew. Roger DeVries couldn't afford any more mistakes. Not with Caitlin's life—and probably his own, come to that—at stake.

The door slid open suddenly, and Caitlin DeVries whirled where she stood. From her rooms overlooking the south side of Castle Hill, all she'd been able to see of the disturbance that had put the whole Residence on alert was a light show down near the base of the hill.

She vaguely recognized the short, stocky NCO framed in the open door as one of her father's bodyguards. Visible beyond him were two more Planetary Guard troopers, part of the detail that had been watching her quarters since the first day of the coup. Both were obviously edgy at the approaching sounds of battle.

Caitlin drew her robe shut over her pajamas, conscious of the way the man was studying the curves revealed by the gauzy New Kyoto silk. She wasn't particularly shy about her body—nobody who had to work day in and day out wearing the skimpy shorts and cooling vest that were de rigeur in an overheated 'Mech cockpit was likely to retain any shyness about showing a little skin—but she didn't like the look in the man's eyes. "Just what in Blake's name do you think you're doing, Corporal?" she demanded, using her best "governor's daughter" voice as she drew herself up to her full height and fixed him with an icy stare. "Haven't you ever heard of buzzing before you barge in?"

The NCO's expression didn't change. "Never mind that now," he snapped. "You're coming with us."

She backed away as he advanced. "Where? What's going on?"

"Your father wants you. Now move!"

Caitlin took another step away from him. "At least let me get dressed—"

"*Now*, I said!" The corporal's sidearm, a deadly-looking vibroblade, was in his hand. "I said I'd fetch you, but I didn't promise you'd still be in one piece! Get moving!"

Caitlin didn't hesitate any longer. The look in the man's eyes told her he meant business with that vibroblade, and she wasn't about to give him a chance to prove it.

Not until a moment of *her* choosing.

Out in the corridor, the noncom gave a curt order to the two soldiers. "Helipad," he snapped. "Move it!" They took the lead, while the corporal trailed Caitlin, his blade at the ready. The stamp of their booted feet contrasted sharply with the slap-slap-slap of her slippers on the fake stonework of the corridor floor.

The two guards took the turn that led to one of the lifts, and Caitlin allowed herself a smile. The stairs wouldn't have been suitable for what she had in mind.

The lift doors slid open promptly, and the first guard stepped quickly inside. The second was moving aside to let Caitlin and the corporal pass when she stumbled and lurched into him. "Ow!" she complained. "Damn floppy slippers!"

The trooper reached out to help her, and in that instant she used her momentum to carry her past him. Her 'Mech-trained reflexes took over, and with a swift motion she grasped the man's arm and pulled him around so that he was between her and the corporal's vibroblade. He started to shout something and jerked back.

Her left hand speared straight into his stomach, and before he could even double over from the force of the blow she caught him with an open-palmed chop to the bridge of the nose. His mouth worked, but no sounds came out as he staggered back and straight into the vibroblade. It whined as it sank into his back, and Caitlin leaped forward.

The corporal tried to yank the blade free, but she was on top of him first. A chop to the wrist made him release the blade, and soldier and vibroblade together fell to the floor. Then she brought her knee up into the noncom's groin. He doubled over, out of the fight for the moment at least.

Caitlin spun again as the guard in the elevator lunged through the doors, his rifle at the ready. In that split second she flashed on the face of Lieutenant Bergstrom, who periodically instructed the cadets in quick-kill and other martial arts disciplines. Standing sternly before the cadets, he was saying, "The first rule when facing an opponent with better weaponry is to even the odds. Get inside his weapon range and you're back on level ground."

She acted on the thought before the soldier could swing the rifle around to cover her, leaping at him with a loud yell. The man flinched as Caitlin gave him a chop across the throat. Then he was down.

She jerked the vibroblade out of his comrade's back, then turned on the downed soldier, who was slowly, painfully trying to straighten up. "Now, Corporal," she said in low, dangerous tones while prodding him in the stomach with the tip of the knife. "Suppose you tell me just what's been going on . . ."

"This is it!" shouted the driver of the Legion's hover carrier. "Hold on back there!"

In reaction to his warning, Alex Carlyle gripped a strap mounted on the hover carrier's front partition, hastily double-checking the restraints that held the portable computer terminal in place. The carrier skewed sideways as it came to a stop, and the motley group of technician-soldiers and armed ex-prisoners at the rear of the passenger compartment were piling out before the turbofans had shut off completely. Julio Vargas, the aerospace pilot, brandished a Sternsacht pistol as he barked orders.

"Move! Move! Move!" he urged, waving the pistol with one hand and using the other to shove men toward the rear door. With his bristling black mustache and the ammo belts for the team's machine gun draped across his chest, Vargas looked like a stock bandito character from some trideo costume drama.

"Aircraft! Aircraft incoming!" someone shouted.

On Alex's monitor, the three blips that represented the surviving Planetary Guard aircraft were swooping low in another attack run. He could hear the rattle of machine gun fire outside as the lead jet started strafing the legionnaires on the ground.

"Strike One! Strike One!" he called as his hand stabbed the commlink button. "Headshot, get those bastards off us!"

"Roger that, Ghost Leader," the cadet MechWarrior replied, imperturbable. Unlike his father, Cristiano de Villar rarely ever betrayed his emotions. "I've got them."

"Legion strike force, Legion strike force," a familiar voice crackled over the commlink. "Legion strike force, this is Cadet DeVries. Please respond."

Caitlin . . .

Alex checked his automatic impulse to respond to the call. He hadn't seen or heard anything about her since the coup, but the fact that she'd been assigned to the governor's staff just before the whole crisis had erupted didn't look good.

And the governor was, after all, her father. Alex couldn't imagine going against his own parent. How could they trust her now? This had to be some kind of trick.

Beside him, Major King turned quickly and keyed the commlink. "This is King," he said, raising his hand to cut off Alex's protest. "Go ahead, Cadet."

"I've got important information, Major," she said, sounding breathless. "They're getting ready to evacuate—my father and Colonel Walthers. By VTOL from the helipad. I think Walthers intends to take some of the Legion officers as hostages."

"Where are the hostages now?" King demanded.

"Third . . . third floor," she replied. "South wing, I think. I'm heading that way now, but if you can get anyone else up there . . ."

"Understood," King said. "Good work, DeVries."

As King cut the commlink, Alex finally gave voice to an angry protest. "It's a trap, Major! Has to be . . ."

King shook his head. "It was Cadet DeVries who tipped us off to this mess in the first place. Got a message out through one of the Residence service people. Her father probably didn't want to lock her up with the rest of you, but he had her under house arrest just the same. We're damned lucky she got loose when she did." The Tech Major paused, tapping the computer console restlessly. "All right. Cadet, you take half the troops and try to find the hostages on the third floor before they move them again. Captain Vargas and the rest will start a regular sweep of the building. I'll get the other carrier up to support us. Got it?"

"Yessir," Alex said. He drew the laser pistol he'd been given during the short trip to the Residence and checked its charge reading. Then he hurried to the rear door, shouting orders to the astech in command of one of the original assault squads.

One of the jets stooped low overhead, twin machine guns chattering. Across the wide circle drive in front of the Residence building a running figure in Legion battle dress went down, flinging his battle rifle away as he fell. With a shock Alex realized it was Cadet Wemyss, who commanded the cadet company's reconnaissance lance.

From the far side of the military compound an autocannon blazed away at the aircraft. Cadet de Villar's *Rifleman* kept up the steady triple-A fire until the jet was out of sight, then switched to target the next aircraft as it started a fresh strafing run. Now a laser flashed, and Alex's eyes followed the path of the light pulse to the target overhead. In the half-light of the rising sun over the Firth of Dunkeld he saw the jet's left wing leaking smoke from a damaged engine. The aircraft seemed to stagger in midair before it started an almost graceful arc toward the ground, heading straight for the *Rifleman* . . .

Autocannon rounds slammed into the crippled aircraft, shredding away shards of metal and debris, but the shattered hulk continued its plunge, burning now.

It struck the BattleMech like an outsized missile, and in a roar of fire and thunder the 'Mech came apart. Secondary explosions ripped through the ruin from detonating autocannon ammo, spreading burning wreckage over hundreds of meters and setting a nearby building aflame.

Alex stared in sick horror and revulsion at the sight. It had all happened so fast.

And Cristiano de Villar was gone, just like that. He hadn't even had time to punch out.

Vargas shook Alex, hard, with a tight grip on his shoulder. "Snap out of it, kid!" he shouted. "You've got a job to do! Now move!"

Alex tore his gaze away from the smoldering hulk that had been de Villar's *Rifleman* and forced himself to act. But as he led his squad up the steps to the Residence doors he felt like a robot, detached from the action, going through the motions.

No simulation had ever prepared him for the reality of battle.

=== 24 ===

"**I** said *move*, bitch!"

Major Gomez de Villar tried to break free from the grasp of the guard who was holding his arms behind his back, but it was useless. The sound of the open-palmed slap across his wife's jaw was like a dagger plunged straight into his gut.

The blow knocked Freya de Villar backward across the bed, but she rolled and came up on the other side, glaring at Max Walthers as she dropped into a classic quick-kill stance.

But the colonel just laughed. Behind him, another of his mercenaries jerked the bolt back on his SMG and trained it on the angry woman. "Go ahead," Walthers said harshly. "Just give us a good excuse."

Slowly, Freya straightened up, a look of resignation crossing her face. The look she gave de Villar was bleak, hopeless.

"Right," Walthers went on, glancing at his wristcomp. "We're behind schedule. Let's move!"

The guard released de Villar and shoved him toward Freya. At that moment an explosion erupted somewhere outside, far louder than anything they'd heard before. It was close enough to shake the whole room, and the trooper with the SMG staggered and looked around with a wild expression.

Freya lashed out with a flat-footed kick that sent the weapon flying. Breaking his fall on the edge of the bed, de

Villar whirled and sank his fist deep into the stomach of the guard who had pushed him, then followed with an uppercut that smashed the man's nose. As he turned again, searching for another opponent, he saw Walthers drawing his pistol, bringing it up into line with Freya as she turned.

"No!" de Villar shouted, leaping.

The gun spat once, twice, three times, and he felt the impact of each slug as his rush carried him between Walthers and Freya. The force of the shots lifted him sideways, and he rolled over the bed and onto the floor beyond.

He tried to rise, his mind still fixed on Freya and the gun and the overwhelming need to help her . . .

But his arms and legs would not respond, and a tide of black swelled around him, cutting off all else.

All but the memories. The Legion . . . Grayson Carlyle . . . Freya . . .

Freya . . .

Hearing the shot as she rounded the corner from the lift, Caitlin DeVries broke into a run. Her mind was a turmoil of emotions. If only she hadn't stopped in her father's office to warn the Legion . . .

But letting them know the score outside had been vital, too, or so she'd thought at the time. Now, with the prospect of guards killing the hostages, she didn't know what to think anymore.

She reached the door to the room from where the sound of the shot had come, and chambered a round in the battle rifle she'd lifted from the unconscious guard in the corridor downstairs. Then, taking a deep breath, she flattened herself against the wall beside the doorway, slapped the Open stud on the wall control panel, and swung around, rifle raised, as the door slid open.

Colonel Max Walthers spun at the sound, and Caitlin didn't need more than a single look to take in the pistol in his hand and the sprawled body of Major de Villar on the floor. Freya de Villar was kneeling beside her husband, cradling his head, sobbing, oblivious to all else.

Walthers raised the pistol, but Caitlin was faster. Her finger tightened on the trigger and the rifle stuttered, pumping a three-round burst into the mercenary's chest. Another uniformed Guardsman threw up his hands as his commander sagged to the floor with a startled look on his face.

Still sobbing inconsolably, Freya de Villar never even looked up.

Roger DeVries leaned heavily against a railing of the helipad, staring down at the burning wreckage of the *Rifleman* on the other side of the military compound.

How could I let things come to this? he asked himself bitterly. I wanted to spare us . . . this.

"Governor! Governor!" his pilot, a swarthy man from Al Jafr named Zenada, shouted over the sporadic sounds of the combat below. He tapped his wristcomp and pointed at the waiting VTOL. "It's past time! If we're going to get out of here, we've got to go now!"

It was past time, but neither Walthers nor O'Leary had shown up. Or Caitlin. If O'Leary had her and DeVries were to abandon him, what would the mercenary do to her?

Or what if the mercenary had been killed, or had fled somewhere else? Legion troops were already in the Residence, and the fighting elsewhere on Castle Hill had started to wind down. Another jet had been knocked down by the *Griffin*'s PPC at long range, and the last pilot had turned his aircraft away from the fight. He was probably heading back for the aerospace port, or maybe even further.

Down the hill from the Residence, DeVries saw a new BattleMech appear from the recesses of the big 'Mech bay where the Legion's gear was stored. Then another, and a third. Some of their pilots must have escaped from their barracks and powered up their hulking combat machines. Not that they'd make any great difference, now. The battle was all but over . . .

But how could he abandon Caitlin to O'Leary's tender mercies?

As if in response to the thought, the helipad lift opened and Corporal O'Leary staggered out, his face bruised, bleeding from a shallow cut across his belly. The mercenary stumbled once, but stayed on his feet as he crossed the helipad and caught a rung of the VTOL's passenger ladder to steady himself. DeVries crossed the rooftop to meet him.

"The bitch jumped us and got away," O'Leary said, spitting eloquently to punctuate the comment. "You want her, Governor, you go find her, but I'm getting the hell out of here!"

"What about Colonel Walthers?" DeVries asked to cover

the jumble of emotions the merc's words had evoked. "He isn't here yet."

"Then he ain't gonna make it," O'Leary said flatly. "There's already a bunch of Grays in the building. I barely dodged 'em myself. If Walthers hasn't gotten the hostages up here by now, it's because he's been caught or killed." The corporal started to pull himself up the ladder and through the open hatch.

DeVries hesitated a moment longer, then nodded to Zenada. "Let's go," he said curtly, grasping the ladder and following O'Leary up.

Caitlin had escaped.

He wasn't sure if he was happy she had eluded the corporal or angry at the choice she'd made—or simply sad at the fate that had finally driven them apart. At least she'd been spared O'Leary's heavy hand. One way or another, it was over.

He thought of von Bulow's armada and shuddered. No, this wasn't the end. It was only the beginning.

"On the roof! Somebody's getting away!"

Dave Clay heard the warning call from one of the infantrymen and turned his *Griffin*'s scanners to check the top floor of the Residence. Major King had already warned them that some of the governor's men might be trying to escape that way.

Without the *Rifleman* for antiaircraft fire, even a slow-moving VTOL transport might not be easy to knock down. The PPC hit he'd scored on one of the jets had been more luck than skill. BattleMech weaponry was designed to hit tanks or other 'Mechs, slow-moving targets that were easy to track and lock. It took special fire control gear like the *Rifleman*'s to hit aircraft with any degree of consistency.

But they didn't have the *Rifleman* anymore. From now on it was up to Clay and Farquhar.

He plotted fire coordinates hastily, hoping to get off a shot before the VTOL could lift clear of the helipad, then hesitated. King's last transmission had warned that the enemy might be taking hostages out with them. What if Major de Villar or Major McCall was on that thing? Clay couldn't just open fire, not knowing.

He wiped the fire program off his board and took a step back with his 'Mech. He couldn't fire without knowing the score, but there was something else he could do.

His fingers punched in a new control code, triggering the *Griffin*'s jump jets. The armored fighting machine rose from the ground in a move that was half leap, half flight. He hoped the reinforced helipad would be strong enough to take the weight of a 'Mech. If it wasn't . . .

The *Griffin* touched down just as the VTOL was starting to rise from the pad. The roof under the machine's massive feet held, and Clay let out a breath he didn't realize he'd been holding. Then, belatedly, he started forward.

The VTOL hovered for a moment as the pilot revectored the engines. Then it shot away, banking sharply to avoid the 'Mech's outstretched arms.

From the cockpit of his *Griffin,* Clay could only watch, powerless, as the aircraft receded to the east, into the rising sun.

=== 25 ===

There hadn't been much fighting here inside the Battle-Mech repair bay on Castle Hill. Cadet Dave Clay had just come inside from the military parade ground, and the contrast between the ruin outside and the orderly ranks of 'Mechs standing in their repair gantries was startling. It was almost as if the dawn battle had been no more than a nightmare.

Almost.

"Ah, Cadet Clay." An astech sergeant he had last seen in battle dress and blackout makeup crossed the gleaming floor with a computer board in one hand and a harassed expression on his face. He'd found time to change into work coveralls, and the lubricant stains on his face and clothes were considerably more in character than his combat garb. "We've just finished running the diagnostics on your *Griffin*. It looks ready to go. If you'll follow me, I'll show you what we found."

Clay didn't answer, but trailed obediently behind as the tech sergeant led him to the waiting *Griffin*. Cocooned in a repair cradle, the 'Mech was surrounded with gantries to permit repair techs to reach every part of the machine. A handful of techs in the red coveralls of the ordnance department were still working at an open service hatch just below the drum-shaped LRM on the right shoulder, probably double-checking the warheads in the missile locker.

"You lost some armor on the chest where that SRM hit you," the sergeant went on, pointing at the scored, blackened spot on the left chest "Can't replace that yet. It's not a high enough priority, but when we get a chance it won't take long. Meantime, remember you've got a weak spot there, okay?"

Clay nodded, his mind flashing back to the lone Guardsman's fruitless stand with his rocket launcher. All he could think of was the feeling of paralysis that had gripped him, preventing him from simply killing the man, refusing to kill him . . .

Just as he'd refused to fire on the VTOL before it got away.

"I'd also advise you to limit the use of your jump jets for a while," the astech continued. He gestured toward the *Griffin*'s left ankle joint. "We picked up some stress in the joint. You probably came down a little too hard on it when you made that jump up to the roof. That's a job for a full repair crew, and it'd take you off the line for about a week. Major McCall passed the word not to take any 'Mech out of service for anything short of a major fault until further notice, so you'll just have to live with it until he says otherwise."

Clay nodded vaguely, barely hearing the man. If he'd known there'd been no hostages on the VTOL, he could have knocked it out while it was still on the helipad. Instead he'd hesitated again, and Governor DeVries had escaped. Any further mischief the man stirred up now would be Davis Clay's fault, pure and simple.

No wonder he'd been passed over for a MechWarrior's berth time and again. When it came down to a real life-or-death situation, every decision he always seemed to make was the wrong decision.

He went through the motions of consulting with the crew chief, but inside Clay knew all too well that it was pointless. Even if some of the cadets were tapped for combat against the Free Skye invaders, he knew his own prospects for ever piloting a 'Mech again were bleak.

And in one part of him, one shameful corner of his mind that his father would never have understood or forgiven, he actually felt relieved.

It felt good to be back in Legion grays again.

Caitlin DeVries climbed down from the back seat of the UVAC as it set down at the Dunkeld maglev station, then turned to take her kit bag from Cadet D'Angelo. She was just heading for the emelt platform when Major King called her back.

He was sitting in the front passenger seat of the air-cushion utility vehicle, dressed in ordinary tech coveralls and checking a list on his computer board. He seemed relieved to be back in his usual role as the Legion's chief technical officer. "Get your *Centurion* powered up first, Cadet," King ordered. "Then I want you to turn it over to Cadet Galleno."

"Sir? I thought Galleno was bringing in the *Archer.*"

King shook his head. "Galleno's never handled anything bigger than fifty tons before. You've logged a few hours on the *Archer,* so I'd rather have you bring her in."

She nodded. "Yes, Major."

"Good. Let me know if you run into any problems. Dismissed."

Caitlin saluted and turned away, hurrying across the open platform toward the last of the flat-topped emelt cars in the maglev train that had arrived in Dunkeld less than an hour before. The train had brought the second contingent of 'Mechs from the cadet company's base at Brander, five more fighting machines added to the Legion's slim assets around the capital. In addition to her *Centurion* and Alex Carlyle's *Archer,* the load included D'Angelo's *Wolverine,* Hideyoshi Naito's *Crusader,* and the Panther assigned to Cadet Wemyss. Now that he had died in the attack on the Residence, the cadet company's recon lance was in need of a new leader.

Caitlin stopped dead in her tracks. What was she thinking of? If the Legion somehow managed to pull itself together and mount a defense against von Bulow's invasion fleet, there'd be more important things on Major McCall's mind than filling out the cadet TO and E. The cadets probably wouldn't be calling any of those 'Mechs their own from now on. More experienced pilots would be taking them into battle, leaving the cadets on the sidelines.

If they fought at all. Thanks to her father, that didn't look very likely. Major McCall had ordered defensive preparations resumed as soon as the fighting was over around the Residence, but she'd been hearing even veteran legionnaires talking about the futility of putting up any resistance. Certainly the Planetary Guard weren't going to help now.

McCall would probably have to negotiate terms with von

Bulow, and they'd end up harsher than the ones her father had agreed to.

Caitlin reached the emelt car that held her *Centurion* strapped down in a prone position. A technical team was already working on the reactor and troubleshooting the power circuitry. One of them waved casually and came to meet her. Astech Sergeant Stewart was her regular crew chief, and had arrived on the emelt with the *Centurion*. He gave Caitlin a hand up to the car, then led her across to the cockpit hatch without comment. Stewart was a quiet man, never inclined to speech unless he had something to say, but he was one of the best technicians at Brander. There was talk that he was being groomed for a technical officer's commission.

Stewart lifted the hatch open and took Caitlin's kit bag while she levered herself into the cockpit. With the 'Mech lying prone, it was hard to move around in the cockpit area, but she finally managed to squeeze herself into the command couch and then reach back and up to take the bag from Stewart. He swung the hatch shut and dogged it manually from the outside.

Caitlin looked up through the canopy for a long moment. The view showed nothing but sky, but in her mind's eye she was seeing the tableau in de Villar's quarters when she'd burst in and killed Walthers. Another crime to lay at her father's door. Walthers and O'Leary and the rest of the professional mercs in the bodyguard had run wild, and though she doubted her father had played much part in events right at the end, those had been his men. And it had been Roger DeVries' decision to abandon the planet's rightful landholders in favor of von Bulow that had set in motion the whole sad train of events.

McCall and King had both been lavish in praising her actions, but Caitlin knew there were plenty of other legionnaires who suspected her loyalties now. Even Alex Carlyle had been distant when they'd met outside de Villar's quarters just after the fight, and that had hurt worst of all. They'd been teamed together in the cadet command lance since the day Caitlin had joined, and the bond between lance mates was supposed to be too tight to permit such doubts.

She'd turned her back on her father out of loyalty to the Legion, but now it seemed she was losing them both.

Caitlin DeVries shoved the thought aside. For the moment she still had her duty, and she'd do it until the end. It was all she had left.

She strapped herself into the seat, snapped her cooling vest's power cord into the side of the couch, then pressed the four sensor pads than would connect her neurohelmet to her chest and thighs. Finally, she reached behind the headrest of her seat and found the neurohelmet tucked back into its receptacle. Pulling it out and up, she fitted it carefully over her head and shoulders, then attached the other ends of the sensor plugs into the neck of the helmet. With everything in place, she touched the power stud and felt a tingle in her skull as the neurohelmet came alive.

Now it was time to recite the code sequence that the 'Mech's onboard computer had been programmed to recognize and accept. Her birthdate . . . her mother's . . . her father's . . . Without the proper code, the computer's defenses would lock her out of the 'Mech controls altogether. Then it would take a half-dozen technicians and another hour or more to clear the program and start from scratch, as they'd already be doing with the *Archer* to override Alex's Carlyle's ID coding. When the authorization was confirmed, the control boards in front of and above her seat came to life.

Caitlin next punched in the order for a full system's diagnostic, and reported the start-up to Sergeant Stewart over her commlink. She half-turned in the seat to check the cockpit life-support readouts, and that made her think of her kit bag wedged under the front of the seat, out of the way. In battle conditions, she would have stripped down to her shorts, shoes, and the cooling vest in the bag. But today the heat buildup shouldn't be enough to require it. She corrected the air flow inside the cockpit instead, then turned her attention back to the computer readout to check the progress of the diagnostic.

Outside, the technical team was releasing the straps that secured the 'Mech to the bed of the emelt car. Caitlin double-checked the computer readout, gave a single, satisfied nod, and reached for the controls. Raising a prone BattleMech was supposed to be one of the single toughest maneuvers a pilot could attempt, but it was child's play next to the problem that occupied most of her thoughts right now.

Winning back the trust her father's actions had cost her.

* * *

Alex Carlyle was feeling like an outsider as the discussion in the conference room unfolded. With the fighting over and done, the senior staff had reconvened in the Castle Hill command center to consider the situation once more. With planetfall for the first Free Skye ships expected in less than twenty-four hours, things were looking grim.

McCall, as the Legion's senior surviving officer, had already put some defensive measures in motion, but it seemed as if they'd been talking to no good purpose for hours on end. And Alex had little enough to contribute here. There wasn't much for an aide to do, and even less for a cadet MechWarrior.

"The governor's treason has changed everything," Captain Simms was saying gloomily. "I mean, we had a chance when we thought we could present a unified front. But if the Planetary Guard and the whole damned civil administration are going to turn on us, I don't see how we can put up much of a fight."

"I agree," Vargas chimed in. "How can we defend a planet that doesn't want defending?"

"Aye, the bluidy Sassenach bastard has put us in a fell spot!" Davis McCall said. "Tae think he would gae behind our backs tae deal wi' the enemy!"

"With the resources we've got on hand, I don't think even the colonel could mount much of a defense," Major Owens said quietly. "Even if we *had* the cooperation of the locals. Without it, I just don't know what we can hope to accomplish."

"I dinna want tae just gie up," McCall said, frowning. "What aboot the plans we were working on before? Is there nae hope tae any of them?"

Owens grunted noncommittally and touched a stud on the table in front of him. Curtains moved aside to reveal a floor-to-ceiling monitor screen, which lit up to display a map of the continent of Scotia, showing population centers and the maglev rail lines.

"An invader could put down almost anywhere, of course," Owens said. "But practical strategy would demand an initial attack against an area that could support long-term operations. That means a population center where supplies can be assembled and stored, with at least rudimentary spaceport facilities and good logistical links to other targets in the area. This is no lightning raid, to touch down anywhere, make the strike, and then run for home. But by the same token they don't have enough lift capacity in those DropShips to support a full-fledged invasion effort entirely from space.''

He paused, favoring McCall with a challenging look. MechWarriors had the reputation for being unconcerned about the essential but unglamorous military science of logistics, while Owens was known for his devotion to such matters. It was one reason he was on the Legion staff. ''Their ideal move would be to take Dunkeld itself, and that's what they were probably counting on when they got DeVries to cooperate. But it would be a chancy move without on-planet support of some kind. A gusty CO might try it just for the sheer surprise value . . .''

''Not von Bulow,'' Ross said. ''No one's ever accused him of being a military genius. He likes the slow but steady approach.''

Owens cleared his throat. ''Then the logical plan would be to hit an outlying area and then move along the maglev lines to strike at the capital.'' He manipulated the map controls on the table in front of him. ''They won't want to fight a campaign through the mountains, though they might choose a base in a mountainous area and strike into the plains of Buchan or Atholl from there. I'd say we can safely eliminate Invertay and the other towns of Strathtay and Moray as landing sites. The same for Pentland, Mar, and Glencoe . . . they all have significant mountain barriers blocking an advance on Dunkeld. Kelso and Eastport are also unlikely because of the distances involved.''

A number of cities and towns vanished from the map. ''That leaves us with . . . maybe five possibles. Arbroath is closest to us here, and the terrain the attackers would have to cross is favorable. On the other hand, even a cursory look will show von Bulow that the maglev line out that way is in rotten shape for cargo transport. You'll remember we had to tear it up pretty thoroughly when we took out Thane Somerled, and the new thane hasn't seen fit to finish repairs yet.''

''I think he's more concerned with rebuilding the rest of the infrastructure in Buchan. Two consecutive years of famine . . .'' Simms trailed off with a shrug.

''All the more reason why Arbroath's not a good choice,'' Owens said with a nod. ''It'd be damned hard to gather supplies in Buchan these days, and I think they're going to need as many local sources of food and other supplies as they can get.''

"Will they necessarily know that, Major?" Alex ventured hesitantly. "Just how good is their intel likely to be?"

"Very good. You can bank on it, Cadet." Owens fixed him with a steely stare. "If Ryan and Richard Steiner have been planning this move for any time at all, you can be sure they've had plenty of scouts checking us out already. That merchant ship that passed through the system last week, now. I bet it carried a few observant passengers . . . probably picked up some new ones here with lots of useful items of information." He looked back at the computerized notes on the terminal in front of him. "If I can continue. . . ? Yes. I doubt Arbroath as a target, and Scone as well. It's too far away from Dunkeld to make a good supply base for a major campaign. But I don't rule either one out entirely. More likely, though, are these three. Halidon and Loch Sheol were both major mining centers in the early days of the Glengarry colony. Both have very good port facilities, though neither one has seen much use lately. A good crew of techs could have them up and running in a few days, though.''

"They're both in pretty rugged country," Captain Dumont observed.

"But if they could get in quick and take control of the passes, the terrain would be as much to their advantage as ours," Owens responded. "The only thing that would make it dicey is if we were there in any strength."

"It seems tae me, laddie, that yon von Bulow mayna want tae tak that risk, either," McCall rumbled. " 'Tis nae a good idea tae rely on enemy blunders, but we canna forget that he's planning a campaign against the Gray Death, and that might be enough tae make him a wee bit overcautious. 'Twouldn't be the first time we were overestimated.''

There were scattered chuckles around the table. Even Owens permitted himself a tiny smile. "True enough, Mac," he acknowledged.

"That's four possible sites, and none of them given much chance," Dumont observed languidly. "Don't tell me you think we'll keep the bastards up in orbit by sheer force of reputation?''

Some fresh chuckles answered the sally. Owens answered him by setting one of the town symbols on the map to blinking. ''The other site I could think of is Coltbridge,'' he said, going on as if Dumont hadn't interrupted. ''There's no major port facility, but it's a damned good emelt terminal, and the flat terrain would do well enough for a wilderness landing. Coltbridge is one of the closest sites of all to Dunkeld, and even if von Bulow couldn't grab the port fast enough to offset their logistics problems they could probably set up all the port facilities they'd need around the initial landing area in fairly short order.''

Alex stirred uneasily. ''Forgive me, sir, if I'm asking a stupid question,'' he began slowly. ''But doesn't this boil down to a case of just not being able to tell which site to cover? I mean, Coltbridge is good in some ways, and so are Halidon and Loch Sheol. Or von Bulow might just as well decide to set down in Strathtay or Moray and risk a longer campaign. I don't see how we can really predict where they're going to land.''

''He's right,'' Simms said. ''With all due respect, Major, your fancy calculations lead exactly nowhere. We've got less than a day left, half the locals stirred up against us, and a good chunk of the Legion ready to give up to boot. If we can't predict where the bad guys are coming in, we might as well just forget it.''

Owens shrugged. ''Well, maybe you're right. If I had to, I'd vote for Coltbridge, but it's a pretty thin line.''

''But—'' Alex started to say.

Freya de Villar spoke up at the same time. She'd insisted on attending the meeting, but had sat through it silent and withdrawn. Now she cut in with a voice as cold as a glacier. ''Are you saying that everything that's happened was for nothing?'' she asked. Her tone was even, but taut with suppressed emotion. ''I can't accept that. My husband and my son died a few hours ago, and I'm not about to go along with any decision that says their deaths didn't count for anything.''

No one answered her for a long time. Then McCall cleared his throat. ''I agree,'' he said slowly. '' 'Tis nae what the Legion stands for, tae turn tail the noo.''

That brought a dozen simultaneous responses from around

the table, everyone trying to take the floor. McCall's voice cut through it all. "Enough! this isna getting us anywhere!" When some of the noise subsided he went on. "I think we need tae tak a wee break. Reconvene in five minutes."

Alex stood up as the hubbub erupted anew. The atmosphere in the room was suddenly oppressive, and he wanted nothing more than an excuse to get away from it, if only for a few minutes.

McCall gave him just that as he gestured for his aide to join him. The Caledonian had found a seat in a quiet corner of the next room, and he watched Alex with a critical eye as the cadet sat down. "Sir?" Alex ventured after a long, awkward silence.

"Ye had something ye wanted tae add back there, laddie," McCall said.

Alex nodded. "Just . . . a thought, an idea, I guess. We can't predict where they'll land, but it seems to me we could be ready for them by persuading them to land exactly where we want."

"By pretending the governor won, is that it?" McCall leaned forward, his face taking on an intense expression Alex had rarely seen.

"Yes, sir. Major Owens said it himself. Von Bulow wants to take the capital, but he wouldn't be likely to land here unless he thought he had some local help. It wouldn't take much effort to persuade him he still had it. We don't have Governor DeVries, but we could surely find someone who could pretend to be sympathetic. Maybe we could claim the governor died in the fighting, but that the Guardsmen put down the cadets who led the attack." He hesitated "Maybe Caitlin could speak in his behalf. She'd be in their intelligence files."

"It might work, laddie," Mccall said. " 'Tis the kind of idea your auld faither might hae come up with." He frowned. "But as divided as we are . . . I dinna ken."

Alex didn't respond. The weapons master sat for a long time, his staring making Alex feel decidedly nervous under the scrutiny.

Finally McCall spoke again. "Even if de Villar was still alive, I dinna ken if he could hae pulled this lot together after a' that's happened. I canna even blame the ones who dinna think we should fight. And I ken fu' weil that I canna get them tae change their minds. None of us on the staff have much credibility left after de Villar seemed tae gie in tae von Bulow, and there isna time left tae educate people tae the contrary. And that's just inside the Legion. No Legion officer will hae much pull as far as getting the people on our side, and wi'oot them there's damned little hope we can fight.''

"So you think we have to negotiate, sir?'' Alex tried to hide his disappointment. He'd thought McCall, at least, would want to tough it out.

The major shook his head slowly. "There's ain man, and ain only, on Glengarry today who has a prayer of making a stand, young Alex," he said. "And that's you.''

"Me? But, Major . . . I'm just a cadet. Not even a full MechWarrior yet. None of them will follow me!''

"You're also a Carlyle, lad," McCall said gruffly. "Remember what we were discussing a few days ago? In your auld faither's absence, ye are the landholder-resident and the owner of the Gray Death Legion. And for many of these people, that counts far more than experience. Ye can speak tae the Legion as your faither's son, and tae all Glengarry as representing the legitimate holder. None of the rest of us can.''

Alex Carlyle swallowed once, stunned. "I . . . I don't know if I can do it, sir. I mean . . .'' He trailed off.

"If you canna do it, lad, then no ain can. And the Legion, everything Grayson Carlyle ever fought for, is finished. It winna recover frae this.''

Alex looked away. McCall was right. His father's whole career had been built on a reputation for invincibility, even in the face of overwhelming odds or seemingly insurmountable obstacles. The loss of Glengarry and the surrender of the very core of the Legion would be a death blow to the outfit. Grayson Carlyle might try to rebuild around the troops on Borghese with Major Khaled, but it would never be the same Gray Death.

A gallant stand, even if ultimately futile, wouldn't tarnish the Gray Death's honor the way mere surrender would.

He looked back into McCall's sad eyes. "I'd need help,'' Alex said reluctantly. "Yours, and a lot more. I just can't believe they'll all follow me the way they would my father.''

"You'll get help aplenty, young Alex,'' McCall said, his

mouth twitching into a smile. "And they'll follow you if I hae tae persuade each ain of them with a club!"

Alex grinned despite himself. "Well, even if it's just you and me against the whole damned armada, we'll give them hell, Major."

"Aye, that we will . . . Colonel Carlyle."

=====26=====

"**T**hey're holding steady on descent profile. Twelve minutes . . ." It was a voice from the control tower of Dunkeld's aerospace port and the news made Acting Colonel Alexander Durant Carlyle smile despite the butterfly feeling in his stomach.

Sitting in the darkened cockpit of his *Archer* not far from the starport tower, Alex reflected that General von Bulow, whatever else he might be, was a punctilious man. He had announced that his ships would be landing at precisely 0100 hours Terran Standard Time—a few minutes after 0930 according to Dunkeld's local time—and from the tracking data coming in to the starport control tower it sounded as if he intended the first ship to ground right on the dot.

That was an important datum to add to what the Legion knew about their opponents. Von Bulow was reputed to be stolid, unimaginative, methodical, and cautious, and the events of the past two days certainly tended to confirm those reports.

The armada had been in orbit for more than a local twenty-six-hour day now, but the Free Skye force had not moved swiftly after making planetfall. Evidently von Bulow had been slow to accept the stories coming out of the Residence, a tale concocted by Alex and McCall describing a failed Legion counter-coup that had ended in the death of Governor DeVries and the elevation of a Planetary Guard junta to control of the capital. The "junta" was claiming to accept the agreement made between DeVries and the Free Skye high command, and warned of a few renegade Legion elements operating in the hinterlands. It had all been calculated to encourage von Bulow to go ahead with a landing at the capital, where the Legion could strike a blow, but for a while it had looked as if the general would be too careful to fall into the trap.

From orbit, though, von Bulow's people would have seen plenty of indications to support the story they were getting from the surface. The remainder of the cadet company was stationed around Brander, openly maneuvering their 'Mechs through Brander Pass and into the uplands of Braemoray in what everyone in the Legion hoped was a credible simulation of a small guerrilla force seeking refuge in the hills. A company of Legion infantry had mounted a mock attack on the WTC itself, setting fire to some of the buildings and generally making it look as if Planetary Guard forces were trying to shut down the Legion post.

The same kind of activity was going on the vicinity of Loch Sheol, one of the potential landing sites Major Owens had identified as a likely Free Skye target. Captain Simms and his 'Mech company had been dispatched there, northwest of Dunkeld, to create the impression of combat in the hill country around the mining center. Halidon, a similar town to the southeast, was under Captain Dumont's command.

That left only the Gray Death Companions, the Legion's 'Mech HQ company, to spring the trap at the Dunkeld starport. Alex had been reluctant to divide his forces in the face of the enemy landing, a cardinal sin in every military textbook, but McCall had maintained that it was a necessary risk. The success of the plan depended as much on surprise as firepower, and so visible signs of Gray Death activity in Loch Sheol and Halidon would make von Bulow more likely to believe an unopposed landing in Dunkeld was possible. The object, as McCall had repeated several times when they were first hammering out the operation, was to give von Bulow a bloody nose. They couldn't expect to win a decisive battle, whether they had the entire Legion or a single 'Mech company. But if they could hit von Bulow hard enough he might back off and give the Legion a short breathing space to organize a proper defense.

Alex could only hope the old weapons master was right. For all the claims that Grayson Carlyle's heir was in control

of the Legion now, it was McCall who was really calling
the shots. The other senior officers had accepted the elevation of Cadet Carlyle to command with varying degrees of
enthusiasm. Owens and King had been supportive, and so
had Captain Vargas. The company commanders, Dumont
and Simms especially, had been cooler, but at least they
were cooperating. In some ways it was a relief to have their
'Mech companies out of the capital. At least Alex didn't
feel like they were always looking over his shoulder, dis-
agreeing with everything he did or said.

That didn't mean he was convinced he wanted to face this
battle with the slender assets left in Dunkeld. The Gray
Death Companions were the Legion's elite, but they were
short a lance—the command lance, which was with the elder
Carlyle on Tharkad—and the only way to make up the difference was for Alex to form an ad hoc command lance of
his own. He'd first thought of taking veterans from some of
the other companies, but again McCall had advised that the
less they disrupted the existing organization the better it
would be. Breaking up teams that were used to working
together would cause chaos at a time when the Legion
couldn't afford even a hint of confusion.

So instead the new command lance of the Companions
was made up of MechWarriors Alex himself could count on
as a team—Major McCall in the massive, powerful *Highlander* he hadn't taken into real combat for five years, and
Dave Clay and Caitlin DeVries, Alex Carlyle's long-time
lance mates from the cadet company. It wasn't exactly an
outfit to inspire great confidence, as far as Alex was concerned. Especially given its commanding officer, who had
held his newly established rank of Acting Colonel for less
than two days . . .

"Final check, people." McCall's voice sounded tense
over the comm system. The three lances of Companions,
and the single platoon of tanks assigned to support the operation, were scattered in four different shuttle hangars
around the port. The reinforced ferrocrete structures were
supposed to shield the waiting legionnaires from detection
by the enemy fleet, and as an added precaution their fusion
drives were powered down, leaving the 'Mechs to operate
minimal life support and command functions off the reserve
batteries. Even communications were being protected by using cables to hook into Dunkeld's land-line au-

dio/video/data net instead of broadcasting over open radio frequencies.

But they were still running a big risk. Alex hoped that neither heat sources nor errant broadcasts would betray them, but he knew plenty of other things could still go wrong. Obviously McCall was thinking along the same lines. The edge in his voice was something Alex Carlyle wouldn't have expected from the canny old veteran MechWarrior.

"Loki One, ready," Lieutenant Freida Bergstrom replied. Carlyle wondered how she could put up with the waiting in the cramped cockpit of her tiny *Valkyrie*. Everyone said that the blonde, blue-eyed woman from Wotan had ice water rather than blood flowing through her veins, but Alex had often heard his father comment that she resented any situation that tied her down. As commander of the Companions' recon lance, Bergstrom was usually able to range far and wide from the main line of battle, scouting, harassing, staying mobile. It must have been sheer hell for her, sitting in a darkened 'Mech inside a hangar waiting for something to happen rather than being able to get out and *make* things happen herself.

Alex found himself wondering if he wouldn't have been better off sending the recon lance with one of the other companies and holding back an extra fire support unit instead. It would have gone against McCall's advice, of course, but in the upcoming battle wouldn't firepower count more than the speed and agility of the lightweight recon 'Mechs?

"Hammer One," another voice added a moment later. Carlyle knew it was Lieutenant Andrei Denniken, the fire lance CO, but only because of the call sign. Denniken's duties had kept him mostly out of sight until now, and Alex knew him mostly by reputation. He was called "the mad Russian tinker" behind his back—and often to his face—and served as a liaison between the Companions and Major King's technical staff when he wasn't leading his lance into combat. Obsessed with the technical side of modern warfare, Denniken was supposed to be a topnotch tech and an absolutely brilliant gunner, but there were those who said he got on better with machines than with people. Alex couldn't be sure how the eccentric officer was likely to perform in the coming battle.

Of course, he could say that about a lot of people, himself included. At least Andrei Denniken had *earned* his slot in the Companions.

"We're ready here, Major," Denniken continued. "But I'm still not too happy with this cold-start order."

"That's the way we're doing it, laddie," McCall growled. " 'Tis aye the ainly way."

"Storm One, ready," Captain Radcliffe reported a moment later. He was in command of the tank platoon in person, although the rest of his company had left Dunkeld to join the two diversionary forces. Ethan Radcliffe hadn't made any secret of his opposition to the entire ambush plan, but he'd been firm in insisting that if any of his men were going to be committed to a suicide mission he'd be in there right alongside them. "And Lucci just signaled me that her people are all in position, too." Lieutenant Darlene Lucci commanded the first platoon of Ross' Armored Infantry Company, six tough commandos trained in the anti-'Mech warfare techniques that Grayson Carlyle and Sergeant Ramage had first pioneered more than three decades ago, back on Trellwan where it had all begun.

"All units reporting ready, Colonel," McCall announced formally. As long as they were tapped into the land lines, they were all sharing a single channel, and the weapons master was being very careful to use Alex's adopted rank. Was McCall maintaining a polite fiction, or did he really regard his old commander's son as his proper leader? Alex had no way of being sure.

He checked his cockpit chronometer. Nine minutes to go . . . "All lances, hold position and stand by," he ordered. "Ghost Lance, report readiness." He should have given that order sooner, while the other units were checking in, but he'd forgotten. A fine CO he was turning out to be!

"Ghost Three, ready and waiting," Dave Clay said. He sounded tense and excited all at once, and Alex wondered if his roommate was looking forward to the chance of fighting a real battle alongside the Companions. Major King's report on the operation to free the hostages from Castle Hill had contained nothing but praise for Clay's performance, from the organization to the final execution, and Alex was glad to see his friend finally getting the recognition he deserved after so many bad breaks. Clay's *Griffin* was the lightest 'Mech in the command lance, which Alex hoped wouldn't put his friend at too much of a disadvantage in the coming battle. The last thing Clay needed right now was to run into unexpected problems when he finally had the opportunity he'd been waiting for.

"Ghost Four, standing by," Caitlin DeVries reported. Alex frowned at the flat monotone of her voice. She'd been withdrawn and moody ever since the battle for Castle Hill, and he still didn't know exactly why. Was it because she'd been forced to side against her father? Or had some word of Alex's doubts about her during the Castle Hill fight gotten back to her? He didn't know, but Caitlin had enough things to worry about without any of that emotional baggage. Her *Centurion* had developed a computer fault, and McCall had decreed a shuffling of 'Mech assets to put her into the seventy-five-ton *Marauder* that Captain Dumont usually piloted. Dumont was in another 'Mech of the same model, the *Marauder* previously piloted by Major de Villar. That 'Mech featured extra computer and communications gear for its role as a battalion command unit, and Dumont was in charge of de Villar's battalion now. Caitlin was fully checked out on the larger 'Mech models, but this would be the first time she'd ever piloted one of the temperamental *Marauder*s except in a simulation.

"Roger, Ghost Four," Alex said. "How's it feel to be the big frog for a change?" He hoped the comment would break her out of the mood she was in, but Caitlin didn't even reply.

"Ghost Two," McCall's voice crackled in his ears. "Ready and waiting, Colonel."

"Seven minutes thirty," the port tower reported dispassionately. "Descent still nominal to profile."

"All units, all units," Alex said. "Review your battle plan one more time. If you've got any questions, this is your last shot at settling them before the bad guys start shooting back."

There was silence on the comm line, and for a moment Alex was afraid something had gone wrong with his hookup. Then he realized that it only meant no one had any questions. The Companions were the Legion's elite. Even if they disagreed with the plan, they weren't the sort to dispute it now . . .

"Anything you want to say, Major McCall?" he asked of the darkness.

"Nae, Colonel. Except I think ye should keep in mind what happened at Innesford."

Alex thought he heard a chuckle on the line, probably Dave Clay. For a moment he couldn't place the reference. Then he remembered, and felt his face redden under the neurohelmet.

It had been a tactical problem for the cadet class a few months earlier, an opposed river crossing against suspected but unconfirmed opposition. As cadet commander, Alex had put his troops in motion: recon 'Mechs to scout out a good crossing point, the cadet fire lance to cover them, his own unit in reserve. Everything had been unfolding with textbook precision until Cadet Mzizi, acting commander of the recon lance for that exercise, had reported in. Though he'd found a spot that looked good, Alex sensed he was unsure of himself and had begun reviewing the plan in detail to make sure Mzizi knew what was expected of him.

Trouble was, Mzizi had stopped everything while listening to the review, and McCall's simulated defenders had turned around and launched a simulated surprise attack that cut the recon 'Mechs into equally simulated ribbons.

Alex swallowed once. The lesson of Innesford had been embarrassing. *Don't talk the plan to death. Just do it.*

But for the next seven minutes he could neither talk nor act. Waiting in the darkness, he turned to the only other thing he could think of to fill the time.

He prayed.

27

"**S**teady . . . steady at the helm, damn you!" Weltall-hauptmann Alvin Lippard of the Free Skye DropShip *Anastasia* gripped the arms of his acceleration couch, furious at the helm officer's inattention. "The eyes of the whole fleet are on us today, Schmidt, so for God's sake pay attention to your board!"

"Aye aye, sir," the unlucky helmsman responded.

Lippard tried to force himself to relax, but he was too nervous. The vanguard position for the occupation force should have been an honor, or so the Weltalladmiral had assured him several times, but Lippard couldn't quite shake the feeling that it was an honor better passed to someone else.

The locals were supposed to have surrendered, and that meant an easy, unopposed landing. But if everything was going so smoothly, why had they waited in orbit so long before finally committing a landing force? And why was the force so small? The *Anastasia,* a *Union* Class DropShip, carried one company of BattleMechs and a pair of fighters. Her consort, the *Leopard* Class *Raven,* was much smaller, with a 'Mech lance and two more aerospace fighters. The extra squadron of fighters assigned to cover their approach was staying at high altitude, and wouldn't be able to support the landing for several minutes if something did go wrong.

Sixteen BattleMechs and a pair of fighter squadrons weren't much to work with, not when there was a reinforced regiment up there in orbit to draw from. It looked suspiciously like General von Bulow was planning to use his force as a sacrificial lamb to try drawing fire from the ground before sending the bulk of his strength into harm's way.

And even if that wasn't the case, Lippard was uncomfortably aware of the attention his ship would be getting from the flagship throughout the operation. One mistake and his career could be over. The atmosphere in the Free Skye military was thick with plots and counterplots, divided loyalties, and zealous political officers seeking out any sign of heresy among the troops. A commander who bollixed an important operation like this one was ripe for a spot on the general's next purge list.

Lippard shifted uncomfortably in his command chair. After nearly twenty years of service in the aerospace arm of the Tenth Skye Rangers, he wasn't about to stand by and watch his career crash and burn. It was bad enough that the Rangers had mutinied en masse against the Federated Commonwealth government. Not seeing any way to oppose the regimental command, he'd gone along with the bulk of the officer corps in supporting the decision. Now he wasn't about to do anything that would make the duke's men mistrust him and turn him into a double outcast with no future at all.

"Give me another sensor scan of the port," he snapped impatiently.

"Aye aye, sir," the sensor technician replied hastily. Everyone on the bridge knew his mood by now, and they were all quick to obey to avoid his anger. "Still no change, sir. One *Union* Class DropShip on the pads, tentatively ideed as the *Europa*. Another *Union,* probably the *Medea,* in a repair berth. They're both powered down, and the one in the yard is showing open hull plating around the drive area. No sign of combat units on the ground, but I can see a block of people, some of them with weapons, formed up outside the administrative building."

"Reception committee," the exec muttered. "A bunch of these damned locals all lined up to beg us to recognize their so-called government."

"Well, the general's orders were pretty specific," Lippard replied absently, studying the descent profile on his monitor. "We'll let Oberst Streiger deal with them. As long as those bastards down there don't do something stupid, everything will work out just fine."

Weltallhauptmann Alvin Lippard found himself wondering if his reassuring words were meant for his bridge crew, or for himself.

"One minute to touchdown."

Alex Carlyle ran his fingers over the control board, activating the 'Mech's main fusion power plant and switching on bank after bank of onboard systems that had been shut down throughout the long morning of waiting. The Free Skye force was committed now. Even if their sensors could penetrate the hangar walls of the Dunkeld spaceport, to pick up the sudden eruption of heat sources and power emissions, it was too late for them to change course. Those ships would have to touch down, no matter what they detected.

The object now was to draw the enemy out.

Outside, Alex knew, a party of technicians were disconnecting the land line hookups so that the four command lance 'Mechs could maneuver. The same thing would be occurring in each of the other ambush sites. By the time the two enemy DropShips were on the ground, the Legion would be ready to strike.

Seeing all his monitor readouts showing green, Alex nodded in satisfaction. Everything was ready, at least on the mechanical side. Whether or not the human side of the equation was up to the confrontation was another matter. That was something that wouldn't become known until the battle was joined.

"Thirty seconds," the tower reported. "Tracking reports four aerospace fighters bearing zero-one-two degrees, range eighty-zero kilometers, angels thirty. They seem to be circling."

Alex bit his lip. Major McCall had told him to expect fighter cover, but it still complicated the battle plan. Those four fighters could spell trouble.

As the seconds crawled by, each one was an eternity of doubt. What right did Alex Carlyle have to lead these men into a battle that was all but hopeless from the outset? He wasn't even half the MechWarrior his father had been in the early days. Besides, shouldn't the man who had brought them all together in the first place be the only one to lead the Gray Death Legion?

"Touchdown," the tower reported. Alex could picture the scramble up there, as the technical team that had been monitoring von Bulow's approach abandoned their posts for the safety of an underground shelter as quickly as they could manage it. In a few moments, as the enemy commanders became aware of the ambush, the tower would no doubt become a major target. The party lined up out on the tarmac in simulation of a reception committee would be scattering, too.

"Right," Alex said on the commlink command channel. "Execute Phase One!"

Sitting in the cockpit of his *Warhammer,* Oberst Wilhelm Streiger watched the 'Mech bay ramp drop away with the same cold indifference he'd felt throughout the approach to the Dunkeld spaceport. Back on Skye where the plans for Glengarry had first been hatched, Streiger had been looking forward to matching arms against the famed Gray Death Legion. The Tenth Skye Rangers didn't boast the reputation of Carlyle's mercenaries, but they were a proud and respectable unit. Their tradition went back over a thousand years, to the days before the discovery of star flight. Today's regiment traced its descent directly to the famous Black Watch of ancient Britain, and the unit remained fiercely proud of that heritage.

A match-up of the old against the new, the pride of a long, distinguished lineage versus the arrogance of a brief but brilliant record. It had been exciting to contemplate the conflict ahead.

Now, it seemed, the Gray Death was incapable of offering even token opposition, at least here in Dunkeld. If they resisted at all, which was doubtful at best, according to the latest briefings Streiger had attended before the landing was finally ordered—it would be a disjointed and haphazard affair. Meanwhile his company of the Tenth would have to be content with rousting whatever rabble might oppose the regiment here at the port. A sad comedown . . .

The ramp hit the ground with a metallic clang audible through his external audio receptors, and Streiger grasped the steering yoke to start his 'Mech out of the belly of the DropShip. His seventy-ton WHM-6R *Warhammer* stalked down the incline onto the tarmac with a slow, measured pace that Streiger thought of as proud and regal. The rest of the company would be issuing from other ports spaced around the perimeter of the DropShip, ready for anything.

At last report, "anything" meant nothing more than listening to some gabbling speeches of welcome from a flock of quaking "dignitaries" assembled to give away their planet to the conquerors.

Streiger paused and checked his video display, puzzled. The so-called "reception committee" should have been just off to his right, between the *Anastasia* and the berth where the *Raven* was slowly settling to the ground. But there was no sign of anyone out there. Strange . . .

"Vanguard One, Anastasia," Lippard's voice crackled in his headset. "There's something going on out there. The locals have dispersed, and we're reading a power surge on board the Gray Death DropShip on the far side of the port. Looks like they're trying a cold start-up on their fusion plant."

"What the hell are they playing at?" Streiger demanded. "They don't seriously think we'd let them take off, do they?"

"Don't ask me, Oberst," Lippard snapped. "Just get your men clear so I can get this bucket aloft. We'll cut them off in the air, and you close in on the ground. Remember the orders. We want to try to capture as many aerospace assets as possible."

"I know the orders," Streiger shot back. Lippard was the kind of fussy old maid Streiger hated most. He was known behind his back as "Mother Hen." Switching commlink channels quickly, Streiger tuned to the company's general channel. "All units, disperse by lances. The DropShip's dusting off."

As he guided his massive war machine out of range of the DropShip's engine wash, Streiger's mind was already racing ahead to formulate the next move. Two DropShips trying to flee the port at the last minute, and a party of local dignitaries scattering before the first 'Mech could descent from the DropShip. . . . There was more going on here than just those isolated events. And far more than Lippard's limited imagination could envision. Perhaps the Gray Death wasn't quite so supine as they'd been led to believe.

Streiger allowed himself a grim smile. This duty might just be worthwhile yet.

"They're taking the bait. Looks like the *Union*'s buttoning up for dust-off, and the 'Mechs on the ground are start-

ing to form up to head for the ships,'' came Lieutenant
Lucci's voice crackling over Alex's commline.

"Roger that, Phantom One," he replied. Lucci's troopers
were serving as the Legion's eyes outside, and her report
made him feel a little better now. So far the invaders were
reacting just the way they'd anticipated.

He switched to the command frequency. "All units, from
Ghost Leader, Phase Two . . . now!"

Outside, the massive hangar doors began to slowly roll
back, the grinding of their machinery overpowered by the
ringing footsteps of four armored BattleMechs starting forward into battle.

Over his command channel, Oberst Streiger heard the
panicked voices of his men. "Multiple targets! Multiple heat
sources becoming visible! Three . . . no, four different
bearings!"

"It's a trap!"

"Clear the channel!" Wilhelm Streiger rasped. "Standard tactical deployment five! Get your butts in gear!"

The babble of excited conversation died, and Streiger's
tactical map showed the company starting to fan out in response to his instructions. Whoever had planned this little
surprise had pulled it off brilliantly. They hadn't caught the
slightest trace of the Gray Death forces in the capital all the
way down from orbit, but now four different hangars had
disgorged hidden defenders. Each of the blips on his monitor represented a fusion power plant, a 'Mech, or an AFV.
Sixteen were showing, with no way to be sure if others
might be lurking out of sight.

They were scattered in a rough arc all around Streiger's
'Mechs, and the Oberst realized in a flash that the encircle-
ment was completed by the Legion's *Union* Class DropShip
on the opposite side of the port. On the ground or in the
air, that ship could direct massive firepower down onto his
troops while the Gray Death blocked a breakout attempt.

A good plan, but as with any good plan, there were holes.
Streiger smiled to himself. He'd taken the measure of the
Legion. Now to counter their thrust.

"Anastasia, this is Vanguard One," he said, switching to
the DropShip's commlink frequency. "Suppress that *Union*
Class ship. We've got a combat situation on our hands down
here."

"But the mission orders—" Lippard came back, sounding unsure of himself.

"Damn the mission orders!" Streiger snapped. "The security of my men comes first!"

The face of the administration building was suddenly scoured by a particle beam that seemed to come out of nowhere. Shards of ferrocrete clanged off the *Warhammer*'s armor from the explosion, and the concentration of raw heat and power left the structure twisted, melting. Streiger cut the commlink without listening to Lippard's arguments and played his fingers across his targeting board, searching for the PPC that had missed him by less than ten meters.

So he *was* going to get his confrontation with the Gray Death, it seemed. The smile still on his face, Streiger found his target and returned fire.

This would be a day to remember, after all . . .

28

"**D**amn it! I missed the bastard!" Caitlin DeVries muttered under her breath. She'd had a clear shot at the big *Warhammer* that had to be the enemy command 'Mech, but her PPC beam had gone wide. The *Marauder* was reputed to be one of the finest BattleMechs in the entire Successor State arsenal, but she was finding the controls hard to manage after the easy responsiveness of her *Centurion*.

Caitlin started to line up a second shot with her left-hand PPC when the *Warhammer* opened up. A PPC beam washed across the *Marauder*'s left leg, and a second particle beam impacted against the wall of the hangar behind her. As her *Marauder* lurched back under the impact of the hit, a pair of lasers scored hits on the machine's chest armor, followed by a volley of short-range missiles raining down on her position a moment later.

Caitlin muttered another curse. That *Warhammer* pilot was going for broke, firing off his full arsenal in a single massive attack. It took guts to fight like that, risking a rapid heat build-up in order to saturate an opponent's defenses.

She checked the computer's damage board. Laser and missile hits and flying debris from the near-miss behind her had left the *Marauder*'s chest and back armor and one arm-mounted PPC pockmarked with half a dozen small, shallow pits, but none was particularly threatening. The enemy PPC had caused the worst damage, scoring away armor in a wide crater on the 'Mech's leg just above the knee joint. It hadn't penetrated, but another hit or two in the same area was likely to take out the whole leg and leave the *Marauder* helpless.

Stepping sideways awkwardly, she started retargeting frantically. The *Warhammer* was slightly lighter than her *Marauder*, but just about equal in armaments. And that pilot was no cadet. He knew his business, all right.

"Ghost Four," she said, trying to keep her voice even. "I need help. That *Warhammer*'s out for my blood."

Even before she could finish reprogramming her firing controls, the *Warhammer* cut loose again.

"Ghost Three, this is Leader," Alex Carlyle said through clenched teeth. "Give Caitlin a hand! That *Warhammer*'s too much for her to tackle on her own!"

"Roger, Leader," Davis Clay came back. "I'm on it!"

Alex had to fight down the impulse to focus on the fight between the *Marauder* and the *Warhammer*. Much as he wanted to back up Caitlin DeVries, that wasn't his role now. The battle plan required that his *Archer* do more important work than merely slugging it out toe-to-toe with the enemy on the ground.

He switched to the special-purpose commlink channel that had been set aside for the 'Mechs and tanks tasked for special duty. "This is Ghost Leader," he said. "Commence Operation Skysweep . . . now!"

Alex was feeding instructions into his targeting computer even as he spoke. Operation Skysweep was designed to discourage the Free Skye DropShips lifting clear of the port from lending anything more than moral support to the troops on the ground. McCall had suggested it first, and the plan was as simple and elegant as any really good one had to be. Most commanders regarded DropShips as their most important assets, preferring to keep them out of danger unless absolutely necessary. So Skysweep called for the Legion elements equipped with long-range missile batteries to focus all their attention on the enemy ships until they decided that the battlefield was too unhealthy a place for their craft.

But they couldn't afford to spend too much time on the two DropShips. Not with a reinforced company of 'Mechs on the ground.

"Targeting," he announced. "Nolans, Hansen, you stick with the *Leopard* until McCall or I say differently."

"Locking on now," MechWarrior Sergeant Rachel Nolans responded. Her *Cataphract* and Paul Hansen's *Dervish* were part of Denniken's fire lance, and both were well-suited to the role of engaging the smaller DropShip. The probability of doing serious damage to either ship was low, but repeated bombardments by missile salvos would make any ship captain nervous.

"Commencing fire," Hansen added a moment later. Then, "Missiles away!" Alex saw the swirling trails leaping skyward from the fire lance position off to his right.

"Captain Radcliffe, concentrate on the *Union*." Radcliffe's tank platoon included a trio of Harasser missile platforms, two fitted out with SRM launchers, the third mounting a heavier LRM system. Although they lacked the punch of the fire-support 'Mechs, the hover tanks had the advantage of being fast and maneuverable. They could get in close, take their shots, and withdraw again quickly before the DropShip gunners could react—or at least that was the plan. Combined with sustained fire from Carlyle's *Archer,* they would certainly make the crew of the *Union* Class notice the Legion.

Alex waited for the targeting cross hairs to flash red, then hit the firing studs for both missile racks in quick succession. The *Archer* staggered under the multiple recoil of forty missiles streaking from the tubes.

Slow and stately, the DropShip was lifting off, but it gathered speed as it rose from the tarmac like some impossible prehistoric flying beast disturbed from an age-long slumber. There was a rippling of explosions near the underside of the spherical vessel as some of Alex's missiles found their mark, but he didn't even bother with the BDA readouts. He knew the attack wouldn't cause enough damage to penetrate the thick armor. Not yet.

While waiting for the green lights on his board to register the end of the automated reloading cycle, Alex was struck by another thought. He switched to the private channel that linked him to McCall. "Major," he began, feeling foolish and worried all at once. "Are you tracking those fighters the tower reported?"

"They're nae on my screen yet, laddie," McCall replied. "But I'm aye watching for them. When things get hot doon here ye can bank on yon bastards tae call them in tae cover their asses." The major paused, then went on. "You tend tae the business at hand, young Alex. I'll watch the skies."

Alex glanced left out of the cockpit, his eyes lingering on the towering form of McCall's *Highlander*. It was an old design, mounting a highly accurate Gauss gun with tracking and fire control gear even better than a *Rifleman*'s. They were scarce as hen's teeth in the Successor States even today, having fallen out of use long ago as Star League technology disappeared, but the schematics had been contained with the other data in the Gray Death memory core that McCall had helped Carlyle's father retrieve all those years ago on Helm. The Caledonian hadn't been able to resist the notion of driving such an aptly named 'Mech into battle, and most of his share of Gray Death profits over the years had gone into buying the fighting machine, which he'd named Bannockburn in honor of a famous Scottish victory on ancient Terra. He'd painted it in a tartan color scheme for the Day of Heroes festivities, and there hadn't been time to change it since. Now it stood like a gigantic clansman, weapon mounts slowly traversing back and forth as McCall scanned the skies for the first signs of enemy fighter support.

Alex wrenched his attention back to his own control board. He couldn't afford any distractions now. The battle was at hand.

Half a dozen red lights were showing on Caitlin's board, and a warning klaxon was sounding in her ears. Half-blinded by the sweat dripping into her eyes, she squinted and tried to line up another PPC shot on the *Warhammer*.

Her fist clenched around the trigger on the left-hand side of the throttle, but there was no reaction. Then she saw the red light over the left PPC status monitor, and she cursed. The *Warhammer* had slammed her *Marauder* with two more devastating attacks in quick succession, while she'd gotten off only a single reply. The computer was reporting that her armor was nearly burned through in two places, and the onboard cooling system was failing fast. Now this.

Her one hope of escape was the heat the enemy *Warhammer* had been building up in its savage attacks. No coolant system could handle the full output of so many energy weapons firing in unison, and if the pilot didn't cease fire and let his heat sinks go to work soon he'd be running the risk of a computer-controlled shutdown. If she could just move back behind the shelter of the nearest hangar . . .

Too late! A hulking Free Skye *Crusader* was moving up to support the *Warhammer*. Another sixty-five-ton 'Mech would make short work of her, damaged as the *Marauder* already was.

Still backpedaling awkwardly, trying to compensate for the weakness in the leg actuators damaged by a missile strike on the cratered armor above the right knee joint, Caitlin switched from PPCs to the powerful autocannon mounted above her cockpit. She canceled the computer targeting and traversed the weapon by eye, squeezing off a full cassette of AP rounds in rapid succession.

The enemy *Crusader* stopped as the projectiles raked across its path. One shell slammed into the big 'Mech's arm, and another caught it in the chest.

In that moment, as the enemy pilot was raising a massive arm to bring a battery of LRMs to bear on her, another 'Mech seemed to appear out of nowhere. Fire flamed from twin jump jets as Dave Clay's *Griffin* sailed over the admin building and settled onto the tarmac thirty meters behind the *Crusader*. Caitlin winced as the 'Mech staggered on landing; she knew the ankle joint was supposed to be weak. Clay had taken a hell of a risk using his jump jets now.

But the sudden leap had caught the *Crusader*'s pilot by surprise. Clay kept control of the *Griffin* and brought his PPC to bear. Before the *Crusader* could fire, Clay had lined up his target and opened up.

It was a perfect shot, catching the *Crusader* right in the weakest armor around the rear of the cockpit assembly. Debris spouted high into the air from the force of the blast, and the 'Mech's head seemed to snap forward. For a long moment nothing happened, but then the huge fighting machine swayed and toppled, falling with a crash Caitlin could feel vibrating through the ground under her own *Marauder*'s feet.

Wilhelm Streiger stared at his monitor in disbelief as Leutnant Wellman's *Crusader* fell. That had been an incredible shot . . .

The *Griffin* that had delivered that savage stroke was no match for a *Warhammer* in a stand-up fight. But Streiger's boards still showed his 'Mech's heat above the red line. He couldn't fire again until more of that heat dissipated. Meanwhile he was nothing but a huge target standing here in the open.

Right now his only alternative was to break off. Reluctantly, Streiger turned left and ducked behind the cover of the admin building, shifting to a run to put some distance between his 'Mech and his two opponents. It rankled to turn his back on a fight, but he didn't intend to be gone for long.

"This is Vanguard One," he said over the lance channel. "Croydon, Coleman, form on me. Coordinates Green Five."

When his heat was back to a tolerable level, he'd make sure that neither of those Gray Death 'Mechs survived the rematch.

29

The entire ship seemed to shudder as the *Anastasia* took another barrage of missiles from the spaceport. Wincing as he clutched the arms of his command chair, Weltallhauptmann Lippard glared across at the exec's position.

"Damage report!" he snapped.

"Still no major hits, sir," the DropShip's executive officer responded. "All decks reporting minor damage, mostly from shifting of unsecured objects. 'Mech Bay Three is showing a red light on the external ramp, and we have minor hull penetrations in three locations. Nothing serious . . ."

"Not *yet,*" Lippard shot back.

"More missiles incoming!" the sensor tech reported.

"Weapons officer!" the exec barked. "Can't you return fire yet?"

"Most of the possible targets are still operating too close to our own 'Mechs, sir," the woman at the weapons board responded. "The only ones we could try to hit without risking our own people are some of those hovertanks, and they're moving around too fast for us to get a clear shot."

"We've got to tell Streiger to either get in there and take care of the bastards himself, or to pull back and let us deal with them, sir," the exec told Lippard.

Lippard shook his head. "I'm not sticking around down here any longer," he said. "We're not going to risk the ship just to nail a few 'Mechs. Helm, climb to twenty thousand and hold. Pass the word to the *Raven* to do the same. And launch all fighters. They can get down and dirty with the 'Mechs without risking our boys.''

"Sir, Streiger's counting on us to intercept the enemy DropShip.''

"The fighters can handle that, too,'' Lippard countered angrily. "If that bastard gets high enough that it looks like it might escape, we can go after him then. But I'm not staying down low and taking this pounding. The *Anastasia* wasn't designed for that little game.''

There was a long moment of silence. "Well, don't just sit there,'' Lippard rasped at last. "Execute the orders!''

"I've got a fault showing in the injectors, Skipper!'' reported Ensign Outhwaite to the rest of the DropShip *Europa*'s bridge crew. "Aborting start-up procedure.''

Lieutenant Evan Fowler cursed under his breath but tried to keep from showing his impatience to the rest of the crew. A cold start on a fusion reactor was one of the most difficult tasks a shipmaster had to face, and it was no fault of Outhwaite's if the systems balked. There were some things even the best engine tech couldn't control.

But that didn't make the delay any easier to accept. The timing of the whole Gray Death operation around the Dunkeld starport depended on getting the Legion's sole spaceworthy DropShip aloft while the invaders were still reacting to the changing situation around them. He would have been happier if they could have moved the *Europa* away from the port long before the arrival of the enemy armada, but he'd been overruled in the war council. Crippling the Legion's aerospace assets was almost certain to be von Bulow's top priority, and the ambush plan depended on having the DropShip in plain sight from orbit, bait to encourage von Bulow to commit his forces to a landing.

But at the same time, the *Europa* was far too valuable to simply abandon. The DropShip still had an important part to play—if they could get her off the ground before the enemy started to turn their attention her way.

Fowler checked his tactical monitor. Both enemy DropShips were starting to climb away fast. The Gray Death battle plan had originally intended to force the withdrawal of the enemy vessels to create an opportunity for the *Europa* to make her big move. Now, obviously, they were falling behind schedule fast. The DropShip couldn't lift until the fusion plant was on-line . . .

Fowler knew the old military axiom only too well: No battle plan survives contact with the enemy. He hoped Alex Carlyle and his staff would be flexible enough to respond to the breakdown of this plan before everything came unglued.

The alternative was disaster, pure and simple.

"Signal Command that we're still stuck on the ground," Fowler ordered quietly. "And re-initiate start-up sequence."

"Have to clear the injectors first," the engineer responded, sounding distracted. "Two minutes . . ."

"Make it one," Fowler told him.

Outhwaite gave him a grim nod.

"The *Europa* reports she's still on the ground," Alex Carlyle told McCall over the private commlink channel. "The cold start's taking longer than it was supposed to. If we don't get her up soon . . ."

"Aye," McCall said. " 'Twill nae be a pretty sight. And we hae more problems, too, laddie. The escort fighters are on my screens and closing fast, and I think the enemy DropShips are opening their fighter bay doors for a launch as weil."

"We can't let them get in here with those fighters," Alex said grimly. "We've got to go straight to Phase Five."

"Aye," the Caledonian repeated. "Even if it means sacrificing Fowler . . ."

Alex swallowed hard. This was still the worst part of the commander's role as far as he was concerned. Any decision he made could result in his people dying.

But it had to be done. Fowler's *Europa* might still win through, even if they accelerated the rest of the battle plan before the DropShip was off the ground and ready for action. On the other hand, if those enemy fighters got in among the defenders at the port, 'Mechs and men would certainly be lost.

"Right," he said at last, trying not to betray the tightness in his throat. "You're still on overwatch, Major. Do what you can against those fighters." He switched channels without waiting for a response. "All units, all units, this is Ghost Leader. New orders. Go to Phase Five and execute as planned. Repeat, execute Phase Five . . . now. Europa, lift when ready, but go to Phase Five *now*. Do you understand?''

Lieutenant Fowler's voice came back. "Understood, Leader," he said gruffly. "Hope you know what the hell you're doing . . .''

So do I, Alex thought grimly. So do I.

Captain Julio Vargas ran his eyes over his cockpit readouts one last time before keying in his commlink. "This is Dragon Leader," he said. "Ready to launch."

"Roger that, Dragon Leader," the voice of the *Europa*'s flight controller came back. The man sounded tense. He had every reason to be. "Transferring battery power to Launch Control."

"Dragon Leader," Vargas responded, reaching out to flip the line of switches that would power up the engines of his aerospace fighter. "Initiating launch sequence. *Now*."

He cut the commlink and muttered a short prayer. Vargas wasn't ordinarily a religious man, but this launch was no ordinary mission. Not anymore, not since young Carlyle's orders to skip ahead to Phase Five.

The original battle plan had called for keeping the Legion's fighter assets under cover until Phase Four, when the *Europa* lifted off. The fighters were supposed to support the DropShip, keeping enemy fighters and DropShips busy while Fowler carried out his part of the operation. In Phase Five, with the DropShip's role accomplished, the fighters were supposed to mix it up more generally, providing air cover or ground support as needed. Now they were going straight into general combat action immediately, before the DropShip was up.

The difference between running interference for Fowler or plunging into the thick of the battle wasn't the part that worried Vargas. It was the launch procedure itself. He and his wingman had loaded their *Slayer* aerospace fighters aboard the *Europa* before the Free Skye armada had shown up in orbit. According to the orderly progression of the original battle plan they would have launched after takeoff to give the DropShip the kind of close support it was likely to need, while the other four fighters in the Legion's tiny arsenal took off from a concealed hangar at Castle Hill to link up a few minutes later.

Instead they were now taking off while the DropShip was

still on the ground, and that was dangerous. The eighty-ton
Slayer was designed for staying power, not maneuverability, and it would take skillful handling for the two Legion
pilots to clear the buildings beyond the port compound after
their high-speed catapult launch.

It was exactly the kind of situation Vargas dreaded most.
Yes, he projected the image of the classic daredevil fighter
pilot to his comrades in arms, and in any normal combat
situation he could put aside all doubts or fears and bury
himself in the moment-to-moment needs of combat flying.
But as seconds ticked away on the automated countdown
sequence, all he could do was sit in the cockpit and think
of everything that might go wrong.

Vargas didn't fear death. Any fighter pilot quickly came
to accept the idea that each battle might be his last. But
Julio Vargas had a morbid dread of injury, a serious, disfig-
uring injury that might leave him something less than what
he was. Of course, modern bionics and plastic surgery techniques were supposed to be able to erase almost any wound,
but the thought of living out his life with artificial limbs
or pseudo-organic skin was repugnant. Men like Davis
McCall, with bionic limbs or organs, made him nervous.
To be that way himself . . .

And a crash on takeoff was just the sort of accident that
might leave Vargas alive but crippled.

Light flooded into the fighter bay as the two airlock doors
of the launch tube rolled back. The seconds continued their
inexorable march down to zero . . .

Then acceleration slammed Vargas back into his seat.
Flung outward by the launch catapult, the *Slayer* hurtled
into open air, and the computer automatically cut in the
fighter's thrusters. Vargas hauled back on his control stick
and pressed the throttles full forward. The gee-force tore at
him despite his protective gear, but the fighter's nose came
up, up, up, the *Slayer* rocketing over the closest building,
gaining altitude fast.

His sensor board lit up with targeting traces, all hostile,
closing fast, but Vargas let out a sigh of relief nonetheless.
These were dangers he could handle with scarcely a second
thought.

"Dragon Leader, good shot, good shot," he announced.
"Dragon Two, cleared for launch. Get up here and join the
fun, Danny-boy!"

"Launch sequence initiated," Ensign Daniel McMasters, his wingman, responded. Though the younger pilot's voice quavered a little, McMasters sounded almost eager to join his companion.

Vargas turned to port as his computer identified a hostile fighter launching from the Free Skye *Leopard*. He thumbed the weapons selector switch to autocannon and waited for the computer to lock on the target. The cross hairs drifted across his HUD until they centered on the fast-moving image of the lightweight enemy *Sparrowhawk*. As they flashed red, Vargas tightened his finger on the firing stud and the autocannon barked.

Shots stitched across the *Sparrowhawk*'s wing as the enemy pilot tried to roll left and up. Vargas followed the maneuver with the cannon still blazing. Suddenly the wing started to shred, and the Free Skye fighter spun away out of control. Vargas saw the pilot punch out, his chute opening seconds after the *Sparrowhawk* had plunged into a warehouse on the banks of the Earn where it meandered through the center of Dunkeld. The explosion sent fire and smoke billowing up from the heart of the Glengarry capital.

"One for the Dragonslayer!" Vargas whooped over the commlink. He'd bestowed the name on his fighter years ago, during the last Legion campaign against House Kurita. "Come on, Danny-boy, if you want a piece of the glory!"

"Launching now!" McMasters replied. There was a moment of silence.

Then the flight controller's voice cut in from the bridge of the *Europa*. "Pull up, Dragon Two! You're too low! Pull up—"

Then a scream drowned out the words, followed by utter silence.

Vargas shuddered. He knew what had happened even before the flight controller's shaken report. "Dragon Two . . . didn't clear the buildings."

He tried to blank out the horror that went with the thought that McMasters' fate might so easily might have been his own. More targets were on his screen. What he had to do right now was deal with them . . .

Alex Carlyle studied his 'Mech's tactical display with a frown. The carefully timed battle plan he and McCall had patched together over the past days had taken less than ten minutes to begin falling apart, and now it looked as if the Legion was in danger of losing everything.

The problem with the *Europa*'s power plant was only a tiny part of it. From the looks of things, the Steiner commander hadn't been caught off guard as much as they'd hoped, or else he'd managed an especially skillful recovery. Instead of falling back from the ambush toward a hole left by the *Europa*'s lifting off, the opposition had evidently considered the DropShip's weapons to be the greater threat and had concentrated on holding the line against the Gray Death 'Mechs. And with nearly half the Legion force committed to the Skysweep portion of the plan, that had given the invaders a substantial numerical superiority on the ground.

Somehow Caitlin and Davis Clay had managed to destroy a Free Skye *Crusader* and forced the other 'Mechs of what had tentatively been identified as the enemy command lance to draw back, but that wasn't likely to continue much longer. Denniken's *Cataphract* and the *Shadow Hawk* belonging to his lance mate, MechWarrior Lowdowski, were holding their own—barely—in an uneven matchup against three Free Skye 'Mechs, another *Crusader,* a *Rifleman,* and a *JagerMech.* Accordingly to the battle map another enemy 'Mech in the same area, an *Archer* like Alex's, had retreated a hundred meters behind the others and was now standing in the shadow of a hangar, apparently preparing to engage with long-range weapons in support of the rest of the Free Skye company.

Off to the extreme left of the crescent-shaped battle front, near the main gate of the Dunkeld spaceport complex, four more enemy 'Mechs were advancing fast. Opposing them were Freida Bergstrom's recon 'Mechs, but the disparity in sizes put the Legion at a sharp disadvantage. One of Radcliffe's tanks, a Pegasus, was trying to lend its aid to Bergstrom's leap-frogging retreat, but there wasn't that much it could do. The recon lance could delay the enemy, but it wouldn't be able to stop them. And if the fighting went on much longer Bergstrom's 'Mechs would start taking unacceptable damage.

On top of it all, there were still four Free Skye 'Mechs off the *Leopard,* which so far had not taken part in the fighting. They'd touched down well back from the battlefield and started off toward the *Europa*'s landing berth, but partway through the fighting had turned, evidently in response to instructions from the enemy commander, and were about to join in. Their weight would be decisive wherever they hit Alex's thin line. And the enemy fighters hadn't added their authority to the battle yet, either.

Alex cursed under his breath as he studied the display. He'd gambled with the lives of his father's best soldiers, and it looked as if he'd already lost. If they didn't get the plan back on track soon, it would all be over. The other Legion outfits would be destroyed piecemeal unless they recognized the hopelessness of their situation and surrendered first.

"Ghost Leader, this is Europa," came Fowler's voice interrupting Alex as he wrestled mentally with the problem of shoring up the failing defensive perimeter. "We have engine start. Lifting off now."

"I copy that, Europa," he replied. It wasn't much to set against all the problems, but Alex could hardly restrain himself from cheering. "Follow the plan. You won't have the fighters, but do your best."

"Affirmative, Ghost Leader. We'll make it."

The blip that marked the DropShip on his monitor changed from green to blue to indicate that the vessel was now airborne, and the tiny symbols alongside it started changing rapidly as the *Europa* gained altitude and speed. The ship was moving southeast, over the city of Dunkeld and across the River Earn, leaving the battlefield far behind. In moments it was no longer visible on Alex's screens.

Whether it could elude enemy pursuit as easily remained to be seen . . .

Meanwhile, Alex Carlyle had a battle to fight. With the *Europa* now out of the picture there was a chance, just a chance, that they could still force the Free Skye troops back far enough to switch over to Phase Six—the final phase of the plan.

He keyed the channel reserved for the units tasked for Skysweep. "This is Ghost Leader," he said, his mind racing ahead as he framed the words. "The *Europa*'s off. I think we can still persuade the bad guys they're outclassed if we concentrate our fire target by target. A couple of saturation attacks might make the difference."

"Aye, that's a bonnie notion," McCall said. "They'll nae want that kind of attention for long."

Heartened by the major's support, Alex went on. "All LRMs to concentrate on one target." His fingers danced over his targeting computer, calling up the coordinates of the cluster of 'Mechs he thought belonged to the enemy command. "I'm feeding the data through the net now. Execute on my command."

He finished punching in the firing program for his own weaponry, then hesitated, his finger poised above the firing stud.

This was a last-ditch effort, Alex knew that. What he didn't know was if it would work.

30

Oberst Wilhelm Streiger checked the heat levels on his
Warhammer and gave a thin smile. The cooling system had
finally done its job, and the 'Mech was ready to re-engage.
This time, he was sure, the results would be decisive. His
tactical map showed the enemy falling back to the left and
right of the Dunkeld spaceport, and Major MacLeod's fresh
'Mech lance was moving up to join the fight. When the
fighters arrived, the Tenth could give the Gray Death a
knockout punch.

"Vanguard One, this is *Anastasia*," Lippard broke in
from the DropShip. "The Legion DropShip has lifted off."

Streiger rechecked his monitor quickly. With the ship
showing every sign of having problems with the cold-start
process, he'd put it out of his mind as a major factor. A
DropShip without fusion power couldn't use energy weapons at all, and it would take most of the ship's battery power
to use missiles. He had just about discounted it as a potential force in the battle.

Now it was powered up, and that might mean trouble.

But the DropShip was already moving off his monitor,
heading southeast and gaining speed and altitude fast. Apparently its crew had decided to abandon a hopeless fight
instead of staying around to support their comrades on the
ground. So much for the vaunted Gray Death comaraderie.

"*Anastasia*, can you intercept him?" Streiger asked. "We
don't want to lose that ship if we can help it."

"It would be chancy unless we sent some of the fighters

after them,'' Lippard replied. "He's got the same speed we do, and he's headed toward mountain country. I imagine Carlyle's pilots know the ground a hell of a lot better than we do, and I don't intend to play follow-the-leader through mountains in a DropShip.''

Streiger hesitated a long moment. The landing-force fighters could catch and probably bring down the ship, but he wanted those fighters here to support his 'Mechs. He could order up more fighters from the armada, of course, but he didn't know if von Bulow would be willing to grant the assistance. The general had used the landing force to spring a trap, and he wasn't likely to throw more troops into it now.

He let out a breath. "No, we want the fighters here, where the real danger is. That DropShip doesn't have anywhere off-planet to go. Track his movements, and we'll follow up on it later.''

Lippard's relieved sigh was audible. "Understood, Vanguard One. We'll keep an eye on the bastard. Anastasia out.''

Streiger turned his attention back to his immediate surroundings. "All right, kids, let's show them what the Black Watch can do!'' he said over the lance channel.

His *Warhammer* began lumbering forward, back toward the site of the earlier fighting. On his map he saw that neither of the Gray Death 'Mechs from the earlier encounter had moved far since he'd broken off. Now that Streiger had Croydon's *Thunderbolt* and Coleman's *Griffin* with him, the Legion 'Mechs wouldn't be able to hold out for long . . .

"Incoming! Incoming!'' Croydon shouted, her voice suddenly sharp and urgent over the commlink. "Multiple missiles incoming!''

And then the sky fell in on Wilhelm Streiger.

"That's our cue,'' Davis Clay shouted as the missiles stretched toward the enemy *Warhammer*. The sheer exhilaration of combat had washed away his doubts and fears, and all that was left was the desire to wade in among the enemy and fight. "You with me, Caitlin?''

"If the old girl'll get me there,'' Caitlin DeVries responded. "Lead on, MacDuff . . .''

"And cursed be he who first cries hold . . .''

"Enough!'' Caitlin joined in on the last word.

Clay considered using his jump jets again, then quickly rejected the idea. He'd been lucky that his earlier maneuver hadn't shattered the weakened ankle joint, and it would be tempting fate to try it a second time. The leap behind the *Crusader* had been his only option when Caitlin had called for help, but now he had to be more careful, instead of jumping, he steered to join the *Marauder* in moving alongside the admin building to follow the enemy 'Mech that had broken off earlier. Alex's new firing plan had targeted the *Warhammer* and his two companions, and Clay and Caitlin were perfectly placed to exploit that devastating barrage of LRMs.

They rounded the corner just as a salvo of missiles dropped among the three Free Skye BattleMechs. Blast after blast went off all around them, and Clay saw shards of armor whirling away from the right-hand BattleMech, a *Thunderbolt*. He stopped his *Griffin* where it stood and raised the PPC clutched in the 'Mech's right fist. With his other hand he quickly programmed his own missile salvo to add to the fury falling on the enemy from the unseen 'Mechs of the Legion's long-range strike force.

Somehow the *Thunderbolt* pilot managed to get off the first shot, but the laser beam barely grazed the *Griffin*'s right arm near the shoulder. The momentary contact caused armor to melt and slough, but in the next instant Clay was returning fire with far more devastating effect. The PPC caught the *Thunderbolt* square in the chest, and the 'Mech staggered back under the force of the particle-beam explosion.

But the chest armor was too thick to penetrate, even with the damage the enemy machine had already suffered from the falling missiles. Clay cursed, and kept cursing as his missiles went wild and detonated harmlessly fifty meters beyond his target.

Now the enemy *Warhammer* was stalking forward, slow, ponderous, its built-in PPC arms swinging up to draw a bead on Clay's *Griffin*. He took a step back, then realized the nearest cover was too far away to reach in time. He'd have to use his jump jets again . . .

Twin hammers of raw power slammed into the *Warhammer* just as Clay was reaching for the jump jet controls, and the bigger 'Mech never fired. Clay watched, stunned into immobility for an instant as Caitlin's *Marauder* strode past him, both PPCs firing again. The heat cost would be ruinous, especially with some of her coolant systems already damaged in the earlier encounter with the *Warhammer,* but she kept advancing nonetheless.

The *Warhammer* backed away, leaving one PPC tube lying on the ground. Caitlin's massive firepower had melted right through the weakest part of the elbow joint, and the damaged arm was trailing myomer fibers, wiring, and random sparks.

Clay snapped out of the spell that had frozen him and retargeted on the *Warhammer* himself, letting off another PPC round that scored a deep hit in the bigger 'Mech's chest armor.

"My heat's past the red line," Caitlin reported grimly. "But if we back off now we'll be flapping in the breeze."

"Yeah," Clay grunted, firing again, this time at the enemy *Griffin* that was running forward to the support of its damaged consort. The beam missed, but in that moment another missile strike landed among the three hostile 'Mechs. The *Griffin* held its ground and snapped off a shot that caught Caitlin's *Marauder* in the chest, but the other two had obviously had enough. They turned and headed away from the Gray Death 'Mechs at a run, leaving their comrade to fight as rear guard.

When Clay and Caitlin started forward together as if to challenge the *Griffin* pilot to close combat, he triggered his jump jets and bounded back, getting off one last parting shot before all three enemy 'Mechs disappeared beyond the shelter of a blast berm.

Clay didn't choose to pursue.

At Dunkeld spaceport's main gate, Lieutenant Darlene Lucci held her hand up as the tall, angular shape of the fifty-ton *Enforcer* strode across the compound, its autocannon blazing away at Lieutenant Bergstrom's retreating *Valkyrie* just outside the perimeter fence. Behind her, the other members of First Squad waited, silent, motionless, almost invisible amid the rubble of the gatehouse. This was just the kind of work the Gray Death's elite armored infantry trained for, in the tradition that had made Grayson Carlyle a legend before his mercenaries had even owned a single BattleMech.

The *Enforcer* rushed forward as Bergstrom headed for the cover of a warehouse in the industrial park that butted up against the port. The pilot was clearly determined to catch up with the last of the recon lance BattleMechs before Bergstrom, like her three subordinates, vanished into the city.

If he noticed the three infantry troopers by the gate at all, the *Enforcer* pilot obviously didn't regard them as any threat to the mountain of metal that surrounded him. A typical 'Mech jock, Lucci told herself with a grim smile. They never thought much about the infantry.

Bergstrom's *Valkyrie* paused in its flight and let off a volley of missiles. They overshot by a good two hundred meters, which wasn't usual for the recon lance's commanding officer. She'd practiced this sort of fighting in conjunction with the armored infantry before, shooting wide on purpose to keep from jeopardizing Lucci's troops as they prepared to go into action.

But her shots served their purpose. The *Enforcer* pilot, seeing his chance, stopped his headlong rush as he tried to bring his deadly autocannon to bear. As he did so, Lucci brought her upraised hand down in a short, sharp chopping motion. "Now!" she shouted over the commlink, and instantly the two troopers followed her out of the rubble in a sprint across the open tarmac toward the enemy 'Mech.

Individual men, even men wearing combat armor, looked pitifully small and helpless in the shadow of a BattleMech, but looks could be deceiving. As she ran, Lucci triggered the jump pack on her back and jumped. The rocket-assisted leap left her clinging to the side of the *Enforcer*'s right leg, and in a few swift, well-practiced motions she attached the demo charge to the 'Mech's vulnerable knee joint, then let go, using her jump pack again to bound clear of the action. The other two troopers went through the same drill, Olsen planting his charge on the right leg opposite hers, while Tjore set his on the left knee.

The enemy pilot must have realized the danger by then, but it was too late. A light laser stabbed toward the infantry as they scattered, barely missing Lucci. Then the charges detonated.

Tjore's went off first, not seeming to do much damage. Then the two on the right leg went off almost as one, and as Lucci ducked behind a half-ruined wall she could see the *Enforcer* staggering. The kneecapping charges didn't leave much outward sign of damage, but they could wreck the workings of a BattleMech's joints when properly placed.

The *Enforcer* took a tentative step forward, swayed, and paused. Clearly the pilot was having trouble making the leg work properly. He'd be trying to realign the actuator circuitry, trying to find a quick fix that would let the 'Mech move freely again. Without mobility, BattleMechs were nothing but massive, heavily armed targets . . .

The pilot was so busy he didn't see Bergstrom's *Valkyrie* and Ryoo's *Javelin* leaping over the fence to land less than twenty meters away. The two light 'Mechs opened fire with everything they had at close range, and in a matter of seconds the *Enforcer* was riddled with a dozen major hits. Lucci saw the pilot punch out just before the autocannon's magazine blew. She didn't even need to give the orders for Tjore and Olsen to close in and disarm him before he could get disentangled from his escape chute.

"Thanks for the assist." Bergstrom's even voice in her suit headphones didn't betray a hint of emotion. "Let's move right and see if we can help Lewis next. You game for it?"

Lucci smiled and waved. "Bring 'em on," she said.

Some day, maybe, 'Mech jocks would learn not to take the mudfeet so lightly . . .

Julio Vargas pulled back sharply on his joystick and pushed forward on the *Slayer*'s throttles. Gee-forces pressed Vargas back into his seat as the fighter angled skyward. His situation board showed two of the five enemy fighters, a pair of thirty-ton *Sparrowhawks*, pursuing him while the other three turned back toward the fighting on the ground.

Vargas muttered an oath under his breath. He'd hoped they'd see him as more of a threat, at least send the heavier *Lucifer*s after him.

But Vargas was a card player, and he always did his best with the hand he was dealt.

He set up a random evasion program on the flight computer and turned his full attention to the weapons board. The *Slayer* mounted a single rear-facing laser among its other armaments, and Vargas let the autopilot do the flying while he worked to line up the cross hairs for a clear shot. His fighter was weaving back and forth under the computer's guidance, but the target lock system compensated automatically for the evasive pattern. All he had to worry about was whatever his two opponents might be doing to dodge his fire—at least until their own computers matched up the *Slay-*

er's programmed maneuvering with something they could recognize and predict.

Captain Julio Vargas didn't plan to give them that much of a chance.

One of the *Sparrowhawk* pilots was pulling ahead of his comrade. Vargas brought the cross hairs down onto the image of the fighter on his rear monitor. It flashed red as the targeting computer locked on, and Vargas tightened his finger on the firing stud.

The rear laser flashed, catching the *Sparrowhawk* dead center across the cockpit. In one smooth motion, Vargas overrode the autopilot and pulled the *Slayer* into an overhead loop. His left hand danced over the weapons controls, setting up his forward-facing weaponry to fire simultaneously when he next pressed the joystick trigger.

The *Sparrowhawk* loomed large up ahead, banking left and down as the pilot reacted to the hit that had burned a deep, jagged gouge in his cockpit armor. The evasive maneuver was blocking the second *Sparrowhawk* from seeing exactly what was going on, and that gave Vargas the perfect opening.

His hand tightened around the trigger as the HUD cross hairs were turning red, and five lasers lanced out as one. The heavy autocannon in the nose chattered, adding a full cassette of high-explosive shells to the havoc erupting around the enemy fighter.

Vargas pushed the nose down, diving steeply under the *Sparrowhawk* as it blossomed into a fireball and came apart. Most pilots would expect an enemy to climb over an exploding aircraft, and that was exactly what Vargas was counting on.

He grinned under his flight helmet as a pair of laser bolts ionized the air above the collapsing fireball. The second *Sparrowhawk*'s pilot had tried to anticipate him, firing without even waiting for a lock. A few shards of burning debris rattled off the *Slayer*'s fuselage and wings, but otherwise he was undamaged . . . and diving straight under the surprised enemy.

The *Sparrowhawk* started a belated turn to chase him, but Vargas pushed the throttles even further forward, pulled out of the dive, and banked sharply right. Seconds later he was squarely on the *Sparrowhawk*'s tail.

It took three shots before enough lasers penetrated the

armored tail and started melting through engine circuitry and control surfaces. The Free Skye pilot punched out as his fighter came apart around him.

"Whoa, there, Dragonslayer!" a familiar voice crackled through Vargas' headphones. Lieutenant Joseph Diskin sounded like he was running on pure adrenaline. "Save a little bit of that action for your buddies, skipper!"

"It's about time you slackers showed up!" Vargas shot back. The other four fighters had finally made it, and that made the odds look a whole lot better all of a sudden. "Let's get down there and bag us some bad guys!"

"Right with you, Captain," Lieutenant Gillian Lockhart chimed in. "Let's party!"

Vargas fell in with the loose diamond formation and turned toward the port. Lockhart spoke for all of them. It was time to party . . . and the invaders were the guests of honor.

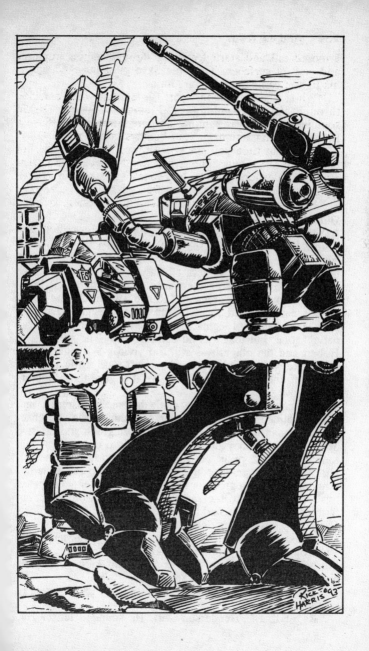

=31=

"**F**ighters closing, fighters closing," Weltalleutnant Sean Ferguson said, chanting the warning like a mantra. "Bearing three-four-two degrees . . . Range fifteen, closing . . ."

"I see them, Red Leader," answered Reggie "Lancer" Peck, his voice cool, calm. It reminded Ferguson of Hobart's patient tone, but that was no comfort now. The memory of Hobart and the others was still too vivid. "All right, boys, looks like we don't play ground support for a while after all. Break off and get some altitude. We'll engage those fighters from above."

"Understood." Ferguson made his reply absently, and barely noticed Chevalier Henderson echoing the response. Weltalleutnant Peck had watched his wingman and the two *Sparrowhawks* from the *Raven go* down to the guns of that lone Gray Death pilot, but it didn't seem to faze him at all. His thoughts seemed focused entirely on the job at hand, with no time for regret, for doubt . . . or for fear. Ferguson wished he could do the same, but his guts were churning with emotion and he had to make an effort to follow Peck's *Lucifer* up toward the clouds.

"Troika attack pattern," Peck announced a moment later. "I'm on the point. You two rookies give me cover, or I'll personally climb out of this cockpit and kick your butts while we're still in the air. You got it?"

"Troika pattern," Ferguson answered. "Chevalier, you're on the right."

"Roger that," Henderson said. He sounded tense. He,

too, was probably picturing those last moments before the Gray Death JumpShip had taken out Hobart and the others.

The three fighters settled into the loose triangular wedge and started a long, shallow dive toward the enemy fighters. Ferguson double-checked with his weapons board and muttered a prayer he hadn't used since childhood.

War to the knife. It was a fine phrase but didn't convey anything of the fear, the brutality, of combat.

"Heads up!" Peck shouted over the commlink. "Here they come!"

A pair of *Corsair*s led the enemy squadron, long, needle-sharp, like two daggers pointed straight at the Free Skye wedge. Each one carried a pair of heavy lasers in nose mounts, with several lighter lasers backing up the two main weapons. They weren't as large or as well-armored as the three Free Sky *Lucifer*,s but their pilots showed no signs of fear as the distance closed between the two formations.

Both *Corsair*s focused all their firepower on Peck's craft, and as they flashed past, Ferguson unloaded most of his weaponry at the right-hand fighter. His BDA sensors reported several hits on his target, but nothing crippling. He fought back the urge to break formation and go in pursuit. The troika attack pattern was designed to provide mutual support and concentrated firepower, and breaking up the wedge at this point could leave Peck and Henderson in trouble.

But Henderson was evidently letting his enthusiasm override his common sense. The third *Lucifer* was already pulling away from the wedge and turning in pursuit of the *Corsair* that had just shot past him.

"Red Two! Red Two! Get back in formation!" Peck shouted.

"Chevalier!" Ferguson added his voice to the call. "Not yet! Troika pattern!"

Henderson didn't reply. He already had his hands full with two Gray Death *Sparrowhawk*s that had spotted his move and sheered off to concentrate their attention on him.

"He's under attack, Leutnant," Ferguson said. "We've got to support him . . ."

"Too late!" Peck shot back. "I'm taking fire from the *Slayer*. Give me a hand, Shadowcat. That first pass screwed up my targeting computer!"

"Shadowcat! Shadowcat! Christ, Sean, they're all over

me!'' That was Henderson, his voice wild. ''Can't fight all of them off!''

Ferguson hesitated for an instant. Peck's opponent was the heavy *Corsair* that had already taken out three of their fighters. With his targeting computer off-line, Peck would have to fire blind, trusting to instinct and training to get him any hits. And Peck was his superior officer and had given Ferguson a direct order to support him.

But Henderson was up against the two *Sparrowhawks* and the *Corsair* he'd been chasing, with the second *Corsair* still unaccounted for. Henderson, his wingman . . . his friend since college . . .

He jerked the joystick hard over. ''Hang in their, Chevalier!'' he said. ''I'm on the way!''

''Red Leader, Red Leader, get your ass back here!'' Peck ordered harshly. ''I need assistance—''

Static crashed over the commlink, and Peck was gone. Ferguson's sensors showed the fireball where Peck had been a moment before, and the *Slayer* and one of the *Corsairs* rising triumphantly through the shower of debris. Peck was gone . . .

And Ferguson was in command now.

''Chevalier!'' he shouted. ''Chevalier! Break off the action, Chevalier! Return to base!''

Sean Ferguson wasn't going to hang around to let the Gray Death claim any more victories today.

''All units, all units,'' Streiger said harshly over his 'Mech's command frequency. ''Re-form on me. Repeating, all units to re-form on me!''

As he uttered the words Streiger knew the bitter taste of humiliation. He had underestimated the determination of the Gray Death defenders, a cardinal sin in a military leader. They had lived up to their reputation for unpredictability— and for fighting skill—to the fullest, and now the Black Watch vanguard was falling apart.

They had lost at least four 'Mechs, not counting Sokol's *Archer*, which had stopped transmitting but that Mech-Warrior Lawson had seen moving under its own fire a few minutes earlier. Three more, including his own *Warhammer*, were in bad shape. And now the fighter support had broken off, leaving the defenders in control of the skies over the Dunkeld spaceport.

Not that the defenders could be doing very well either

at this point. They had confirmed kills on three Free Skye 'Mechs, and a fourth probable, along with a hovertank and the fighter that had crashed during launch. Some of the other Gray Death machines, like the *Marauder* he'd been playing tag with right from the start, must be hurting by now. The losses didn't match up, but the Gray Death had started with fewer assets and didn't have an entire regimental combat team in orbit overhead to draw on for reinforcements.

And the battle still wasn't over. If the Rangers could just hold out for a little while longer, there was still a chance to turn things around.

Streiger checked his tactical map as he hurried the *Warhammer* toward the center of the port, away from the ragged skirmish line that marked the Gray Death's front. With their DropShip fled—evidently Grayson Carlyle's aerospacers were as unreliable as the ones who'd abandoned Streiger—the Legion no longer had the landing force completely boxed in. What Streiger needed now was some kind of secure cover they could use to keep the fighters and long-range 'Mech weapons from pounding them until Lippard could bring down the *Anastasia* for some serious fire support.

The DropShip captain wouldn't be eager to bring his vessel back into the fight, but he'd do it. Even an old woman like Lippard would know that it was the only way to salvage a victory from this mess now.

Streiger stopped the scrolling map display and allowed himself a tiny smile of triumph. That was the answer—the disabled DropShip still on the field back toward the open side of the enemy crescent. It was big enough to provide shelter for all the Black Watch BattleMechs, and the Gray Death, crazy as they might be, would never deliberately damage something as valuable as a DropShip. Not without a lot of debate and soul-searching first—exactly what would buy Streiger the time to bring in Lippard. "All units, all units," he said, speaking rapidly. "Take up positions around the crippled DropShip at grid coordinates White-six."

Then he switched to the DropShip channel, already mentally rehearsing what he would say to Lippard.

* * *

"They're doing it, Alex!" Davis Clay shouted over the commline.

Alex Carlyle couldn't help but grin in response to the elation in Clay's voice. Finally, the rest of the battle plan was falling into something that resembled what they'd wanted in the first place.

"Don't count your chickens yet," Alex warned. He'd been burned once already. Now he wasn't taking too much for granted.

"My sensors say they're all weil within the zone, laddie," McCall reported. It was a measure of how hard the fight had been these last few minutes that the old weapons master had forgotten to address Alex formally over the open channel. "I dinna think we should wait . . ."

Alex double-checked his own display before answering. "I'm with you, Mac," he said. Someone chuckled, probably Caitlin DeVries, and he realized he'd just called his dour tutor by the nickname even Legion veterans didn't dare to use.

Well, McCall could string him up by his own insides when the battle was over. For now there were more important things to worry about. "This is Ghost Leader," he said slowly. "Execute Operation Petard. Repeat, execute Petard."

Alex could well imagine what must be going through Lieutenant David Longo's mind as he heard those words. The idea had first come from McCall, and King's technicians had been the ones to set up the mechanics, but in the end Longo had been chosen to carry out this last, most crucial phase of the battle because it was such a personal matter for him.

In the underground bunker where the erstwhile port control crew had gathered, Longo's hand would be poised over an improvised red switch, waiting for the command. And now the man's hand would be coming down, but not without a last thought of everything that had gone before, years of service aboard the *Medea,* the ill fortune that the ship should be the one stuck on the pad when the invasion came . . .

Yet at least a man should have the option of shooting his own dog.

Suddenly the ground was rumbling, and a thunderclap like an enormous sonic boom ripped through the port complex. Explosion after explosion was tearing through the crippled DropShip's hydrogen fuel cells, spewing fire and smoke and huge chunks of debris in all directions. And the 'Mechs of the Free Skye landing force were standing right there, right at ground zero. Any that survived the *Medea*'s death throes would be in no shape to offer resistance afterward.

But Alex doubted many of them would survive.

32

"So there I was, just me and my little *Panther* up against the two of them. I tell you, man, it was looking bad. This *Shadow Hawk*'s all over me like stink in a Kurita sewer, right up until one of those infantry boys jumps up and plants a big one right on his ankle joint . . ."

Alex Carlyle took a sip of his glass of wine and listened to MechWarrior Ehland continuing his tale. Here in the cavernous ballroom of the Residence the traditional postbattle war stories made the fight for the port sound sufficiently remote that the battle might have been something glamorous, glorious even. Perhaps that was what separated the veterans from rookies like him. All Alex could remember was death, destruction, and the certainty of failure, right up to the moment when the *Medea*'s explosion finally clinched the victory for the Gray Death.

A victory, but a costly one. Three BattleMechs had been destroyed, one from Denniken's fire lance and two of Freida Bergstrom's lightweight recon 'Mechs. All three pilots had died fighting in their machines to the last. One of the four hovertanks, Sergeant Wilkie's Pegasus, had been wrecked as well, and both Wilkie and Ethan Radcliffe had been lucky to escape the burning hulk before the enemy *Firestarter* 'Mech had closed in to finish them off. And two of the precious fighters and their pilots were gone, MacMasters in his *Slayer* and Ensign Quil's *Sparrowhawk*, the latter shot down as he pressed too far in pursuit of the fleeing enemy craft and came under the fire from one of the Free Skye

DropShips. Five of the armored infantrymen, almost half of Lucci's force, had also been killed or seriously wounded. Beyond that, the cost in civilian lives and property damage in Dunkeld was incalculable.

Yes, it had been a victory of sorts, though the Gray Death had lost close to a quarter of their force to win it. Alex thought he knew now exactly how that ancient Greek general must have felt when he said, "Another such victory and we'll be undone." Pyrrhus, that was his name—the man who had given military science the concept of a Pyrrhic victory. That was exactly what the battle at Dunkeld had been, a success the Gray Death Legion couldn't really afford.

The detonation of the fuel cells aboard the *Medea* had finished off most of the invasion force in one blow, and sustained fire from LRMs and the fighters had finished off the rest. The Gray Death had a handful of prisoners locked up in the same cells—hastily rebuilt to repair battle damage—that had held the Legion's officer corps during Governor DeVries' short-lived coup. And the defeat of the first landing force had evidently made General von Bulow think twice before committing more troops. He had longer purse strings to work with than the Gray Death, more men and machines to spend as he pleased, but von Bulow's masters back on Skye would not be pleased if he lost more troops needlessly.

For tonight, it seemed that Glengarry was in no immediate danger, but McCall had assigned a full watch crew to monitor the skies from the underground command center, while technical crews were already hard at work trying to repair the battle damage to the 'Mechs and tanks that had survived the battle. There was no way of knowing how soon the enemy would be back.

They had held a memorial service for the dead that afternoon, but now the somber mood had given way to a celebration. Not only had they dished out far worse damage than they'd taken, but word had come from the Glencoe Highlands that the *Europa* had made good her escape from the battle and found a safe haven—the last crucial goal of McCall's battle plan. Buoyed up by both facts, the officers and men not required elsewhere had gathered at the Residence to drink, swap stories, and toast the triumph of the

Gray Death. And of their new colonel, who they praised as the man responsible for it all.

Thinking about the causalities, about the way the whole battle had nearly come apart, Alex would have preferred to duck responsibility than take credit for it.

Without realizing it, he'd finished his wine all the while his mind had been turning over the butcher's bill. He stared absently at the empty glass, barely aware of the celebration anymore. Finally he shrugged to himself and started across the room toward the bar.

Lieutenant Denniken intercepted him halfway there. "Here's the man of the hour!" he said loudly, then plucked a glass from a passing waiter's tray, thrusting it into Alex's hand and putting the empty on the tray. "I've got to admit it, I thought the idea of meeting them with just the Companions was suicide, but I was wrong. Who would've thought a cadet could put together a battle like that?"

Five or six officers close by, including Lieutenant Lucci and Julio Vargas, added a chorus of agreement. "Those bastards never knew what they were getting into," MechWarrior Hansen, the *Dervish* pilot from Denniken's lance, chimed in. "Then it's whoosh, bang, and they're dead. Just like that . . ."

Alex felt himself blushing at the unwanted attention, and took a swallow from the glass Denniken had forced on him. It was Earn Valley scotch, far more potent than the wine he'd confined himself to so far this evening. He had to fight to keep from gasping as the fiery liquid seared his throat.

"Your father'll be proud of what you did today, kid . . . er, Colonel," Rachel Nolans said, slapping him on the back. She piloted the *Catapult* that was the third survivor of the fire lance. Lowdowski's *Shadow Hawk*, the fourth in the unit, had been destroyed.

Alex found his voice at last, hoarse from a morning spent shouting orders, the overwhelming attention here, and the effects of the scotch. "It was McCall's plan," he protested. "And it wasn't anything to cheer about, anyway. Von Bulow will be back, and next time he won't be pulling any punches."

Vargas shrugged. "Maybe so. Maybe tomorrow we've all had it. But we kicked some butt today, and you know damned well we wouldn't have even tried if you hadn't come forward the way you did. McCall planned it, but you had the guts to carry it out.''

''But—'' Alex felt a hand on his arm and turned to meet McCall's dour stare.

''If the colonel can spare a wee moment . . .'' As the major's tone didn't leave much room for refusing, Alex trailed the big man to a quiet corner of the ballroom.

''What is it, Major?'' he asked, feeling like a cadet called on the carpet again.

''Dinna be sae quick tae damp doon their enthusiasm, young Alex,'' McCall said softly. ''They all ken as weil as you or I what we're up against. But they've won a wee little tulzie today, and they deserve the chance tae let off some steam withoot being forced tae think aboot what might happen tomorrow.''

''It's just . . . what kind of victory did we win today, really? Von Bulow's not going to just apologize for the inconvenience and jump on out of here. And we lost some good people out there that we can't replace for the next fight. We shouldn't be celebrating . . .''

''Aye, we should, laddie. We should. Dinna forget, we got the *Europa* awa' and hidden safe in the mountains, and we took oot better than a full company of 'Mechs in one blow. That's the sort of thing your auld faither would hae done, if he had been here . . . and 'twas you, not me, who first brought up the idea of luring the landing force into a trap. 'Tis that kind of sideways thinking that'll keep us going, no matter how hard the road gets doon the way.''

''You really think we have a chance?''

McCall shrugged. ''In the long run, I doubt we could hold everything they can throw at us. What we hae tae do is slow things doon, force yon Skye rebels tae pay dearly for all they wish tae gain. It will cost us, laddie, maybe more dearly than you can imagine, but the more time and effort Duke Richard invests in us, the less damage he can do elsewhere. And we willna be alone forever. The rest of the Legion will come, and then these bastards'll pay double for attacking us at home. That I can guarantee.''

''But a lot of these people will be dead by then. Maybe all of us. I'm not sure I can live with that on my conscience, Major.'' Alex looked away. ''Maybe DeVries was right in the first place.''

''If you give it a' up the noo, then the ones who've already died did it all for nothing. You don't want deaths on your conscience, laddie, but how much worse is it tae travel only partway doon the road and then just roll over and give up when things start tae look grim? That would be the real waste. Because if you surrender too soon, if there's nae spark of resistance tae keep the duke and his cronies occupied here, than it may be this rebellion will work after all, and everything we've worked for, everything Grayson Carlyle has ever believed in, could come crashing doon in payment for one lad's delicate sensibilities. Think on that, if you dare, before you talk again of DeVries being right.''

Alex studied the other man's scarred face, surprised at the depth of the anger he heard behind McCall's speech. ''I . . . I'm sorry,'' he stammered. ''I guess I didn't think it through. But I told you before, I'm not cut out to be the leader. You should go ahead and take command yourself instead of us continuing this farce of me in charge.''

'' 'Tis nae farce, laddie,'' McCall said. ''They willna follow me as they'll do for a Carlyle. You're the ain man who can keep the Legion together in these straits, young Alex. I ken weil that you can do it. But you maun ken it too . . . and 'tis a lesson you'll hae tae learn aye soon.''

''I'll try, Major,'' he said quietly.

McCall's sudden grin took Alex by surprise. '' 'Mac' was guid enough in the field, laddie. You sound a wee bit less like some whelp of a cadet when you use it . . . just sae lang as you dinna get too much used tae it when things get back tae normal and you're back in my class at Brander. The cadet who calls me 'Mac' tae my face dies a horrible bluidy death, you ken.''

Alex found himself grinning back at the old weapons master despite his doubts. There was something irrepressible about McCall, an indomitable confidence that made it impossible to doubt his words. As long as Davis McCall still believed the Legion had a future, Carlyle thought he should at least try to take him at his word.

But it was hard, right now, to picture a day when things would truly return to normal on Glengarry, when he'd be back to being one of the cadets at Brander, with nothing more pressing on his mind than coping with McCall's next field maneuvers.

The weapons master turned away then, crossing the floor to greet Freya de Villar. Alex didn't rejoin the party right away. He continued to stand quietly in the corner, alone with his thoughts, sipping his scotch and listening to the snatches of conversation that rose above the general babble from time to time.

"Well, I'm here to tell you, things didn't look too good just then." That was Dave Clay, standing a few steps away in a circle that included Caitlin DeVries and two of the Harasser tank jockeys, among others. "I mean, the lady was having problems of her own and that *Warhammer* out-massed me by twenty tons, and the indicator light's blinking on the ankle joint where it was already too damned weak. So I said to myself, 'Dave, my boy, you'd better come up with a good one this time . . .' "

Alex shook his head slowly. The older cadet was sounding just like the veterans now, telling war stories and waving his hands to illustrate his tale.

Maybe in the long run it wasn't the gap between rookie and grizzled old-timer that was so enormous, but the one that separated those who followed and those who led.

"Transmission completed, sir," the communications officer reported. I just hope to God the message gets through."

Captain Rodland didn't reply, but he agreed inwardly with the prayer. After everything the *Gray Skull* and her crew had gone through, there was still no guarantee that the message they'd brought from Glengarry would do any good.

The *Gray Skull* had jumped from Glengarry into the Skye system at the last possible moment, and by some miracle the damage they'd taken from the Free Skye fighters hadn't knocked out any crucial systems. They'd come out of jump fearing the worst, but luckily there'd been no sign of hostile ships close enough to cause any problems. Long-range sensors showed a lot of activity in the system; Free Skye military forces were apparently getting ready to launch still another armada to points unknown.

Rodland hadn't lingered any longer than it took to reprogram the *Gray Skull*'s navigational computers and jump again, though it meant arriving at Mizar with the storage cells drained. That had required nearly a week for recharging in space, but fortunately they'd encountered no activity anywhere in this system either. Rodland had been tempted to hook in to the Class B hyperpulse station on Mizar to send out the message to Grayson Carlyle on Tharkad, but this ComStar facility was not one supervised directly by the Federated Commonwealth government. Blake only knew which side of the Free Skye rebellion ComStar might decide to support. The risks were just too great.

So instead they had made the jump to the New Earth zenith jump point, transmitting the message from here, as originally instructed. The system was another link in the chain of military bases in Victor Davion's effort to establish a loyal military presence in the Skye region, only recently designated as home to a battalion of MechWarriors from the well-known NAIS academy on New Avalon. The Federated Commonwealth also controlled the ComStar facility on New Earth and it was now part of the government-controlled communications stations that bound the far-flung F-C holdings together. The *Gray Skull*'s sensors had confirmed that the NAIS was still in control here.

The planet was another likely target for Free Skye invasion, but it was also the Gray Death's best hope of getting word of the attack on Glengarry to Colonel Carlyle and Prince Victor. Rodland could only hope that the message—and the *Gray Skull* as well—would already be on their way before the separatists turned their attention this way.

"Maybe we should stick around," Ilse Martinez remarked as she unstrapped herself from an unused station nearby. "Get in touch with Kommandant Staab and let the NAIS people know what's going on."

Rodland shook his head. "We've done what de Villar told us to do. The message is on the net, and Colonel Carlyle can decide who else to pass it to. If we start talking with the big wheels here, we could end up getting commandeered by the Federated Commonwealth High Command. If that happens, we don't get to Khaled on Borghese, and that's the only ace we've got left in the hole if the rest of this deal goes sour."

Martinez studied him for a long moment. "You're right, of course," she said, nodding reluctantly. "It's good to see you putting the Legion first." With that she pushed off, floating through the open hatch to the ladder that led below.

Rodland stared after her. Carrying out the next part of the mission would get the *Gray Skull* still further from the Skye rebellion, and that was what really mattered now. Or was it? Thinking back over the eventful week since the Day of Heroes, he couldn't help but want to make sure those men and women back on Glengarry got the help they needed.

The messages had to get through, and Captain Einar Rodland, late of the Rasalhague Republic Navy, would be the one to see that they did.

== 33 ==

Planetary Orbit, Glengarry
Skye March, Federated Commonwealth
7 April 3056

General-Kommandant Wilhelm Freidrich von Bulow set his hand computer terminal on the desktop carefully, making sure the velcro pad on the bottom of the device caught on one of the holding surfaces properly. Zero gravity was one inconvenience after another, and with the engines powered down while the DropShip *Asgard* and her consorts rode in orbit around Glengarry each of those petty inconveniences was an irritating reminder that they should have been on the ground by now.

Instead they were no closer tonight to even getting a toe-hold on the planet, thanks to the Gray Death's well-laid ambush and the sheer incompetence of a handful of his officers.

Von Bulow sighed and looked across the table at his aide. "All right. What's next on the list, Johann?"

Hauptmann Albrecht checked his wristcomp readout. The younger man managed to maintain his parade-ground rigidity even when it took a lap belt to keep him in his chair. "The matter of the DropShip captains . . . Lippard and Neice."

"Ah, yes. The gentlemen who left the ground force without fire support because they were afraid of a few missiles." Von Bulow massaged the bridge of his nose, wishing he could find time for a few hours' sleep. The preparations for the first landing op had taken days to put together. And now he could look forward to putting in even more time trying to come up with a way to redeem the campaign on

Glengarry. "Neice has the *Raven*, correct? The junior officer?"

"Yes, *Herr General*," Albrecht responded.

"Well, he might have shown more initiative, but the decision to withdraw was Lippard's. Put a reprimand in his file and have the political officer look into his background . . . just to be sure." Duke Richard Steiner's political officers, attached to every military unit in the Free Skye Movement's growing military, were supposed to weed out the officers whose loyalty was questionable. Von Bulow had no reason to think the captain of the *Raven* had acted out of treachery, but the duke might not see it that way. Best to let the PO check the man out thoroughly.

"And Lippard, *Herr General*?"

"The political officer can deal with suspected traitors," von Bulow said harshly. He made a quick chopping motion with one beefy hand. "I deal with incompetents. For the moment, the *Anastasia*'s exec can have the command. See that he knows how and why he got it—and what we expect of him if he's to keep it. This man Lippard, any political connections we need to worry about?"

"No, *Herr General*."

"Then you needn't worry about the formalities too much. Have him shoved out one of his ship's airlocks as an example to the rest."

Albrecht didn't even flinch. "Yes, *Herr General*."

And maybe the next DropShip captain who put his precious ship above the good of the mission would think twice when it came time to launch the next landing, von Bulow thought.

"There's also the question of the two fighter pilots who broke off without orders, *Herr General*," Albrecht went on after a moment's consultation with his wristcomp.

"Names?"

"Ferguson and Henderson, *Herr General*. From the remnants of Red Squadron, off the *Merkur*."

"Hmph." Von Bulow frowned. That had been his mistake, assigning those two to fly high cover for the landing. He probably should have sent in a larger aerospace contingent to start with, holding the two survivors of the battle with the Gray Death JumpShip in reserve until he was sure they were ready for action again. But all the intelligence reports had checked out, and there was as much humiliation in being the general in charge of an elaborately executed overkill as there was in letting the enemy give you a bloody nose. He'd been sure the vanguard could handle whatever minor resistance the city might offer, but he'd been wrong. "Both new men, if I remember correctly."

"Yes, Herr General. Freshly assigned from the cadres on Skye. The battle after the jump was the first action for both of them. The veteran in the squadron was caught in the jump wash."

"The senior man, Ferguson . . . he should be taking a space walk right alongside Lippard for running from the battle." Von Bulow shook his head slowly. "But it's a hell of a lot easier to replace a DropShip captain than it is to scrape together trained aerospace pilots. Demotion in grade, a reprimand in his record. And see that his name manages to come up on every shithouse assignment we've got until he's had a chance to show he can do better."

Albrecht noted the instructions, nodding slowly. "It will be done, Herr General."

Pulling his own terminal free of the desk, von Bulow called up the list of reminders he had made earlier. "Now, Albrecht, what is the status of the search for the enemy DropShip that escaped the fighting?"

"No progress, Herr General," the aide replied uncomfortably. "The *Raven* tracked the ship into the southern mountains. Captain Neice's original evaluation was that she was heading for Halidon. There's a fairly good port facility there . . . you'll remember our discussions of the city as a base if we couldn't land directly in Dunkeld."

Von Bulow waved an impatient hand. "Yes . . . yes, I'm familiar with the geography. From your choice of words it seems Neice guessed wrong eh?"

"Yes, Herr General. Lippard refused to allow the *Raven* to conduct an active pursuit on the grounds that the enemy would have the advantage if it came to flying through mountain passes, and a DropShip wasn't worth risking in that."

"Lippard again," von Bulow muttered. "I wish I could have him executed twice." He looked up at his aide. "Continue, Johann."

"Yes, Herr General." Albrecht consulted his wristcomp again. "Unfortunately it seems the mountains in that region are thoroughly laced with heavy metals deposits that make it very difficult to detect a ship on the ground. They must have landed the DropShip in a narrow valley somewhere well away from any populated area, then used camouflage to hide it from visual detection. We are continuing over-flights by reconnaissance fighters in hopes of spotting something, but frankly, Herr General, it is unlikely we'll find that ship as long as they choose to remain concealed.''

"Hmph," von Bulow snorted. "That may mean they've set up some sort of prearranged return trip by the JumpShip that escaped. With the right timing, they might evacuate their leaders and a few 'Mechs, run the orbital blockade, and hook up with the JumpShip before we could mount an interception. That means we'll need to maintain a tight watch on close orbit and atmosphere, and keep an eye out for any sign of incoming JumpShips as well." He frowned. "We may need to request some additional aerospace forces from His Grace to serve on picket duty until we can track the ship down on the ground."

"I doubt His Grace will be eager to part with any more forces, Herr General," Albrecht said seriously.

"True enough. We don't have all that much to work with, and there are plenty of other planets to secure." Von Bulow tapped the side of the hand terminal thoughtfully, turning over the problem in his mind. "The real answer, of course, is to get down to Glengarry's surface in force. Once we've done that, we'll find all their hidden assets and neutralize them. But they're obviously better prepared for resistance than we thought. They took us by surprise this morning, using the double-blind of the governor's negotiations and that story of putting down a coup. I'm beginning to think the whole thing was a lure, from the moment DeVries first contacted us. The story of a fight between the governor and Carlyle's people wasn't the typical sort of bait for a trap, and it threw me off my guard. Devious . . . those people down there are too damned devious."

Albrecht cleared his throat uncertainly. "Forgive me, Herr General, but I'm not sure the facts support the idea of DeVries being part of the trap. Just before I came in I had a note from Communications. They're monitoring a station in Eastport, a city on the far eastern end of the continent of Scotia, in the district they call Teviotdale. Apparently Governor DeVries and a number of government people loyal to him have turned up there and are trying to reestablish some degree of control over the area."

"Have they tried to get a message to us?"

The aide shook his head. "Not so far, Herr General. They only went on the air a short time ago."

"It could be coincidence, I suppose," von Bulow said slowly. "Or they could be thinking they'll trick us a second time. Eastport is too isolated to serve as a solid base of operations, and they'd love it if we landed there and had to slog all the way across the continent." He chuckled humorlessly. "Even making us waste our time reconnoitering there would buy the bastards more time than we can afford to give them. Well, keep monitoring the situation, but we won't waste any more effort on a lost cause. DeVries had his chance. When we land on Glengarry, it won't be in any spirit of compromise and compassion, I guarantee that right now."

Albrecht nodded. "I thought that would be your reaction, whether DeVries was serious about surrendering or not." He made another note. "That was all I had, Herr General. Have you any further instructions for me?"

"Call a full staff meeting in the Intelligence Conference Room at 0900 TST," von Bulow told him. "Pass the word to Major Heinkel that we will want to review updated plans for Operation Trident."

"Trident. Yes, Herr General." Albrecht's tone was carefully neutral.

"You disagree with the choice, Johann?"

"Er . . . of course not, Herr General . . . but I was wondering . . ."

"Go on, Johann."

"Trident calls for a division of our troops, Herr General. Is that wise? Concentration of force is one of the first military maxims, and against opponents of the caliber of these Legion officers, it seems to me that we're risking defeat." Albrecht looked uncomfortable, as if he'd said more than he'd intended to.

"The objection is valid enough, Johann, under most circumstances," von Bulow told him, smiling. "But the intention behind Trident is to saturate the defense. Our chief advantage right now is in numbers. They can't cover every viable landing site in sufficient strength to stop us from getting a drophead *somewhere*, even if they win one or even two fights along the way. Trident forces them to commit the bulk of their troops to battle, and to take losses they cannot

possibly afford, if they want to oppose the landing at all.
And no matter how good they are, in the end they'll run out
of men before we do, and we'll open up the defense like
cracking an egg.'' Von Bulow returned the terminal to its
spot on the desk top. ''You see, Johann, the only way to
properly use a deep purse is to spend from it until you buy
what you want. No amount of tricks or clever strategy can
beat out the laws of attrition, as long as you have the will
and the resources to stick with it.''

''Ah, Carlyle. Come in . . . Baron,'' said Prince Victor
Davion, seated in his Royal Offices on Tharkad.

Grayson Death Carlyle passed between the two Federated
Commonwealth guards at the door and entered Prince Victor Davion's private office. Like the man, the room was
spartan, with few outward trappings of royalty. But from
this room, or its twin on New Avalon, the affairs of humanity's largest interstellar state were decided.

''Your Highness, I must speak with you,'' Carlyle began,
bowing perfunctorily before taking the seat the Archon
Prince offered him with a wave of a hand. ''It's a matter of
some urgency . . .''

''You're here about the situation on Skye,'' Prince Victor
said blandly. ''In particular, the news from Glengarry that
you received yesterday.''

''Then you've already had word, sire?''

Victor nodded curtly. ''My idiot cousins Ryan and Richard Steiner seem determined to play the demagogues. I assume the private message that came for you off the
hyperpulse net concerned the situation?''

''Yes, sire . . .'' Carlyle hesitated, then went on. ''My
officers reported an invasion armada that fired on Gray Death
ships. One of my JumpShips just barely escaped to bring
out the news. Do you have anything more recent?''

''Yes, it seems that the previous Baron of Glengarry,
General von Bulow, I believe is his name, objected to losing
the fiefdom to you. With Ryan's blessing and Richard's clandestine help, von Bulow has gone to reclaim Glengarry.
Current intelligence puts the opposition as the Tenth Skye
Rangers and supporting troops.''

''The Legion . . .''

''They're seriously outnumbered, Carlyle. But knowing

your people . . . well, you tell me. What are the odds they're still holding out?''

"De Villar and McCall were in command. Neither one of them would give an inch. I'd say they're still fighting—if there's anything left to fight with." The mercenary leader leaned forward in his chair and locked eyes with the prince. "As you know, the rest of the Legion is with Major Khaled on Borghese. With your permission I can take my command lance there, assemble the battalion, and mount a relief expedition. Two weeks from now, three at the outside, we'll be back on Glengarry letting the bastards know who they're up against.''

"I've already sent orders to Borghese to have your people mobilized, Carlyle. They have priority on all jump routes and should be in system in about twelve days. But I'd rather you didn't go with them.''

"Sire?''

"The Tenth was the only regular Skye unit to mutiny. The others are watching and waiting. If I send regular Federated Commonwealth troops, the rest of the Skye military will go into full-scale rebellion. And regardless of your reputation, you and a single battalion won't be enough to defeat the Tenth Sky Ranges. So, in your name as Baron of Glengarry, I've contracted a few regiments of the Northwind Highlands. They'll be ready to move in three weeks and be in the Glengarry system in four. I want you to lead *them* back to Glengarry to crush this rebellion.''

"Sire . . . surely I'd be better employed with my own people.''

"That's not the way I see it, Carlyle. We don't even know if there'll be any force left to relieve on Glengarry. I can't waste one of the best officers in my service on a possibility and I cannot gamble with Federated Commonwealth control of Skye.''

"Then you're . . . writing them off?'' Carlyle looked away. "Sire, my son is on Glengarry.''

"I know. And I'm sorry, but we're not abandoning any of them. Your Major Khaled is a good man. Provided someone is still putting up a fight on Glengarry, his troops—your troops—can make one hell of a difference. But when the rightful Baron of Glengarry returns, he must come with an overwhelming force. I need you to make sure this rebellion is crushed dead.''

Grayson Carlyle didn't answer immediately. So this is the price for the title and the ceremony and the cheers of the crowd in court, he thought bitterly. If he refused Victor's orders now, he'd be breaking the oath of fealty he'd taken less than a week ago. And the Archon Prince was perfectly capable of denying him any help for the defenders on Glengarry.

"Very well, Your Highness," he said at last. "I'll do it."

Victor Steiner-Davion smiled. "Good. Good. With your people tying the bastards in knots on Glengarry and you coming in with the Highlanders on the counteroffensive, Skye will be saved."

Grayson Death Carlyle rose slowly and bowed once more. He hoped the Archon Prince of the Federated Commonwealth was right.

And he also hoped that somewhere, somehow, Alex Carlyle knew that his father's thoughts and prayers were with him.

34

Dunkeld, Glengarry
Skye March, Federated Commonwealth
11 April 3056

The status board on the *Archer*'s cockpit display showed half a dozen red warning lights, and the shrilling of an alarm drowned out the voices of Alex Carlyle's men as they implored him to come to their aid. But he couldn't help them. Wave after wave of enemy attackers were on their way, and there were no more legionnaires to throw into the fray.

Alex Carlyle jerked awake, sitting upright in one violent motion with a cold sweat prickling his forehead. For a long moment he couldn't shake the dream, the same one that had plagued him every night since the battle at the port. It grew more real, more vivid, each time, and he always awoke expecting to find himself in the midst of the fighting with his friends and comrades screaming his name.

It took him several seconds to realize that the shrilling sound wasn't just an echo of the dream. No, he was safe in his quarters in the Residence on Castle Hill and it was only the intercom panel beside his bed warbling urgently. He reached out with an unsteady hand to tap Accept Call. "Carlyle," he croaked. He swallowed and tried to get a better grip on himself before repeating his name, more clearly and confidently this time. "Carlyle. Go ahead."

"Colonel, this is Longo in the command center. We've picked up changes in the delta-vees on four of the Drop-Ships in orbit. Looks like it's about to go down, sir."

The former DropShip captain's words brought Alex to full wakefulness. "On my way, Lieutenant," he said. "Alert

Major McCall and put out a general readiness alarm. Alpha Detachment to stand ready to move out.''

"Yes, sir," Longo said. "Command center clear."

Alex rolled out of bed and crossed to his closet, dressing hurriedly. It was nearly four full days since the battle at the spaceport, and they'd been expecting some sort of enemy action long since. Now that the wait was finally over, he wasn't sure if he was relieved or afraid of what was about to come.

All the while he finished dressing and then headed for the command center far below the Residence building, Alex turned over and over in his mind the prospects for success. Now that the Gray Death had stood up to the Free Skye armada once, there was no hope of suckering them into another ambush, and that put the Legion right back where it had been after de Villar died and Governor DeVries had fled the capital.

There were still several good landing zones available to an enemy invasion force, and too few of the Legion to cover them all. The abrupt appearance of Governor DeVries and two battalions of his Planetary Guard at Eastport in Teviotdale had complicated the situation further, since there was always the possibility that von Bulow would opt to land where he already had local support and then mount a longer ground campaign. But the original prime target sites of Dunkeld, Coltbridge, Loch Sheol, and Halidon still remained the most likely places for an enemy strike. But which would it be? And how could the outnumbered Legion cover them all?

Alard King had come up with the best answer to the second question. Two days after the fighting in Dunkeld, the far-flung detachments of the Legion had returned to the capital, bringing with them every emelt train they could commandeer along the way. Now the entire Legion force on Glengarry, minus a few infantry and armor outfits left behind to watch the possible landing sites, was assembled in the heart of the city around the hub of the maglev transportation network. One batch of 'Mechs was already loaded up on emelt flatcars, ready to move out on short notice to any point on the emelt net. The others remained ready for battle around Dunkeld itself, but could be quickly loaded and shipped out at need.

The idea was to create a rapid response to any landing,

wherever it might occur. In a matter of hours, Legion
'Mechs could be moving to battle at any of the towns von
Bulow might choose as his next target, and with luck that
would bring the Gray Death into action before an enemy
DZ could be fully occupied and prepared.

Alex could only hope it would work.

By the time the lift doors snapped open to let him into
the command center, he had his features composed and his
bearing as relaxed and confident as he could manage. Longo
met him as he left the elevator.

"We've just had an update, sir," he said without preamble. "The computer's predicting a landing to the north,
in the Strathtay or Glensheol regions. Of course, they could
still modify their flight profiles . . ."

"That's right," Alex said, cutting him off. After three
days of studying the map and debating strategy with McCall
and the others, he was all too familiar with the various ways
the enemy could use to keep matters in doubt until the last
possible moment.

They still had no clear notion where von Bulow was likely
to strike. To all appearances the Free Skye general was
snubbing Governor DeVries' efforts to arrange a truce and
fresh negotiations, and that made Eastport look unlikely.
But Free Skye fighters had been overflying Loch Sheol,
Coltbridge, and Halidon every few hours for the last two
days, while steering clear of Dunkeld itself. Was that a clue
that von Bulow was trying to divert attention away from the
capital before repeating the direct approach that had failed
before? Alex doubted it, and McCall seemed certain that a
second battle at Dunkeld was the last thing the invaders
wanted now, but there was always that nagging doubt.

"What about the intruders last night?" Alex asked Longo
as they crossed to the Snake Pit.

The DropShip captain shrugged. "Nothing more since
the briefing at twenty-three hundred, sir. We had the one
DropShip on the screens, tracing an arc that brought it over
Loch Sheol, Coltbridge, and Halidon in succession. The
ship had too many fighters escorting it, so Captain Vargas
couldn't try an intercept. There was no landing, and the
ship rejoined the rest of the armada after the flyby."

That had put them all on alert for a while, until it became
clear that the incursion wasn't part of a full-scale landing
effort. Alex sat down at a monitor position and studied

Longo thoughtfully. "Mac—Major McCall thought the ship might have been carrying pathfinders. Any indications of that from any of our people?"

"No, sir." Longo shook his head. "Of course, good pathfinders don't give themselves away, and I expect these troops are good."

Alex nodded. A full-scale landing on a hostile planet was usually preceded by the deployment of pathfinders, scouts and elite infantrymen who could study the situation on the ground up close, clear automated defenses and sensors, spot enemy units and generally smooth the way for the landing to follow. Von Bulow hadn't used pathfinders at Dunkeld because he'd believed there would be no resistance. He'd be crazy not to use them this time around, but there was no way of telling where they might have gone in. Using high-altitude/high-opening parachutes and personal jump belts for the descent, pathfinder troops could be inserted almost anywhere without being detected on the way down.

So von Bulow probably had troops on the ground already, and those four ships were now following them in. The trick was to be sure of where that landing would come. If the Gray Death waited until the Free Skye forces were already committed to one definite target, they'd lose the advantage of mobility that the maglev lines gave them.

Your call, Colonel Carlyle, he told himself, the thought mockingly. Your call, and a bloody mess if you're wrong.

Behind him, Alex heard the elevator doors open again. He turned in his chair to see McCall striding across the chamber, his unkempt hair and sleepy expression making the man look like a bear disturbed from hibernation. "Does yon computer hae a projected DZ yet?" the Caledonian asked as he came up, cocking one eyebrow at Alex.

"So far, it looks like Loch Sheol," Alex said. "If the projections hold up, that is."

McCall sat down next to Alex and studied one of the computer monitors intently. "Hae you made a call yet, laddie?" he asked quietly.

Alex shrugged. "You know what we're up against. I keep wondering if I'd be better off throwing darts at a dartboard to figure out where the bastards'll set down."

"My gut says the projections are right," McCall told him. "Loch Sheol is well nigh pairfect for a landing, and I dinna think our esteemed opponent is the kind tae play at suddenly

switching targets. He'll ken weil that we've drawn back tae
the capital, but I dinna think he'll be counting on us using
the maglev net to shift 'Mechs. So he had nae reason tae
try tae sucker us that way. He'll be expecting us tae move
after he's on the ground anyway.''

"You might be right," Alex said slowly. "And that could
give us the chance we need to smash those troops fast. He's
only starting out with a small force to grab the DZ, just like
he tried here. If we redeploy north fast enough, we might
catch them with their pants down.''

"Aye, maybe," the Caledonian said. "Maybe . . . but I
wonder what we're overlooking. Only four DropShips in the
first wave. Hae y'seen any more starting down, Lieutenant?''

"No, Major," Longo replied. "They've got a fair-sized
fighter screen, though. Twelve so far.''

"I dinna like it," McCall said sourly. "If it was a full-
scale attack, they'd be sending in more than four ships. I
dinna think von Bulow would run the risk of anither bluidy
nose like the last ain.''

"Still, four DropShips with that kind of fighter cover . . .
that could mean enough 'Mechs to take on everything we've
got, with the rest of their force held in reserve.'' Alex
frowned. "Or it could be a reconnaissance in force. There's
no guarantee all those ships are full. We know of two that
don't have any 'Mechs aboard anymore, and we don't know
if all of them were carrying full loads in the first place.''

"Aye," McCall agreed. "Could be 'tis a ploy tae lure us
tae pounce on a token force while the real landing comes
doon somewhere else.''

"So, we can respond and leave the real DZ open. Or we
can sit tight, and find out too late that this is the real DZ.''
Alex shook his head slowly. "Either way, we're done for.''

"We canna risk losing the initiative, laddie," McCall told
him. "We maun send troops tae support the lads we've got
in place, and it's got tae be enough tae fight it oot. But I
think we'll want tae hold back the second wave until we see
what we're really up against.''

"Dividing in the face of the enemy . . . don't like it
much, Mac.'' Alex frowned again. "But I guess we don't
have a hell of a lot choice.''

"Who's on first wave?" McCall asked Longo.

"Captain Dumont, sir. With the battalion HQ lance and one full company."

The weapons master turned back toward Alex. "Dumont's a good man, laddie, but I think you'll be wanting someone who kens better what you want to tak command on the spot. I think we should divide the command lance. Send me ain of the others, say young Clay, with the response force while you stay here and keep an eye on things until we ken better if we need tae commit the rest of our lads."

Alex shook his head. "It's a good idea, Mac, but you've got it backward. You're the one with the judgment to decide how to handle the reserve. I'll go with Dumont."

"But—"

"I know, I know," the younger man said quickly, holding up a hand to forestall McCall's protest. "I have to learn to delegate. Well, that's exactly what I'm trying to do here. The best man to handle the reserves is you, Mac. You've got the experience to do the job, and I don't. But I *can* take command in the field. That's what you've been training me for."

McCall didn't answer right away. Alex held his eye with a steady gaze, and he could almost read the older man's mind in the sudden silence. McCall really was better suited to make the decisions that would send the reserves in motion as they were needed, but despite his experience in the port battle—maybe even because of that experience—Alex himself remained an unknown quantity when it came to exercising an independent command, away from McCall's guidance. The fact that Henri Dumont was one of the least enthusiastic supporters of Alex's advancement to the head of the Gray Death would only add to the possible problems. But McCall couldn't very well protest openly without publicly proclaiming that Alex wasn't fit for the job, undoing everything the weapons master had worked for.

Finally McCall gave a quick, sharp nod. "Aye," he said. "Aye, 'twill hae tae do."

Alex mustered a thin smile. "Good. Then that's settled." He turned to Longo. "Pass the word to load up my *Archer* with the other first-wave 'Mechs. And . . . uh, make it the *Centurion* as well. Inform MechWarrior DeVries to get to the assembly point ASAP."

"Caitlin?" McCall rumbled. "Are you sure it shouldn't be young Clay?"

He shook his head. "Last report from King was that Dave's *Griffin* would need another twenty hours of work to put that ankle joint right. But Caitlin's *Centurion* is back at a hundred percent, and since they had to scrap the *Marauder,* she's best for the job."

"Aye, I suppose you've got the right of it." McCall didn't sound convinced, though, and Carlyle could understand his reluctance. The governor's daughter had gone into the fight at the port moody and withdrawn, and having her BattleMech very nearly knocked to pieces around her couldn't have helped either her confidence or her competence much. But Clay's 'Mech was on the verge of a major failure unless it was repaired before it went into battle again. This would give Caitlin a chance to prove herself once more. Alex Carlyle knew only too well how one failure could destroy a MechWarrior's self-confidence, and he was afraid part of her problem stemmed from the doubts he'd voiced about her during the fight with her father's troops. He couldn't leave her out of this op without risking more bad feelings, more uncertainties, more doubts that would ruin her chances of ever being an effective MechWarrior again.

Alex stood up suddenly, thrusting all his doubts and worries behind him. "I daresay it isn't perfect," he said. "But it's a plan, Major, you're in command here. I'm on my way to the assembly point. Mister Longo, pass the word for the ready force to saddle up and be ready to move out for Loch Sheol. And somebody get hold of the CO of the pickets up there and brief him on the situation."

He strode quickly toward the elevator before anyone had a chance to reply. It felt good to finally have the chance to take action, after the long wait.

Alex only hoped that the action would be the right one.

Captain Giles Montclair braced his elbows against the rough sandbag-and-earth berm of his observation post outside Loch Sheol and raised his field imager to his eyes. It was set for a standard visual scan in the bright morning light, and the tiny glowing red indicators in the lower left-hand corner of the viewer showed that both the recording and transmitting functions were active. Montclair thumbed the touch pad on top of the imager to increase the magnification and adjust the focus. He centered the view on the nearest of the four DropShips that had grounded less than ten minutes earlier on the port tarmac in the valley southwest of the mining town of Loch Sheol, three kilometers below his position on a long ridge spur.

It was a *Fury* Class DropShip, designed to carry troops and light vehicles. Montclair tried to remember the exact capacity of the *Fury,* but he couldn't remember the stats because it wasn't a ship in use by the Gray Death. Probably about a hundred men and a platoon or two of light armored vehicles—about the size of his own force. The comparison might have been heartening if not for the other three DropShips looming beyond the first vessel, two *Union* Class 'Mech carriers and a battle-scarred *Leopard.* That meant a potential force of better than two full companies of BattleMechs—not to mention the fighters circling overhead.

Monitor situation and fall back on Benmor Pass, the orders from Dunkeld had said. *Avoid combat unless absolutely necessary for the preservation of your command.* Montclair smiled grimly. Combat against two companies of Battle-Mechs was not exactly likely to preserve his small command.

He scanned the port slowly, the imager catching a tableau of Free Skye soldiers clustered around one of the mines his men had left behind when the withdrawal orders first came through. It was one of the big anti-'Mech jobs, set to analyze seismic data and detonate when something as big as a medium-sized 'Mech moved into the device's effective blast radius. A few of the mines had gone off when the DropShips had first set down, but the hull damage had been minor. A 'Mech, though, would find those mines hard to handle. They could be nearly as effective as the Gray Death's patented knee-capping techniques.

For the moment, fear of those mines was keeping the bigger DropShips buttoned up. The *Fury* was unloading troops, and as Montclair watched, the big ramp doors in the bottom of the DropShip dropped to allow a Galleon light tank to roll ponderously down to the tarmac on clanking treads. Nearby, a party of sappers was manhandling some combat engineering gear—it looked like a mine-sweeping and bomb-disposal rig to Montclair—into position near another of the mines.

It would take the invaders an hour or more to track down

all the explosives and render the port safe for anything larger than a *Stinger* or a *Wasp* . . . and in that hour, the reinforcements Major McCall had reported on the way from Dunkeld would reach Benmor and start unloading from their emelt cars.

Montclair lowered the field imager and switched it off. "So far, so good," he told Lieutenant Elphinstone, his senior platoon commander. "Now let's get our people set up to screen the pass. It's going to be a long morning."

=== 35 ===

Near Benmor Pass
Glengarry, Federated Commonwealth
11 April 3056

As the emelt approached Benmor Pass, Alex Carlyle checked the chrono function of his wrist computer for what seemed like the hundredth time. Despite the speed of the maglev train, the trip north seemed to be taking several eternities. As time continued to creep by, Alex was becoming more and more impatient—and more concerned at what the enemy might be doing in the meanwhile . . .

But it couldn't be helped. The trip from Dunkeld to Loch Sheol took just over two hours no matter how much he wanted it to go faster, and after that it would take another hour or more to get the Legion unloaded and ready for battle. That would have to be fast enough.

He considered contacting McCall on his commlink, but rejected the notion. Alex had already checked in three times in the past hour. Too blatant a show of anxiety by the Acting Colonel would only cause morale trouble, something he couldn't afford now. If there was any change in the current situation, McCall would let him know. For the moment it seemed that nothing else was going to happen for a while. There was no sign of further movement among the ships in orbit, and the troops at Loch Sheol were still reporting the enemy's deployment proceeding at an almost leisurely pace.

Alex plugged his wristcomp into the monitor screen in front of his seat and called up the Legion's detailed survey maps of the Glensheol region. Studying the terrain and the tactical situation might keep him from thinking about the battle as anything more than just another abstract problem like the ones McCall gave the cadets to work out in the classrooms of the Brander Wilderness Training Center. He might even come up with some useful stratagem at the same time.

Glensheol was a wide region of bleak highlands, roughly triangular in shape, which lay between the Grampian Mountains and the Braebuchan Range. The third side of the triangle, to the north and east, was bounded by ocean. Steep cliffs and rocky shallows gave the coastline a forbidding, barren aspect, and few colonists had settled there even in the heyday of Glengarry's colonial expansion.

The heart of the region was Loch Sheol, the big, ragged lake that nestled between the arms of the two mountain ranges. The original colonial surveyors had named it Loch Shiel, and the region Glenshiel, after famous landmarks in old Scotland on Terra. But the settlers had altered the names by associating them with Sheol, an archaic name for hell. The new names were far more appropriate.

Glensheol lay directly over a major fault line, and was one of the most geologically active areas on Glengarry. Frequent quakes shook the region, and five active volcanoes and plenty of older, burnt-out cones also dotted the area. The hot springs that fed Loch Sheol were well known on and off the planet. The highlands around the loch stank of sulfur and were usually swathed in a steamy, humid mist.

But the area had drawn colonists despite its unpleasant conditions. The Grampians were heavily laced with rich metal deposits from Invertay to the Monaghan Highlands, and Glensheol was one of the best mining areas of all. A sizable town had grown up on the southern shores of Loch Sheol during colonial times, and even now it was still home to a thane and his people, who often behaved as if the wealth and remoteness of their uplands gave them license to claim virtual independence from the rest of the planet. The Gray Death Companions had fought three short, sharp campaigns in the land between the mountains before they'd finally disabused the thane of that misguided idea. A report in Alex's file on the area noted that 'Mech campaigning around Glensheol, especially in the lower-lying areas close to the loch, could put an unexpected strain on a 'Mech's coolant capacity because of the high temperatures that frequently prevailed there.

The traffic in heavy metals had prompted the early colonists to construct an independent port facility near the town of Loch Sheol, and the maglev line had been pushed through high mountain passes to service the town in the years when the colony was still expanding. As the early strategy sessions in Dunkeld had brought out, the Loch Sheol port could be either a perfectly secure base of operations for an army, or—if the passes out of the uplands were held by an enemy—a perfect trap.

Alex studied a detail map of the area south of Loch Sheol and tried to put himself in von Bulow's place. The town and port were in a valley right along the lochshore. The town lay to the west of the Sheol River, with the port proper on the eastern side. Less than twenty kilometers south, under the towering volcanic peak of Benmor, the pass leading down to Buchan snaked through the mountains. A conventional road and the maglev line both led through Benmor Pass, spanning the river at the Bridge of Benmor and then turning straight north toward the town. The terrain between pass and town was a whole series of humpbacked ridges, nasty terrain for any kind of large-scale battle. The Sheol River cut a valley through the obstacle course, while the road itself passed over lower, more even ground.

It was terrain that favored the defense, and in an ideal war Alex would have opted for standing back near Benmor Pass and letting the invaders fight their way up to his lines, taking casualties all the way. But a defensive battle wasn't practical for the Gray Death, not in their present situation. Success depended on rapid action, before the enemy's superior numbers could become a deciding factor. And as long as better than two-thirds of the enemy armada remained uncommitted in orbit Alex could not afford to become bogged down facing any one enemy formation.

That meant the Gray Death would have to do the attacking, and it was up to Alex Carlyle to find a way to make that attack, in that terrain, feasible.

He checked his chrono function again. Numbers, terrain, even time itself seemed to be taking sides against the Gray Death . . .

Hauptmann Ann Ison-Price coughed, inwardly cursing at the noisome atmosphere of the Loch Sheol drop zone. Even in a MechWarrior's shorts and cooling vest the heat made her uncomfortable. She didn't even want to think what the fully uniformed sapper officer in front of her must be suffering.

"As long as you keep to the areas we've marked out on the tarmac, you 'Mechs should be safe enough," Leutnant Samuel Rusk was saying, somehow blending the diffidence expected of a junior officer with the arrogance of a specialist the op commander couldn't do without. "The port itself was mined, but sparsely. We've found no traces of mines away from the tarmac area. I doubt they had many to spare."

Ison-Price nodded. "Good. I want you to concentrate on the route across the river and into town next. I know, I know, you don't think they had any mines to put down. But I want the route checked anyway, and if a mine so much as scratches the paint on one of my 'Mechs I'll give permission for the pilot to dance a flamenco with his BattleMech right through the sappers' barracks. You get my drift, Leutnant?"

"Yes, Hauptmann. I'll issue the orders right away."

Ison-Price smiled as he hurried away, then turned to the 'Mech bay officers from the *Katerina* who was hovering nearby. "Mister de la Pena, commence the unloading. I want the patrol lance deployed first, so don't let Leutnant Wills or Feldwebel Geraci talk you into giving them priority." She didn't wait for a response, but turned away and bent over the portable tactical computer terminal the infantry CO had set up here in the shadow of the *Katerina,* the *Union* Class command DropShip.

Before she could adjust the display, though, the commlink portion of the terminal buzzed insistently. Sighing, Ison-Price keyed the Accept key. "Incoming message from the *Asgard,* Hauptmann," the voice of the *Katerina*'s communications tech announced.

A moment later the terminal monitor lit up with the heavy features of General von Bulow. "You are falling rapidly behind schedule, Hauptmann," he rumbled. "Did I make a mistake in assigning this mission to you?"

"Herr General, the sappers have finished clearing the mines and the 'Mech unloading has commenced," Ison-Price said hurriedly. "I will be throwing a screen of scout 'Mechs south along the road and maglev line within another quarter-hour, while we unload the rest of the company."

"Hmph," von Bulow grunted. "I suppose that will have to do. But be aware that we've detected the Gray Death

Legion moving a force toward you. High-speed maglev trains carrying about a company of 'Mechs. Very creative, these legionnaires . . . no one on my staff had considered the mobility of the maglev lines for anything except logistics. So you have no more than a few hours to deploy for a possible battle.''

"Yes, Herr General," Ison-Price replied. The weltalloberst commanding the covering fighters had reported the maglev movement to her almost a half an hour earlier, but she didn't think it would be wise to point this out to von Bulow. Instead she wiped the sweat from her forehead and went on. "If the general could authorize the fighters to strike the maglev line just south of Benmor Pass, we could knock out most of their column in one stroke, and restore the original timetable at the same time."

The general shook his head. "No. The purpose of Operation Trident is to encourage the enemy to commit as many troops as possible as rapidly as possible. We may be forced to push up our deployment timetable, but this bit of ingenuity actually plays into our hands quite well. At any rate I do not wish to see the maglev infrastructure damaged. Our forces will need it to deal with the logistical problems of an advance on Dunkeld. Not to mention the later occupation."

"Yes, Herr General," Ison-Price repeated, but she was seething within. Ever since touchdown the entire landing force had been subject to von Bulow's micromanagement, and she was weary of being nothing more than a pawn on his larger strategic chessboard.

But she also knew such was the fate of the modern warrior. She would follow her orders, win or die, because that was the code of the MechWarrior.

RICK HARRIS '93

36

"**C**ommunications check," Alexander Carlyle said, his fingers entering the proper code sequence on the keypad for his *Archer*'s comm console. "Channel one . . . channel two . . . channel three . . . channel four . . ."

He finished the sequence and returned to the base frequency. His crew chief, Technical Sergeant Newkirk, started running through his part of the drill. "Channel one, check," the astech said. The *Archer*'s computer switched channels to match the signals Newkirk was transmitting. "Channel two, check. Channel three . . . your transmission's a little ragged on three. Better take it off-line. Channel four, check . . ."

Finally it was done, with no further communications problems, and they moved to the next part of the check list, running the *Archer*'s targeting systems through a series of test problems to make sure it was ready for combat. Each step was absolutely necessary, and the process could be hurried only so much without risking a catastrophic oversight. Nevertheless, Alex begrudged every minute of the process.

The emelt train had stopped near the very top of Benmor Pass, high on the slopes to the east of Ben Mor, and for the past half-hour they'd been unloading and checking the 'Mechs as fast as men and machines could work. And all due speed was crucial. Though the narrow confines of the pass gave them some protection from the enemy fighter cover that periodically circled overhead, Captain Montclair's infantry pickets had been falling back for nearly an hour in the face of an advance by a lance of light recon 'Mechs that had crossed the Sheol River from the port into the town of Loch Sheol and then followed the road and maglev line south toward the pass. Alex's force was in danger of being caught by exactly the sort of preemptive attack the mobility of the maglev line was supposed to have given the Legion.

"Ah, Ghost Leader, Dingo One 'ere," came a voice over the commlink, interrupting Alex's ongoing exchange with Newkirk. Alex told the technician to wait, then switched to channel six to respond to the call.

"Go ahead, Dingo," he said.

"My boys are all up and runnin', mate," Lieutenant John "Dingo Jack" Murphy said. His accent, the product of his origins on Botany Bay far out in the Periphery, was as thick and colorful as McCall's, but usually easier to follow. Murphy commanded the recon lance of Dumont's Dreadnoughts, the 'Mech company that had drawn the Loch Sheol mission. He was independent, irreverent, and often irritating, but he was also a brilliant scout and light-'Mech tactician. Which made up for a great many sins. "Thought maybe you'd like us to go walkabout and see what we can turn up."

Alex smiled at the man's cocky tone and expressive turn of phrase. "Not just yet, Lieutenant," he replied, trying to keep from laughing over the open channel. "Move up to the head of the pass and take up defensive positions for now. You'll be the rallying point for Montclair's boys and girls if they have to fall back any further."

"Can't say as I agree with you, mate, but I guess you're the boss," Murphy told him. "But I'd rather be out there doing the hunting instead of crouching up in the rocks and waitin' to be caught like a 'roo in the billibong."

"You'll get all the freedom you need, Murphy," Alex said. "But it'll have to wait until more of the 'Mechs are ready to take over the line. Ghost Leader, clear."

He returned to the check list, running through the remaining items rapidly. The astech had just pronounced his 'Mech combat-ready when another call diverted Alex once more.

"Ghost One, this is Chevalier One." The stiff, formal tones belonged to Captain Guillaume Henri Dumont, the elegant, aristocratic young officer who had taken command of First Battalion in place of de Villar. "Please respond."

"Ghost Leader," Alex answered shortly. Dumont had made it crystal clear that he was not happy to be taking orders from a jumped-up cadet, and the dislike was mutual. The captain wasn't well-liked among the rest of the Gray Death officers because of his prim manner and aristocratic airs and the way he looked after his own comfort even in difficult field conditions, but everyone agreed he was a top-notch MechWarrior with a flair for the kind of tactics that had made the Legion famous.

"I just had a report that Lieutenant Murphy's lance has started moving forward. When I requested an explanation from Lieutenant Rammadutta, he indicated that Lieutenant Murphy claimed to be acting on orders from you."

Alex frowned. "That's right. I've ordered him to hold the mouth of the pass until the rest of the company is ready to relieve him."

"If you *please*, Colonel," Dumont said, his voice tight and clipped. "If you please, in future I would appreciate it if you would adhere to the chain of command. Perhaps your training has not yet encompassed the matter, but I assure you it is of the utmost importance, particularly when dealing with an officer like Lieutenant Murphy. He is all too eager to take advantage of any ambiguities in the command structure in order to indulge his own taste for glory."

"I . . . see," Alex said slowly. He should have realized that Dumont would be a stickler for the chain of command. Properly, the order for Murphy's lance to go forward should have gone from Carlyle to Dumont, then to Dumont's replacement as CO of the Dreadnoughts, Lieutenant Joshi Rammadutta.

He was aware of the chain of command, but the Legion's freewheeling style didn't generally make much of an issue out of it . . . except, obviously, in Dumont's outfit.

"I regret any appearance of impropriety, Captain," Alex went on, choosing his words with care. "However, I'd appreciate it, in turn, if you'd keep in mind the need for flexibility in this operation. I won't always be able to consult with you on every decision I make." He cut the channel before the battalion commander had a chance to reply. Then he keyed the commlink again, switching to the channel reserved for the technical staff and breaking in on a conversation between one of the crew chiefs and the battalion's senior technician, Captain Almonte. "Status report," he said when the tech was on the line.

"Eight 'Mechs on-line, Colonel," Almonte told him. "The four recon 'Mechs, two from the fire lance, and the two belonging to you and Cadet . . . er, MechWarrior DeVries. The rest of the fire lance will be ready to go in another five minutes."

"And the ETA for the whole unit?"

"Twenty, maybe twenty-five minutes," the technician said. "Less if we don't run into any problems. We've been lucky till now, so I'm not going to count on it. There's always at least one problem . . .''

"All right, keep at it. Concentrate on speed. If you hit a snag, go to the next 'Mech and leave the hard stuff for last."

"Yes, sir," Almonte said. After the exchange with Dumont, it felt good to be dealing with someone who didn't sound as if he had an outsized chip on his shoulder.

Alex called up the tactical map. The feed from Montclair's infantrymen showed the four enemy 'Mechs within a kilometer of the Bridge of Benmor, and that was uncomfortably close to the legionnaires. Something had to be done about them before they became a major threat.

But Alex was even more concerned, right now, over the things that didn't show up on the battle map. None of the Gray Death infantry was in a position to overlook Sheolport any longer, and the marching lines of ridges concealed whatever his opposite number might be doing out there. They'd spotted two *Union* Class DropShips and a *Leopard* on the ground, enough to carry a short battalion of 'Mechs. That wasn't quite twice what Alex had with him, but enough to make the odds damned uneven. Particularly since Vargas and his four fighters, though scrambled and ready to come to Alex's assistance, were no match for the enemy air cover.

They couldn't afford to let the enemy threat develop further. The Legion had to strike quickly, but first they needed to know just what they were up against.

How had Murphy referred to it? Time to go walkabout, to scout out the enemy instead of staying here and letting the bad guys seize the initiative . . .

He switched to the general commlink channel. "This is Ghost Leader to all units. New orders. Lieutenant Murphy, prepare to move out on my command. Lieutenant Obote will move the fire lance up to relieve the recon lance at the head of the pass. Ghost Lance and Dingo Lance are going out to probe toward Loch Sheol and see if we can deal with those enemy scouts. Captain Dumont, you will take command here, deploy all available BattleMechs, and take whatever defensive measures you consider necessary to secure the unit until the reconnaissance is completed. Captain Montclair's force to draw back to support the 'Mechs here. Any questions?''

There were none. Alex breathed out a small sigh. If McCall had been there, he probably would have argued against Ghost Lance participating in the recon effort, but Dumont was probably glad to have his inexperienced CO out of his hair for a while. He suppressed a twinge of guilt at the thought of McCall's likely reaction. Alex needed first-hand information on the enemy before he could plan the next move. And there was also the question of how reliable Dingo Jack Murphy was likely to be if given too free a rein.

But at the core of it, he knew that his real reason for going in was his reluctance to send the recon 'Mechs into unknown danger while he stayed back in safety and waited while his men started dying again.

MechWarrior Feldwebel Hermann Franke paused his *Wolverine* and checked his long-range sensor array. According to the aerial recon reports, there were enemy Gray Death BattleMechs beginning to deploy along the high ground of the Benmor Pass fifteen hundred meters to the south, but his readings were inconclusive. The high metal content of these mountains obscured the magnetic anomaly detectors, while the high atmospheric temperatures that prevailed in these volcanic uplands brought infrared scanners to the verge of electronic nervous breakdown. And without MAD or IR to go on, even a hulking metal monster like a BattleMech was damned hard to spot if it didn't want to be seen.

''What's the matter, Sarge?'' MechWarrior Ryser asked. Her *Cicada* was on the left flank of the loose, diamond-shaped patrol formation, with her teammate's *Whitworth* off to the right. Franke had taken the point position himself for this patrol, leaving MechWarrior Jaten and his *Dervish* to bring up the rear and provide fire support if they ran into trouble.

So far, all they'd spotted were a couple of parties of infantry hastily falling back toward the pass, plus a fast-moving Saracen hovertank that had skittered away out of range before the 'Mechs could target it. He had expected a more active resistance from the vaunted Gray Death Legion, and the fact that it hadn't materialized yet was starting to make him edgy.

"Just a feeling, Ryser," he said. "Look, increase dispersion by fifty percent. Ryser, I want you to advance to the crest of the hill off to your ten . . . Hill Two-one-five, according to the map. You should have a pretty good view of the river valley and the two bridges from there. If those mercenaries are planning to fight at all, they'll be covering the bridges so that their troops can cross over the gorge there." He paused. "But for Blake's sake be careful. If they've got heavy stuff—LRMs or PPCs—at the mouth of Benmor Pass, you'll be in range. So be ready to fall back if you come under fire."

"Don't worry 'bout me, Sarge," Ryser told him, sounding cheerful.

Franke would have liked to feel as nonchalant as she sounded.

"Colonel Carlyle, I can see those four 'Mechs now. Another couple of minutes and they'll be in sight of the bridges."

Sitting in Benmor Pass in the cockpit of his *Archer,* Alex acknowledged Lieutenant Elphinstone's signal. Her platoon was drawn up on the slopes of Ben Mor west of the mouth of the pass and high enough to command a good view of the road from the bridges all the way to the outskirts of Loch Sheol, though the port was hidden by intervening high ground.

He hesitated for an instant. The enemy 'Mechs were closer than he'd thought, and that put everything at risk. If they decided to destroy the road where it spanned the Sheol River, it would almost certainly render a Legion attack impossible. The river wound through a steep-banked gorge nearly forty meters deep where the road and maglev bridges crossed, and neither infantry, hovertanks, or 'Mechs without jump jets would be able to cross. A battle here could prove disastrous.

But it was still possible to change the equation, provided he acted in time.

"Murphy," he ordered urgently. "I want you and Bodnar to use your jump jets to drop down into the river. Stay tight against the north bank to avoid being seen, and make your way along the river to a point behind the enemy column . . . say, five hundred meters downstream. Royale, Lovell, you two are with me." He hesitated. "You too, Caitlin."

Like his *Archer* and Caitlin's *Centurion*, neither Royale's *Commando* nor Lovell's *Raven* were equipped with jump jets. With the river as cover the other two could maneuver without being spotted, but the less mobile 'Mechs would have to play the role of bait in the interim.

Alex shifted to a flat-out run and thundered across the bridge, with the *Raven* and Caitlin's 'Mech close behind and Royale bringing up the rear in the tiny *Commando*. Once across, he veered sharply to the left. His rear monitors showed Murphy and Bodnar descending into the gorge, out of sight.

They had just to hope none of the enemy fighters came in close enough to spot them from above.

"Ghost Leader calling Dragonslayer," Alex said, switching commlink channels. "Vargas, I need a diversion that'll keep their fighters busy for a minute or two. Can do?"

"Can do, Colonel." the squadron leader acknowledged without hesitation. "Let's see how serious they are about keeping us out of the DZ."

Four remaining fighters matched up against twelve or more Free Skye craft, odds that made Alex shudder. This time Vargas wouldn't be able to count on the elements of surprise and confusion that had netted him all those shoot-downs over Dunkeld.

"Enemy in sight," MechWarrior Royale warned.

Alex glanced at his screens, saw the *Cicada* clambering into view on a hill a few hundred meters north and on the other side of the road. "I've got him. Lovell, it's time to give them a little symphony, don't you think?"

He could almost hear the anticipation in the man's voice. "Hope they like the music," Lovell said. "And a one, and a two . . ."

The *Raven* was a scout 'Mech designed especially for electronic warfare. It carried sophisticated sensors and a wide range of special targeting systems, plus an array of jamming gear. Though no form of ECM could defy computer-driven redundancies and switching systems for very long, the *Raven*'s ability to break down an opponent's command and control for a few crucial seconds could be a tremendous advantage in a firefight.

Alex programmed his fire controls. "Let's let 'em know they're not welcome," he said, and tightened his finger on the firing stud of his joystick.

His port-side LRM battery fired, sending a swarm of missiles arcing toward the exposed 'Mech on the hill. "Lovell, Royale, split up and take cover," he ordered, firing the starboard-side battery hard on the heels of the first volley.

As the missiles began to fall around the *Cicada*, Alex broke into a run again and headed for the partial cover of one of the thick ferrocrete pylons that supported the maglev line. He was willing enough to risk damage there, if it would draw attention away from the bridge. Even if the Legion lost at Loch Sheol today, the invaders might finally make their own job more difficult if they ended up wrecking the maglev line, thus paralyzing their own logistics capacity.

Explosions rippled all around the *Cicada*, but the pilot withdrew before Alex's BDA sensors could determine how much damage the strike might have done. That particular model wasn't very well-armored, and with luck those missile hits might have rendered the 'Mech useless or nearly so. He hoped so. This battle had to be short and sharp, over before any of the enemy's other assets on the area could come up and join the fight.

"Here they come," Caitlin reported.

Through a gap in the undulating terrain on either side of the road, Alex could pick out the loose skirmish line of 'Mechs moving forward at a trot. A *Wolverine* . . . a *Whitworth* . . . and the *Cicada*, with a ragged hole in its right torso and obvious internal damage, but still moving, and still potentially dangerous.

And all three were heading straight toward the bridge, ignoring the Gray Death 'Mechs entirely.

37

"I don't know! First the jamming cut in, and then I was under fire! I didn't see where it was coming from!"

MechWarrior Feldwebel Franke cursed under his breath. Ryser's voice was ragged with static, but even the distortion caused by the Gray Death jammer couldn't hide the thin edge of panic. "Easy, Ryser," he said. "We know they've got positions up on the ridge. All we have to do is flush the bastards, then let Jaten work a little of his counterbattery magic on them."

From their position near the Bridge of Benmor, the three 'Mechs left Jaten's *Dervish* behind, moving past the hill where Ryser had come under fire. Franke felt every nerve, every muscle going taut within him. It was times like this, when the enemy's positions were close by but unknown and with no way to predict how much firepower might rain down at any moment that a MechWarrior often regretted his choice of career. These metal mountains, heavily armed and armored, might be the kings of the battlefield in a stand-up fight, but in a situation like this they felt more like incredibly slow, incredibly large and lumbering targets just begging to be smashed by incoming fire.

"Full speed!" he shouted. "Run for the bridge!" That was the best way to draw a reaction. Once the scout 'Mechs were over that bridge, they'd be able to take advantage of the rugged mountain slopes beyond, and jump jets and high maneuverability would compensate for superior enemy numbers until they could pinpoint their opponents' dispositions and call in support from the *Dervish* or the covering fighters.

It would be the best way to draw a reaction, but also the best way to commit suicide, if they didn't move fast.

"Damn!" Alex spat out. "Lovell, Royale, attack now! We've got to divert the bastards!" His whole strategy was falling apart. "Caitlin, circle left in case their fourth 'Mech is coming in over that ridge on the other side of the maglev line!"

He stepped out from the cover of the pylon near the Bridge of Benmor and lined up his shot, aiming for the *Whitworth* this time. The enemy 'Mech was slow, but well-armed and equipped with jump jets, and in this kind of fight probably the most dangerous 'Mech out there.

As Alex hit the firing studs on each side of his joystick simultaneously, both LRM launchers roared as one.

"Incoming! Incoming!" Feldwebel Franke shouted as his sensors picked up the missiles arcing in from the right flank. "God damn, those mercs are already across the river!"

He wrenched the *Wolverine* to the right, nearly losing the 'Mech's footing on the slick surface of the road. A *Raven*, its elongated cockpit giving it the beaklike head of its namesake, sprinted from cover with both arm-mounted lasers firing. One beam caught his lower leg, but didn't penetrate the armor. Franke triggered his jump jets for a sideways leap, unloading a full autocannon ammo cassette as he landed. Shells tore into the *Raven*'s stubby left arm.

"I'm hit! Christ, Sarge, I'm—"

MechWarrior Anuskiewicz never finished his last transmission. Missile after missile had slammed into the right torso of the *Whitworth*, blowing away armor in huge chunks and exposing the skeletal internal structure underneath. Then a new wave of explosions rocked the 'Mech, the fury of the attack detonating LRM warheads still in their loading rack. The *Whitworth* swayed for a moment, then collapsed in a heap of useless, twisted metal and half-melted plastic.

Alex Carlyle barely noticed the effect of his fire on the *Whitworth* as he shifted his targeting cross hairs toward the *Wolverine* that had shattered Lovell's starboard laser, but the voices on the commlink were quick to respond.

"That's one for the Colonel!" MechWarrior Royale whooped. "Give 'em hell, Legion!"

Royale's little *Commando* raced across the open terrain between the maglev line and the road, trying to close the range with the damaged *Cicada* before the enemy pilots could recover from the sudden onslaught. But at that moment a cloud of missiles arced over the hills from the north, and the MechWarrior's shouts turned suddenly to a wordless cry of fear and pain. Another wave of missiles fell on the *Commando,* and this time multiple warheads slammed repeatedly into the cockpit.

MechWarrior Winston Royale never ejected.

Alex swallowed sour bile and fired on the *Wolverine,* but the fast-moving 'Mech was already bounding backward on flaming jump jets. His missiles didn't even come close. He muttered a curse and started to set up the targeting program again.

A warning alarm shrilled. Alex glanced at his status board, saw the traces on the tactical monitor that showed incoming missiles targeted on his *Archer.* He took a few steps forward, but too late to clear the target zone. The first two warheads were near misses, the force of their explosions making the *Archer* stagger as he fought for control, barely keeping the 'Mech upright to the sound of whining, overloaded gyros.

Then a missile slammed into the *Archer*'s left arm. The blast only scored the armor plating above the elbow joint, but the force of it shook Alex up. He lost track of the rest of the strikes, but at least three more struck the 'Mech.

And as abruptly as it had started, the barrage was over. Alex shook his head to clear the ringing in his ears, then wished he hadn't. Through a haze of pain and disorientation, he squinted at the damage board. There were no red lights, but his comm board was showing an amber warning signal that indicated partial failure of the commlink systems, and he'd lost a lot of armor from the damaged arm. A few more bombardments like that one would send him down the same grim road Royale had just traveled.

Still groggy, it took him a long moment to recognize the motion outside his cockpit as the Steiner *Wolverine,* now bounding toward him on its jump jets, ready to take advantage of his weakness . . .

"Alex! Alex! Ghost Leader, respond!" Caitlin DeVries al-

most screamed into the commlink mike. Her rear monitors had
caught the missile attack on the *Archer,* and though the hulking
BattleMech didn't seem too badly damaged, it was neither moving nor firing, and Alex wasn't answering . . .

She hesitated. Her *Centurion* was near the crest of the
ridge Carlyle had ordered her to cover. According to the
computer's counterbattery tracking function, she'd have a
clear shot to engage whatever was firing those missiles once
she reached the top.

But Royale's *Commando* was gone, and the *Raven* was
damaged. And neither of those light 'Mechs would be much
good supporting Alex Carlyle against the *Cicada* and the
Wolverine working together.

Another volley of missiles arced straight overhead. If
somebody didn't do something about the LRM battery on
the other side of the ridge, Alex wouldn't have a chance
anyway.

Grim-faced, Caitlin DeVries continued climbing.

Alex Carlyle forced himself to shake free of the lassitude
that had gripped him since the first missile attack. More
LRMs were coming in, but their targeting was off this time
and they hit fifty meters beyond his position, kicking up
dust and debris with each impact. Sluggishly at first, but
then with increasing confidence, he backpedaled slowly over
the uneven ground and tried to line up his targeting reticule
on the fast-moving *Wolverine.* Trading his missile batteries
for the *Archer*'s two arm-mounted lasers, he opened fire just
as the enemy 'Mech was finishing a jump, catching the enemy squarely in the center torso with both pulses.

Neither shot penetrated, but they pitted the *Wolverine*'s
thick chest armor enough to give the pilot something to think
about. The *Archer* outmassed and outgunned the other
BattleMech, but only if Alex could keep his opponent at a
distance so that his LRMs could take their toll.

Out of the corner of his eye, he could see Lovell's damaged *Raven* trading shots with the *Cicada* and apparently
getting the better of the fight. If they could just get those
hidden missile batteries beyond the ridge out of the picture,
the odds were still in the Gray Death's favor . . .

Caitlin DeVries reached the top of the ridge and surveyed
the valley below. The enemy 'Mech was right out in the

open, a *Dervish* standing still to conserve heat while it fired as quickly as its missile launchers could recycle between shots.

The *Dervish* was only slightly heavier than her *Centurion*, though the design was better armed and included jump jets that would make it a slippery opponent. But this time she didn't hesitate. Arming her own missiles and the *Centurion*'s autocannon, she started down the slope with guns blazing.

Almost immediately the *Dervish* pilot reacted, jumping eastward and shifting its batteries to face the new foe. Missiles streaked toward the *Centurion*, but went wide in the enemy pilot's haste to shift from indirect to direct fire. Her autocannon stitched a line of shell craters across its armored torso.

And then, abruptly, the scene was transformed. In an instant the *Dervish* was bracketed by two more BattleMechs bearing the crest of the Legion settling down on pillars of fire on either side of the fighting machine. Murphy's *Wolverine* opened fire from close range with a battery of Harpoon SRMs, and a moment later the *Jenner* added its vote with four laser beams all aimed straight at the target's cockpit.

As the *Dervish* toppled, Caitlin's only thought was of how she had made the wrong choice. She had left Alex to face the enemy alone, though Murphy hadn't needed her help here to deal with the *Dervish*.

She only hoped her bad judgment hadn't left Alex Carlyle to die unaided.

Alex fired off his missiles and swore once again as the *Wolverine* jumped away. The speed and maneuverability of his target just about made up for his own advantages of size and firepower, and the result was little short of a stand-off. That other pilot was good, damned good, and Alex was beginning to think he'd never be able to pin him down.

At least the missiles from the far side of the ridgeline had stopped falling. It looked, too, as if Lovell had finally found the *Cicada*'s weak spot and hammered it hard enough to put the damaged 'Mech out of action for good.

If only he could put an end to his own duel the same way.

Alex traded LRM shots yet again, missing the target but taking more damage of his own. This whole operation was turning into a debacle. An *Archer* should have been able to take out a comparative lightweight like a *Wolverine* without even running up its heat levels too much.

Alex was trying to line up another shot when Murphy and Bodnar appeared on the crest of the hill where they'd first spotted the *Cicada*. He felt like cheering, but he also felt like a fool, being bailed out by the recon lance because he couldn't deal with the enemy himself.

The *Wolverine*'s pilot finally recognized defeat when Caitlin's *Centurion* materialized on the road. He popped the cover on his canopy and ejected, leaving his 'Mech standing like a brooding war memorial in the middle of the devastated field. Bodnar's *Jenner* touched down nearby to take the man prisoner before he could fade into the underbrush and attempt an escape back to his friends at Loch Sheol.

Loch Sheol . . .

For all the fighting, for all the sacrifice, Alex was still no closer to learning what awaited them at Loch Sheol.

38

Hauptmann Ison-Price frowned as she checked the cockpit scanner readouts. This pesthole she'd drawn as her station in the general's Operation Trident made most of her sensors unreliable, but some deep instinct told her that the enemy wasn't far away.

Damn Franke and his lance! she thought bitterly. A single message, heavily laden with static, had reported the patrol lance taking fire near the head of Benmor Pass. After that, silence. Company B was operating in the dark, and Ison-Price didn't like it one bit.

She let out a sigh of resignation. The general's orders had left no room for initiative or second thoughts. With the patrol lance out of touch, it was her duty to take her troops out of Sheolport and engage the Gray Death as soon as possible.

"Move out, people," she ordered sharply, and swung her *Crusader* around. With the rest of the company command lance following, she led the way toward the bridge to Loch Sheol, where the four 'Mechs of the fire lance were already waiting. As she started over the bridge, the driver of the Hetzer wheeled assault gun guarding this section of the port perimeter waved nonchalantly. She envied the infantry and armor in the landing force. Their job was easy—secure the port perimeter and wait for further orders.

But easy or hard, she had her duty, and Hauptmann Ison-Price intended to see it carried through to the end.

* * *

"That's only four more, Colonel Carlyle," said Dingo Jack Murphy over the command channel. "I can't believe we could've missed an entire company or more. If we've overlooked so much as a deserter taking a crap behind a tree then it's time I give it up and go back to hunting 'roos for a living!"

Alex Carlyle nodded slowly, but of course Murphy couldn't see him. His commlink was back on line, after a fashion, but it would take a full overhaul before he'd be exchanging voice-and-image messages. "Yeah, I know what you mean," he said, frowning at his monitors.

Following the battle with the enemy recon 'Mechs, Carlyle, Murphy, Caitlin, and MechWarrior Bodnar had continued their interrupted scouting mission, leaving Lovell's *Raven* to wait on the road for Dumont to start bringing the rest of the Legion force across the river. The battalion commander had managed to imply that Alex had run a whole range of unnecessary risks in the fight by the bridge, charges that had done absolutely nothing to improve Alex's mood.

That had been more than an hour earlier. Since then Murphy had shown Alex and Caitlin a shallow slope down to the riverbed that he'd discovered during his flanking attack on the enemy lance. On Dingo Jack's suggestion they'd decided to conduct their probe along the river rather than using the more exposed road. The river had the advantage of cutting straight through the rugged terrain between the pass and the port facility, so it was almost as good as a highway for the four BattleMechs as they probed the unknown territory in search of the enemy.

They'd been lucky so far. Vargas and his pilots were still playing cat and mouse with the Free Skye fighter cover, but none of the enemy aerospacers had overflown the winding river since the scouting party had started using it. Meanwhile, the heat and magnetic disturbances continued to play merry hell with onboard sensors. Though Alex was exasperated at not being able to use them, he knew his force would never have been able to work their way this close to the enemy DZ otherwise.

Now Murphy's *Wolverine* had advanced to a position where he could hide behind a tumble of rocks and actually watch the Sheol port bridge, while the rest of the party waited further back and studied the situation from video signals relayed to them from the *Wolverine*'s cameras.

They'd visually identified only eight BattleMechs around the port. Were the others lying in ambush, waiting for the Gray Death to walk into an ambush? Or were they still aboard ship, delayed in unloading for some reason or other? Or . . .

"Murphy," Alex said with sudden urgency. "Can you get a visual on any of those DropShips from where you are?"

The scout didn't answer right away, but the video image blurred as he tried to swing his cameras to view the port. Alex cursed under his breath as he realized there just wasn't an adequate line of sight . . .

Then, suddenly, the monitor image went wild. It took Alex several seconds to realize that Murphy had just triggered his jump jets and leapt upward, out of the ravine. "Damn it, man, what are you doing?" he shouted.

"Just gettin' you what you wanted, mate," came back the imperturbable reply.

The *Wolverine* had touched down on the port tarmac, landing within a few meters of a Galleon class light tank and a cluster of surprised-looking riflemen. Murphy's weapons were already blazing, but even as his autocannon slammed round after round into the Galleon, his cameras were zooming in on the massive DropShips across the open surface of the landing field.

"Bodnar, Caitlin, get up there and give him some support," Alex snapped, angry at having this new fight suddenly forced on him, yet grudgingly admiring Murphy's freewheeling initiative. No wonder Dumont had sounded so disapproving when talking about the recon lance commander.

He started aiming his missile batteries to give Murphy covering fire, but his eyes were on the video images while his finger played over the keyboard. His own comm panel had already been programmed to record the images from the *Wolverine,* and after a moment he switched from the live feed to a playback. As one of the *Union* Class ships filled the screen he froze the frame and zoomed in.

Alex remembered that ship. The name, *Anastasia,* had been partly blacked out by the scorching marks of a missile detonation, but the computer verified that the registry numbers below were the same as the ones on the ship he'd attacked at Dunkeld.

It was theoretically possible to transfer 'Mechs between DropShips in orbit, but it was a long, laborious process and not something to be undertaken lightly. Odds were that the DropShip had touched down empty, since none of her 'Mech contingent had escaped the first landing.

He hastily checked the *Leopard,* and felt a sinking sensation deep in his gut. It was the other refugee from Dunkeld. Two empty DropShips . . .

The whole landing here at Loch Sheol had been a decoy after all. One company of BattleMechs lightly supported by ground troops, enough to simulate a major effort and draw a disproportionate number of legionnaires north to face them.

Which meant the real landing was yet to come.

"Those explosions are coming from the port!" Hauptmann Ison-Price stopped her *Crusader* and turned to head back toward the battle that had suddenly erupted behind the little 'Mech column at Loch Sheol. "Damn them! It's like fighting an army of phantoms!"

Her commlink crackled. "Trident One, Trident One, this is Asgard." General von Bulow's voice was curt, abrupt. "We have reports of fighting in the drop zone. Confirm."

She switched to the frequency of the ground-to-orbit relay. "Affirmative, Asgard," she reported. "They must have come in up the river and attacked as soon as they knew we were moving out. I have no details to report, but I confirm firing around Sheolport. More to follow . . ."

"I am ordering *Anastasia* and *Raven* to lift, Trident One," the general told her. "And the other two DropShips will move to the designated emergency retrieval point, since you can't cover the port itself. Your priority at this point is to keep the enemy engaged as long as possible, then withdraw to the retrieval point and pull out with whatever forces you can lift out. Do you understand your orders?"

"Yes, Herr General," Ison-Price grated. With almost a quarter of her force already lost and an oversized Gray Death company in the field, the chances of breaking off the action and getting aboard DropShips was narrow at best. "Request you release fighter support to assist us, sir."

"Negative, Trident One." The simple words sounded like a death knell in her ears. "Trident Two is commencing operations now and requires the fighters."

"But—" Ison-Price bit back the protest. As of now, her company had become expendable. As long as they kept the Gray Death contingent occupied here, von Bulow had no particular need to support them. "Orders acknowledged, Herr General," she said mechanically.

The channel went dead.

Hauptmann Ann Ison-Price considered her options. She could surrender now or she could fight on, with little hope of bringing more than a handful of her troops out alive.

She had always prided herself on upholding the honor of her regiment, on obeying orders and carrying out her duty no matter what. And others in the regiment were depending on her to fulfill her role at Loch Sheol and pin down the enemy while the rest of the Operation Trident unfolded.

But the force the Gray Death had sent north was already committed, wasn't it? A losing battle here would buy no more than a few hours' time and a few extra Legion casualties. In the long run would that really be enough to make a difference in the rest of the campaign?

She reached for her commlink board and switched channels to one of the frequencies reserved for diplomatic contact. Ison-Price had never let her troops down before. She didn't know if what she was about to do would change all that, but it was the only choice that made any sense to her now.

"Gray Death Commander, Gray Death Commander, this is Hauptmann Ann Ison-Price of the Tenth Skye Rangers. I wish to discuss terms of ending this . . . situation."

Alex heard the incoming message, but could hardly believe what his ears. For a sickening moment he wondered if he had made a fatal mistake, missed additional enemy 'Mechs on the ground after all. Perhaps the scout force was already surrounded.

But the four DropShips at the port were all lifting off, and except for some desultory resistance from the tanks posted around Sheolport there was no sign of an enemy counterattack. His scanners showed nothing, nor did a quick look around him using eyeballs and video cameras, the only reliable sensor gear he had left.

"Gray Death Commander, please respond," the call went on after a moment. "I wish to . . . I wish to surrender my force to save further unnecessary bloodshed."

She was surrendering . . .

Then those other ships had been decoys, and the 'Mech landing at Loch Sheol a diversion.

Or his opponent was trying to trick him.

He switched to the diplomatic channel. "Free Skye Commander, this is Colonel Carlyle, commanding the Gray Death Legion." Maybe if they thought Grayson Carlyle was on Glengarry after all, the invaders would be less inclined to debate matters. Certainly they might rapidly change their minds in favor of a fight if they knew that they were up against a half-trained cadet pretending to be the famous Colonel Grayson Carlyle. "If you're serious about surrender, then call off your infantry and armor immediately and recall those DropShips to the ground. And bring your BattleMechs and fighters back to Sheolport where I can see them." He hesitated, unsure of how far to push the bluff. "Any further sign of hostile action will result in the destruction of your entire command."

He shifted channels quickly. "Ghost Leader to Chevalier One. Dumont, get your forces moving toward Loch Sheol ASAP. Ghost Two will update you on the situation. Caitlin, you've been monitoring?"

"Yeah . . . Do you think they're serious, Alex?"

"I don't know. We'll soon find out." He switched back to the diplomatic channel just as his opposite number replied to his transmission.

"Colonel Carlyle, I have instructed the forces at Sheolport to suspend hostilities provided your troops do the same. But I have no authority over the aerospace forces, and cannot control their actions. My 'Mech company is preparing to cross the Sheolport Bridge. Do I have your guarantee of a truce until we conclude negotiations?"

Alex didn't reply right away. If it was all an elaborate deception, he could be leaving his exposed force open to disaster. But a chance to finish this confrontation without further losses was something he just couldn't pass us.

"You have it," he said at last. "My word of honor that we will only renew the battle if attacked first. Good enough?"

"Grayson Death Carlyle's word is good," she said. That made him wince. Was it bad faith for him to let that misconception stand? He didn't see that he had any choice. Not yet, at least.

"Very well," he said. "I will reestablish contact when I'm sure our terms have been met. Carlyle clear."

He paused to order Murphy to withdraw from the port. The scout returned to his previous position, with Mech-Warrior Bodnar's *Jenner* posted close by. Then he issued more detailed orders to Dumont, and listened gravely to a report from Vargas that indicated the enemy fighters had abruptly broken off and headed south and west, away from Glensheol.

"What are your orders, Colonel?" the pilot asked when he'd finished.

"For now, I want you flying cover here. If you pick up any sign of trouble, let me know. Ghost Leader, clear."

"Dragonslayer, on the way."

Then, and only then, did Alex make the call that he'd been wanting to make for what seemed like hours on end. "Ghost Leader calling Glengarry Command. Put me through to Major McCall."

"This is McCall," the major answered promptly, sounding harassed. " 'Tis aye guid tae hear your voice, laddie . . . Colonel. We've got troubles . . . big ones."

"Another landing?"

"Aye. Ainither four ships hae just changed their delta-vees. Computer says Coltbridge this time."

"The landing here turned out to be a diversion, Mac," Alex said quietly. "Two empty DropShips and a reinforced company that was nothing but bait. Von Bulow seems to have cut them loose pretty thoroughly now that he's launching the real attack. We've knocked out four 'Mechs and some infantry and armor in a couple of skirmishes, and now their CO is talking about surrender."

"Sounds like you and your lads and lassies hae been busy," McCall said, sounding impressed. "But by taking you north tae Loch Sheol, the enemy's got what they wanted whether their decoys surrender or not. The more time you spend there, the worse it is for us doon here."

"You're mobilizing Hannibal's Cannibals to head for Coltbridge, aren't you?"

"Aye . . . and the Companions who are left, too. But I dinna like it. If this is the real strike, they'll hae a' the advantages. And they still have not committed everything, either. There are aye more troops up there in orbit, lad, who can still complicate things more."

"Then I have to wrap it up here as soon as possible and get the Dreadnoughts south again. We can either reinforce you or cover another landing, if we have to."

"Aye, 'twould be the best. Dinna let them spin oot the negotiations for lang." McCall chuckled. "Aince upon a time back in auld Scotland, aince upon a time, Robert the Bruce tied doon an army ten times his ain size for over a month just by negotiating a wee surrender. Dinna let them dae as weil wi you . . . we dinna hae a month tae waste."

"I hear you, Mac. We'll be down there to back you up as soon as I can manage it. And it won't be a month, that much I'll promise."

"We'll be moving oot in ainither half-hour, lad. Good luck. You've done your auld faither . . . and your auld teacher . . . proud."

39

"**S**urrender!" General-Kommandant von Bulow slammed his fist down on the table in front of him, dislodging his hand terminal. It floated free on the bridge of the Free Skye DropShip *Asgard*, but neither he nor his aide paid it any heed.

"Yes, Herr General," Albrecht said tentatively. "Apparently Hauptmann Ison-Price opened negotiations about half an hour ago. We didn't pick it up at first because we haven't been monitoring the diplomatic channels regularly."

"Incompetents and cowards! The whole damned Tenth Skye is falling apart because the officer corps is made up of nothing but incompetents and cowards." Von Bulow made an effort to get his anger under control. "But maybe it's not as bad as it seems. Ison-Price might actually buy more time by stretching out the negotiations than she would have on the battlefield."

"It's possible, Herr General," Albrecht said. "But on this orbital pass the visual sensors have spotted the maglev trains in Benmor Pass starting to reload some of the equipment they were unloading last time we were overhead. I'd say they're planning to shift some of their forces south again soon."

"Can we mount a strike on the maglev line and cut them off where they are?" von Bulow asked.

"Herr General, that would mean weakening the fighter screen over the Coltbridge DZ or sending down a DropShip. But we haven't accounted for all their fighters yet, or for the

DropShip that got away. It might take a major effort to do any good, and it could certainly undo all the plans for the rest of Trident.''

Von Bulow glared at his aide, then nodded suddenly. ''You're right, of course, Johann. If we start trying to second-guess things at this point we'll end up with a hopeless muddle. I had hoped that more of their force would go north, and that they'd be tied up longer. But even if they manage to leave Glensheol early this afternoon it would take a miracle for them to do their compatriots any good.'' He smiled coldly. ''And when the real blow comes, they'll never be able to stop it.''

''Yes, Herr General,'' Albrecht responded dutifully.

Von Bulow reached out to pluck the floating terminal box out of the air just as he would pluck this planet from his enemies in another few hours.

Alexander Carlyle lifted the neurohelmet from his head and unstrapped from the *Archer*'s cockpit chair. He reached behind it to pull out his kit bag before slapping the touch pad beside the hatch. The lock opened and he scrambled out onto the immobile 'Mech's shoulder. Slinging the bag over his own shoulder, Alex started down the flexible ladder that had dropped from hatch to ground when the cockpit opened.

At the bottom, Technical Sergeant Newkirk gave him a quick thumb's up. ''Good job today, sir,'' he said with a grin. ''But you sure as hell destroyed the paint job when you took those missile hits.''

''Yeah,'' Alex answered him distractedly. ''Look, when you get her strapped down see if you can patch up the armor there some way. I want her ready to fight when we get to Coltbridge.''

''No guarantees, sir,'' Newkirk said. ''But we'll do what we can.'' He scrambled up the ladder. The astech would handle the shutdown procedure once he'd maneuvered the *Archer* gingerly down into the improvised cradle on the flatbed emelt car. That left Alex free to concentrate on other matters . . . like trying to plan what to do next.

By the time Dumont and the rest of the troops had approached the southern end of Loch Sheol, the Hauptmann at Sheolport had been willing to capitulate without haggling about terms. Probably it was the sight of the Dreadnoughts' fire lance, led by Lieutenant Obote's massive four-legged

Goliath, that had finally convinced them. The eight enemy
MechWarriors had stood down from their fighting machines
and surrendered, together with the infantry and the three
surviving tracked AFVs at Sheolport. Before surrendering,
however, the enemy 'Mech pilots had frozen out their neu-
rohelmets to keep the Legion from taking over their 'Mechs
immediately. But that was only a minor inconvenience, for
a competent electronics tech could have them up and running in a matter of hours.

That would have to wait, however. Alex had concluded
the negotiations entirely by commlink, and let Dumont, with
his flair for the proprieties, handle the formal aspects of the
surrender. The Free Skye prisoners, including the survivor
of the battle at the Bridge of Benmor, had been rounded up
by Legion infantry, disarmed, and confined in Loch Sheol.
Captain Montclair and his original force would remain in
the area to guard the prisoners and stand watch once more,
but the rest of Alex's command had barely waited for the
surrender before they were on their way back to Benmor
Pass. A lot of stores, reloads, and technical support gear
had already been going back aboard the emelts before the
'Mechs returned, and the process of hastily preparing the
unit to ship out once more was already well under way.

Once again Alex knew the agony of waiting. The last
word he'd received from McCall was of a 'Mech drop of
unknown strength around Coltbridge and of the old Caledonian's efforts to get his troops there in time to contain
them. Vargas and his fighters were patrolling between Loch
Sheol and Coltbridge in case the enemy tried to launch an
air strike along the maglev route. That had been McCall's
doing; Alex had never even considered the possibility—and
here were reports from the eastern part of the continent
that Governor DeVries was on the move again, though no
one knew what his intentions were at this stage. And in the
face of all these threats and rumors and potential disasters,
Alex was powerless to do anything until the techs finished
loading up the 'Mechs and gave the go-ahead for the move
back toward Dunkeld.

He couldn't help but wonder if any of it would make a
difference in the long run.

I was never cut out for this, Davis McCall thought bit-
erly, staring at his 'Mech display without using it. This is

work for the colonel . . . or for Cris de Villar. But not for
me . . .

The second Legion strike force had arrived at the maglev
junction near Coltbridge in just under an hour from the time
the first emelt car left Dunkeld, and the task of unloading
and prepping the 'Mechs as they reached their destination had
gone surprisingly well. The entire force, Captain Simms' company plus the much-reduced Gray Death Companions, had ren-
dezvoused with the infantry and armor deployed outside the
town. Commanding them was a former officer of the Planetary
Guard who had joined the Gray Death, a captain with the unlikely name of Lochinvar Fraser.

Fraser had tracked a 'Mech drop from low orbit down to
the ground. Instead of sending in their BattleMechs aboard
DropShips and unloading them on the surface, this wave had
come in fitted with ablative shielding, parachutes, and special shock-absorbing landing gear. Like outsized paratroop-
ers, the 'Mechs had descended individually, then spread out
over a wide area. It gave the Legion the advantage of having
the invaders dispersed during the first stage of the ground
fighting, but also made the task of locating the enemy and
predicting his next move considerably harder. And since
Coltbridge didn't have a port to serve as a focal point for
the landing, there was no simple way for McCall to outguess his foe. All the invaders needed in order to bring in
support troops and supplies was an open field large enough
to handle DropShips. And there were plenty of those around
Coltbridge.

That left the maglev station just outside town as the only
logical place to focus his own efforts. If the invaders planned
to use the maglev net for supplies, they'd aim to secure the
station before pushing on to the capital. Without it, they
couldn't master the computer-controlled switching or power
distribution systems that operated this segment of the net
work.

So in one way McCall's job was easy. He had a single
point to defend, and plenty of men and machines to mount
that defense. But they'd lost track of the enemy as their radar
signals were lost in ground clutter, and there was no way
of knowing from where the major blow would come—if and
when it came at all. McCall was worried that this landing
like the one at Loch Sheol, might have been a feint. With
all but a handful of the Gray Death drawn out of Dunkeld

perhaps General von Bulow was planning to land his main strength there after all.

McCall muttered an old Gaelic curse under his breath. He'd never claimed to be a tactician, nor had he ever been happy waiting on the defensive. It made him nervous. The Gray Death Legion had always been a strike force, carrying the battle to the enemy. Sitting in one place and waiting for the axe to fall wasn't his idea of how to make war. If Grayson Carlyle had been on Glengarry, McCall thought unhappily, he wouldn't have been forced into this uneasy waiting game.

"Major, I've got MAD readings to the northeast," Freida Bergstrom reported, icy calm as ever. Her 'Mech was posted two kilometers out from the station as an early warning post. "They're not ours . . ."

"Any other signs of trouble?" he asked.

None of the other recon 'Mechs had any similar reports to make. So either the enemy was coming in from the one direction, or they were staying out of reach until the battle was under way.

He made his decision quickly. "All recon 'Mechs to form on Lieutenant Bergstrom," he ordered. "Armor and infantry will dig in around the terminal and watch for other enemy columns. Captain Simms, prepare to move out."

The Legion was at its best when fighting a mobile battle. McCall would try to strike that enemy column quickly, before this turned into a static defensive situation.

He would do everything possible to win the day, but Major David McCall still wished it was Grayson Carlyle and not him in command.

40

"There they are," McCall said, in his cockpit video display, the enhanced image from the closest enemy Battle-Mech—still several kilometers away—filled the screen as if the fighting machine were close enough for the Bannock-burn to touch.

"Jesus, Mohammed, and Blake!" someone muttered over the commlink. "A *Zeus* . . . a *BattleMaster* . . . a *Cyclops*. . . ."

"I count three *Archer*s out there," another voice added. It sounded like Captain Hannibal Simms, McCall's second-in-command, his voice tinged with something between surprise and fear.

"They're really throwing in their big guns this time," Freida Bergstrom commented coolly. "I'm almost afraid to go in there, for fear they'll step on me."

"Quiet on the channel," McCall rasped. But he understood how they felt. Most of the Free Skye BattleMechs were heavy or assault models, weighing in at anything from seventy to ninety tons and bristling with weapons and armor. By contrast, the Gray Death had only a handful of 'Mechs massing more than fifty tons in the field, and only McCall's ninety-ton *Highlander* could equal a *Zeus* or a *BattleMaster* for sheer overwhelming power. If Grayson Carlyle had been in charge, McCall would probably have been making the same kind of comments as the others.

But he was in charge, and no amount of talk would change the equation that faced them now. The Gray Death had more

'Mechs in the field today, but they were lighter than their opponents and no match for most of them in a stand-up fight. This was the kind of situation where superior mobility counted the most. If they could manage to concentrate on just a few of their opponents at a time, they might have a chance. But they'd take serious causalities doing it.

And that kind of mobile running battle was ill-suited to the basic goal of protecting the Coltbridge maglev terminal. As long as the enemy kept advancing, they'd ultimately force McCall to make the choice between abandoning the terminal entirely and settling in for a defensive battle he couldn't possibly win.

What would Grayson Carlyle do? McCall asked himself, still staring at the images in his monitor.

He couldn't answer the question, but with each passing moment the two 'Mech forces drew closer to the fatal collision.

Leutnant-General Leonidas Brannock, commander of the advancing Free Sky forces, smiled as he studied his opponents. As expected, the Gray Death hadn't been content to stay on the defensive. They'd sallied forth from their perimeter to meet the advancing Free Skye force near Coltbridge, but he could just imagine how they would be reacting to their first sight of Brannock's 'Mechs. From the looks of it, only one of the 'Mechs out there was bigger than a seventy ton *Warhammer,* an odd-looking ninety-tonner that his computer's Warbook program identified as a *Highlander,* though this was the first time Brannock had ever seen or heard of such a 'Mech. And he could see a lot of smaller fighting machines—*Valkyries* and *Griffins* and the like—mixed in with the handful of decent-sized opponents.

Brannock had been skeptical of the orders from von Bulow putting him in charge of this portion of Operation Trident. It was, essentially, just another preliminary to the main thrust, but as commander of the Tenth Skye Rangers, Brannock believed that the place of honor at the head of the largest landing force should have gone to him.

Now he could see the wisdom of his superior's planning. His four lances were hard-hitting, powerful units, and even though outnumbered they would make short work of the opposition here. And if the Legion had additional reserves to throw in to the battle, Brannock's heavies would take a lot of punishment, but they'd deal out more death and destruction than they suffered along the way. Even if he didn't have the biggest force, Brannock could look forward to being the first of the Skye Rangers to enter Dunkeld once the fighting here was over.

The commanding officer of the Tenth Skye Rangers smiled coldly under his neurohelmet's face shield. These mercenaries hadn't even begun to see everything they were up against this time. With the fighters assigned to support his landing, he could break that rabble out there without so much as exposing his own 'Mechs to more than casual damage.

With the merest hint of a satisfied smile, Brannock reached for his comm board.

"All fighters, all fighters, prepare to execute Coltbridge ground support mission Beta Three."

Weltalleutnant Sean Ferguson bit his lip nervously and obeyed the strike leader's call. He banked his *Lucifer* left, checking the position of Henderson's fighter behind and to the right, then pushed his throttles forward into the red afterburner zone.

Ferguson felt as if he'd been in the air continuously for days on end, though in fact it had been only a doubled patrol shift. His superiors had made it clear that it was by only the narrowest margin that he'd missed arrest and perhaps even execution for his ill-timed retreat from the fighting over Glengarry's capital. It seemed his punishment was to fly mission after mission, until he was finally so exhausted he'd commit a fatal error and crash his fighter somewhere far from help or hope of rescue.

Despite the punishment, Ferguson knew that the fear he'd felt in that last fight would never go away. He wasn't sure anymore if he could carry out the orders his superiors would give him, if he could face another dogfight, another attack run through hostile fire. The thought nagged at the corner of his mind all the time, in the cockpit or floating weightless tethered to the bulkhead in his quarters aboard the *Merku* between missions.

But if he disobeyed again, he'd be a sure candidate for court martial. That is, if they didn't just space him out of handy airlock to save the ship's political officer time and paperwork.

"Targets! Targets, airborne, bearing zero-six-eight!" Henderson's tone was crisp and precise, by the book all the way. He shared Ferguson's black cloud, but to a lesser degree.

Ferguson checked his radar. Four blips, racing toward the ten fighters covering the Free Skye drop zone. Even before the computer predicted their identities based on speed, size, and configuration, Ferguson knew they were the four Gray Death fighters they'd tangled with over Dunkeld. This time the Free Skye force enjoyed a clear-cut numerical advantage, and they were ready for action, but Ferguson's mouth still went dry as he remembered the wild dogfight over the city. All by himself, one Gray Death pilot had accounted for half the Free Skye losses in the air that day. And here he was arriving for a return engagement . . .

"Strike Flight, Strike Flight, this is Strike Leader. We will engage the enemy fighters first." There was a pause. "Red One and Two will continue with the ground attack profile." Ferguson could almost hear the thought behind the bald order. The professional pilots didn't want any amateurs or cowards flying beside them when they went into battle.

"Red One, roger," he said, not sure if he was relieved or disturbed by the orders. "Ground attack profile."

His hand tightened involuntarily around the joystick as he dropped the *Lucifer*'s nose and led his wingman toward the last reported position of the enemy 'Mechs.

I won't be afraid, he told himself. I won't be afraid . . .

"Fighters! Fighters! Fighters!"

Davis Carlyle Clay heard Lieutenant Denniken's chanted warning and felt his throat tightening. As if the enemy didn't have enough firepower in those hulking 'Mechs looming in the distance, now they were bringing in fighters again. In his mind's eye he kept seeing the aircraft crashing into Cristiano de Villar's Mech. He even had visions of the Omnifighter attack that had claimed his father's life.

Vargas and his reduced squadron were on their way to support the defense at Coltbridge, but the invaders had enough craft in the air to neutralize them and still launch ground attacks that could crack the Gray Death 'Mechs open long before their heavies on the ground opened fire.

McCall had spread their BattleMechs out in a loose skirmish line, with the lightest machines far out on the flanks where they could use their superior mobility to dart in and out of the fighting once the two forces came together. Clay's post was near the center, close alongside McCall's *Highlander*. He could see the other 'Mech's guns tracking the approaching fighters, opening fire even before they were in visual range, trying to lay down a deadly pattern of airbursts in hopes of catching one of them with a lucky hit.

Suddenly two massive aerospace fighters, like flying BattleMechs, dropped down from the clouds on a low-level attack run. Explosions blossomed on the plain as they dumped their ordnance. Clay saw Denniken's *Cataphract* take a hit, while a missile swarm overshot his *Griffin* by scant meters. As he staggered, trying to keep his balance, he saw the *Highlander* continuing to blaze away as fast as its weapons could recycle between shots.

The fighter bringing up the rear seemed to lurch in midair as the *Highlander* found its mark. Smoke erupted from one of the engines, and a moment later it was spinning out of control toward the far bank of the Earn River. A parachute blossomed as the pilot ejected.

Clay let out a sigh of relief. "Good shooting, Major!" he whooped.

He felt safer now, knowing he was under McCall's guns.

"Red One. Good chute! Good chute!"

Leutnant-General Brannock heard the call, but right now it didn't much matter whether the pilot of the damaged fighter had ejected safely. Dead, captured, or just scrambling for cover on the ground, it all added up to the same thing. Most of the fighters had hared off after their Gray Death counterparts, and he was down to only one pilot to maintain the bombardment he'd been counting on from ten.

And that *Highlander* was nearly as good as a *Rifleman* for laying down antiaircraft fire. They had to neutralize the big BattleMech fast or risk losing the other fighter as well.

"Sparta Lance with me," he snapped, shifting the big *Zeus* into a lumbering run. Most pilots thought of the *Zeus* as a stand-off weapons platform, but Brannock had always found that the psychological advantages of engaging in close outweighed the arguments for staying back to take advantage of the LRM launchers and large laser mount. The best way to neutralize the enemy was to overwhelm him. The regimental command lance would break the enemy line i two right at the center, and then the fighter could close in for another run without having to run the gauntlet of those deadly accurate guns. Meanwhile the rest of his force would exploit the initial breakthroughs at every possible opportunity.

"Here they come!"

McCall looked up from his scanners to see the four biggest enemy 'Mechs bearing down like runaway juggernauts, straight toward the center of the Gray Death line. Nearby, Denniken's *Cataphract* took a few quick steps forward, all four lasers flashing while the torso-mounted autocannon slammed round after round into the *Cyclops* on the let flank. A moment later Hansen's *Dervish* and Nolans' *Catapult* joined the lance leader in concentrating fire in the massive machine, according to the tactics McCall had sketched out after studying the enemy battle line. When possible, all 'Mechs of a lance will engage a single target . . .

It would work, but only until the engagement became general, or until the Gray Death took enough losses to make ganging up on individual targets impractical.

The massive enemy *BattleMaster* was caught in a crossfire from 'Mechs of the fire lance from Hannibal's Cannibals, a *Warhammer* and a *Crusader* among them. McCall saw the *Warhammer*'s PPCs score a pair of hits on the *BattleMaster*'s left leg. That would weaken the limb considerably, something to keep in mind in case he had a chance to engage the assault 'Mech later.

Then McCall didn't have any time to spare to watch the other fights erupting around him. The Free Skye *Archer* had halted at optimum missile range and was opening fire. Though the first volley went wide, McCall had to act quickly to protect himself. And the *Zeus* was still running, coming straight toward the *Highlander* under the cover of the *Archer*'s firepower as if to challenge McCall's BattleMech to some archaic hand-to-hand brawl.

He lowered his Gauss gun and opened fire, but the shot went wild and missed the target. As the *Zeus* closed in, McCall resorted to the uncanny mobility of his massive BattleMech, triggering jump jets to bound sideways and back away from the *Zeus*' mad charge. Jump jets were rarely mounted on something the size of a *Highlander,* and the 'Mech's ability to jump often took an opponent completely off guard.

Clay tried to maneuver his *Griffin* forward to get off a PPC shot at the cockpit of the *Zeus*, but he rushed the shot and the range was too short for the finicky PPC targeting system. Almost casually the enemy pilot cut loose with his large laser, and Clay fell back quickly before a second shot ripped his 'Mech apart.

McCall gritted his teeth and aimed his Gauss gun for another shot. It looked like it was going to be a long, hard fight . . .

"Red One, this is Sparta One." The words crackled over Sean Ferguson's commlink. "Repeat your attack run."

Ferguson shuddered. He didn't want to go down there again, not after what had happened to Henderson . . .

"Do you read me, Red One? This is Sparta One." The general's voice sounded breathless, impatient. "We are engaging their antiair 'Mech. Repeat your attack run while we have their ground fire neutralized."

For long seconds Ferguson couldn't force himself to move the stick. Even the general's reassurance didn't make any difference. He had reached the breaking point, and the thought of running the gauntlet one more time had him paralyzed.

I will not be afraid, he repeated to himself, a silent mantra. This is the last chance. I *will* not be afraid!

And somehow, he found the courage to haul the stick over and bank sharply left, swinging his fighter around to make the attack run.

"Lieutenant Bergstrom! Captain Simms! The major needs help!" Clay's throat was so tight it was almost impossible to force the words out. The *Highlander* was a good match for the enemy *Zeus*, and McCall was handling it brilliantly, but no one was dealing with the *Archer* that was still lobbing volley after volley toward the Major's 'Mech.

He triggered the *Griffin*'s jump jets, thankful that King had found the time to repair the damaged ankle joint. His 'Mech bounded forward, and he drew a bead on the *Archer* with his PPC. If no one else would help, he must do what he could.

Explosions erupted around him, and Clay's wild look across his scanners showed a Free Skye fighter skimming low straight up the ragged defensive line toward him.

For an instant he froze again, the old, automatic reaction. Then something inside Dave Clay snapped, and he raised his PPC barrel skyward. He didn't have the sophisticated tracking gear the *Highlander* mounted, but a PPC hit would definitely give that fighter pilot something to think about.

Clay fired, cycled, fired, and fired again. His heat indicators shot up fast, and he heard the extra cockpit air coolers cut in to try to fight the sudden temperature surge. But he ignored all that, ignored everything except the enemy fighter and the sudden need to shoot it out of the sky.

Ferguson gaped as the tiny *Griffin* at the edge of his vision swelled rapidly in the screens of his fighter's cockpit. The 'Mech was standing stock-still, legs braced apart, arm upraised, making the air sizzle with bolt after bolt of raw energy from the PPC.

For a moment Ferguson couldn't react, and a moment was an eternity in the life of a fighter pilot. Steering a straight, level course, not even remembering to maintain his fire, Ferguson didn't realize what he was dong until it was too late.

The *Lucifer* bucked and rocked as it flew straight into the PPC pattern. Red lights lit up his damage board, and an alarm shrilled a warning in counterpoint to the screech of armor melting and twisting as the PPC shots played across the fighters belly.

All the commotion finally snapped Ferguson out of his trance. He scanned the damage readings quickly, but the sluggish feel of the joystick told him more about the damage to control surfaces on the underside of the wing than any pattern of red and amber lights could. The battered *Lucifer* was going down, and there was nothing he could do to stop it.

Infantrymen clustered around the terminal building gaped up at the stricken craft as it passed over the maglev station and the wide, sluggish River Earn. Awkwardly, he fumbled for the ejection mechanism, yanked back hard on the lever, and closed his eyes.

Wind whipped in his face as the cockpit canopy blew and his seat slammed upward into his spine.

A moment later he as floating gently down to the ground under a spreading parachute and straight into the arms of an infantry patrol bearing the skull patches of the Gray Death Legion.

For Sean Ferguson, the war was finally over.

McCall grunted in satisfaction as the twin medium lasers in the *Highlander*'s left torso mount found their mark. The hit didn't do much more than scorch the heavily armored *Zeus,* but at least it was a score.

Another missile barrage streaked toward him, and he barely had time to trigger his jump jets and leap clear before the ground where he'd been standing erupted under the impact of forty warheads exploding simultaneously. That *Archer* was more dangerous, at this point, than the *Zeus,* at least as long as the *Zeus* pilot continued to insist on close combat. A sardonic, detached part of McCall's mind remembered the lecture he'd given young Carlyle after the training exercise with the simulated *BattleMaster.* Apparently Alex Carlyle wasn't the only MechWarrior who had catapulted to high rank without learning the value of using his weapons to best advantage instead of indulging foolish preferences for some particular, limited combat style.

"Scratch one overstuffed bastard!" Andrei Denniken whooped. McCall allowed himself a quick glance down the line. The hulking Free Skye *Cyclops* was still as a statue, with one arm off at the shoulder and lying in the grass nearby and a pillar of smoke roiling from the ruined remnants of its cockpit. Denniken's crack shooting had scored again.

"Hey, Russki!" McCall called. "If you can stop patting yoursel' on the back, I could aye use some help dealing with yon *Archer.*"

"Cossacks to the rescue again," Denniken replied. "In case any of you in the fire lance couldn't understand him, our fearless leader wants that *Archer* taught a lesson or ten. I've got a flask of vodka for the gunner that brings the bastard down!"

"Major," Lieutenant Bergstrom warned. "The rest of their line is starting to move."

McCall muttered a Gaelic oath under his breath. his duty as commanding officer required him to stay above the fight, direct the battle as a whole instead of letting himself get caught up in the battle madness. Wasn't that just the thing he'd lectured young Carlyle about, an eternity ago? If not for Bergstrom's alertness, he might not have noticed the second wave starting forward until it was too late.

He unloaded all his weapons at once in the direction of the *Zeus* and took two quick bounds back toward the Earn. "Get clear, Ghost Three!" he called. The *Zeus* wasn't maneuverable enough to catch up with either McCall's *Highlander* or Clay's *Griffin* if they made a determined effort to stay out of reach. The big threat was that the frustrated enemy pilot would shift to using his formidable long-range arsenal.

McCall switched commlink frequencies hurriedly. "Captain Fraser, send in the Harassers!"

It was the same tank platoon, short-handed now, that had supported the defense at Dunkeld, three Harasser hovertanks armed with missile launchers. They weren't quite the equal of the enemy *Archer* contingent, but they'd be a damned good equalizer all the same. If only McCall and his men could hold the line until the Harassers arrived to lay down a sustained barrage, he could start trading ground for time.

But somewhere in the back of his mind, McCall knew that sooner or later he'd run out of both.

A *Wolverine* jumped toward Clay's *Griffin*, its autocannon firing as it settled to the ground barely fifty meters away. A pair of rounds slammed into the *Griffin*'s shoulder, but Clay gritted his teeth and answered the shot with a PPC bolt. It chewed deep into the armor on the enemy 'Mech's right arm. Clay made a quick jump of his own past the other 'Mech, then turned quickly as he touched down and fired again.

The maneuver took his opponent by surprise, and he was slowly turning. Clay's next PPC shot caught the *Wolverine*'s relatively weak rear torso armor before the pilot could swivel, and the burn-through exposed the skeletal outlines of the 'Mech's framework and sparking, arcing cables that writhed as if with a life of their own. The *Wolverine* pilot didn't wait to argue points of honor. His next jump was away from Clay, but not far enough to escape the third shot that took the right arm off entirely.

Clay hoped his father was watching him from whatever Valhalla the veterans of the Gray Death Legion inhabited. For the first time, he truly felt like a MechWarrior, and he thought that perhaps, just perhaps, Delmar Clay might have the grace to utter a few sparing words of praise at the way his son had finally lived up to the family name.

Suddenly a pair of enemy *Griffins* were flashing toward him, and there was no more time for such thoughts. Clay was no more suicidal today than his erstwhile opponent in the *Wolverine*, and he triggered his jump jets to fall back in the face of the sudden advance.

"Bergstrom, Yuhas, get those lighter 'Mechs clear!" McCall ordered. As the heavier enemy BattleMechs closed the range, the recon lances would be in the most danger. Some of the 'Mechs in the invaders' arsenal could put one of the Gray Death's lightweights out of action with a single shot.

Missiles were still falling near his *Highlander*, but at least that first *Archer* had retreated under the onslaught of Denniken's lance. Unfortunately, they in turn had retreated from a *Marauder,* a *Caesar,* and the somewhat battered *BattleMaster* that had finally managed to disengage from Lieutenant Zetterling's *Warhammer.*

Now that both enemy fighters had been shot down and the Harassers were starting to make their presence known, the battle had started to develop a seesaw quality. A Gray Death lance would combine to destroy or drive back one of their Free Skye opponents, only to come up against some combination they couldn't handle. Then the Legion 'Mechs would give way in turn.

"Start a leapfrogging withdrawal on the terminal," McCall ordered curtly. Now that the battle was heating up, he was most afraid of being caught out here and forced into a toe-to-toe slugging match. By falling back, he might just induce the enemy to start scattering, and that would give the Legion a fresh chance to catch a few of the more foolhardy pilots flapping in the breeze.

If he could just keep everyone working together, all would be well . . .

The heat in his cockpit suddenly surged alarmingly, triggering alarms and warning lights. Reacting more by instinct than design, McCall jerked the BattleMech sideways to pull away from the laser beam that had just grazed his cockpit armor. He cursed aloud this time. While he'd been focusing all his attention on the big picture, one of the little pictures—that same damned *Zeus*—had caught him completely off guard. Less than a meter to the right and it would have burned right through.

As it was, he didn't like the looks of the damage board. It was showing short-circuits in the environmental controls and his ejection system.

All at once the environmental monitoring board to his left started to smoke, then spark, and then the overloaded systems simply blew, smashing McCall sideways. His harness held him, but his helmeted head was snapped back, hard, and David McCall went hurtling into darkness.

41

"**M**ajor McCall! Major!" Dave Clay shouted the name over and over, but the weapons master didn't reply.

"He's been hit," Captain Simms said. "All units, fall back. Harassers, pour on the missiles! Go! Go!"

Clay ignored the retreat order. He cut in his jump jets and leaped straight toward the unmoving *Highlander,* determined to save his father's friend or die trying . . .

Leonidas Brannock checked the BDA sensors of his *Zeus* and frowned. According to his computer's best estimate, his laser shot hadn't been enough to cause any serious damage to the *Highlander.* But it stood there, unmoving, while all around the Gray Death fell back.

A trick? He wouldn't have put it past that pilot, who seemed to have a charmed life and an ideal sense of the ebb and flow of battle. But if that was the command 'Mech, which all the signs indicated that it was, its sudden immobilization certainly seemed to have spread dismay among the rest of the legionnaires. Would the 'Mech pilot resort to a trick like that even though it could backfire and cause a full-scale panic?

Or was the retreat just another of the Legion's famous tactical tricks, too? At the NAIS Academy Brannock had studied military history from the Greeks all the way through the last Succession War, and he could think of any number of battles that had hinged on a feigned retreat that lured a foe into ambush. Hannibal had done it at Cannae, and the official accounts of William the Conqueror's triumph at Hastings claimed that he had ordered the same stratagem, though the feigned panic had probably turned all too real at the time.

Grayson Death Carlyle was notorious for doing the unexpected, and his subordinates had learned from him. Caution was the wisest course, and yet Brannock knew that unleashing his BattleMechs as the enemy fled in disorder could win the victory here and now.

He didn't waste much time thinking about it. The only sure way to keep the enemy on the run was to press them hard and make damned sure their leader really was dead.

"All units, all units," he called over the commline. "General chase. Run 'em down and start collecting trophies, boys!"

Moving forward in his *Zeus,* Leonidas Brannock was ready to deal with the *Highlander* once and for all.

Clay's last jump brought the *Griffin* down close alongside the stricken *Highlander.* Hastily looking the 'Mech over, he noted the scorched and scoured armor along the side of the cockpit. There was no obvious breach, no reason to suppose McCall had been hit.

Except, of course, that the older warrior neither moved nor answered the commlink nor even attempted to punch out, as he would have if the *Highlander* had been crippled.

Davis Carlyle Clay debated what to do, knowing he couldn't just abandon McCall out here.

Missiles slammed into the rising ground just behind him, and Clay looked up to see the running form of the enemy *Zeus* bearing down on the two Legion 'Mechs. The *Zeus* was nearly twice his mass and almost impossible for one small *Griffin* to even scratch without more luck than Clay figured he had left. But he still wasn't about to abandon McCall until he was sure of his fate.

Slowly, deliberately, he moved the *Griffin* forward, like a small animal defending a larger but wounded mate. It was David facing Goliath, a slingshot against a giant.

Frowning, Alexander Carlyle studied his *Archer's* tactical display. Just a few minutes ago the Gray Death had been conducting a careful, orderly consolidation around Coltbridge. Now it was fast turning into a rout.

And there was no response from McCall on the private tactical channel. Alex had intended to make his approach as stealthy as possible, then get a quick sitrep from the weapons master before suddenly going on an open frequency and confusing an already chaotic situation by seeming to appear from out of nowhere. Now Alex didn't know what to do. Judging from what he could see, he'd be hard pressed to establish any kind of control, and just trying could complicate the situation further.

It was an ironic end to a well-executed transfer operation. The maglev had carried his strike force from Benmor Pass to a point a few kilometers from Coltbridge, where they had reactivated and unloaded the 'Mechs in record time as each emelt car reached the assembly point. From there it had been a short march overland to just northeast of Coltbridge. Now Carlyle and his men were poised squarely behind the invaders, ready to deliver an unexpected blow.

But everything was falling apart on the battlefield, and Alex's intervention now could end up doing more harm than good.

"Alex, those two beacons closest to us . . . that's Dave and the Major!" Caitlin DeVries jerked him out of the his reverie. "And look at what they're up against . . ."

He checked the readouts on the tactical map and felt his blood run cold. The decision wasn't hard to make any more.

"Let's move!" he shouted. Quickly programming his LRMs, he fired two quick volleys in the general direction of the *Zeus* that was slowly advancing on his two lance mates. They probably wouldn't hit, but at least they'd send the Free Skye invaders a signal that they suddenly had a whole new battle on their hands.

The missiles streaking toward Brannock's *Zeus* seemed to be coming from out of nowhere, and for a moment he thought that one of the missile-carrying hovertanks had worked its way around behind the Free Skye lines. But then he saw the readings on his MAD sensors and he knew the truth. More Gray Death BattleMechs. At least ten, by his first quick count. His first guess had been right after all. A trap—and he had fallen neatly into it.

"Break off and re-form," he ordered, terse, angry. "All units, break off pursuit and re-form on me! We have multiple targets bearing zero-three-nine degrees, closing! Break off pursuit and re-form on me!"

The impudent little *Griffin* that had been helping to bait

the trap was still standing in plain sight, almost challenging Brannock to do his worst. But Leonidas Brannock had other things to worry about now. Maybe there'd be a chance to deal with that audacious pilot some other time. For the moment that warrior wasn't going to tempt Brannock any more today . . .

McCall became aware of the ache in his head first. Groaning, he tried to shift in his seat, but he found that his arm—his bionic arm—wouldn't move. He couldn't feel anything from the shoulder down, either. It brought back memories of the days after they'd amputated his original mangled limb, following the Clan attack on Sudeten. For weeks after the surgery, he'd had that curious sensation, the dull, remote feeling of a limb that wasn't really there.

Groggy, he used his good arm to lever himself upright, the motion making his head spin. McCall probed the side of his scalp gingerly, felt the warm stickiness of blood matting his hair. The neurohelmet was supposed to be padded against this kind of injury, but no protection was perfect. One of the built-in headphones had ruptured and given him a deep, bleeding gash, but he didn't think it was a serious injury. Certainly it wasn't as bad as losing the use of his arm. He could pilot the 'Mech one-handed, but in the heat of battle the injury would slow him down.

If, of course, the explosion hadn't crippled his controls entirely. Carefully, he settled the neurohelmet back in place and checked his status board. There were reds and ambers showing, mostly minor systems. One heat sink was off-line, and his cockpit air coolers were out. Things were likely to get pretty damned hot if he got back in the battle.

Slowly, almost hesitantly, McCall raised the 'Mech's right arm. It responded. He sighed, relieved. There might still be some fight in the old warhorse after all . . .

"Major? Do you read me, Major?" Dave Clay's voice on the commlink was panicky. "I saw you move your arm. Are you all right? Do you read me?"

"Easy, there, laddie," McCall replied. "Dinna fash yourself sae much."

"When you didn't answer . . . God, Major, everything's happening so fast . . ."

McCall called up his tactical display and whistled in surprise. Clay was right. His troops were dispersed and in disorder, while the Free Skye forces were forming up in a circle less than a kilometer to the south and west of the *Highlander*. But, of all miracles he'd given up hope of seeing, the 'Mechs of Alex's force were streaming in across the same undulating terrain the enemy had crossed less than an hour before.

If not for that, the battle would surely have been over. Even now, there was no way to tell whether or not they could get the 'Mechs down by Coltbridge reorganized in time to do any good.

"Second battle . . . same bluidy odds," he muttered. He groped for his frequency switch. "Ghost Two tae Leader. Are you there, young Alex?"

"I'm here, Mac," Alex Carlyle replied. "But for a few minutes there I was afraid you weren't."

"I'm the last of a lang line of Highlanders, laddie. We fight wi' each ither when we've nae ithers tae fight, we wear kilts in freezing weather and eat sheep's stomachs as a delicacy, and we toss tree trunks around in the name of sport." He paused. "A wee bump on the heid willna slow one ae us doon for lang, young Alex. 'Tis the least vulnerable part of the body tae us."

"Well, Mac, how's about lowering that hard head of yours and seeing how much damage you can do to the bad guys. You up for it?"

Leutnant-General Leonidas Brannock watched the newcomers as they closed in from the northeast. This force was only slightly smaller than the other, and it included several heavy 'Mechs. The fight wasn't going to be a picnic, after all.

If only the fighters hadn't gotten involved in a duel with the Legion's air cover. Brannock shook his head. If he was going to wish for the impossible, why not wish that pompous ass von Bulow had concentrated on a single landing using overwhelming force? They would have taken heavy causalities in a stand-up fight with the full force of the Gray Death Legion, but Brannock knew what the causality lists looked like for this campaign already. At least one decisive battle wouldn't have wasted good men in sideshow operations.

There was little point in considering the maybes or the might-have-beens. What was left was the need to act.

"All units, form line abreast, standard open terrain intervals," he said on the general commlink channel. "The Black Watch will advance!"

And twelve BattleMechs moved out in unison, spreading out and beginning a slow march straight for the enemy. This would be the decisive moment . . . victory or defeat, and no middle ground.

42

"**O**bote, Dumont, to the front!" Alex snapped. "Let's show them they're not the only ones with firepower around here."

Dumont's *Marauder* somehow managing to convey its pilot's neat, precise, economical way of walking as it moved, took a few paces forward. Further down Alex's uneven skirmish line, Lieutenant Bhekampi Obote also advanced. His *Goliath* was an unusual 'Mech design, walking on four legs instead of two, and resembling nothing so much as one of Mother Terra's long-extinct pachyderms. They were the two biggest 'Mechs, aside from McCall's *Highlander* facing the enemy force, and they had the firepower to trade blows with the heavy 'Mechs that faced them.

So did the *Archer*. "The rest of you, fall back, disperse, and then harass the enemy as the opportunity presents itself. Keep away from these big boys unless you're built to take it." Under the forced calm of his tone, Alex's heart was racing. He knew their luck wasn't likely to hold once the battle was joined. The smaller 'Mechs would end up like Royale's *Commando* back at Benmor, shattered and crushed under the weight of a single, well-placed volley.

McCall had claimed the Gray Death could win even against the odds. But the price they could end up paying today would give them just another Pyrrhic victory. More lives lost in the face of the seemingly endless supply of von Bulow's troops. In a war of attrition, victory went to the side most willing to sacrifice its troops. And Alex Carlyle was finding it increasingly hard to spend that precious coinage.

"Fire at will," he said, and hit the firing studs on his console.

For the second time today destruction reigned supreme in the field northeast of Coltbridge.

A plasma bolt from one of the Free Skye *Marauder*s ionized the air less than five meters from her *Centurion*'s cockpit, but Caitlin DeVries concentrated on her own target, hardly aware of the near-miss.

She had deliberately stayed close to Alex's *Archer* despite his orders for the lighter 'Mechs to avoid contact with the heavies. Caitlin had left his back uncovered in the fight by the bridge at Benmor Pass, and she was determined not to repeat the mistake.

Mistakes . . . At every turn, Caitlin had somehow made the wrong choice, or so it seemed now. In the battle at the port, she had managed to fight a first-line *Marauder* right into the ground, then let a smaller 'Mech virtually wreck her. One wrong move after another . . .

Starting with her father. She had sacrificed everything to become a MechWarrior even her father's love. And yet now she was turning out to be a failure in her chosen path. Maybe the first wrong move had been siding with the Legion after she'd discovered her father's coup.

Or maybe it had been her decision to join the Gray Death in the first place.

But the past . . . was gone. Dead. Her only family was the Legion now, and Caitlin DeVries was determined never to let that family down again.

She held her fire, watching as the slow-moving *Battle Master* with the missing leg armor stalked relentlessly forward. Chance had placed it opposite the position Alex had chosen, and the 'Mechs were trading shots faster than their heat sinks could dissipate the high temperatures generated each time one of them fired or moved.

Caitlin tracked the larger 'Mech, keeping the cross hair centered on the cockpit, holding her fire until she was sure the shot would count.

And then something slammed into her side, knocking her off balance. The *Centurion* staggered, fell to the ground. Caitlin could see the damage board lighting up. Another

PPC shot, this one a hit. It hadn't penetrated, but the next one that struck that side surely would.

The *BattleMaster* kept on coming, and Alex had an uneasy feeling of déjà vu as he watched it striding slowly forward. He had suffered burn-throughs in three places, losing a laser and a pair of heat sinks to plasma bolt hits since the fighting had started. But the Free Skye force was taking its share of punishment, too, especially from Obote's *Goliath* and McCall's *Highlander*. The latter was using his jump jets to skirmish with the enemy, always staying on the move, darting in close to make an attack, then jumping clear of danger. Two of the enemy 'Mechs were gone, but he wasn't sure what kind of casualities the Legion had suffered.

He targeted the *BattleMaster*'s plasma gun and fired everything he had. Missiles and beams streaked toward the metal behemoth, and for a moment the ripple of multiple explosions obscured his view.

As the smoke cleared, he saw that the pilot had jettisoned his PPC. He was flexing the 'Mech's massive hand slowly, as if getting used to the controls.

And still it kept on coming.

"I'm hit! I'm hit!" That was Cadet Farquhar's voice coming over the commline. His *Phoenix Hawk* had been added to the battalion command lance as part of the reorganization after the death of Major de Villar. Now his screams were hardly recognizable. "Oh, God . . . I'm—"

Then he was gone.

"The kid bought it," MechWarrior O'Dell, one of his lancemates, reported grimly. "That *Zeus* just walked up and caved in the whole front of his cockpit, punching him."

"Ashburn bought it, too," someone else said.

They were like the voices of his conscience, reminding Alex of each of the fallen. Accusing him . . .

A kind of rage took over, and he ignored his missiles and lasers. Suddenly he wanted to do to one of the enemy what they'd just done to Farquhar. He started forward, going to meet the *BattleMaster* halfway.

Caitlin fought to lever the *Centurion* up off the ground. It was a tricky maneuver at the best of times. Now, with her 'Mech damaged and a battle raging all around, it was well-nigh impossible, but she finally managed to roll the massive machine over and get up on all fours.

Then she saw the *BattleMaster,* just coming to grips with Alex's smaller *Archer.* Those huge fists could make short work of her friend's 'Mech.

The enemy 'Mech was half-turned away from her now, exposing the damaged leg. She could see the latticework of internal structure through the gaps in the armor. And she knew she had one chance to intervene.

Caitlin raised her arm-mounted autocannon and opened fire. Round after round slammed into the chamber; round after round poured into the damaged leg.

The *BattleMaster* staggered back, off balance. She fired again, and suddenly the whole lower half of the limb dropped away. And the *BattleMaster* fell.

She let out a sigh of relief as the autocannon magazine ran dry. Though it might have turned out differently, this time she hadn't let her family down.

The fall of the huge *BattleMaster* brought Alex back to his senses. What had he been thinking of? In those few moments, everything McCall had ever taught him about command had gone out the window . . .

He took a moment to glance at his tactical board. The Gray Death skirmish line was crumbling in several places as the lighter 'Mechs were overwhelmed and destroyed or forced back. At least three were out of action, and he doubted if any of the 'Mechs were still fully operational after the punishment of the firefight.

And all the while the Legion was going down, he'd wanted nothing more than to grapple with a single enemy.

There were more traces appearing on the southwest side of his tactical screen now . . . Mechs from McCall's force, coming back into battle as they realized the fight was still going on after all. Denniken had rallied them, somehow; Captain Simms, according to the readouts, had punched out when his *Shadow Hawk* took multiple hits from the *Archer* earlier, before Alex's troops had come on the scene.

Alex swallowed. His troops were wavering, but there were reinforcements in the offing again, not fresh, perhaps, but not so tired as the men around him.

And not as tired as the enemy must be by now . . .

One last effort. That's what they needed. One final effor

to turn the tide of this bitter fight once and for all. If only he could make them all see what had to be done.

Alex mustered his strength. "One more attack, Legionnaires!" he shouted on the general commlink channel. "One more attack! For the Gray Death Legion!"

And he turned the *Archer* slowly, deliberately, opening fire as he started forward, pushing through the Free Skye skirmish line with all weapons blazing at once. One more attack . . .

Other voices took up the call. "For the Gray Death Legion!" someone yelled. "Give the bastards hell!"

Carlyle! Carlyle! Carlyle!" others chanted. "Carlyle and the Gray Death Legion!"

In that one moment, Alex Carlyle finally learned what it was to be a leader of men.

Hours later, the battle of Coltbridge was over.

The worst of the firefight had ended in minutes, but the fighting had gone on long afterward. The enemy general had been tenacious, regrouping and attacking again each time it seemed he couldn't possibly sustain another battle. Armor and infantry had come up, too, but the Gray Death 'Mechs still able to fight had made short work of them.

Late in the evening, the invaders had finally pulled back behind a screen of medium BattleMechs and armor, and Alex had let them retreat. None of the Gray Death 'Mechs was in any condition to press the pursuit very closely, although Freida Bergstrom and Dingo Jack Murphy, their depleted lances temporarily united into one makeshift unit, had followed at a discreet distance to keep tabs on the foe and discourage any notions of renewed fighting. At last report, though, they'd fallen back to a field fifteen klicks north of Coltbridge and had started loading up aboard a pair of DropShips.

Julio Vargas had reported in only a short time ago. Two of the four Gray Death fighters had made their last flight, but six of the enemy had been sent to fly an escort into the afterlife, and the long aerial action had kept them from returning to influence events on the battlefield.

The attack had been repelled, but as Alex brought his *Archer* into the defensive perimeter around the maglev station there were early reports of yet another Free Skye landing, this time at Halidon, in the southern mountains.

He was exhausted, unable to even contemplate the new threat. Glancing at his chronometer he saw that the hour was closer to dawn than to midnight.

When the *Archer*'s power cut off so Newkirk and and his crew could go to work repairing whatever damage possible, Alex climbed down from the cockpit, weary and discouraged. Except for the eerie illumination of work lights set up around the station, it was pitch-black outside. He didn't really know where the rest of the senior officers were, nor did he much care. All he wanted right now was a place to stretch out and a chance to sleep after his long day in the cockpit.

"Colonel?" He turned as Captain Fraser, the infantry commander at the compound, came into the light and saluted stiffly. "Sir, there's an emelt train coming in along the east line."

"Emelt?" Alex repeated vaguely, swaying where he stood. "From Dunkeld?"

"No, sir," Fraser said. "It . . . sent a message ten minutes ago, sir. Governor DeVries is on board. He's asking for a safe-conduct through our lines. Says he needs to talk to you about a matter of extreme importance."

"The governor . . . here?" Alex blinked, suddenly more alert. "He was in Eastport . . ."

"He's on the way here now, Colonel. Do we give him his safe-conduct? Or do you want us to go after the car? One of the hovertanks could take it out easily enough, if you want." Fraser had been an officer of the Planetary Guard once, Alex remembered, but he didn't seem to care much for the man he'd once pledged to protect.

"No . . . no, tell him he has my word he can come and go safely. But check the emelt when it comes in. It would be just like von Bulow to use DeVries as a Trojan horse just when it looks like we've won this round."

'Yes, sir."

"And see if you can track down Major McCall and any other staff officers you can turn up. I'll want them to be in on whatever DeVries has to say . . ."

"Yes, Colonel. Ah . . . Captain de Villar arrived from Dunkeld half an hour ago, sir. With Major King and the rest of his techs. She says she has information on the Halidon landing for you."

Alex made a vague gesture of dismissal. "Not now . . .
No. Wait. Point me in the direction of some blackroot tea
and let me wake up. Then send her to me."

"Yes, Colonel," Fraser repeated. He called one of his
sergeants over and turned Alex over to him, then saluted
and vanished into the darkness.

Alex tried to force his brain to work again as he stumbled
after the NCO toward the untidy campsite on the other side
of the terminal building. More news about Halidon, and
now here was DeVries with some mysterious errand. It
seemed as if the burden of command never let up.

This side of leadership was a far cry from the excitement
of knowing your men were behind you on the battlefield.
That had been almost like a drug, heady, powerful. But off
the field, counting the butcher's bill or planning the next op
. . . that part of command was grim.

He carried the name, but Alexander Durant Carlyle wasn't
sure how much longer he could shoulder the burden.

43

Coltbridge
Glengarry, Federated Commonwealth
12 April 3056

Alex met Governor DeVries in one of the offices that had
survived the damage to the maglev terminal building at
Coltbridge. DeVries came alone, apparently willing to accept the promised safe-conduct, or perhaps not caring anymore what happened to him. He had a drawn, hunted look,
and his elegant clothes were rumpled and dirty. But his
bearing was still stiff and proud.

"Well, you've come a long way from the cadet barracks,
Colonel," DeVries said quietly after Lieutenant Obote had
escorted him into the room and Alex had motioned him to
a chair. "I never thought the Legion would do this well."

"Obviously," McCall grated. The Jacobite's bionic arm
had shorted out after the hit that almost blew open his cockpit, and he had it in a sling until a medtech could have a
look. McCall, Vargas, and Freya de Villar were standing
behind Alex. Though Alex would have preferred not to have
Freya at the meeting, she was the one who'd been doing
most of the intelligence work for the Legion since the fighting had started, and was the officer best suited to evaluate
whatever DeVries had to say. He could imagine what she
must be feeling, standing there looking at the man whose
hired thugs had killed her husband.

"If we'd had your help in the fight, we'd have done ever
better," Alex told DeVries. "You damn near cost us every
thing. So why are you here now? Did you pals send you to
negotiate another neutrality deal?"

DeVries looked away. "What I did, Carlyle, I did be

cause I thought it was best for Glengarry. Maybe I was wrong. But if your mercenaries had been reasonable and given the agreement a chance, many who are dead now would still be alive. Which of us really cost our people more?''

Alex ignored the sharp hiss of Freya de Villar's indrawn breath behind him. ''It's a little late for this debate, Governor. You told my men that you had something important to discuss. Let's discuss it, and leave the recriminations to the history books.''

The governor shrugged. ''As you wish. First off, for the record, I'm here on my own initiative. After Dunkeld, I'm afraid General von Bulow doesn't regard me as one of his friends. Apparently he thinks I was involved in the ambush you set. Or perhaps he's afraid I'd be part of a new one now.''

''My heart fair bleeds for you,'' McCall muttered.

DeVries spared him an angry look. ''No, I came here because we can still do each other good, Carlyle, despite what's happened.''

''Get to the point,'' Alex said harshly. He was suddenly tired of all the verbal fencing. After the savage fighting at Coltbridge, all he wanted now was to sleep for a month or two.

''You've heard about Halidon by now, of course.''

Alex nodded wearily. Freya de Villar had brought the word in herself, from Dunkeld. While the fighting was still going on at Coltbridge the Free Skye forces had landed a third force, much larger than either of the first two, at the mining town of Halidon. The Gray Death infantry and armor were already falling back rapidly before the superior forces, and they'd lost control of the all-important pass that led down from the Monaghan Highlands into the plains of Atholl. Control of that pass made the enemy's drop zone all but impregnable. Von Bulow's troops were on the ground at last, and it would take a miracle to dislodge them.

''From what I've heard,'' DeVries went on, ''I'd say your campaign is just about over. Now that von Bulow has a secure base of operations on the ground, it's only a matter of time before he launches a drive against the capital. You can still put up a fight, of course. You might even win another battle or two. But do you really think, Carlyle, that you can actually win in the long run? You're outnumbered, and von Bulow can call on reinforcements from Skye if he has to. Where is your relief force? On Borghese? That's a long way off—if they ever come at all.''

"So we're back to the same old tune, is it?'' Vargas mocked. "Give it up now, and let His Excellency the Governor play the quisling again and rule the planet for Duke Richard?''

DeVries spread his hands. "I told you before, I'm in no position to deal with von Bulow any longer. Look, I'll admit it, I thought Richard Steiner might have kept me on to govern if I cooperated. But the truth is that I wanted to see Glengarry spared of this fighting, and I thought that I'd be a hell of a lot better as the intermediary between Glengarry and Skye than some outsider who'd treat the place as a spoil of war.'' He leaned forward, his eyes intense. "I can't save the planet, and any ambitions I had are useless. I'll probably be treated just like the rest of you, once von Bulow wins.''

"Then what do you want from us?'' Alex asked.

"Prolonging the fight is just going to lead to more death and destruction. But there's an alternative. *Not* surrender— but an alternative that would let you get the core of your outfit off this planet intact. You and your top people and your best 'Mechs, Carlyle, could all escape and live to fight again another day. Join up with the other half of your outfit . . . find your father and reorganize.''

"How?'' McCall asked, curt and harsh.

"My people in the capital tell me you managed to get one DropShip out during that first fight. The ship hasn't turned up at any of the towns where my people have contacts, and I know for damned sure there weren't any JumpShips to take it out, so I'd guess you've been hiding it up in the mountains somewhere. The metal deposits would mask her, providing you did a good job of camouflage.''

"And if that's what we did?'' Alex asked cautiously. They had concealed the *Europa* in the way DeVries had described, holding her back as an ace in the hole. If nothing else, her 'Mech bays would give them a repair platform for their BattleMechs even if they lost control of Castle Hill and the other Gray Death bases on Glengarry. He was reluctant to give too much away to DeVries. God alone knew what kind of double game the man was playing, or what he'd do if he knew for sure the whereabouts of the Drop-Ship.

"You have a DropShip hidden in the wilderness, and no way to use it." DeVries smiled thinly. "I, on the other hand, am in contact with a merchant JumpShip that came in system day before yesterday. The owner's an old friend of mine, and he owes me a favor or two. But he's not the sort of fellow to risk his own cargo DropShips running von Bulow's blockade. On the other hand, with your fighters and your own DropShip and a little bit of luck, I think you could break through the Free Skye bunch and rendezvous with him, if you were so inclined."

"By this time, any JumpShip that's been spotted out there will be drawing von Bulow's fire like a 'Mech draws missiles," Alex said. "Even if they don't blast your buddy out of space, they'll be watching him. And it would take us days to reach the jump point." He shook his head. "There's no way we could make it work even if we wanted to do. And I don't see why we should anyway."

"I know a little bit about space travel, Carlyle," DeVries said quietly. "Captain Hill is jumping out again tomorrow to avoid . . . entanglements. But if I sent him the right signal, I could set up a rendezvous for later. He could jump out, recharge, then come back in at a pirate point close enough to Glengarry to cut down on the travel time by quite a bit. And knowing when he was coming back, we could run the blockade before the Free Skye force even knew there was a ship coming."

"It would work," Vargas commented. "Assuming the guy could be trusted to keep the rendezvous."

"He can be trusted," DeVries said.

Alex rubbed his forehead with a grimy hand. "Your word isn't exactly a guarantee any of us would trust, Governor. But you've left the really big question unanswered. Why should we want to do this?"

"I said it before. You're going to lose in the end, and a hell of a lot people are going to die along the way. But if you evacuate your leadership and your best equipment, at least you keep a nucleus of your unit intact. And the rest . . . they could disperse. Hide out for a while. Maybe even come out of hiding and mount a fresh campaign when you round up the rest of the Legion and are ready to come back . . . if that's what you decide to do.

"The point is, as long as you're a threat to the Free Skye rebellion, von Bulow is going to keep coming after you with everything he's got. He'll crush you one by one if he has to, and along the way he'll destroy a lot of innocents who deserve better. It made sense to fight when there was no other way out, but if you can save lives by retreating from a hopeless campaign, doesn't it make more sense to do that?"

"You seem to have developed a remarkable concern for our safety all of a sudden," Vargas remarked. "Or is there something in it for you?"

"I want passage with you," DeVries said. "There's nothing left for me on Glengarry anymore."

"Aha!" Vargas exclaimed. "So much for altruism, eh?"

The governor flushed, directing his angry stare at the cocky pilot. "Yes, I want passage, and you people are my only ticket out. But that isn't my only reason. Not by a long shot."

"Name another," Vargas replied.

"My daughter, for one," the DeVries said flatly. He looked back at Alex, his expression softening for the first time. "Is it wrong for me to worry about her safety, Carlyle? She's cast her lot with your Legion, and she'll stick by that decision to the end. I don't want the end to be what your damned heroics might give her." He paused, glancing at McCall and Vargas. "If you're determined to play Horatio at the bridge and fight to the bitter end, then at least give your people, Caitlin included, an option. Let the ones who don't share your bloody-minded convictions leave . . . and for God's sake let me take Caitlin out of this. She's all I care about now."

Alex couldn't meet the other man's eyes. "I understand how you feel, Governor," he said quietly. Something in what DeVries said had struck a chord, and suddenly all his doubts were back in full force. "Go back to you emelt car. I'll . . . we'll let you know our decision." Staring down at his desk, Alex barely noticed the door closing behind the governor. The silence in the shabby room was thick and brooding.

"You're not really going to consider his proposition, are you?" Vargas said, breaking the stillness at last. "For all we know his 'friend' is piloting a Free Skye ship and just waiting to round us up out in deep space, where we'd be completely helpless.''

"He sounded sincere enough, aboot his daughter if nothing else," McCall observed soberly. "I dinna fear a trap sae much as I fear what his plan would do tae the Legion."

Alex turned in his chair to face the old Caledonian. "What can this do that von Bulow won't do a hell of a lot more thoroughly? DeVries had one thing right, at least. As long as we continue to put up a fight here, the killing will go on. And one day we're going to run out of blood and guts and BattleMechs, and what difference will it have made? What kind of difference will our little handful of people make in the long run? We're no army, to decide the fate of the whole Federated Commonwealth. Richard'll either win and Skye will become independent, or Victor will crush the rebellion and hold everything together for a few more years. But whatever's going to happen, it's going to happen no matter what we do here. And meanwhile, if we keep on fighting, we keep on dying too."

"We're soldiers," Vargas said, shifting uneasily in his seat. "Fighting . . . dying . . . that's part of the job."

"Hasn't this fight already cost too much?" Alex shot back. "Everyone aboard the *Antelope* . . . Lowdowski and Royale and Farquhar . . .'' He met Freya de Villar's cold eyes. "Your husband and your son. Every time we go out there, we're going to lose a few more. *I'm* going to lose them. Some day it'll be Dave Clay or Caitlin, or you, Mac, and it'll be my fault, because I didn't know when to quit. Because I tried to take my father's place, and those people out there are so loyal to him that they'll just keep following me from one damned blood bath to another."

He stood up slowly. "Look, I need to be alone for a few minutes. I'll be outside . . .''

Alex left the room without a backward glance. The sun was just coming up over the eastern horizon. Staring off into the distance, it was possible to blot out his vision of the battle ravages around him, and see the rugged beauty of Glengarry again, the way it had been the morning he'd watched the sunrise from the balcony of the Residence, back on the Day of Heroes.

I'm not Grayson Death Carlyle, he thought, still staring off into the distance. I tried to be, but I'm not. I can pilot a 'Mech in battle. I can even manage to pull off a few good tricks in planning a battle or two. But I can't keep leading these people to the slaughter. I should never have let McCall talk me into taking command.

He thought back to the day before the crisis had erupted, to the exercise at Brander and the mistakes he'd made trying to cover Cadet Gates and refusing to send someone else into danger. McCall had told Alex afterward that he couldn't be a leader if he wasn't willing to make life or death decisions for his followers.

Well, he'd tried. He'd led men into battle three times now, and through it all nothing had changed. The battle plan had nearly blown up in his face at Dunkeld, and a quarter of his force had died. At Loch Sheol he'd gone in with the scouts, and it was only by a miracle that the invaders hadn't cut them to ribbons before Dumont's people arrived in the field. And at Coltbridge . . . if Alex had arrived just a few minutes later, McCall and all his people might have been lost. The victories were all hollow, and now that von Bulow's troops were secure on the ground, hollow victories wouldn't mean a thing anymore. What kind of leader did that make Alexander Carlyle?

"A human being, pairhaps, laddie," McCall's distinctive voice said behind him. Alex started. He hadn't realized he'd spoke that last thought aloud.

"If we didn't send any 'Mechs, a lot of the outfit could get out aboard the *Europa*," he said, still watching the sun gradually rising in the distance "A few of us could keep the fight going here. How many would go, if we gave them a chance?"

"A few," McCall said. "Not many. I told you aince, lad, that these people look to the Carlyles tae lead them. Even if you ordered them tae go, most would volunteer tae stay wi' you."

"Yeah. That's the problem. As long as I'm the figurehead they look to as their leader, they'll stay with me because they think it's their duty. Well, I thought my duty was here, to stay and fight for the Legion and for my father. Now I'm not so sure. If we keep on like this, I'm more likely to destroy the Legion than save it. And if we can't make a difference on Glengarry, where's the sense in that? Von Bulow's going to win, tomorrow or next week or next month The Skye rebellion will succeed or fail on its own merits whether we all die with our cooling vests on or we cut and run today.''

''That would be true, lad, if you were right in saying that we canna make a real difference. But I think we can. More than you think.''

''That's what you said before, after the first fight. I even believed some of it then. Now I just don't know. I can't see *how* we can have any impact on things here, much less on Skye or Tharkad.''

''After today, you can say that?''

''What about today? What are you talking about?''

''Laddie, you arrived here in the nick of time. An hour later and we would hae been doon for the count.''

Alex nodded. ''I was just thinking that. Don't try to convince me that I had anything to do with winning today. We were lucky, pure and simple.''

''Aye, 'twas luck. Luck and the fact that the Free Skye people decided tae surrender at Loch Sheol instead of fighting it oot. Laddie, if that woman up there had held on for ainither hour, Dave Clay and I would be daid along with everyone else doon here. And you would have walked right into those enemy 'Mechs here wi'oot us tae provide a disraction. Do I hae the rights of it?''

Alex nodded slowly. ''I guess so. Yeah, I suppose it wasn't all luck.''

''Weil, then, if you gie it up here, what fight will von Bulow be able tae show up at in the nick of time and turn the result against Victor Davion? What Free Skye stronghold will hold oot because of it? Resistance tae a foe is never in vain, laddie. Von Bulow may hae more troops than we do, but the Davions hae aye more. That means the Free Skye troops will soon be fighting a campaign like ours here, trying tae shift scant resources tae where they're needed most. But if they dinna hae the use of these troops here—if they come tae fear us tae the point of calling for more—then think what that does tae the rest of the war effort.''

Freya de Villar had appeared in the doorway behind McCall. ''He's right, you know,'' she said somberly. ''What you said earlier, about the price we've paid. Maybe no one knows that more than I do—I'd give anything to have them back again. But they died for something important . . . for their *home*. Glengarry is our home now, and Cris and Cristiano died fighting to keep it from falling into the hands of those barbarians. So, the way I see it, as long as one of us, just one of us, is willing to fight against the odds, the war on Glengarry will go on. And if that helps stop Ryan and Richard Steiner's damned rebellion, then it's worth doing. Even if we have to pay the price that they've paid . . . that I've paid.''

She turned away, and neither Alex nor McCall answered her.

Finally Alex spoke again, low-voiced, more to himself than the other two. ''Barbarians . . .'' Grayson Carlyle had often talked about holding back the barbarians at the gates. It was a losing battle, he had once told his son, but it was a battle they had to keep on fighting. ''If we let them win, the Federated Commonwealth falls apart. Civil war. Anarchy worse than anything we had before the Clans came. And the barbarians like von Bulow, the ones who spend their men's lives like so many pawns on a game board, they win the bigger victory. There won't be any lights left to save man from the dark age they'd give us.''

''Aye,'' McCall agreed softly. '' 'Tis that which your auld faither has always said we're fighting against.'' He chuckled without humor. ''If you were like von Bulow, laddie, you wouldn't care about the ones who died. But if you were like him, they wouldna follow you in the first place.''

''Mac, I don't know if I can be the kind of leader the Gray Death needs,'' Alex said. ''I've made a hell of a lot of mistakes already, and I'll make more . . . and mistakes cost lives. What right do I have to send people out to die fighting my battles?''

The Caledonian shrugged. ''What right does Victor Davion hae? Or Richard Steiner? You're a leader because your faither was. And because, whatever you think aboot it yourself, you hae what it takes tae make men willing tae die for you. 'Tis a powerful responsibility tae bear, and it can be too damned much sometimes. But let me turn the question around. What right do you hae tae turn your back on your responsibilities? You hae a cause worth fighting for, and the chance tae make a real difference . . . and the talent to motivate people tae follow you. Coltbridge proved that, if nothing else did. You can sit on the sidelines, though you ken fu' weil that there's work tae be done. Or you can do the work and tak the consequences, the bad and the good together. That's something only your conscience can decide.''

Alex turned his eyes back to the east, to the rising sun. McCall was right. He had been letting his decisions come from others for too long now. McCall had talked him into taking charge after de Villar's death, and again after Dunkeld. But the doubts had come from outside, too. He hadn't wanted to accept the responsibility for the men who died. That wasn't a part of the ''glory'' of war, thinking about the friends or comrades who would never come back from the battlefield.

That responsibility, though, cut both ways. If the Gray Death couldn't make any difference to the war, then continuing the fight for honor or glory or because others might disapprove of surrender or retreat was foolish. But if they *could* make a genuine difference by fighting on, the equation wasn't so simple. More than just the Legion could be lost if he didn't fight. Some things demanded that warriors shed their blood . . . like holding back the tide of anarchy if only for a few years more.

His decision, and no one else's, right or wrong.

''All right,'' he said. ''We'll fight . . . we'll fight von Bulow every step of the way, with everything we've got and for as long as we can.'' He paused. ''But we should let anyone leave who wants to, Mac.''

''You'll give DeVries the ship?''

Alex shook his head. ''No . . . anyone who wants out can take to the hills, like DeVries said they could if we pulled out. But I think we'll be needing the *Europa*, Mac. I've got an idea for tackling Halidon after all, but it needs the *Europa* to make it work . . .''

A guard in the kilts of the Planetary Guards opened the door at the rear of the governor's emelt car. Caitlin DeVries swallowed and stepped through. Her father looked up from the desk that had replaced the ordinary passenger seats that were normally there.

''Caitlin . . .'' He trailed off, looking wistful. ''I'm . . . I'm glad you came.''

''I almost didn't, Dad,'' she said slowly. ''After everything's that happened . . . I didn't think I wanted to see you again.''

He looked away "I know. I know, Kit. I bollixed everything up, and us most of all."

"Alex told me about the JumpShip. And said he couldn't agree to it."

He nodded. "He called me a little while ago. Stupid pride . . . Why can't any of them see reality?"

"And why can't you allow anyone else to have principles, Dad? I believed it when you said you wanted to keep the war away from Glengarry. You think peace is more important than anything else, and maybe if more people thought like that, we humans wouldn't spend so much time and effort trying to tear ourselves to shreds. So you put your devotion to peace ahead of the Legion, ahead of the fealty you owed to the Carlyle family . . . ahead of me, even. Why can't you see that other people value their own principles, whatever those might be, just as highly?"

"It's different . . ."

"No, Dad, it isn't. The Legion happens to stand for order in the face of chaos, and that's a pretty damn good principle too. You talk about seeing reality? Well, war is reality. Aggression. Petty ambition. Alex and the others know that most people out there don't share your dedication to peace, so they fight to keep some kind of order. That's seeing reality, if you'd like."

He sighed. "They've convinced you, at least."

She nodded. "Yes, Dad, they have. It killed me having to choose between you and the Legion. Being a MechWarrior is something I've wanted for as long as I can remember. And I have friends in the Legion, good friends like Alex and Dave. But you're my father, my blood." Caitlin paused, studying her father's face, but hardly seeing him for the tears threatening to spill from her eyes. "But I also believe in what the Legion stands for, Dad. And you're the one who taught me to put my principles first."

Roger DeVries took his daughter's hand. "I pleaded with Carlyle to make you leave them, Cay," he said slowly. "But he said it was your decision to make, not his . . . and he also said you'd already made it."

She nodded and wiped her eyes.

"Knowing you're out there fighting, that you could be the next one to die . . . that tears *me* apart. I want to be able to reach out and protect you, and I can't." DeVries stood up slowly and took a tentative step toward his daughter

"But whatever I think about your choice, however much I wish you'd give it up . . . Cay, you're doing what you believe in. I'm proud of you for that."

Father and daughter embraced, and for a few moments there was no war or the thought of it. Only a peace that had been a long time coming.

Epilogue

Gray Death DropShip Europa
Dunkeld Aerospace Port, Glengarry
Isle of Skye, Federated Commonwealth
13 April 3056

"The last 'Mech is loaded up, Colonel."

Alexander Carlyle looked up at Lieutenant Fowler's drawn features and nodded. "That was quick work, Captain," he said with a thin smile. "How soon until we can lift."

"Ten minutes, Colonel."

He looked around the DropShip's control room. The crew was busy with the final pre-launch checklists. None of them seemed concerned at the prospect of another battle with the invaders. If anything, there was an air of anticipation, almost of eagerness, on the bridge. If the Legion was going to fail, they would fail together, fighting to the end. That was what counted now.

The *Europa* had returned to Dunkeld by flying low over the mountains from her secret hiding place and making the dash for the capital while the bulk of the enemy fleet was on the far side of the planet. She'd leave the same way carrying the Companions and Lieutenant Obote's fire lance from Dumont's Dreadnoughts. The rest of the Legion, under the command of Davis McCall, were headed by maglev to the Free Skye base at Halidon with Davis McCall in command. The DropShip would, everyone fervently hoped, give them an unexpected edge in the battle to come by putting the Legion's force down on the enemy flank, where they could launch yet another patented Gray Death ambush, like the ones at Dunkeld and Loch Sheol and Coltbridge.

They might not win. The terrain and the numbers wer

both against them this time. But for Alexander Durant Carlyle, the doubt and indecision were over. Freya de Villar had been right from the start. As long as one of them was willing to fight, the war on Glengarry would go on. The Gray Death would hit von Bulow's men at Halidon, and again after that, and again until they'd pushed the invaders off their homeworld for good . . . or until everyone in the Legion had died trying. And Alex would lead them, win or lose, because his place was with his father's people . . . with *his* people.

And when this war was over, when the rest of the Legion returned to Glengarry to relieve the survivors or to bury the dead, Alex hoped his father would be proud of what they had tried to do.

He realized Fowler was still there, waiting for him to speak again.

"Well, Captain, looks like it's time we lifted. The Legion is waiting for us . . . and I don't intend to let them down."

"Yes, *sir*!" Fowler said with a grin. He turned away. "All hands to launch stations! Prepare to lift ship!"

Within minutes the Gray Death DropShip *Europa* was rising from the Dunkeld spaceport on a pillar of fire, the Gray Death Legion's course set for battle—and for the unknown.

CRUSADER

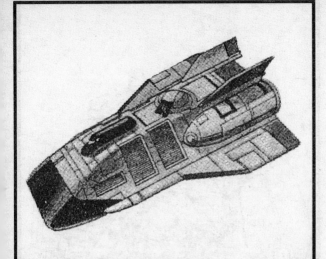

LEOPARD CLASS DROPSHIP

UNION CLASS DROPSHIP

LOCUST

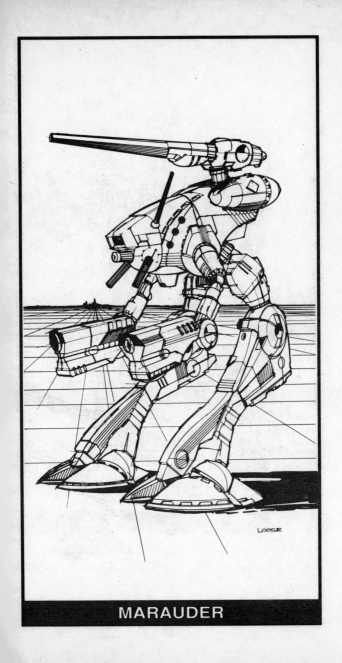

MARAUDER

PHOENIX HAWK

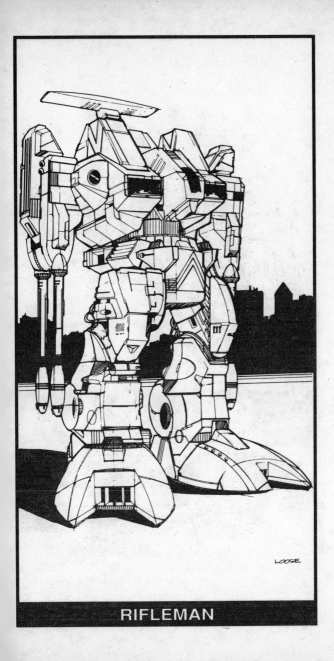

LOOSE

RIFLEMAN

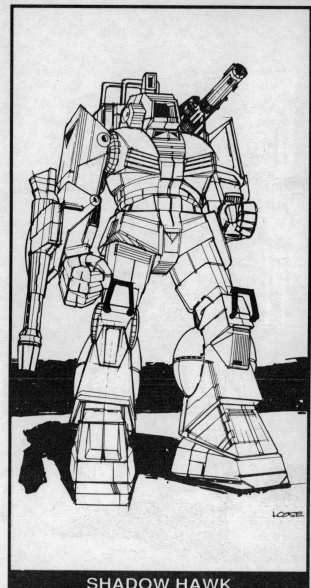

SHADOW HAWK

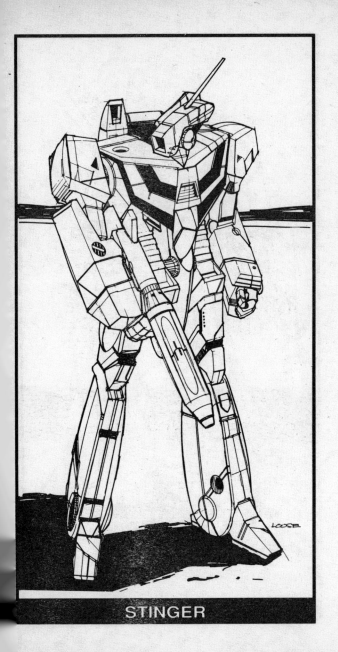

STINGER

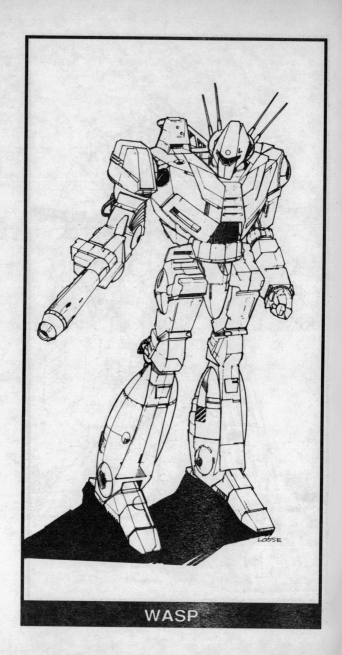

LOOSE

WASP

LOOSE

WOLVERINE

**Exploring New Realms
in Science Fiction/Fantasy Adventure**

Shadowrun™

Titles already published or in preparation:

Never Deal with a Dragon
Robert N. Charrette

In the year 2050, the power of magic has returned to the earth. Elves, Mages and lethal Dragons find a home where technology and human flesh have melded into deadly urban predators.

Choose Your Enemies Carefully
Robert N. Charrette

As Sam searches for his sister, he realizes that only when he accepts his destiny as a shaman can he embrace the power he needs for what waits for him in the final confrontation.

and:

Find Your Own Truth
Robert N. Charrette

2XS
Nigel Findley

Changeling
Chris Kubasik

Never Trust an Elf
Robert N. Charrette

Into the Shadows
Edited by Jordan K. Weisman

Streets of Blood
Carl Sargent

Shadowplay
Nigel Findley

Night's Pawn
Tom Dowd

RoC

**Exploring New Realms
in Science Fiction/Fantasy Adventure**

Battletech®

Titles already published or in preparation: